LA T-
7.48

COLD STORAGE

BARBARA A. KIGER

COLD STORAGE

BARBARA A. KIGER

Tallahassee, Florida

Copyright © 2012 by Barbara A. Kiger

Cover art © 2012 by Annie Butterworth Jones

All rights reserved. No part of this book may be reproduced in any form or by any means, electronic or mechanical, including photocopying, recording, or by any information storage and retrieval system, without written permission in writing from the publisher, except for brief quotations contained in critical articles and reviews.

Inquiries should be addressed to:
CyPress Publications
P.O. Box 2636
Tallahassee, Florida 32316-2636
http://cypresspublications.com
lraymond@nettally.com

Cover photograph courtesy of Brenda Kiger

Library of Congress Control Number: 2012950933

ISBN 978-1-935083-41-2

First Edition

Dedication

To Chuck, who taught us more than we needed to know about guns. You are missed.

Acknowledgements

A big thanks to my family and friends who patiently answered my questions, especially when they didn't fit the topic being discussed. Despite my frequent interruptions, your answers clarified many a muddled thought. Several of you also helped with the necessary research, without which I might have put a dolphin in one of Michigan's northern lakes or shot my victims with a musket. Rita Jason helped me avoid the first and Douglas Davey advised me on the second.

The music played at the Valentine Dance came to you courtesy of Pat Kiger, and Chuck and Wayne Kevin Kiger supplied the information on the cars and other vehicles. Suzanne Muellner sent me several brochures on snowmobiles, and Geoffrey Liebrandt answered my questions about helicopters.

Barbara Ross helped research the setting, and Jeanette Schaal advised me on the plot issues involving human trafficking and migrant laborers.

My companion during the writing of this book was Dottie McCarron, and when we finished, Paula Kiger edited the "almost" final draft. My editor and publisher Lee Raymond once again turned my words into a book, *Cold Storage*. Here are a couple of words that never need editing: Thank you.

If it's right, I listened to what each of you had to say. If it's not, I didn't.

Chapter One

"Do you know who she is?" I asked.

"Can't say for sure without seeing more of her face."

I took a deep breath, more shudder than breath, and shifted my eyes from the man's weather-worn face to the freezer, seeing again the frosted body that lay within.

"Is there someone you want me to call, Miss Arthur?" the man asked.

Call? Names and faces raced through my mind. Steve, a surgical resident, could not get away from the hospital on such short notice. Besides, if things went as planned, he would be here in a day or two. Thelma was baby-sitting the offices of Arthur and Arthur Security. It was a job she was extremely good at, but she couldn't do it long-distance. As for Larry Rhodes? I looked at the man standing before me. Did I really need another police officer?

I shook my head. "Thanks. I drove up alone, but a couple of friends will be joining me in a day or two."

The man, who had identified himself as Sheriff Duncan, nodded. "Judge Marfield called me," he said, naming the woman in whose house we now stood, a winter retreat where I had come to recuperate from a recent gunshot wound. "She asked me to check on you."

His words explained his unexpected arrival. His timing was less obvious. Sheriff Duncan had knocked at the door only minutes after I had made the gruesome discovery—before I even had time to think of what to do or whom to call.

He patted the closed freezer lid. "Don't think the judge was expecting anyone to leave you a house-warming gift."

The man's humor, in what was not a humorous situation, surprised me.

Having been told I would not be spending the night in what the man with the weather-worn face was calling the "crime scene," I headed for the stairs. "I'll get my suitcase," I said.

"My deputy's on the way. She can get it for you when she gets here. Don't want you wandering around in here any more than you already have." His eyes swept the room, as if looking to see what I might have disturbed, then settled back on me.

"I hate to roust you out on such short notice, but . . . I'll give Mrs. Braun a call, she runs the local motel, and let her know to expect you."

Duncan pulled a cell phone from his jacket pocket and speed-dialed a number. From outside came the snow-muffled sound of a car engine. Bringing his conversation to an end, Duncan snapped shut his cell phone and swung the front door open.

A woman, as tall as my own five-eight, came through the door. A patterned stocking cap covered her head, and an apple-red down-filled jacket was zippered tight against her chin.

"Damn, but it's cold out there." She stamped her feet, ridding her boots of snow.

"Deputy Johnson," Sheriff Duncan said, "this is Miss Arthur."

"Ginny," I said, extending my hand.

"Myra," the deputy said. She pulled off her glove and gave my hand a firm shake.

"Seems someone left Miss Arthur a house-warming gift." The sheriff opened the lid of the chest freezer and stepped back, allowing his deputy an unobstructed view.

Johnson stared into the freezer, her face taking on a grim expression.

"Any idea who she is?" Duncan asked.

"Could be the Shouldice girl." Johnson's jaw tightened, deepening the lines around her mouth. "Cindy Shouldice had blonde hair."

Sheriff Duncan slammed the lid shut. "Or maybe the Leggit girl?" he suggested.

Myra Johnson shook her head. "Too small. Josie Leggit was bigger-boned." The deputy paused. "And Josie had brown hair."

Cindy Shouldice? Josie Leggit? The two were guessing. They did not know who the girl was.

They moved back from the freezer. "Doc Wacker's on his way, and I've called in Bryant," said the sheriff. "You and Kev can process the crime scene. I've taken all the pictures you'll need." Duncan handed Myra Johnson the camera that hung around his neck. "But first you need to get Miss Arthur's suitcase." The sheriff shot me a questioning look.

"In the bedroom," I said, answering the unasked question.

"Then you can take her to Braun's. Linda's expecting her."

I tried to tell the sheriff I had a car, but he waved my words aside. "You don't need to be driving in this weather."

Deputy Johnson headed for the stairs. The silence that followed her leaving was broken by the raucous cry of what sounded like a pair of embattled wildcats.

"What the hell!" Sheriff Duncan looked around the room.

"The cats," I explained, heading for the garage.

The caged pair acknowledged my approach with another protracted howl. Ignoring their complaints, I picked up the wire cage. A sharp pain gripped my shoulder. Grimacing, I started for the laundry room. In objection to their going airborne, the pair redoubled their vocal efforts.

Sheriff Duncan took the cage.

"Thanks," I muttered, rubbing at the pain. "Will they be welcome at the motel?" I asked, wondering what the alternative would be if he said no.

"These two won't be welcome anywhere if they don't stop that caterwauling." Sheriff Duncan quirked an eyebrow in my direction. "I presume once you've taken care of them they'll settle down?"

Eager to demonstrate what I hoped was true, I pointed the way to the laundry room.

After closing the door behind us, I pulled the litter box from beneath their traveling cage, opened a can of cat food, and freed the Siamese pair. Zeus preceded Hera, sniffed at the cat food, meowed his approval, and headed for the litter box.

"You can always leave them at the vet's for a couple of days," he said.

"Are you saying I'll be able to get back in here in a couple of days?"

"Depends on how fast our crime scene team can get the job done. This is a big place. That shoulder bothering you?" he asked as we left the laundry room, shutting the door behind us.

The hand with which I had been massaging my shoulder froze. "Some," I admitted.

"It isn't just the gunshot wound that takes time to heal. Most of us tend to carry along a load of guilt with the scar." A loud knock cut off the sheriff's philosophical musings, and a few long strides carried him to the door, where a draft of cold air ushered in two snow-covered figures.

One wore a bright-red down-filled jacket similar to Sheriff Duncan's and Deputy Johnson's, the other a muted black-and-green wool car coat with a knit scarf wrapped twice around his neck. Both wore wool caps pulled tight over their heads.

The sheriff motioned to the younger man. "Miss Arthur, Deputy Bryant."

"Kev Bryant," the deputy said, extending his hand.

I offered mine, which the deputy shook vigorously. He was well over six feet and, although the layers of clothes made it difficult to tell, looked to be on the lean side. His face, which seemed more naturally suited to smiling, wore a somber expression.

"Jim Wacker," said the second man. A wave of his hand as he hurried by acknowledged my presence. "Where's the body, Rick?" he asked. The doctor looked around the room as if expecting any number of bodies to put in an appearance.

"In the deep freeze, Jim." The sheriff motioned to the freezer, which was now the focus of four pairs of eyes.

"Could just as well been left outside, cold as it is," Wacker mumbled. He set the bag he was carrying on the floor before shedding coat, hat, and scarf and dropping them over a chair back. "You looked at the body?" Wacker asked, pulling on a pair of latex gloves.

"And Deputy Johnson and Miss Arthur," the sheriff answered.

"Miss Arthur?" Jim Wacker snapped the cuffs of the gloves against his wrists and turned to look at me, his second look a bit longer than the first.

"She found the body," the sheriff said.

With a muttered, "I see," the doctor lifted the lid of the freezer. A look of concentration settled on his face as a cloud of cold air escaped.

Whistling a tune I could not name, Jim Wacker bent over the body. Being no more than five feet six or seven, the Pine City Coroner all but disappeared inside the freezer.

"She's dead all right." Wacker straightened, his face reddened by the cold. He looked at the sheriff. "Got all the pictures you need?"

Duncan nodded an affirmative.

Wacker grunted approval and looked to where Deputy Bryant stood. "Kev, how about you spreading out that body bag and giving me a hand?"

The deputy did as Doc Wacker requested, and the two soon had the dead girl out of cold storage.

Sheriff Duncan stared at the body for several long minutes. "Either of you know who she is?" he asked finally.

I edged forward, making myself a part of the threesome. She lay on her side as she had in the freezer and was, as Duncan had said, young and blonde, the long hair hiding all but her chin and the tip of her nose. A light blue sweatshirt covered the upper half of her body, jeans and dirty Converse sneakers her legs and feet. The young victim's face and hands were so white as to appear almost blue, and the one eyebrow visible through the strands of hair showed fringes of frost.

Bryant stared mutely for several seconds. "Could be one of that Frazier bunch," he said, then shook his head. "I don't know," he finished.

"I'm thinking she could be the Leggit girl," Duncan offered. "But Myra said the hair color's wrong. She's thinking maybe Cindy Shouldice."

Doc Wacker stared intently at the body. "Hair color is easy to change."

He pushed aside the blonde hair. "Don't look like either the Leggit or the Shouldice girl to me." The frown he wore deepened. "She does seem to favor that Frazier bunch."

He looked to where Bryant stood. "You might be right, Kev. Hard to tell, been a few years since I've seen any of them."

Myra Johnson, my suitcase in hand, reached the bottom of the stairs. Moving forward, she jockeyed into position between Bryant and Wacker, the men shuffling sideways to give the newcomer a better view.

"Recognize her?" the sheriff asked.

"Not sure." Johnson's expression changed from curiosity to puzzlement. "She looks like . . ." Myra's voice trailed off. Deputy Johnson shook her head. "I don't recognize her, Sheriff."

"Care to hazard a guess as to how she died, Doc?" the sheriff asked, turning his attention from his deputy to the doctor.

"The condition she's in, can't really tell much of anything."

"There's some bruising on her neck. Strangled, maybe?" Duncan suggested.

Wacker shrugged. "I saw that, and you could be right, but . . ."

". . . but you're not committing to anything until after the post."

Doc Wacker grinned. "Nothing until after the post."

At a signal from the doctor, Kev Bryant zippered the body bag closed.

"Shouldice, Leggit, Frazier, or whoever else you people think she might be, we need to get her into the van." Doc Wacker looked around for his coat, hat, and scarf. "With any luck she'll thaw out in two or three days. Give me another day for the post." He wrapped the scarf around his neck, shoved his hands into the sleeves of his coat, and pulled the cap over forehead and ears. "Ready?" He gave Bryant a questioning look.

Bryant was, and the two shifted the body bag to a waiting stretcher.

"You ready to go, Miss Arthur?" Duncan asked.

"I'll get the cats," I answered.

One was prowling along a shelf filled with an assortment of sports equipment. The other surveyed the room from a shelf that held a jumble of mismatched hats, scarfs, and mittens.

Grabbing a catnip mouse from their traveling cage, I dangled it enticingly as I advanced on the wily male. Ignoring the bait, Zeus leaped from the shelf and slipped past me.

Surprising all who watched, especially me, he marched across the floor and with a twitch of his erect tail entered the wire cage.

His female companion rose from her perch, placed a dainty paw on each lower shelf, and slowly made her descent. Gaining the floor, she entered the cage.

Hardly believing my luck, I fastened the wire door behind them and slid the litter pan into place.

As if expecting the two might change their minds, Sheriff Duncan lifted the cage.

I struggled into my coat, grabbed my shoulder bag, and followed the sheriff. Deputy Johnson, my suitcase in hand, brought up the rear.

Behind us Kev Bryant unfastened the case filled with the tools of a crime scene tech.

Chapter Two

Leaving behind the warmth of Marsha Marfield's north woods retreat, I stepped into arctic cold and blowing snow. I sucked in a lungful of numbing air, pulled the hood of my parka tight around my head, and followed Sheriff Duncan through what, if not already a blizzard, was fast becoming one.

A pair of SUVs, their contours blurred by several inches of snow, sat one behind the other in the driveway. Bubble lights grew from their roofs, marking them as police vehicles. Slowing my pace, I looked to see if the garage door was shut. It was. I picked up my pace. The Honda, bought only weeks ago to replace the Ranger which had proved too costly to repair after its encounter with a snowplow, was safe inside. That other night had been much like this. Only that night had ended with a game of chicken with a monster truck. I shivered, as much from the memory as the present cold.

Ahead, a glow of light gave a diamond-like sparkle to the blowing snow. I slit my eyes against the stinging fury and worked my way toward the open rear door of what proved to be a Chevy Suburban, arriving as Sheriff Duncan shoved the wire cage with its protesting occupants into the cargo area.

Deputy Johnson, close on my heels, handed my suitcase to the sheriff. With an economy of motion, he shoved the suitcase in beside the cats and slammed the door shut.

Trailing the Suburban's length with my gloved hand, I found the front passenger door and climbed aboard. The engine sprang to life before I had the door shut behind me. Shivering, this time it was from the cold, I fastened my seatbelt and waited for warm air to start circulating.

Johnson shifted into reverse and backed slowly into the turn-around before heading down the driveway. She hesitated as we came to the road. Except for the Suburban, there were no other vehicles in sight. Who else but cops, county coroners, and dead bodies would be out on a night like this? Me, I thought ruefully.

"Something wrong?" Johnson asked.

Surprised, I turned toward the deputy. Were my thoughts so transparent as to be read by a virtual stranger?

"You were shaking your head," she explained.

Despite the horror of the last few hours, I laughed.

"I say something funny?" Johnson slowed as we approached a curve in the road.

"Nothing funny. Just glad to know it was my body language you were reading and not my mind."

Johnson touched the gas, and the SUV accelerated into the straightaway.

The falling snow, the warm air blowing around us, and the drone of the tires against the wet pavement invited an intimacy our short acquaintance would not otherwise have permitted. Trading on the moment, I asked, "How many girls have gone missing from up here?"

"Runaways," Johnson corrected, which was not really an answer.

I waited, but Myra said nothing. Evading?

"Two that I know of," she said at last, and followed the words with a long sigh.

"Both from here?" I persisted. Pine City was not a large community.

Johnson nodded.

"Shouldice and Frazier?"

"Shouldice and Leggit," Johnson said. She stared through the clear fan-shaped patch of windshield left by the back-and-forth swipe of the wiper blades.

"What about Frazier?"

"Not from here, at least not anymore. The whole family moved to the Upper Peninsula a few years back."

"Whole family?" I prompted.

"Mother, father, two or three sons and their families, maybe a brother or two. I don't know how many, but there was a bunch of them."

Another silence, and again I waited as Johnson slowed for a series of curves. The road straightened, and Myra Johnson drummed a rapid rat-a-tat-tat on the steering wheel.

I watched the steady rhythm of her fingers. Was the conversation making the deputy angry, or was it more specific, like not being able to identify the dead girl?

Johnson's fingers relaxed, curled back around the steering wheel. "We don't know who the dead girl is. So who can say if she has or hasn't ever lived around here?"

"Deputy Bryant seemed to think it could be the Frazier girl," I offered, playing the devil's advocate.

"And the sheriff thinks it might be Josie Leggit, and I'm partial to Cindy Shouldice, but who can tell? We only got to see the side of her face."

A halo of light shimmered in the darkness. "This is it." Johnson swung the Suburban into what, to my untrained eye, looked like a field of unbroken snow but was according to Johnson an unplowed road. At least she said it was, and what choice did I have but to believe her?

Despite her reassurance, I said a silent prayer. Used to Marion City's well-plowed streets, the uncharted wilderness held no allure.

Snow flew from beneath the Suburban's wheels as we continued to move forward. Myra Johnson, her face far from being an open book, continued to stare through the windshield.

"You don't agree with Deputy Bryant?" I pushed, hoping to learn more about missing and/or runaway girls.

Myra Johnson turned to look at me.

"About the dead girl being a Frazier," I said.

Johnson studied me for a long moment. "Kev has a lot of crazy notions," she said, and returned her attention to the unplowed road. Minutes later, the faint glow of a lighted sign came into view.

"We're here," Johnson said. She swung the SUV around a circular drive, stopping at the front entrance. "I'll leave the Suburban here. Doubt there'll be any complaints about where I park tonight." Johnson pushed open the driver's door and disappeared into the blowing snow.

Eager for the comfort of four walls and a roof, I opened the passenger door and slid into the snow. The cold whiteness worked its way down my ankle boots and up my pant legs. Brrr . . . but I wasted no time shivering, just hurried after the Pine City deputy.

"Be right with you," a voice called from across the lobby as the two of us pushed through a set of double doors. True to her word, a woman of about forty, judging from the spray of fine lines at the corners of her eyes and a pair of deeper lines that framed her mouth, hurried toward us.

"Welcome to Braun's." Her smile grew. "Linda Braun," the woman said, extending her hand in greeting.

"Any port's a good port in a storm," I said, "and this looks like a winner."

"Best in Pine City," Linda Braun assured.

"Only one in Pine City," Myra Johnson countered.

The three of us laughed. It was a good sound, one that reached into the corners of the room and eased the tension in my taut muscles.

The lines on Linda Braun's face faded as she smiled, making her look younger than the forty years I had originally guessed. Thirty? Thirty-five?

"Sorry it had to be under such circumstances. Sheriff Duncan called to say you were on your way. You made good time." Linda directed the last to Myra Johnson.

"Not much traffic out there tonight," the deputy said.

"Don't I know it." Linda Braun looked in the direction of the motel's dining room and lounge.

"Don't complain. With all this snow, you'll be turning customers away tomorrow," Johnson said.

"Okay . . . okay, you're right," Linda said, replacing the threatening frown with another smile.

"Sheriff Duncan thinks she, Miss Arthur," the deputy corrected, "should be able to get back into the Marfield place in a couple of days."

"Ginny," I corrected.

"Stay as long as you like, Ginny," the motel owner said.

"However long you stay, you'll need your suitcase, and I'm sure not going to baby-sit those cats." With this pronouncement, Johnson pushed back through the set of doors we had just entered as Linda led the way to a counter that ran along one wall. "Let's get the formalities over. Then get you settled. You hungry?" Linda went behind the counter and began punching keys on a computer keyboard.

"Hungry?" she repeated, looking up. An overhead light caught the movement of the woman's shoulder-length hair, turning the darker blonde of age into a youthful gold.

"You know, I think I am," I confessed. The quickie fast-food hamburger and fries I had eaten on the way north were now but a memory.

We finished the registration process just as Myra Johnson banged through the front door. Cold air and a pair of loudly protesting Siamese cats accompanied her.

"You do take pets, don't you?" I looked anxiously from the caged pair to the woman behind the counter.

A grin spread across the innkeeper's face. "Sheriff Duncan warned me about those two," she said. "But seeing we're not busy tonight, they won't be disturbing anyone but you."

"Is she here yet? Did she really see the body? Was it really in a freezer?" A matched set, a pair of girls who to my unpracticed eye looked to be about thirteen or fourteen, burst through a door near the end of the registration desk. "Did you?" they chorused, staring at me in wide-eyed curiosity.

"What on earth are you talking about?" Linda demanded of the pair who, at first glance, looked much like the older woman.

"Oh, Mother."

Mystery solved, I thought, as the girls rolled their eyes in typical adolescent fashion.

"Don't oh, Mother, me. I asked you a question."

"Jimmy was in the emergency room when Doc Wacker arrived with the body," one of the matched set offered. "He called and told us all about it."

"Jimmy told *you* all about it," her sister corrected.

"Should have expected something like that," Myra Johnson muttered. "Keeping a secret around here is like carrying water in a sieve; can't be done."

"Do you know who she is?" the girls asked, shifting their attention from me to the deputy.

Myra held up a restraining hand. "Back off, you two. This is police business. How can we solve the crime if everyone in town knows more about it than we do?"

"Crime? Was she murdered?" asked one of the girls.

"Of course she was murdered," said the other twin. "You don't think she climbed in that freezer by herself, do you?"

"Enough, enough," their mother ordered. "Miss Arthur, in case you haven't already guessed, these two are my daughters, Kimberly and Deborah."

"Mom always introduces Kimberly first," said the twin whom I presumed to be Deborah.

"That's because I was born first." Kimberly dug an elbow into her sister's rib. "And everyone calls us Kim and Deb."

"That's enough," Linda commanded. "You two show Ginny to her room and help her get settled."

As if seconding the motion, the Siamese pair howled agreement.

"I'll take the cats," Kim or Deb said.

"I guess that leaves me the suitcase," grumbled the other twin, who I'd bet was Deb if I were a gambler.

"There's some chili in the kitchen, Ginny. Will that be okay with you?" Linda asked.

I said it was and hurried after the fast-disappearing twins. In a town where girls went missing and bodies turned up in freezers, who knew what might happen if they were to get out of my sight?

Chapter Three

I FOLLOWED THE EXCITED CHATTER of the girls and the plaintive meows of the cats, stopping when they stopped before a room at the far end of the hall. The suitcase-carrying twin (Deb?) swiped a key card through the electronic lock of Room 110.

"Quick, Ginny! Close the door, so we can let the cats out," Kim said, or maybe it was Deb. Hell, it was late, I was tired, and . . .

"We can let them out, can't we?" the other asked somewhat hesitantly.

I nodded and watched the Siamese make their escape.

"They're adorable," one said, as both grabbed for the feline pair.

I watched the chase, sure of the outcome before the race had hardly begun. The girls did look like their mother, but. . . . Their legs were long, promising a height greater than hers, and while the woman's hair was a faded blonde, the girls' hair was darker, brown not blonde. Their eyes, too, were different, not the vivid blue of their mother's, but a rich chocolate brown. The father had obviously contributed much to their gene pool.

"What are their names?" the twin who was settling a cat in her lap asked.

"You have Hera, and the one stalking the corner of the spread is Zeus."

"Greek gods," the twins chorused.

"How clever," one added.

"I didn't name them," I said. "They came already named."

"Then whoever had them before was pretty smart," the other said.

I said nothing. The cats had belonged to a couple, one a murderer, the other a victim.

"Which one are you?" I asked instead, looking at the twin who was stroking Hera.

"Deb."

"And I'm Kim," Kim said, flopping across the bed. "What can you tell us about the murder?" Kim rolled on her side, propped her head in her hand, and gave me an expectant look.

"Jimmy thinks he's so smart, but he only got to see the murdered girl, and here we are, talking to the person who found the body," Deb said.

Kim frowned. "You didn't kill her by any chance, did you?"

"Of course she didn't, Kim," Deb said. "Ginny only got here today, and the dead girl was frozen stiff. Jimmy said she was all folded up, sort of rounded, like she was trying to keep warm."

"What else did Jimmy tell you?" I asked, wondering who this Jimmy, this font of information, was.

"Nothing," Kim answered. "That's why we're asking you."

"Like you said, I just got here. What could I possibly know?"

"Her name for starters," Deb said, "or if not her name, you can at least tell us what she looks like."

"I bet the sheriff knows who she is," Kim declared.

"Oh, Kim, be still. If Sheriff Duncan knew who she was, he would have told Doc Wacker, and Jimmy says they logged her in as a Jane Doe."

"Didn't anyone even have a guess as to who she was?" Kim persisted.

"Deputy Bryant thought she might be a Frazier," I offered.

"Frazier," Deb screwed her face in concentration. "Wasn't that the family that moved to the Upper Peninsula a few years back?"

"You might be right," Kim said, "but I don't remember if there were any girls . . ." Kim broke off in mid sentence. "How old was she, Ginny?"

"She was young, I'd guess maybe a year or two older than you two."

"Fifteen? Sixteen?" Kim shook her head. "Can't think of any girls that age named Frazier who used to live here."

"We can ask at church on Sunday and at school Monday," Deb said.

Zeus, tired of battling the spread, sprang up on the bed, stalked around Kim's prone body, and proceeded to knead a pillow into shape.

"Here, kitty, kitty," Kim coaxed. Zeus ignored the girl's entreaties and settled into the pillow. "Be that way," Kim scolded.

"If you want a cat to cuddle, you'll have to talk your sister into sharing Hera. Zeus isn't the cuddling type," I said.

Kim nudged aside her twin's hand and began to stroke Hera's back. "Good kitty," she crooned. She looked at the other cat. "See what you're missing?"

Zeus's tail switched. Annoyance? Contempt? Knowing Zeus as I did, I guessed the latter.

I zippered open my suitcase and pulled out the bag of toiletries. The clothes I'd leave. If I were only going to be here a couple of days . . .

The telephone rang. Being closest, I answered. It was Linda, telling us the chili was ready. "We'll be right there," I promised.

"Mom?" Deb asked.

"Mom, and she said if we didn't get ourselves over there, she'd throw the chili out."

The girls deposited Hera on the bed and headed for the door. "We'd better get moving then," Kim said, "or she just might do that," the two finished together.

We headed back the way we had come, bypassed the lobby, and ended in the dining room. The twins called a greeting to the woman serving plates of food to a couple in a booth. Another pair, both males, sat on stools at the bar. Each held a can of beer in his hand.

"We're here, Mom," called one of the twins. As Deb was no longer holding Hera and Kim was no longer lounging across the bed, I was back to not knowing who was who.

"In here," Linda Braun's call preceded her appearance in the doorway. "We're eating in the kitchen. Is that okay with you, Ginny?"

I said it was and followed the twins and their mother into a brightly lighted kitchen.

A large commercial range, flanked on either side by a pair of ovens, dominated one wall. On the opposite wall four single-unit sinks and a pair of dishwashers looked equally impressive. Another pair of doors, which I later learned were a walk-in refrigerator and freezer, was at the end of the room. Did everything around here come in pairs?

An island with wooden counter-tops and a center sink filled the middle of the room. Pots and pans of every conceivable size and shape hung overhead.

There were, however, three things that caught my immediate attention. One was a man of indeterminate age, resplendent in a large white apron and chef's hat, chopping vegetables at the middle island. Another was the unmistakable aroma of chili simmering in a large pot on the stove. The last was the man who rose from the chair in which he had been sitting.

"Just dropped by to make sure you were settled, Miss Arthur," Sheriff Duncan said.

"I invited Rick to eat with us," Linda said, exchanging a warm smile with the sheriff. "It's late, and there's no sense in him having to go home to an empty house and cook a meal."

"Can't hardly refuse Linda's chili," the sheriff said.

He settled again at the large round table that could easily accommodate eight to ten. A coffee mug sat on the place mat before him. Four other place mats with napkins and cutlery were circled around the table.

Linda added a basket of French bread, along with a bowl each of sour cream and grated cheese.

"The bowls are on the counter, girls. Please dish up the chili." Her words were not a command, just a request, but it was obvious she expected they would be obeyed.

They were, and I watched the girls fill the bowls. Moving in and around each other in a well-practiced dance choreographed just for them, they placed the bowls on the table. The mother had taught her girls well. Linda motioned me to a seat between Kim and Deb.

"So, are you settled in?" the sheriff asked.

"She is," Kim answered.

"And so are Zeus and Hera," Deb added. "They're named for Greek gods. Isn't that clever?"

"Sheriff Duncan is talking to Miss Arthur." Linda looked at her daughter. "Let's give her the opportunity to answer his questions."

"I am settled in, and so are my cats," I said.

"Zeus and Hera," Deb repeated.

I laughed, was joined by the twins, then by the sheriff's deeper rumbling, and finally the mother's musical-sounding laugh.

"They'll run over you if you let them, Ginny." Linda looked from one daughter to the other.

"Any guess as to how long it will be before I can get back in the Marfield place?" I looked at Sheriff Duncan as I spooned up more chili, sipping at the edge before placing the spoon in my mouth.

"I'm still hoping a couple of days, but I'm not promising anything."

"We'll take good care of you, Ginny," Deb said. Her words carried the cheerful assurance reserved for the young. "You can have your meals with us here in the kitchen, and Kim and I will take you out on the snowmobile, and we can go skiing. Do you like cross-country or downhill?"

Linda frowned at her loquacious daughter. "Give Ginny time to catch her breath. Maybe she came up here to get some rest or be alone."

"Ginny's on vacation, Mom. No one likes to be alone on vacation," Deb said.

"Ginny told us the murdered girl might be a Frazier," Kim interrupted. "Is that true, Sheriff Duncan?"

"Who said anything about her being murdered?" Rick Duncan said.

Kim snorted. "Nobody climbs in a freezer and pulls the lid shut behind them."

"And who said anything about her being in a freezer?" Duncan looked at Ginny.

"Don't blame me," I protested. "I'm not the informant. You have an effective grapevine up here, of which, I can assure you, I am no part."

The sheriff looked from one twin to the other. "So, where did you get your information?"

"Jimmy," Deb said without hesitation. "He was in the hospital when they brought in the girl's body. Only he said they logged her in as a Jane Doe, and Ginny said Deputy Bryant thinks she might be one of the Fraziers who used to live around here."

"We don't remember them, but then it's been a while since they lived here," Kim added.

"We're going to ask the kids at church on Sunday if anyone remembers there being a Frazier girl about our age who moved to the Upper Peninsula," Deb finished.

The air left my lungs as I listened to their rapid-fire delivery. How do they do it? I wondered, gulping in air.

"Jimmy Wakefield?" Sheriff Duncan asked, returning the conversation to its starting point. He was obviously used to the twins' high-velocity delivery system.

"Jimmy Wakefield," Kim answered. "He's a hospital volunteer."

"He took the course they give. He wants to be a doctor." Deb offered the information with pride of ownership.

"If he's going to be a doctor, he'd better learn to keep his mouth shut," Duncan said.

"Is it true?" Linda said. "Does Kevin Bryant think she might be a Frazier?"

"That's what he said, but we don't know. Haven't had time to check it out yet. I'll get Juanita started on it first thing tomorrow."

"I seem to remember there being a family of Fraziers around here, maybe three, four years ago. I remember they moved away, but I don't know where they went."

Linda's eyes took on a faraway look. Was she remembering something else that happened three or four years ago? Watching her face, I doubted it had anything to do with the Fraziers. Sheriff Duncan, too, must have sensed her withdrawal.

"Linda," his voice was gentle. His hand covered over the work-roughened hand that lay on the table between them.

Linda shook her head as if to clear it and murmured a faint, "Sorry," before drawing her hand from beneath his.

I watched the interchange, wondering as I did how many late-night suppers these two had shared either with or without benefit of twin chaperones.

"Don't you think it's a good idea we ask if anyone remembers a Frazier girl about our age?" Kim asked.

"No, I don't," Sheriff Duncan said, "and I don't want to hear anything about either you or your sister asking any questions about anything connected with the case." Duncan looked from Kim to Deb.

"This is police business, serious police business, and I don't want you two putting your noses in it," he added, his voice harsh.

I looked from one twin to the other, seeing first the surprised look on their faces, then the look of determination that flashed in their eyes. It was the last that held my attention.

"Understand?" The sheriff's voice rang with authority, much as it had when directed at me earlier that day.

The girls slowly nodded their heads. I wouldn't say for sure, but I had the distinct feeling both had their fingers crossed.

Apparently satisfied, Sheriff Duncan rose from his seat. "I've got to hit the road, Linda." He moved around the table, stopping beside my chair. "You'll need to come by Headquarters tomorrow and give us a statement," he said. "Any time will do, late morning, afternoon. If we don't get any more snow, the county will have cleared the roads by then."

"My car . . ."

Duncan waved my words aside. "Give me your keys. One of my deputies will bring it over in the morning."

I fished the keys from my purse, voicing my thanks as I handed them over.

Linda called a good-bye to the chef who had finished his chopping and followed the sheriff through the door that led into the dining room, the couple's voices growing faint in the distance.

The silence around the table was broken by the clank of silverware and bowls bumping against bowls, homey sounds of a table being cleared. Another sound, a sigh, intruded.

"Do you suppose we got Jimmy in trouble?" Deb asked.

Chapter Four

Tired as I was, sleep did not come easily. When it did, nightmares intertwined with dreams made me wish I were still awake. The girl, her face hidden by long strands of blonde hair, held center stage. Like a ball she lay curled among the frozen meat and vegetables, her limbs folded tight against her middle. If pushed, would she roll?

I struggled, trapped in a tangle of sheets. Sleep, I needed sleep. No! Mustn't sleep. The girl . . .

Pain, biting, persistent, drove sleep away. I shifted my weight off my shoulder, found the scar, and massaged gently. A unicorn, suspended on a chain around my neck, insinuated itself between my fingers.

A phone rang. One . . . two . . . three times! I reached out, grabbed my cell without knocking it to the floor, and brought it to my ear. Savoring the silence, I didn't answer.

"Ginny?" a voice asked.

"Larry?" I asked cautiously. Was something wrong? Why was he calling so early? Sleep fled, taking with it the last vestiges of the dream.

"It's not early," he said, answering my thought. "It's after eight."

I struggled to a sitting position. The drapes were closed, lending the room an artificial darkness. My eyes found the bedside table. The digital clock read 8:11.

I yawned. "I had a busy day yesterday."

"So I hear. Moving in and out of cabins and motel rooms can be rather tiring," said Larry Rhodes, a lieutenant in the Marion City Police Department and, since Uncle David's disappearance, my self-appointed caretaker.

"And what did you hear?" I fought for calm, but had already lost the battle.

"That you're up to your old tricks."

"I presume you're talking about the body in the freezer?" I said in a measured tone, but my words were loud in my ear.

"You're damn right I'm referring to the body in the freezer."

"Are you inferring I put the damn thing in the freezer?" I gave my anger full rein.

"You should have called me. I didn't appreciate hearing about it from Judge Marfield."

And like falling dominoes, his words fell into place.

"She thought you might need someone with you." He paused. "I didn't mean to yell at you." His voice lost its edge. Sounded, well . . . almost apologetic.

"You call me at eight o'clock in the morning, jump my frame, and. . . . What did you think? That I had put the girl in the freezer or, worse yet, that I had killed her and then stuffed her in the freezer?" Whatever load of guilt he was selling, I wasn't buying.

"Ginny, you're not making sense."

"About as much sense as you are." Another thought demanded attention. "How did you know I was at the motel and not the cabin?"

"Sheriff Duncan told the judge . . ."

". . . and Judge Marfield told you," I interrupted, watching another domino fall.

"Ginny?" He paused. "How are you really?"

"I'm fine. Could have used more sleep, but . . ." I let the sentence dangle, let the anger drain away.

"Okay, okay. I said I was sorry."

"You said you didn't mean to yell at me," I corrected.

Rhodes sighed. Ours was definitely an adversarial relationship.

"When is Steve coming up?" he asked.

"Sunday."

"Are you sure? His schedule isn't that reliable." He hesitated. "And MacPhearson?" Rhodes asked, naming the Marion City detective who had all but lost his life in a shoot-out last November during the city's annual Santa Claus parade.

"He's coming up," I said. This being another touchy subject, I didn't elaborate.

"I guess you know what you're doing."

Which is what I've been trying to tell you, I thought, but did not say. I pushed the cell phone tighter against my ear. Was Rhodes grinding his teeth?

"You've still got a ways to go with that shoulder, and MacPhearson . . ." If nothing else, Rhodes was persistent.

"Drop it," I said.

Heavy breathing sounded over the phone. Rhodes was not having a good morning. The thought lifted my spirits. One way or another, I meant to break the tie that binds.

We said our good-byes, surprisingly pleasant given the circumstances.

I wavered between staying in bed or getting up. Getting up won. A shower first, I decided, then breakfast, after which I'd tackle Sheriff Duncan and the Lake County constabulary. Setting the plan in motion, I swung my legs off the bed, dumping the Siamese pair from my lap.

The couple from last night were having breakfast in the dining room when I passed through, but the drinkers from the bar were not there. I shared a smile with the couple. They were about my age, but despite our shared smiles, it was obvious they were more interested in each other.

The kitchen, though no beehive of activity, showed more action this morning than the night before. The chef was back, slicing and dicing at the center island, along with a short but sturdy middle-aged man who offered a welcoming smile as he filled a mug with coffee from a large urn on a side counter. Linda sat at the round table, a ledger and several file folders near at hand. Her blonde head lifted as I came through the door.

"Grab some coffee and come join us," she called in welcome. "This is Juan Torres. He does the heavy cleaning, and his wife Rosa does the rooms."

"Hi, Miss Arthur," a voice called from near the walk-in refrigerator. "I'll see to your room now that you're up." Near the same age as Juan, who was now leaning against the counter drinking his coffee, I took her to be his wife Rosa.

I filled a mug and brought it to the table.

"Bacon and eggs," Linda asked, "or are you a fruit and cereal girl?"

"How about some toast?" I said.

"Bagel with cream cheese?" Linda tempted.

"A bagel will be fine."

Rosa joined us, bringing with her a pitcher of orange juice and several glasses. "Will your cats mind me coming in the room?"

"Not a bit, but just leave some towels and don't bother with changing the sheets. I'm only staying a couple of days."

"As long as you're our guest, Rosa will do your room," Linda said. "We're not as fancy as some of the big city hotels, but our service is four star, and that includes fresh linen and Ted's cooking."

The chef brandished his chopping knife. "Ted Williams," he said, the smile on his face belying the menacing blade in his hand.

I laughed. "Okay, I'm yours to pamper. Rosa can do my room, and Ted can toast my bagel."

"Coming right up." The cook, who with his short stature and bulky frame bore no resemblance to the baseball super-star whose name he shared, set a bagel with an assortment of cream cheeses before me.

Linda ran a pencil down the list lying before her and exchanged it for another. "We're about filled up tonight," she said.

"How many rooms do you have?"

"Just over a hundred."

I looked at Rosa. She was short like her husband, but not as sturdy. "I hope you'll have some help tomorrow. A hundred rooms makes for a lot of cleaning."

"We manage with a skeleton staff when we're not busy but bring in additional help when we need it," Linda explained. "Up here you learn to go with the flow, but this snow will bring out the snowmobilers, cross-country skiers, and the ice fishermen."

"No downhill types?"

"Cadillac gets most of that market, but we get the overflow. We'll never be millionaires, but this place provides a comfortable living," Linda said.

"And Linda's a good employer. Wouldn't want to work anyplace else," Rosa said. She drained her coffee mug and headed for the first of the four sinks. "Hera and Zeus?" she asked. She rinsed her mug and placed it in the dishwasher.

My mind on motels, guests, and winter sports, I missed the question.

"Zeus and Hera? The cats' names?" Rosa repeated.

"Right," I said, and was rewarded with a smile from the woman whose swarthy complexion spoke more of sunshine than snow.

"Your car's out front." Linda fished a set of keys from the pocket of her jeans and laid them on the table. "Kev Bryant dropped it off about an hour ago."

I thanked Linda for playing messenger, picked up my dishes, and took them to the sink. Rinsing them as I had seen Rosa do, I placed them in the dishwasher.

The bed was made, fresh towels were on their racks in the bathroom, and a pair of Siamese cats slept in the pool of sunlight that poured through the sliding glass doors that led to a snow-covered patio. I didn't stay long. Just grabbed my parka, checked to see if my hat, gloves, and scarf were in the pockets, and let myself back out the door.

What with the scarcity of cars in the lot, the Honda was not hard to find, the blue color shining gem-like against the white snow. I thumbed the remote and slid behind the wheel. Though still not as user friendly as my Ranger, it had a new car smell and several amenities, like automatic door locks and a heater that produced instant warmth, to both of which I had become addicted.

Houses appeared along the highway, replacing the oaks, birches, and maples as I drew nearer Pine City. A convenience-store-cum-gas station marked the beginning of the business section. Several small specialty stores abutted snow-banked sidewalks, their windows reflecting the morning sun. A traffic light signaled me to a stop. I was obviously traveling Pine City's main street, and just as obvious was the corner street sign that labeled it Pine Street. What else?

Another block brought me to my destination, the Lake County Sheriff's Office. I pulled into the parking lot and found an empty visitor's slot.

The building, a nondescript, single-story cinder-block edifice, boasted few windows and a flat snow-covered roof.

A uniformed officer looked up as I pushed through the door.

"Ginny Arthur," I said. "Sheriff Duncan asked that I come by and fill out a report this morning."

"Deputy Schmidt," he said. "The sheriff is expecting you."

I approached the desk. Older and several inches shorter than Kevin Bryant, Deputy Schmidt offered a thin-lipped smile. "I'll tell him you're here." Schmidt disappeared through a door behind the desk, leaving me alone in the small reception area.

Before I had time to settle into what looked like all the other chairs in all the other waiting rooms I'd ever been in, Schmidt was back. "Through here, Miss Arthur," he said, holding the door wide.

The room behind the door was easily two to three times larger than the reception area and held four desks, two deputies—one male, the other female—and one sheriff.

The sheriff came forward, his hand held out in greeting. "You prefer to dictate your statement or type it out on one of these computers?" he asked without preamble. His smile grew large. "We tend to be a bit informal around here, Miss Arthur, but truth is, we don't have anyone who can take shorthand, at least not today."

Our secretary, Carol Whiting, is snowed in and probably won't get plowed out until this afternoon."

"I can type the statement on the computer," I said, thinking it would save someone, the snow-bound secretary no doubt, from having to transcribe my handwritten or recorded notes.

Sheriff Duncan pointed to a nearby computer. "Bentley, show her how to use this thing."

A young black man, a very young black man, wearing the uniform of the Lake County Sheriff's Department, pulled the chair away from the desk and motioned me to sit down. Young though he was, his teaching skills were excellent, and I soon had the keyboard humming. Forcing my mind back to yesterday afternoon, I recorded my arrival at Judge Marfield's vacation home, moving from activity to activity until the fatal moment when, intent on finding the promised dinner Marsha Marfield had told me would be there, I lifted the freezer lid.

I typed quickly, telling of the sheriff's arrival and that of the two deputies and Doctor Wacker, finishing with my leaving with Myra Johnson. I scrolled back to the beginning, read through the document, changed the wording when needed, and finished with a spell check. I pushed away from the computer.

Deputy Bentley was there, leaning over my shoulder. "Ready to print?"

I said it was and watched the printed pages slide into the printer tray. I spent the next few minutes reviewing my work.

"Look okay to you?"

I started at the sound of his voice. For such a big man Sheriff Richard Duncan was very light on his feet. My mind lurched as I pictured another light-footed policeman, this one with hair even more red than mine, slipping through Marion City's crowded streets, passing groups of boisterous parade watchers waiting for Santa and his sleigh.

The sheriff read through my statement. "Looks good," he said, unaware of my trip into the past. He handed me the report. "Sign and date it, and be sure you initial each page."

I did as directed, handing the report to Bentley when I finished.

"Carol will be glad to see this," he said, slipping the pages into a folder. "Besides doing most of the secretarial work around here, she's the receptionist and dispatcher." He waved at a window that showed a large expanse of white. "With all this snow, we're bound to get a lot of tourists, and a lot of tourists means a lot of work for the department." His smile took the edge off his words.

"You're right about the tourists. Linda Braun said the motel's about booked full already." I paused. Looked up at the sheriff. "Does this mean you'll be too busy to finish processing the Marfield place today?"

"Bryant and Johnson should finish tonight or, if not, tomorrow morning. The judge said you were expecting some house guests and had to be back in tomorrow afternoon at the latest."

"If this will compromise your case . . ." I started.

"Not only are Johnson and Bryant fast workers, they're also very good at their jobs. They'll be out of the judge's place tomorrow morning at the latest."

The sheriff's tone brooked no argument, and I moved off the subject. "Were you able to identify the body?" I asked, slipping into my parka.

Duncan shook his head. "Juanita's been on the phone most of the morning checking, but so far she hasn't turned up a thing. If someone has gone missing, nobody's talking about it."

I looked at Juanita, the female half of the pair of deputies I had seen when first entering the room. A set of earphones covered her ears, and her eyes focused on a scrolling computer screen. Being familiar with the latest in integrated computer systems, Arthur and Arthur used only the latest and the best. I knew that what I was seeing was hi-tech, very hi-tech. How, I wondered, did a place as small as Lake County have access to such expensive equipment? Shared time? Government issue? Camp Whiting was, I knew, but a stone's throw from here.

I pulled on my cap and readied the zipper on the parka. "Nothing from Doctor Wacker?" It was a fishing expedition, but Sheriff Duncan wasn't biting.

"Not yet." The sheriff pursed his lips. Gave me a speculative look. "Then I'm not telling you anything you don't already know, am I, Miss Arthur?"

Gentle though it was, I caught the sheriff's rebuke. Was he telling me to back off? And if so, why?

Because it's none of your business, a voice inside my head said.

The sun was nearing the midpoint when I left the sheriff's office. Caught again by the town's only traffic light, I took in the scene around me. Both pedestrian and vehicle traffic abounded, promising a busy week, or at least a weekend, for both the Braun Motel and the Lake County Sheriff's Department. To my right, a brightly painted sign on a nearby store caught my attention. Duncan's Meats it read.

Chapter Five

A PARKING PLACE OPENED UP. On impulse, I pulled in and joined the throng of pedestrian traffic that threatened to bottleneck every storefront and doorway along Pine Street. Not that the array of goods on display wasn't enticing, but intent on reaching Duncan's Meats, my patience was wearing thin.

"Why aren't you out on your snowmobiles or pushing your skis through all that white stuff out there?" I muttered under my breath as I excused my way through the crowd.

"We're taking the snowmobiles out after lunch," one pair chorused to another.

"Excuse me," I said, not giving the second couple a chance to say what they intended to do about snowmobiling after lunch.

The four smiled and drew closer together, allowing me room to slip past. I did, grabbing onto the door handle before another group of sidewalk strollers barred my way.

The meat market was filled with shoppers. Some, temporary cabin dwellers like me no doubt, walked the aisles, pushing carts filled with one of everything Duncan's Meats had to offer. Others gathered two and three deep in front of the meat counter. The glass-fronted cooler stood almost shoulder high. Running the width of the store, it provided space for a great variety of meats. Used to shopping Marion City's supermarkets with their offering of packaged goods, I stared open-mouthed through the protective window.

"You have to take a number," a nearby voice instructed.

I followed the voice's pointing finger to where a stack of numbered plastic cards hung from a rack above the counter.

Another voice, this one close to my opposite elbow, said. "You just looking, or you thinking of buying, Miss Arthur?"

Surprised, I turned in the direction of the second voice. Doctor Wacker, wearing yesterday's plaid coat and knitted scarf, smiled at me.

"Looking," I confessed. "No place to put it if I did buy something." I thought of the freezer with its grizzly contents and knew no matter how many times it was scrubbed, I would never be able to use.

"Jim, that girl you're talking to, she the one who's staying in the Marfield place?" a voice boomed from behind the counter. "If it is, tell her I'll have the new freezer in place by tomorrow afternoon."

What was it with this place? I thought. Did mind reading come with the territory?

"Ardella, meet Miss Arthur," Jim Wacker said.

The arms and shoulders that hovered above the counter spoke of a tall muscular woman; her smile and a come-closer nod of her head showed a welcoming personality.

"Ardella Duncan," she said, offering a meaty hand (bad joke, I know). "The judge called and ordered another freezer and told me to fill it up. Said some folks would be using the place for a couple of weeks."

I found myself shaking the beefy hand (I grimaced inwardly; I knew this joke was as bad as the first). I looked for a smile, found I had one, and offered it to Ardella Duncan. "Thanks," I managed.

"Any particular cuts you'd like me to put in?"

I stared in dismay at the numerous cuts of meats Duncan's offered.

"You want I should put in what I usually do?"

"The usual will do," I said, broadening my smile and reclaiming my hand.

"Sunday afternoon," she promised. Ardella Duncan looked at the rack of reclaimed numbers on the spindle and called, "Forty-seven."

"Here," a voice from further down the counter answered.

I tailed after Jim Wacker.

"Just came in for a loaf of bread," he said, grabbing a loaf of rye from off the shelf. "How about coming home with me and helping me eat some of the ham I have in the refrigerator?" He gave me an amused look, adding as I hesitated, "If you don't, I'll be eating ham for another week."

"Seeing as it's lunch time and I'm hungry, Doctor Wacker, I'll be glad to share that ham with you. Don't happen to have some Swiss cheese and dill pickles to go with it, do you?"

I followed the doctor into the driveway of a large white frame house. Black shutters, relieving the stark whiteness, bordered a pair of oversized front windows located either side of a set of double doors.

We continued around the house. Following Doc Wacker's lead, I climbed from the Honda, crossed a patch of snow-covered grass, and ascended a short flight of stairs.

"Front door's for patients," he said, inserting a key into the lock of a door that was far less impressive than the oversized pair in the front of the house. "Besides," he continued, "this is the part I live in. The other half is for working, and I'm not working today. Today I'm having a lovely lady for lunch."

A smile played over his face, and a merry twinkle lighted his eyes, confirming the man's sense of humor.

"You can hang your coat on the pegs over there, and leave your boots in the bin. Floor's clean, so you won't get your socks dirty."

I did as instructed and, avoiding the puddles of melting snow at the entryway, walked stocking-footed into what I can best describe as a country kitchen. Big, with polished pine cupboards and counter-tops, I was reminded of my Grandma Wickie's kitchen. Feeling like I had come home, I settled into a wooden chair beside a matching table.

"Hope you're hungry," Doc Wacker said.

He pulled ham, not the sliced deli ham I was used to, but a real ham, bone and all, from the refrigerator. Swiss cheese, dill pickle spears, and yellow mustard followed.

"I like mine grilled," he said, setting a large black skillet on the stove. "And you?"

"Same," I said, already tasting the toasted rye bread, warmed ham, and melted cheese.

My imagination did not disappoint, and later, sipping from a mug of steaming coffee, I groaned contentedly. "Are you for hire?" I asked.

"You need a doctor?" Wacker teased. He laughed, and I laughed with him.

"How long have you been living here?" I asked.

"Just over thirty years. Mary Ellen and I came here right after I finished my family practice residency. We bought this place about a year later." The doctor stared into his mug. "Sometimes it seems like it was yesterday, and other times I'd swear it was a lifetime ago."

"Mary Ellen is your wife?" I said, happy to know the name of the woman who had created this pleasant room.

"Was," Doc Wacker corrected. "Mary Ellen died last year."

"I'm sorry," I said, offering the apology in the embarrassed way people do.

"No need, Miss Arthur. You couldn't have known." He took a long sip from the mug he cradled in his hands. "Ovarian cancer," he explained. "We thought it was a stomach or bowel upset. When we got around to doing other tests it was too late. The cancer had spread. The drugs that might have helped her if we had caught it earlier didn't help."

"Did Mary Ellen do the kitchen?"

"Not only did Mary Ellen do the kitchen, she did the whole house." The doctor laughed. "You should have seen it around here. She had the whole damn place torn up for months—hell, years." He laughed, wiping the corner of his eye with his fingertip. "We moved the office to the front half of the house and kept the back and second floor for ourselves."

Doctor Wacker's combined office and living arrangements reminded me of the Marion City office building that housed the Arthur and Arthur Security Agency. A combination of business offices and a penthouse apartment that had, until his disappearance almost three years ago, been Uncle David's home.

"Worked out real well, especially after the girls were born, seeing that Mary Ellen was wife, mother, nurse, and office manager," the doctor continued. "That is until she got too sick to work."

"Do your daughters still live at home?"

"Oh, no, they're long gone. Both girls live in California, around San Diego. They prefer perpetual sunshine to snow and cold." He sighed. "I can be glad of one thing, though, at least I know where my girls are."

"You're referring to the Shouldice and Leggit girls?" I asked.

"Cindy Shouldice and Josie Leggit. Gave them both a school physical when they started junior high."

"This is a small community," I said. "Don't you think it strange two girls would go missing at the same time?"

"If you're suggesting anything more than they ran away . . ." The doctor's voice trailed off. "The sheriff did everything he could to find them, and it's still an open case."

I sipped at my coffee. Like Myra Johnson, Doc Wacker had Cindy Shouldice and Josie Leggit pegged as runaways. It was time to change the subject.

"What about the Fraziers? Do you have any record of there being a girl who would be about fifteen or sixteen now?"

The doctor drained his coffee and placed the mug on the table. "Hard to say. It's a good-sized family, especially if you count all the aunts and uncles. But I don't have any record of having seen any of them in the past four or five years."

He pushed away from the table. "How about more coffee?"

I said yes, and we continued to talk, progressing from Miss Arthur to Ginny and Doctor Wacker to Jim. At last, feeling like I'd more than overstayed my welcome, I rose to leave.

"Stop by any time, Ginny, and if my nurse tells you I'm too busy, you just tell her I said to make time."

Promising I would, I headed back into town.

The motel parking lot was full, and I was forced to park at the back of the lot. As the lot had been plowed, Juan's work most likely, I had no trouble getting to my room. A pair of cats, hungry cats from the sound of them, and a blinking message light on the phone welcomed me.

I took care of the cats, then grabbed a bottle of water from the fridge and picked up the phone. The message was from Steve. Settling my backside on the bed and a smile on my face, I dialed my lover's number.

Chapter Six

The call did not go well. The near blizzard conditions that had plagued Pine City had vented their remaining fury on Marion City. The residents, who somehow never seemed to adjust to the vagaries of northern winters, slipped and slid into each other both on foot and in cars. It was the cars that caused the most damage, and Mercy Hospital, being the city's designated trauma center, received all of the major traffic accidents and a goodly share of the minor ones.

"I'm up to my neck, Ginny, and it's impossible for me to get away. Maybe next weekend . . ."

"What about MacPhearson?" I asked, hoping the shift in subject would ease my disappointment.

"It's all arranged. MacPhearson will be there tomorrow. He'll leave here sometime after noon. He wants to make sure all the roads are clear."

"He? Who's driving him up?" I straightened, freeing myself from my nest of pillows. "Not Rhodes," I protested.

"Stop worrying, Ginny. It's all arranged. MacPhearson will be there tomorrow afternoon."

I didn't stop worrying. Steve knew I wouldn't, and despite his assurance, I continued to nag until a persistent page called him away.

I finished the bottle of water I had been nursing and stared into space. I was disappointed by the turn of events, bitterly disappointed if truth be told. This was not the first time Steve had canceled, nor would it be the last. Being the Chief Resident, not only was he responsible for his own considerable workload, he was responsible 24/7 for the interns and first year residents who rotated through the emergency/trauma areas, and things would not be getting any better. Steve had applied for advanced training in trauma surgery, and the best training centers were a long, long way from Marion City.

I swung my legs over the side of the bed, giving Hera an affectionate hug in passing. No sense in venting my frustration on the innocent cat. I headed for the bathroom. What I needed was a shower, a cold shower.

I sat alone in a corner of the dining room at a table for two. Why am I not surprised? In this place almost everything, except me, came in pairs. Proving the point, Kim and Deb materialized beside me.

"The beef stroganoff is your best bet," one said, offering a menu.

"With apple pie and ice cream for dessert," said the other, pouring my water.

"How about a glass of house red for starters?" the two chorused.

Despite my resolve to revel in self-pity, I laughed. "Whatever you say." I handed back the menu. "What have the two of you been up to today? Snowmobiling? Skiing?"

"Don't we wish? Mom's had us working all day, morning and afternoon. First it was help Rosa, then Ted, then Juan, and here we are now helping Maggie." Both girls answered, one after the other in what I had come to recognize as their customary machine-gun style.

"But we'll have extra help tomorrow. Want to go skiing?" the twin who handed me the menu asked.

"Can't. I'm expecting to get back in the cabin tomorrow, and the butcher promised to deliver a new freezer full of meat."

"Too bad, we know some good trails, ones the tourists don't know about," said the twin with the water pitcher.

They turned, ready to leave. "Wait," I called. "When is Mass and where is the church?"

The twin with the water pitcher called over her shoulder, "Be in the lobby by nine-thirty. You can go with us."

I met the Braun family in the motel lobby at the appointed time and rode with them in a much-used Ford Explorer to St. Paul's. Built of red brick and stone, the church blended into its wooded surroundings and looked as I imagined it had looked when it was built nearly one hundred fifty years ago. Not large by Marion City standards, the church held the Pine City congregation with several pews to spare.

"You'll like Father Mike," the twin who wore a bright red scarf said, naming the local pastor.

I guessed her to be Kim when the other ran off to where a boy wearing a big smile waited. "Jimmy Wakefield?" I asked.

"That's Jimmy," Kim said.

"The informer?"

"What informer?" Linda Braun, who had dropped us at the front of the church while she parked the Explorer, joined us.

"Ginny's talking about Jimmy leaking hospital information to Deb," Kim explained.

"You know what Sheriff Duncan said about that," the mother reminded as she led us into church.

As when I attended Mass with Grandma Wickie, the parishioners at St. Paul's also met for coffee, rolls, and conversation after Mass. The congregation was younger, and the yelling, screaming, running swarm of toddlers suggested the people were as fertile as the rich farmlands and orchards for which the area was known.

Father Mike, short and round-bellied, had a cherubic smile that dared one not to like him. "I hope you don't go by first impressions," he said. He grabbed my hand and smiled even broader as he pumped it up and down. "Dead bodies are not our usual things, Miss Arthur." The pastor's smile faded, and his handshake slowed.

I opened my mouth to speak, but another parishioner pulled at the priest's sleeve and dragged him away.

I took the opportunity to sample a sweet roll, when I felt a hand on my arm.

"I'm Maggie Schmidt," a woman said. Middle-aged with graying hair, she looked decidedly worried. "I saw you at the motel last night. I work in the dining room."

I searched my memory but came up blank.

"No reason you should remember me, Miss Arthur. We weren't introduced."

I smiled, started to speak, but the woman waved my words aside.

"I wanted to ask you about the body you found." Her voice dropped to a near whisper, and she glanced anxiously around.

I pulled back, telegraphing my reluctance to talk about the dead girl. "You should talk . . ."

But again my words were waved aside. "My brother, Norm Schmidt, is one of Sheriff Duncan's deputies. You met him yesterday morning."

I nodded I had.

"He said you found the girl's body." She drew closer. "If you could just tell me what she looked like," Maggie rushed on. "You see . . ." The woman's waving hand grabbed my arm. Her worried look intensified.

"You really should be talking to Sheriff Duncan about this," I repeated firmly. "Whatever it is you want, I'm sure he can help you." I freed my arm and tried stepping back, but the crush of people kept us close.

"I'm sorry I bothered you, Miss Arthur. Of course, you're right. I should talk to the sheriff, but you were here and . . ." Looking defeated, Maggie Schmidt turned away.

Deb, with Jimmy Wakefield in tow, pushed a plate overflowing with sweet rolls and coffee cake in my face. "Your cats need fattening up, Ginny. How about I take this to them?"

I vetoed Deb's suggestion, threatened murder and mayhem if she dared feed the cats anything but cat food, and turned my attention to Jimmy Wakefield. Taller than the twin by several inches, he had the gangling look of many teenage boys, all arms and legs. His smile was tentative and self-conscious, awkward like the rest of him. "Please don't tell me I shouldn't have told Deb about the Jane Doe we have in the hospital morgue," he said. "Everyone in town's already on my case."

I laughed. He was so earnest. "I won't tell you that you shouldn't have told Deb about the Jane Doe in the hospital morgue," I said.

Deb rolled her eyes. "You sure have a nice way of not telling him, Ginny."

"Tell me," I leaned close to the young man. "Has Doctor Wacker started the post yet? Have they identified her?"

Jimmy's face lit up. "You know . . ."

Deb poked the loquacious teenager in the ribs. "Jimmy," she warned.

His face reddened. "I guess you got me," he said.

It was well into the afternoon when we arrived back at the motel. A message from Sheriff Duncan waited, telling me the deputies had finished with the cabin and that the new freezer was in place. Not that I didn't appreciate Linda Braun's hospitality, I hurriedly repacked what few things I had taken from my suitcase. I shoved the cats into their traveling cage and headed for the parking lot.

Several housekeeping carts, pushed by unfamiliar faces, slowed my progress. Excusing my way between the carts, I dropped the cats and my suitcase in the lobby and went in search of Linda.

The dining room wait staff had been augmented by three or four equally unfamiliar faces. The extra help the Brauns had spoken of must have arrived.

I stuck my head in the kitchen, saw Linda, and thanked her for putting up with me and my feline companions. I spent another minute looking but didn't find Ted, Maggie, or the Torreses.

Sunlight, reflecting off the cars in the parking lot, met me as I exited the motel. Squinting in the glare, I slid my sunglasses in place. Another pair of strangers, both wielding shovels, were busy removing snow drifts the wind had blown into empty parking spaces. A wash of fast-moving clouds hid the afternoon sun. Without warning, day became night and the snow shovelers mere shadows.

I clicked the Honda's doors open and shoved the cats and my suitcase inside. Grabbing the snow brush, I cleared the snow from my windshield, watching the men as I did. Their shadows, sometimes long and sometimes short, disappeared and reappeared between the parked cars. Playful shadows, they enjoyed a whimsical game of peek-a-boo with the sun and clouds.

"I have a little shadow . . ." I sing-songed the Stevenson poem into the cold air. The familiar words, favored memories from childhood, brought a smile to my face, and I left Braun's Motel feeling as carefree and light-hearted as the twins.

The cabin looked much as it had when I first saw it Friday afternoon. Hoping it was not quite the same, I parked the Honda in the drive in front of the large two-storied log house. Though referred to by Judge Marfield and the locals as the cabin, it was definitely not a cabin.

The two-story log structure had a great room with a fieldstone fireplace, laundry, and storage area on the first floor. The second floor held another great room with its own stone fireplace. A bar separated the kitchen from the great room. Oversized thermal pane windows and a set of sliding glass doors led to a covered balcony, which overlooked Big Pine Lake. Two wings, one a bedroom wing and the other the garage wing, flanked the main house. It was cabin living on a grand scale.

I inserted the key into the front lock and pushed the door inward. The silence overwhelmed me. It was in fact a bit eerie, and I looked over my shoulder. There was nothing there. Feeling somewhat foolish, I stepped inside.

The first thing I saw was the freezer. I suppressed a nervous giggle.

Refusing to be cowed, I moved forward. Promising I wouldn't scream, I popped the lid and stared into the frosty depths.

A score of carefully wrapped and labeled packages—rib roast, New York strip, ground chuck—stared back. Alongside were several commercially packaged fruits and vegetables and an assortment of what appeared to be homemade casseroles.

I allowed myself a carefully controlled breath and slammed shut the freezer lid. There was no body inside, male or female, frozen or unfrozen.

Deciding a fast getaway would not be necessary, I ran the Honda into the garage and brought the cats and my suitcase into the cabin. The cats quickly claimed the laundry room with its shelves of sports equipment and winter hats, gloves, and scarfs as their own. I hauled my suitcase up the stairs and claimed one of the two bedrooms, the one with the adjoining bath, as my own. First come, first served, I reasoned.

I marveled at the abundance of drawer space, did a slow turn-around in the dressing room, and vowed to make use of the spa tub and the large, very large, shower with its array of showerheads.

I wandered back into the great room. A large map showing Lake County along with several of the surrounding counties covered most of one wall. Unlike most maps, this one identified areas of local interest.

I found Big Pine Lake and its neighbor, Little Pine Lake, and wondered if Duncan's deputy had been able to find the Fraziers who were said to have lived in the area.

Besides the two lakes, the map also marked the locations of several area farms, noting the owners, acreage, and principal crops. Two especially large tracts stood out, one a forest preserve and the other a National Guard base, specifically Camp Whiting.

The name rang a bell. I had heard it before, and just recently. "Whiting . . . Carol Whiting?" I said to the empty room.

Sheriff Duncan's receptionist, secretary, dispatcher? The Carol who hadn't made it in to work the morning after the storm?

My eyes continued to move over the map. Whiting! There it was again. Another large tract, a farm labeled as belonging to Caroline and Roger Whiting. Was this Caroline Sheriff Duncan's Carol?

Tiring of the map, I went into the kitchen. The sweet roll I had eaten after Mass was long gone. I went to the refrigerator. Had Ardella Duncan, the good fairy who had so generously filled the freezer, extended her bounty to the refrigerator? She had.

I found some deli meats, bread, butter, and mayonnaise. I put it all together and took a big bite. Not as good as Jim Wacker's grilled ham and cheese, it filled the empty place in my stomach. I foraged further and found the fixings for coffee. Leaving the pot to brew, I made another trip to the freezer.

I popped the lid. This time without trepidation. Confronted with choices too many to take in, I pulled out the first casserole my hand closed over. To my delight, it was lasagna.

Dinner decided upon, I poured a mug of coffee, chose satellite music, and made my selection. Light classics best suited my mood, and a medley of Chopin waltzes was just finishing when a knock sounded at the front door.

I hurried downstairs, crossed the great room, and threw open the door. Detective Douglas MacPhearson of the Marion City Police Department stood there. His smile was less broad and his eyes less bright than they had once been, but his hair was just as red. I looked past where he stood to a much-used pickup. "Where is Rhodes?" I asked.

Chapter Seven

MacPhearson looked over his shoulder. "Are you expecting him?"

"Rhodes was supposed to drive you up here!" My face grew hot, heralding the familiar rush of anger and frustration. What was there about this man?

"Rhodes didn't drive me up here. I drove myself."

The sun lost itself behind the snow-laden pines, and a gust of wind pulled at the open door.

"Are you going to let me in?" MacPhearson's mustache twitched.

I wanted to slam the door in his face, but settled for yelling about his having made the trip alone.

"I'm perfectly capable of driving myself up here," he said, interrupting my tirade.

I retreated to the center of the room. Another stronger gust of wind followed, raising goose bumps on my arms. "For heaven's sake, come in and shut the door. We're not heating the outside," I muttered, retreating behind one of Grandma Wickie's axioms.

MacPhearson slammed the door shut.

"Want me to get a room at that motel I passed a few miles back?"

"Fat chance, they're booked solid." I threw up my arms. "Why in hell did you make that trip by yourself? If I had known . . ."

"That's why we didn't tell you."

"We?"

"Steve and me. Doc Brock told me I could do anything I wanted as long as I didn't get too tired."

"And who's to say when you get too tired?" I stared into the familiar face. The lines around his eyes were deeper, and his hair still too short to cover the scar left by the surgeon's knife.

"Me, Ginny. It's me who says when I get tired." His eyes darkened to sapphire, and the muscles in his jaw tightened.

I seesawed between wanting to hit him to wanting to hug him. "Since you're not going anywhere, you might as well take off that damn jacket." Needing to distance myself, I headed up the stairs. "I hope you like lasagna, because that's what we're having for dinner."

Glad for something to do, I heated the lasagna in the microwave and tossed a green salad. Ardella Duncan had indeed thought of everything.

Remembering the loaf of French bread in the freezer, I called down to MacPhearson, asking he bring it up.

"Put the bread on that cookie sheet and slide it into the oven," I said when he came into the kitchen.

I watched MacPhearson perform the simple task. Would he remember to put the bread on the cookie sheet before putting it in the oven? Did he look tired? Was he in pain? Did his head hurt? Steve said Mac still forgot things, that he sometimes had headaches, blinding incapacitating headaches.

"Something wrong?" MacPhearson asked. Whatever damage the bullet had done, it had not changed his uncanny feel for a situation.

"Can you drink wine?" I asked.

"I prefer a Bud." MacPhearson smiled, the first real smile since his arrival. "But if wine is all you have . . ."

"Are you on anything . . ."

"Nothing," MacPhearson interrupted.

"If you were, would you tell me?"

"Ginny?" His voice sounded a warning.

I laid the silverware beside the plates. "The corkscrew's in the drawer." I indicated which drawer with a nod of my head, "Or if you prefer, there's Bud in the fridge."

We moved from the kitchen to the great room, where we listened to the crackling fire and watched the flames leap and fall back to caress the logs they were devouring.

Dinner had gone well. Maybe it was the wine, which MacPhearson did drink, or the lasagna, which was very good. Perhaps, though, it was because I didn't tread on the ground rules MacPhearson had established. The redheaded detective had made it clear that he would control his rehabilitation.

Better there be peace between you than war, the voice inside my head suggested.

I shifted uneasily, disturbing Hera who meowed her protest. I waited, but the voice inside my head had nothing more to say.

"That was a good meal," MacPhearson said. He stretched his legs farther into the room as if reaching for the fire. Zeus, who for reasons known only to the cat had claimed the detective as his own from their first meeting, purred contentedly in the police officer's lap.

"That freezer," MacPhearson inclined his head in the direction of the stairs, "is that where you found the body?"

"Who have you been talking to? Rhodes?"

MacPhearson looked at me. "You never learn, do you, Red?"

"It was Rhodes, wasn't it?" I demanded, ignoring MacPhearson's covert reference to my curiosity.

"What difference does it make who told me? Everyone in Lake County knows you found a dead girl in a freezer. All I'm asking is if the freezer sitting downstairs is the one where you found the body?"

"You don't think I'd keep the damn thing in the house after finding a body in it, do you?"

MacPhearson laughed. "Glad to know it's not the same one. Somehow I don't relish the thought of eating food that's been chummy with dead bodies." The smile left his face. "So, how about telling me about it?"

"You mean . . ." I stopped the words before they became the sarcastic remark I had intended and told about finding the girl in the freezer.

"And they don't know who the dead girl is?"

"They have some ideas, but as far as I know, no one has made a positive identification."

"You mentioned a couple of missing girls."

"Cindy Shouldice and Josie Leggit."

MacPhearson stared into the fire. The leaping, dancing flames had settled into a red glow as the logs turned to ash. "Sure seems like a lot of missing persons for such a small community," he mused.

He was echoing my thoughts, and it was the last thing an ailing detective needed to do. "It's not your case, Mac." I spoke slowly, wanting the words to sink in. "So how about we hit the sack and then hit the slopes tomorrow morning? Or would you prefer snowmobiling?" I stood up.

"Does that map show the trails?" MacPhearson lifted Zeus from his lap and walked over to the large map that had caught my attention earlier.

"It should," I said, joining him.

It did, and we picked a snowmobile trail that led from the Marfield cabin to Braun's Motel.

The aroma of freshly brewed coffee woke me, that and the sunlight streaming through the patio doors that led to the balcony. I stretched, luxuriating in the feeling of having nothing to do. A bang on the bedroom door shattered the illusion.

"Wake up, sleepy head." More banging followed.

"It's not locked," I grumped.

"Then get decent, because I'm coming in." The banging stopped, and the door started to open.

"Wait!" Conscious of my state of dress, or rather undress, I sprang from the bed and bolted for the dressing room, slamming the door shut behind me as the bedroom door opened.

I pulled on a terry robe, which fortunately, given the present circumstances, I had thought to pack. When I reentered the bedroom, MacPhearson was sitting on the bed. Propped against an array of pillows, he slathered cream cheese over a toasted bagel. Two mugs, judging from the aroma that drifted upward, held the coffee I had smelled earlier.

"Breakfast in bed sounded like a good idea. Since you fixed dinner last night, I thought I'd do the honors." MacPhearson smiled. "Still drink your coffee black, Red?"

Any number of words crossed my mind, but I swallowed them all along with a bite of toasted bagel heaped high with blueberry cream cheese. It was heaven.

"Been looking over that map out there," MacPhearson said. "Looks like you can get just about anywhere you want to go either by snowmobile or on cross-country skis."

"That's what the girls were telling me. Promised to show me some trails the tourists didn't know about."

"Girls?" MacPhearson leered á la Groucho Marx.

"Not your type." I punched his arm. "But you're in for a treat," and told him about Kim and Deb, and threw in Jimmy Wakefield as a bonus.

"How long you been up here?" MacPhearson asked.

"Since Friday," I answered, before noticing the detective's twitching moustache.

"That curiosity will be the death of you yet," he said, his grin widening.

MacPhearson gathered the remains of our breakfast while I showered. I didn't linger under the multiple heads, but promised to take advantage of them at a later time. Anticipating the day ahead, I dressed in thermal underwear, jeans, and a wool sweater.

MacPhearson was studying the map when I came into the great room.

"It looks like some of these trails run through Camp Whiting." Mac's finger traced a series of lines that ran through the National Guard training camp.

"Is that unusual?"

"Most military reservations are not open to the public," MacPhearson rubbed his jaw, "at least not since 9/11."

"I thought the Guard did most of its training in the summer," I said. "Could be that's why they open it up in the winter. Tourism is big business up here."

"You might be right." Mac moved away from the map. "So where are those snowmobiles, and I trust there's plenty of cold-weather gear up here because I sure didn't pack any."

"Do you even own any, Detective MacPhearson?" I teased. Though I had not known MacPhearson long, the detective did not strike me as a winter sports enthusiast.

"Come to think of it, Red, don't believe I do."

We found what we needed in the storage room. Hera, who had created a nest among the scarfs, took umbrage at being disturbed, but after giving us a good scolding, promptly resettled herself.

It took several minutes to dress for our outdoor adventure and several more to read through the owner's manuals that came with the pair of Polaris Sportsmans. With all the latest bells and whistles, I suspected they could drive themselves. As ready as the equipment was, being novice drivers we took our time familiarizing ourselves with the machines. After several trial runs on trails near the cabin, we deemed ourselves ready and took off for Braun's Motel.

MacPhearson took the lead. Typical male, he claimed to be the superior map-reader. Perhaps he was, but having him in front gave me a better vantage point. Despite his determination to be the master of his fate, I planned on keeping an eagle eye on the stubborn detective.

He did prove a good leader, signaled turns well in advance, and kept to a safe speed. The sun rode low overhead in a cloudless sky, and the trees with their blankets of snow provided us a fairyland of white. We passed others who, like ourselves, were enjoying the winter wonderland. Similarly garbed in multi-hued waterproof jumpsuits, helmets, and goggles, we were as visitors from another planet unknown one to the other.

MacPhearson raised a gloved hand, signaling a turn into Braun's Motel. We coasted to a stop in an area reserved for snowmobiles. Getting off the Polaris proved more difficult than getting on, my long unused muscles screaming a protest.

"Need some help?" MacPhearson asked. Like me he wasn't smiling and, like me, was, in fact, grimacing. "Hell of a lot of hard work driving one of those things," he muttered.

Linda Braun called from an open door and welcomed us into a large coat room.

"Just leave your outerwear in here and join us in the kitchen. There's plenty of hot coffee, and Ted can rustle you up whatever you want for lunch."

"How about a new body," I suggested, gingerly flexing and stretching my arms and legs.

Linda laughed. "Maybe you should just skip lunch and jump in the hot tub instead."

"That sounds like a winner." MacPhearson hastened to pull off his snowmobile suit.

"No bathing suit, no hot tub," I said primly.

Eyes twinkling, Linda led the way into the kitchen. I made belated introductions, noted the twinkle was still there, and promised myself I'd have a talk with her.

"I heard you were here." Linda's smile ratcheted up a notch as she looked at the redheaded detective.

"Sheriff Duncan?" I asked, naming the suspected informant.

Linda nodded. "Rick called. He'll be here for lunch."

Declining Linda's offer of a seat at the table, MacPhearson leaned against a nearby counter. "I hear you're filled up," he said, accepting the mug of coffee she offered.

"We are, but I'm not complaining."

"I see you have the extra help you spoke of," I said.

"We're lucky. A good many of the migrants stay year round."

"Same ones, or is it a new group each year?" MacPhearson asked.

"I see a few of the same faces from year to year, but I don't pay that much attention. Roger Whiting contracts for the migrants in this area. I just pick up the phone, tell him what I need, and he sends them over."

"Linda." Sheriff Duncan's voiced preceded him into the kitchen.

"In here, Rick," Linda answered.

Sheriff Duncan strode into the room, saw MacPhearson and, hand outstretched, moved toward the detective.

"Rick Duncan," he said, shaking MacPhearson's hand, "and you must be Detective MacPhearson."

Introductions made, the sheriff unzipped his down-filled jacket and tossed it over a chair.

Linda suggested the lunch special, bratwurst dogs with slaw and dill pickles. With the addition of a round of Bud, this last being MacPhearson's suggestion, the three of us settled around the table. With a smile and a cheery, "Be right back," Linda left to fill the order.

"I suppose you already know about the body Miss Arthur found," Duncan said. Linda delivered the beer, and the sheriff took a long pull.

"Any luck finding out who she was?" Mac asked. He followed Duncan's example and lifted his Bud to his lips.

"Matter of fact, we have." Duncan set his beer on the table. "Her name is Sarah Frazier."

Chapter Eight

Sheriff Duncan's eyes locked on mine. "And I understand the credit goes to you, Miss Arthur."

"Me?" His words caught me off guard.

"If you're the one who told Maggie Schmidt to talk to me, yes."

"I did talk to Maggie after Mass yesterday, and yes, I did tell her to talk to you." I was puzzled. "Shouldn't I have told her to talk to you?"

Ted Williams set a plate of bratwurst dogs and slaw in front of each of us. Without answering my question, the sheriff picked up his dog and took a large bite. Hoping I was no longer the center of attention, I followed suit and was wiping mustard from the corner of my mouth when the next question came.

"What interests me, Miss Arthur, is why Maggie Schmidt came to you in the first place."

I choked on my sandwich and on the sheriff's tone of voice, which was decidedly unpleasant. That, and the formality of his address, screamed interrogation.

MacPhearson pounded my back, and Linda pushed a bottle of beer into my hands. Her "Drink this" followed close upon MacPhearson's "Are you okay?"

I pushed aside the beer and moved out of reach of MacPhearson's heavy hand. "What are you suggesting, Sheriff Duncan?" I demanded. "I was there. Maggie saw me, and she asked about the body I found in the freezer."

The sandwich, which until a few minutes ago looked appetizing, had lost its appeal. I shoved the plate away, tipping over the beer as I did. Linda grabbed a handful of napkins and attacked the spreading pool of amber liquid.

I stood up, pushing back my chair. "Why don't you ask Maggie? If anyone knows why she chose to ask me about the dead girl, it would be her." I was breathing hard, and my face felt hot.

"Sit down please, Ginny," the sheriff said quietly. He took a swallow of beer and followed it with a heaping forkful of slaw. "No offense, just trying to get to the bottom of things."

I reclaimed my chair. "Well, I'm not the bottom you're looking for, nor am I the top."

Sheriff Duncan pushed the last of his sandwich into his mouth and wiped his lips with a napkin. "No," he agreed. "You're not the bottom, nor are you, as you say, the top, but I sure as hell think you're somewhere in the middle, and it's the middle I'm interested in knowing about." The sheriff's eyes locked on mine. No slouch in the staring department, I stared back.

It was Duncan who broke the tension. "Got to go." He smiled at the three of us, a smile that grew bigger when he came to Linda. "Be in touch later," he added.

Linda sprang to her feet, grabbed the sheriff's jacket, and held it high as he slid his arms into the sleeves. "Ardella did a good job fixing this." She ran a finger over what had been a jagged tear in the sleeve.

The sheriff removed Linda's hand and took another look around the table. "I'll be in touch," he said. This time I didn't think he was talking to Linda.

I pulled the bratwurst sandwich back toward me and fingered the bun. It was cold.

"How about a bowl of potato soup?" Linda offered. She picked up the uneaten sandwich. "Ted's got a pot on the stove. I'll have him bring you a bowl."

"What in hell did you do to get Duncan so riled up?" MacPhearson asked. He was staring at me with the same intensity as Sheriff Duncan had.

"Nothing," I protested.

"Nothing won't cut it, Ginny. You must have done something," MacPhearson said.

I shook my head. "Maggie asked me what the dead girl looked like, and I told her she would have to talk to Sheriff Duncan. That's all. I swear."

Ted set the bowl of soup in front of me. Chunks of potatoes and bits of bacon swam in a thick buttery broth. The delicious aroma reawakened my appetite, and I picked up a spoon and dived in.

"Maggie get you in trouble asking questions about Sarah?" The cook's large hands rested on the back of the chair the sheriff had just vacated.

I shook my head. "She just wanted to know what the dead girl looked like."

The man's hands kneaded the chair back. "It was Norm who put her up to it," he said. "He's Maggie's brother. He's one of Sheriff Duncan's deputies. She asked him about the dead girl, and all he did was get mad. Told her to ask you. Said you were the one who found her."

I lowered the spoon back into the bowl. This last was not new. Maggie Schmidt had said much the same thing when she asked about the body in the freezer.

"Norm can be an ornery cuss when he wants to be," Williams said.

I pictured the thin-lipped deputy I had met at the sheriff's office, and was inclined to agree with Williams' assessment.

"Did Maggie have a special reason for wanting to know what the dead girl looked like?" MacPhearson asked.

"Maggie heard from this niece of hers, Sarah. They were supposed to meet the middle of last week, but Sarah never showed up." The chef's big hands continued to bother the chair back. "When she heard about the dead girl . . . well, she was afraid maybe it might be Sarah."

"Maggie did ask for Wednesday off. Could that have been when she was supposed to meet her niece?" Linda asked.

"Sounds about right." Ted backed away from the table and commenced to rub his hands over the front of his apron. "That's about all I know about it, except I know Maggie's going to be real sorry she got you into trouble with the sheriff, Miss Arthur."

The chef went back to his chopping block, and I lifted a spoonful of soup to my mouth. Damn if I was going to pass up another lunch.

"What I can't figure is why the sheriff thinks talking to Maggie Schmidt puts you in the middle of a murder investigation."

I sighed, recognizing Mac's cop voice. The one that said if I was in the middle of something, he had every intention of joining me.

We waved good-bye to Ted and Linda and made our way to the coatroom. Outfitting ourselves in everything except goggles, we headed for the area reserved for snowmobiles.

MacPhearson rubbed his backside and twisted gingerly from side to side. "Do we really have to get back on these things?"

"You into walking?" I asked.

"You have no mercy." Groaning, MacPhearson swung aboard the snowmobile, adjusted the goggles over his eyes, and revved the motor.

Stifling my own grunts and groans—I had no intention of letting him know how badly all of me ached—I swung aboard my waiting snowmobile.

The sun-bright trails we had traversed early in the day were now filled with dark shadows. MacPhearson reduced his speed and crowded the right side of the trail when meeting other travelers. Our bodies hurting more with each bounce, the ride seemed to go on, and on, and on . . .

The cabin was as we had left it. I did steal a look at the freezer, but curbed the desire to look inside.

Being less sensitive than I, MacPhearson pushed ahead and swung open the lid. "Oh, hell," he exclaimed.

"What?" I froze, metaphorically speaking.

"There's no body in here," he shouted.

Resisting the urge to kill him, I headed up the stairs. "As long as you have that thing open, you might as well pick out something for dinner."

I took my time in the shower, letting each shower head work its magic on my shoulder and other aching muscles too numerous to count.

I pulled on jeans, found a sweatshirt that advertised the Arthur and Arthur Security Agency, and slipped barefoot into a well worn pair of loafers. Feeling considerably better, I went looking for MacPhearson.

"Did you know there was a hot tub on the balcony?" Mac came through the sliding doors, bringing in the scent of charcoal and grilling steaks. I sniffed appreciatively.

"Potatoes are in the microwave, and salad's in the fridge," he said.

"Want me to set the table? Wine?" I started toward the kitchen.

"Wine's breathing, but you can set the table." He leaned into the counter. "Did you know there was a hot tub out there?" MacPhearson was, if nothing else, persistent.

I confessed I didn't and continued setting plates, silverware, and napkins on the table.

"Thought we might have a long soak for dessert."

I looked at him. "No suits . . ."

"Not to worry, the good judge thinks of everything." Reaching behind him, Mac produced a black Speedo brief for himself and an even briefer white bikini, which, I presumed, was meant for me.

I started to shake my head but, seeing the look on MacPhearson's face, stopped. Was it disappointment or amusement? Going with disappointment, I offered, "I'll see."

Dinner went well, very well, and I was seriously considering joining MacPhearson for dessert when a knock on the door interrupted.

With a "Stay put," MacPhearson double-stepped his way down the stairs, opening the door before another knock sounded. A pair of voices floated upwards, one male, MacPhearson's, the other female.

I started down the stairs. When the woman came into sight, I recognized the slender form and graying hair.

"I didn't want to bother you," I heard her say, "but when Ted told me how Sheriff Duncan got on Miss Arthur, I just had to come."

"No need to apologize, Maggie," I said. I offered a welcoming smile and motioned her to a seating area by the fireplace.

Maggie settled on the edge of the closest chair. "If I had any idea the sheriff would act like he did, I would never have bothered you."

"I understand it was your brother, Deputy Schmidt, who suggested you talk to me."

"Norm," Maggie said.

MacPhearson pressed a mug of coffee into the woman's hands. "Did you have reason to think you might know the dead girl?"

After a long minute, Maggie nodded her head. "I was supposed to meet my niece last week. Wednesday it was, but I waited and waited, and she didn't come. She didn't call." Maggie spoke slowly, as if she feared hearing the words.

"Sarah Frazier is your niece?" I said, naming the dead girl.

"One . . . one of my sister Angie's girls." A tear slipped from the corner of Maggie's eye. "She'd been on the road for over a month but was sure she would get here by then."

"How far did your niece have to come?" Mac asked.

"Rocky Ridge. It's a small place in the Upper Peninsula. Angie and her husband, Len, used to live here but moved to the Upper Peninsula a few years back. Said it was too crowded around here. Said they wanted more space so they could do whatever they wanted to do whenever and however they wanted to."

"Did Sarah have a car?" I asked.

"Sarah didn't say, but I don't think so. I think she was hitchhiking."

"Even if she was hitchhiking, it shouldn't have taken her a month to get here," I said.

"Sarah didn't come directly here. She'd stopped when her money ran out and got a job waiting tables. Winter's a busy season. She'd have no trouble getting work. Especially if she worked for tips, which she probably did. I offered to drive up and get her, but she said no. Said she didn't want her folks to know where she was."

"Any idea why she wanted to come down here?" MacPhearson asked.

"She was pregnant," Maggie said with a long sigh. "Sarah never did get along with her folks, especially not her dad. That had to be the reason. Can't think why else she would have left home."

"Did Sarah tell you this?" I asked.

Maggie shook her head. "Doc Wacker." Another tear slid down her face. "He found out when he did the autopsy."

Maggie picked at a loose thread on the sleeve of her jacket. "When you wouldn't tell me what the dead girl looked like, Miss Arthur, I went to Sheriff Duncan like you said I should. I told him about Sarah, about her not being here when she said she would." Maggie shuddered. "That's when he took me to see her."

"How about your brother, the deputy, did he know she was coming?" MacPhearson asked.

"I didn't tell him. Norm would have been on the phone first thing. He's always been thick as thieves with that bunch."

"So as far as you know, you were the only one who knew Sarah was coming to Pine City?" MacPhearson pressed.

"Ted knew," Maggie said.

Chapter Nine

"I LIVE WITH HIM, YOU KNOW," MAGGIE SAID. "When you live with someone, there's not much you don't tell them." Maggie looked from me to MacPhearson. A knowing look spread over her face as if the two of us being here together validated her statement.

Another round of apologies followed as MacPhearson helped the older woman into her coat. Then, as suddenly as she had appeared at our doorstep, Maggie was gone.

MacPhearson and I shared the kitchen cleanup. Strangely, after all Maggie had told us, neither of us had much to say. I was tired and, as was my habit under such circumstances, kept words to a minimum. MacPhearson did little better, communicating with furrowed brow and a few grunts. This being the mood, dessert was not mentioned. I did grab the bikini, determined to check it out with the dressing room mirror before its debut in the hot tub.

My mood was not much improved the next morning. Knowing the dead girl was related to someone I knew, however slightly, was a real downer. I slid out of bed and into the waiting bikini, twisting and turning before the dressing room mirror. What I saw did little to change the direction in which the day seemed headed. Besides the scar on my shoulder, the psychic pain with which I still hadn't learned to live, the angles were round where I would have preferred flat and flat where I would have preferred round.

"Less potatoes and more exercise," I told the girl in the mirror.

I showered, dressed in last night's jeans and sweatshirt, and was sliding into my loafers when I sensed something was wrong. I looked about the room, but everything was as it should be.

I sniffed the air, but smelled nothing. Where was the aroma of coffee? The smell of bacon or at the very least toasted bagels?

I opened the bedroom door and headed up the hall. Except for the shuffle of my feet along the floor, I heard only silence. Where was MacPhearson?

I checked out the kitchen, hurried down the stairs, and made the rounds of the lower level. Zeus and Hera were nosing around their empty bowls, which I promised to refill later. There was no sign of MacPhearson.

I opened the door to the garage. My Honda, MacPhearson's truck, and the snowmobiles were huddled together in the semidarkness.

"MacPhearson," I called.

I took the stairs two at a time. If this was a joke, it wasn't funny. I reached the second floor in a dead heat with the cats. Another look around the open space told me the redheaded detective had not put in an appearance.

"The hot tub?" Neither the empty room nor the cats answered. I pulled open the sliding doors that led to the balcony.

The cover was in place over the tub. My stomach did a flip-flop as I reached out and loosened a corner of the canvas tarp. Common sense told me he could not be hiding in such a confined space, but I wasn't listening to common sense.

The corner I had loosened allowed only a restricted view, and I flung the tarp wide. A cloud of water vapor escaped. I let out a breath and gulped in another.

Dropping the tarp, I reentered the great room and retraced my steps to the bedroom wing. There was but one other place to look. Propriety be damned! I turned the knob and pushed inside.

MacPhearson was there.

I rushed to the bed, called his name as I went. He did not answer. I touched his shoulder and shook it, calling more loudly as I did, "Mac, Mac, wake up."

MacPhearson groaned. I left off the shaking and touched his face. It felt cold and clammy.

I was back again in Marion City, on the street where MacPhearson had been shot. Mac's head was in my lap. Huddled together on that cold November morning, I watched the blood run down his face and puddle beneath his head.

"Talk to me, Mac," I whispered to the pale-faced man who lay on the bed before me. Where had the wind-buffeted ruddiness of yesterday gone?

"My head," he mumbled after what seemed an eternity of waiting. His eyes opened, blank eyes that showed no recognition.

Was this one of those headaches Steve had warned me about? Had I let MacPhearson get too tired yesterday?

I raced from the room, grabbed my cell phone from its charger, and speed-dialed Steve's number. Wonder of wonders, he answered. Sometimes miracles do happen.

"Steve," I took a calming breath, "Mac's . . ." I described his symptoms, started with his groans, and ended with his blank staring eyes. "Is this one of those headaches you told me about?"

"Ask him if his head hurts," Steve said.

The request was so maddeningly simple I almost threw the phone but instead asked, "Does your head hurt, Mac?"

It must have been the right tone of voice, for MacPhearson mumbled what sounded like "Yes."

I relayed the information to Steve and was told to ask Mac about his medication. I did, but Mac did not answer.

"Go through his things," Steve ordered.

I did and found what Steve had told me to look for—a set of pre-loaded syringes.

"You'll have to give it to him," Steve said after I read him the label.

Much as I disliked needles, I did as instructed.

"The drug is fairly fast-acting, and you should notice an improvement in about thirty minutes." Steve walked me through what to expect and then questioned me about Mac's activities since his arrival.

"Was the snowmobiling too much?" I asked.

"Hard to say, but Mac has to learn to judge his activity levels."

Feeling guilty as hell, I broke the connection with Steve and stared down at the man who lay corpse-like before me.

I pulled a chair close to Mac's bed and held his hand, determined to wait for the thirty minutes to pass.

Steve had instructed me not to try and wake him. "Let the medication do its thing."

Like a kid waiting for Santa Claus I checked my watch at ten-second intervals.

Thirty minutes passed. Thirty-five. Forty. Should I call Steve? I clutched the cell phone, finger poised to speed-dial his number.

I felt Mac's fingers move under mine. Beneath the covers, his legs moved. Slowly, oh so very slowly, MacPhearson opened his eyes.

"Ginny?" he asked.

Yes, oh yes, I wanted to shout, but said, "And who else would be in your bedroom holding your hand?" Plenty of others, no doubt, but I dismissed the thought.

His hand moved to touch his head.

"Does it hurt?" I asked.

MacPhearson started to shake his head, seemed to think better of it, and answered hesitantly, "I'm not sure. It's hard to tell."

"Why didn't you tell me you were still having headaches? And why in hell didn't you tell me where you kept your medicine?" I sought refuge in anger. "Or did you think you could still give yourself a shot after you passed out?"

"Did you . . ."

"And who else?" I interrupted.

MacPhearson's eyes almost twinkled, and his lips moved upwards in an honest-to-goodness grin. "Thanks, Red. I owe you one."

"You bet your life you do," I retorted, but my words fell on deaf ears. MacPhearson was asleep.

Chapter Ten

I GAVE MY PATIENT A GENTLE PAT, PICKED up my cell phone—Steve had asked me to call Doctor Wacker and have him check on Mac-Phearson—and headed for the great room. I debated Mac's right to privacy and my need to monitor his condition. Ranking my needs higher than his, I left the bedroom door open.

A pair of hungry cats met me in the kitchen. Responding to their scolding, I saw to their needs before looking for the Lake County Coroner's number in the directory Judge Marfield had provided.

Jim Wacker was not in his office, nor did he answer his cell phone. I left a message, asking he return my call, and started the coffee. I had just popped a bagel into the toaster oven when a knock sounded at the front door. Resigning myself to what would surely be a cold hard bagel, I hurried down the stairs.

Another bang sounded before I reached the door. My hand on the deadbolt, I looked through the peephole. Seeing Sheriff Duncan's face, I swung the door open.

Cold air, a shaft of morning sunshine, and Rick Duncan came into the room. In sharp contrast to the day's bright promise, the sheriff looked like a proverbial thundercloud.

"Is something wrong?" I asked, forgoing the more conventional good morning and how are you.

"You're damn right there is," Duncan yanked at the zipper on his jacket, "and you're right in the middle of it again."

"In the middle of what?" I demanded.

Sheriff Duncan, jacket gaping wide and hands on hips, glowered angrily. "Maggie Schmidt is dead."

I drew back, bumped against a cushioned chair, and fell into the seat. "Maggie Schmidt is dead?" I said in frank disbelief.

I saw her as I had first seen her, serving dinner to the young couple in the dining room of Braun's Motel, and in the social hall at St. Paul's, and here in the cabin last night.

The sheriff started pacing. "She went off the road about a mile from here. Ran over the embankment and through the ice into the lake." Duncan looked around the room. "Where's that police officer boyfriend of yours?"

Still reeling from Duncan's words, I tried to decide if I should stay sitting or try standing. Deciding to reserve my strength for the battle Sheriff Duncan seemed intent on waging, I remained seated.

"If you mean the police officer, he's upstairs in bed. If you mean my boyfriend, he's in Marion City. The former is asleep and can't be disturbed, and the latter is at work but can be reached by phone. Do you want me to call him?" I hoped I sounded exactly how I felt, bitchy. Akin to anger, it was an easier emotion to deal with than grief over the death of a woman I hardly knew.

"How is it that when you show up we get an epidemic of dead bodies?" Duncan asked. He stopped pacing. "What's MacPhearson doing still sleeping? You two have a rough night?"

"Are you inferring we were up all night running people off the road?"

Duncan threw up his hands. "I'm not inferring anything." He chose a chair and dropped into it. "All I want is some answers that make sense."

"How about a cup of coffee?" I stood up. Maybe the battle lines were drawn, but the sheriff seemed ready for a truce. "And for starters, how about taking off that jacket and coming upstairs? We can have our coffee and . . ." I headed for the stairs, relieved when I heard the sheriff's footsteps follow behind.

I poured a couple of mugs of coffee, asked about sugar and cream, which the sheriff declined, and slid a fresh bagel into the toaster oven.

"What time did Maggie leave here?" Sheriff Duncan sipped from his mug while I slathered a generous amount of cream cheese over my bagel.

"She got here just after we finished eating," I said. I took a bite of bagel and ran the numbers in my head. "We ate late, about eight. That means she got here about nine or nine-thirty. She didn't stay long, half an hour, forty-five minutes. So that would have made it somewhere between ten and ten-thirty when she left." I never could do math in my head.

I took another bite of bagel and waited. The sheriff remained silent.

"What time was it when you found her?" I asked. As the sheriff had asked what time Maggie left, this seemed a logical question.

Duncan thought otherwise. Instead of answering my question, he asked, "How much did the three of you have to drink?"

I set the half-eaten bagel on my plate. "And what does drinking have to do with it? Is that why she went off the road? Because she'd been drinking?"

"How about answering my question first?" He lifted the mug to his lips. "How much did the three of you have to drink?"

"Mac and I had a bottle of wine with dinner."

"That's all? No brandy with your coffee after dinner? And what about Maggie? Did she share that bottle of wine?"

"Mac gave her a cup of coffee," I said. I picked up the bagel and took another bite.

"No brandy?"

"Just coffee, and she drank that alone. Mac and I had already finished our coffee before Maggie arrived."

"Not very sociable letting your guest drink alone," Duncan said.

"Maggie Schmidt wasn't making a social call."

The sheriff quirked an eyebrow. "And what kind of call was she making?"

I carried my empty plate to the sink and exchanged it for the coffee pot. "She came to apologize. Said she was sorry about your jumping all over me." I refilled our mugs and returned the pot to its warming plate.

"Ted Williams tell her?"

"Or Linda Braun, but Maggie didn't say, and I didn't ask. What difference does it make? She was upset and wanted to apologize for what had happened."

"You say she was upset?" The sheriff sounded as cop-like as Rhodes or MacPhearson.

I said nothing. Refused to be baited by the sheriff's demeanor.

"Upset enough to drive into the lake?" he persisted.

"How in the hell should I know?" I said, my resolve crumbling. "The poor woman had just learned the dead girl was her niece, her pregnant niece. Wouldn't you be upset?" I waited for an answer, but none came. "Maybe she drove into the lake on purpose, or maybe she just lost control of the car."

I remembered the drive to Braun's Motel the night I had found Sarah Frazier's body, remembered Myra Johnson negotiating the hilly road with its series of twisting curves, and realized either of the two scenarios was a viable option.

"I'm thinking plenty, Miss Arthur, but I don't know a damn thing about what happened last night. Why in hell do you think I'm here?"

"Why, Sheriff Duncan," I said, reverting to my bitchy persona, "I thought you were here to accuse me of getting Ms. Schmidt drunk enough so that MacPhearson and I could run her off the road and into the lake."

"That's just about exactly what I am thinking, Miss Arthur."

"Well, you can forget about the drinking part because she didn't have anything to drink here, and since MacPhearson and I didn't have any part in her drinking, it follows we didn't have any part in running her off the road."

The phone rang. It was my cell phone, which I had placed in its charger on the counter. I left the table and grabbed it.

"Jim, thank you for calling . . ." I turned my back on the sheriff as I explained about MacPhearson's headache and Steve's request that he check on his patient. Wacker said he would and promised to come by later that afternoon.

"So what's wrong with your police officer friend?"

This time Duncan omitted the boyfriend part. "Mac was involved in a shootout last November and is still having trouble with headaches."

"Head wound?"

I nodded. "And the headaches are such that he needs to be medicated."

"And that's why he's still in bed?"

"If I'm the he you're talking about, I'm not in bed. I'm here in the kitchen and I'm hungry. What's for breakfast, Red?" MacPhearson, cocky grin and all, pulled a chair away from the table and sat down.

I looked past the grin to his eyes. If they were the mirrors of his soul, I was looking at a tormented man. Was he in pain? The effects of the medication I had given him? "Should you be up?" I asked.

"What difference does it make?" MacPhearson answered. "I'm up and I'm hungry."

My knee-jerk reaction to MacPhearson's sarcasm was anger, but I held it in check. "Bagel and cream cheese okay?"

MacPhearson nodded, but added, "You're really going to have to come up with something different, Red. Bagels and cream cheese are beginning to pale."

"Just stopped by to see how the two of you were doing," the sheriff said.

"We're doing fine," MacPhearson said.

I busied myself with coffee and bagels and cream cheese and waited for the next lie.

Duncan cleared his throat. "Actually, I came by to ask about Maggie Schmidt."

"She was here last night," MacPhearson said.

I set the coffee on the table and went back to the counter for the bagel and cheese. The two of them switched to telling the truth, making the conversation less interesting, but it being their conversation, I stayed out of it.

Duncan shifted in his chair as if seeking a more comfortable position. "Want to tell me about Maggie's visit?" he asked the Marion City detective.

"You have a reason for asking?" MacPhearson took a bite from his bagel.

The sheriff leaned against the back of his chair. "You have a reason for not telling me?"

MacPhearson shrugged his shoulders.

Damn! At the rate they were going with the questions, it would be dinnertime before either came up with an answer. I was wrong.

"Because Maggie Schmidt died on her way home from here last night," Duncan said.

"Accident?" MacPhearson said.

Duncan shrugged. "She ran off the road and into the lake."

"The last time I looked at the lake it was frozen," Mac said.

"It still is," said the sheriff.

"The car broke through the ice?" MacPhearson asked.

"Did Maggie drown?" I asked.

"Won't know until Doc Wacker does the post."

"Sounds like an accident," MacPhearson said, "and if that's so, why are you here asking questions?"

"Seemed like a good place to start."

"So what is it you want to know?"

Duncan covered the same ground with MacPhearson as he had with me, and MacPhearson gave the sheriff the same answers as had I. Duncan didn't say if he was satisfied with the answers, but satisfied or not, he left shortly afterward.

"He didn't tell us not to leave town," I said.

"Don't hold your breath, Red. I think the good sheriff has you pegged as a serial killer. You didn't happen to go out after I fell asleep last night, did you?"

I heard the bantering tone in MacPhearson's voice and saw the twinkle in his eyes. Mac was back from wherever it was the pain had taken him.

Chapter Eleven

A SECOND ROUND OF BANGING FINISHED as I opened the door.
"Thought maybe the two of you had gone out the back way," Jim Wacker said as he entered the cabin. "Wanted to see where Maggie Schmidt had her accident and, being I was close by, decided to make a house call." Wacker looked around the great room. "Where's the patient? In bed?"

"Upstairs," I said.

"Hope this is a social call, Doc," MacPhearson said, after I introduced him to the Lake County Coroner.

Jim Wacker's eyes twinkled. "Cantankerous sort are you?" Not waiting for an answer, he added, "Truth is, this visit is both social and professional. So how about we get the professional part over so we can get down to being sociable?"

Wacker motioned MacPhearson to a kitchen chair and placed the bag he was carrying on the table. "Now, let's pretend you're the patient and I'm the doctor. That means I get to look you over and you get to answer my questions."

A look of amusement showed on MacPhearson's face. His good-natured acceptance along with a measure of cooperation on each man's part proved a successful combination, and the doctor's exam seemed to have hardly begun before it was over.

"As long as your headaches don't get more severe or occur more frequently, they will just have to run their course." Wacker flipped off the penlight and dropped it into his bag. "Medicine working okay?"

MacPhearson said it was, but Wacker looked at me for confirmation.

"It took between thirty and forty-five minutes before Mac seemed to relax and another ten minutes or so before he fell asleep."

"And how long did he sleep?"

"Not long, an hour, an hour and a half maybe. I didn't keep track." I looked from MacPhearson to Jim Wacker. "Should I have?"

Wacker waved a dismissive hand. "No . . . I would have thought a little longer maybe. I'll give Doctor Brock a call and let him know how his patient's doing." Wacker rubbed his hands together. "Now that the professional part's out of the way, how about getting down to being sociable?"

To Jim Wacker, being sociable meant that I would brew a pot of coffee and that we would eat the bag of doughnuts he fished from his black bag. Amazing the things doctors carry around with them. Besides the sugar high Wacker's offering produced, I soon learned that he carried around a good bit of knowledge about the murdered Sarah Frazier and her recently deceased aunt.

"I heard Maggie came by here before the accident," Wacker said. He hitched his chair closer to the table and pulled a doughnut from the paper sack.

"She was here, stayed about thirty, forty-five minutes. Left about ten or so." MacPhearson chose a doughnut from the sack Wacker handed him. "Duncan was here earlier. He seems to think the two of us filled Maggie full of booze then let her get behind the wheel of her car."

Despite his headache and his having been recently medicated, Mac had a firm grip on the conversational ball, and I let him run with it.

"Do your autopsy findings support the good sheriff's suspicions about Maggie Schmidt being drunk?" MacPhearson asked. He fiddled with his coffee mug, twisting it from side to side. "You have done the post, haven't you, Doc?"

Wacker nodded. "Fact is, that's what I was doing when Ginny called." Wacker licked his chocolate-covered fingers.

"She certainly wasn't drunk when she left here," I said, pushing a pile of napkins toward him.

Smiling a thank you, the doctor switched from licking to wiping.

"Was she drunk?" MacPhearson asked again.

"A little hard to say," Wacker said. "There was a considerable amount of booze in her stomach, but her blood alcohol levels weren't all that high."

"High enough to make her lose control of the car?" MacPhearson asked.

"Blowing snow, slippery roads, who's to say what's enough?" Wacker crumpled his napkin and tossed it on the table.

"Did they find a bottle in the car? Who found the car? What time did the accident happen? Was she killed immediately or . . ." As Jim Wacker had, MacPhearson crumpled his napkin and threw it on the table.

"Sheriff Duncan didn't say if he did or didn't find a bottle in the car," Wacker said amicably, more amicably than I would have, given Mac's aggressive questioning.

"When did she die?" MacPhearson pressed.

"Hard to say, the cold and all," Wacker answered.

"I know cold temperatures can confuse the time of death." MacPhearson thumped his mug against the table. "But I'm hearing that excuse a lot lately."

Wacker studied MacPhearson. "You really are an ornery cuss," he said.

MacPhearson leaned back and crossed his arms over his chest. "Okay, if you can't tell me the time of death, how about telling me when they found the body."

Wacker leaned forward, closing the distance MacPhearson had put between them. "Now, that I can do. It was about five A.M. A couple of ice fishermen wanted to get an early start. Saw Maggie's Volvo sticking out of the ice and called the sheriff."

"Did she drown?" I asked.

"I didn't find any water in her lungs." Wacker shook his head. "She bounced around the front seat, hit the dashboard, the windshield, and of course, the steering wheel."

"No seatbelt?" It was a throwaway question. From what Jim Wacker had said, I already knew Maggie Schmidt had not been wearing a seatbelt.

Wacker shook his head. "Given the condition of the body, I'd have to say no."

"Maggie was upset when she left here," I said.

"I'm sure she was," Wacker said. "I was with her when she identified her niece, and she took it hard."

"I don't think she knew about Sarah being pregnant until you told her." I pictured Maggie Schmidt's thin haggard face, saw the broken veins that ran like spider webs over her cheeks and nose, the limp graying hair that brushed her shoulders.

"Was Maggie an alcoholic?" I reached out, touched Jim Wacker's arm. "She was, wasn't she?"

Wacker stared out the glass doors that led to the balcony. He nodded. "Yes, she was, but to my knowledge Maggie hadn't had a drink in several years."

"My guess is Duncan's thinking either accident or suicide," MacPhearson said. "If one doesn't fit, the other will."

Neither Wacker nor I responded, both of us knowing Mac's guess could be right.

Wacker pushed back from the table and stood up. "Hard on a family when there's two to bury."

"Will they take both bodies up to Rocky Ridge?" I asked.

Wacker shrugged. "That will be up to the family."

"When will the bodies be released?" I asked.

"Far as the Coroner's Office is concerned, and that's me, they can go now."

I closed my eyes against the vision of the teenager's body inside the freezer, of Maggie's tears when she talked about Sarah. "What caused their deaths?" I didn't need to know, but being the curious type . . .

"For Sarah Frazier it was a skull fracture," Wacker answered. "She either fell or was pushed and hit the back of her head against something." Wacker held up a protesting hand. "And before either of you ask, I don't know what that something was."

"What about the marks on her neck? Sheriff Duncan thought she may have been strangled," I said.

"I considered it. Only there weren't sufficient physical findings to support the theory."

"Any evidence she tried to defend herself?" Mac asked.

"We have some fingernail scrapings. When we get a suspect, we can compare the DNA."

"And for Maggie?" I asked.

"Massive head trauma." Wacker leaned forward and picked up the paper sack, empty now, and crumpled it in his hands, then reached for the used napkins scattered over the table. Ready to go, he was cleaning up the mess that lay in front of him. With a rush of insight, I knew it was a job he was used to doing, one that didn't always involve empty paper sacks and crumpled napkins.

MacPhearson walked Wacker to the door, and I cleared the table of coffee mugs and plates. Intent on loading the dishwasher and thinking thoughts of Sarah Frazier and Maggie Schmidt, I didn't hear MacPhearson come up behind me.

"How about having that dessert we missed last night, Red?"

Busying myself with the task of handling mugs and plates, I pondered the suggestion. Should I or shouldn't I? Should we or shouldn't we?

"Well?"

I took my head out of the dishwasher. "Why not?"

I pulled a warm-up suit over the bikini and slipped back into my loafers. Much as I wanted to be the first one in the hot tub, MacPhearson was already there when I exited the sliding glass doors that led from my bedroom to the balcony.

"Water's hot," he called.

I slipped off my shoes and eased down the sweat pants. I debated leaving on the sweatshirt but thought better of it. In a single graceful motion, at least to my inner eye I looked graceful, I stepped over the edge of the tub, pulled free of the shirt, and sank to my neck in the hot steamy water. The sigh I sighed was one of sheer pleasure.

My eyes closed, and I retreated into a Never Never Land of not quite awake and not quite asleep. As with all imagined things, Never Never Land faded into the mist. Reluctantly, I opened my eyes.

MacPhearson, sitting across the tub from me, smiled. "Not bad as desserts go," he said.

He was right, and I said as much.

"That shoulder bother you?" he asked.

Reflexively, my fingers found the scar and massaged around it. "Only when I use it." I laughed, then amended, "It hurts some when I overdo, but it's getting better."

Another silence fell between us, and again MacPhearson interrupted my thoughts. "I see you're still wearing that unicorn," he said.

This time my fingers closed over the silver charm that hung on a chain around my neck. My thumb found the irregular edge of what should have been the mythical beast's horn and rubbed against it. A senseless ritual, I know, but it brought back memories of Uncle David. Not the memory of his betrayal and abandonment, but . . .

I shut my eyes and leaned my head against the edge of the tub. "I still wear it," I said.

"Do you hear from him?"

I opened my eyes and studied the cloudless sky that showed through the pines. "Not since I was in the hospital, and if he hadn't left this," I lifted the unicorn, "I wouldn't have known he had been there."

The unicorn, tucked inside a blue velvet jeweler's box, had been left on the table beside my hospital bed. When I had asked, I had been told it had been left by a tall, good-looking red-haired man.

Only it should not have been there. It should have been in the hidey hole behind the dressing room mirror in Uncle David's apartment. There was no question about it being the same unicorn, its broken horn a dead giveaway. It was me who had broken it when, as a small child, I had used the pointed end to carve my initials in the windowsill of Uncle David's office.

My fingers tightened around the silver charm. Who else but Uncle David could the "red-haired man" have been?

Once again silence fell between us. This time, I spoke first. "Have you considered that Maggie may have been murdered?"

"And why do you think Maggie Schmidt may have been murdered?" MacPhearson said, his voice more conversational than confrontational.

I repositioned my head against the rim of the tub. "Everything seems too convenient," I began.

"Convenient how?" MacPhearson prompted.

"Sarah comes to see Maggie, then Sarah turns up dead. Maggie identifies Sarah's body, and would you believe, Maggie turns up dead."

"As an example of logical thinking, Ginny me girl, that last bit wins first place in the illogical category."

"I'm not your girl."

"I know, you're Doctor Brock's girl."

I wiggled more upright. "I think I've cooked long enough." I was looking at my hands, using my puckered fingertips as an excuse to quit the hot tub. Discussing murder with MacPhearson was okay. Discussing Steve Brock was not.

Mac lifted his head from the edge of the tub. "You think Maggie may have been murdered because you don't like the sequence of events. You think everything's too convenient, a little too pat. Anything else?"

I came fully upright. "We know she didn't have anything to drink while she was here, and judging from how she acted, I don't think she had been drinking before she got here."

"Which means?"

"Which means she did her drinking after she left here."

Chapter Twelve

DINNER WAS ANOTHER OF ARDELLA Duncan's casseroles and dessert a snifter of brandy. By unspoken agreement we did not discuss either Sarah Frazier or Maggie Schmidt, opting instead to watch the vintage movie *Anatomy of a Murder*. Seeing as how the action takes place in Michigan's Upper Peninsula, it seemed a good choice. I went to bed wishing we had a Jimmy Stewart to solve our problems.

The aroma of coffee woke me. The clock on the bedside table said eight. Preferring breakfast in the kitchen to the possibility of another breakfast in bed with MacPhearson, I hurried my shower and was sitting at the kitchen table spreading cream cheese on a toasted bagel by eight-fifteen. Much as I liked bagels, MacPhearson was right, they were beginning to pale. Either I needed to suggest MacPhearson try something new or make my own breakfast. I was deciding on the better course when MacPhearson called.

"Up to trying another snowmobile trail?" MacPhearson was studying the map and drinking a second cup of coffee. "There's a trail that runs through a part of Camp Whiting. It's longer than the one we took Monday. Think you're up to it?"

I studied MacPhearson's face. Gone were the furrowed brow and sunken, dark-circled eyes that had accompanied yesterday's headache. Still, I was not convinced as to the wisdom of MacPhearson's plan. "The question is not if I'm . . ."

MacPhearson raised a hand. "Stop right there. If I didn't feel up to it, I'd say so."

I doubted this last was true, but said nothing.

I poured myself a second cup of coffee and joined MacPhearson, watching as he traced the route he had selected for the day's outing. Camp Whiting covered approximately one hundred fifty thousand acres, and though the map indicated that many of the trails once open to the public had been closed since 9/11, several remained open.

We reviewed the snowmobile checklist and made a couple of preliminary runs around the cabin. Muscles, still sore from our introductory run of two days ago, were slow to respond, and not until MacPhearson was satisfied with our performance did he give the signal to head out.

The ride took us well into the afternoon. Since we had planned to end the day's run at Braun's Motel and stay over for dinner, we stopped for a break midway through the run at one of the trail-side picnic areas. Most were equipped with tables, grills, and ample parking. This one was no exception. Prominent too were reminders that we were in a restricted site, with warnings not to trespass beyond the designated areas.

Opting to forgo the tables and benches that were covered with snow, we munched our way through apples and granola bars astride the seats of our snowmobiles.

"Ever been up here before?" MacPhearson asked, offering a cup of coffee from the thermos he, bless him, had thought to pack.

"Two or three times. Once with my mom and dad. We did the usual camping, hiking, swimming, fishing thing."

"And the other times?"

"Canoeing with Uncle David."

"No camping?"

"We stayed in motels. Uncle David wasn't what you would call the outdoor type." I gathered the trash and stored it in the back of the Polaris as another party of snowmobilers pulled into the clearing. I counted five. Probably all men, but in their bulky suits, helmets, and goggles, it was hard to tell.

We exchanged greetings with our fellow travelers as we readied ourselves to leave. The words were brief, nothing more than "Hello" and "Have a good ride."

Mac and I headed back to the trail, winding our way through the five snowmobiles, which the newcomers had parked in a random rather than ordered fashion. We had hardly left the lot when the strap on my helmet came loose. I motioned MacPhearson back into the rest area and worked at readjusting the errant strap.

MacPhearson parked his Polaris and walked over to where I sat. The repair was minor (I had caught a piece of the chin strap in the metal fastener), and I had the helmet back in place in minutes.

My attention was caught by the five men, who, unlike Mac and I, had chosen to use the facilities provided and were brushing snow from one of the tables and its attached bench.

Three of the five had removed their goggles and helmets and, as if sensing me watching, looked up. Two looked familiar. The beer drinkers from the motel bar maybe?

We headed back the way we had come, retracing the run until we came to the fork that led to the motel. This last was busier than our earlier run through Camp Whiting. It was also a livelier crowd, and the trail rang with cheerful "Hi, see you later" and "Meet you at. . . ." It was a party in the making if I ever saw one.

We left the trail, turned into the motel parking lot, and made for the area reserved for snowmobiles. Glad to be off the bouncing seats, we hurried our aching muscles to the back entrance. The jocular mood we'd encountered on the trail proved infectious, and MacPhearson and I were laughing as we pushed through the door. Big-brother-like, MacPhearson shouldered me aside and was the first inside.

"Must be you two had a good time," Linda Braun greeted.

"You pushed me," I said, pointing an accusing finger at MacPhearson.

"We did," MacPhearson said, answering Linda's question. "You'll have to excuse her; Red's the nagging type."

Linda joined in our merriment, and we were all laughing when we reached the kitchen.

Linda motioned us to the round table with, "It's a little early for dinner, so how about a beer and a nacho platter to hold you over?"

I groaned, thinking of the minuscule bikini. MacPhearson, however, gave a thumbs up. Rationalizing that Mac needed the extra calories for his recovery, I nodded agreement. All right, so this is another example of illogical thinking, but then who's counting? "I am," said the voice inside my head.

"You're not joining us?" I asked, when Linda, after serving the beers and nachos, moved away from the table.

"Too busy," she said, leaning against the back of an empty chair. "Ted's seeing to the funeral arrangements, and with Maggie. . . ." She didn't finish.

"They're not sending her body back to Rocky Ridge?" MacPhearson asked.

"Maggie wasn't from there, and Ted really wanted her buried here." Linda shrugged. "So I guess Norm went along with the idea."

"Will there be a funeral Mass?" I asked.

"Father Mike is saying the funeral Mass at ten on Thursday," Linda said.

I continued pushing the cheese-and-salsa-loaded chips into my mouth. They were beginning to lose their appeal, however, and when MacPhearson asked, "What about Maggie's niece?" I shoved my plate aside. Enough was enough.

"Rick said Norm will be taking Sarah's body back to Rocky Ridge. It will be after Maggie's funeral, but Rick didn't say when." Linda's sigh carried the weight of the world. "Got to get back to work. Roger Whiting sent over some extra help, but they're not used to waiting tables."

Linda left, and Mac continued to pick at the nacho platter. I looked around the kitchen. The activity had picked up, but the atmosphere seemed oddly wrong without the familiar chop-chop of Ted's knife against the cutting board. A friendly smile from Rosa Torres, who today was wrapped in an overlarge white apron, lightened the mood.

"You the cook tonight?" I called.

"Just filling in until Ted gets back," the housekeeper said, lifting the lid of something that smelled mighty good. "I'm not much for waiting tables," the small woman nodded toward the dining room, "but I do know my way around the kitchen."

"Rosa," the twins chorused in unison as they burst into the kitchen, "you can do anything better than just about anybody."

"You two get out there and wait on those hungry people. How do I know what to cook if you don't bring me the orders?" Rosa made a shooing motion with her hands.

The twins hurried their escape, detouring past our table on their way to the dining room. "You must be that detective from Marion City," one said.

"Douglas MacPhearson," said the other.

"Kim. Deb. The dining room," Linda ordered, coming into the kitchen. "Ted not back yet?" she asked Rosa.

"Is it always like this?" Mac asked, laughing. "It reminds me of home." Knowing MacPhearson had grown up with several sisters, the comparison was easy to see.

A commotion from the far side of the kitchen caught my attention. It was Ted Williams. Sensing the activity level was about to escalate, MacPhearson and I sought refuge in the dining room.

Tranquility waited on the far side of the door, and dinner—pan-fried bluegills—proved even better than promised.

Forgoing dessert for the sake of my waistline, and brandy for sobriety's sake as we still had to snowmobile back to the cabin, we were about to order coffee when the twins stopped at our table. Other than taking our order and checking to see if everything was okay, we had seen little of them.

"The Whitings want you to join them for coffee," one said.

"I told them you weren't having dessert," the other explained.

"They're sitting over there by the window," the first twin said, pointing to a middle-aged couple who were looking in our direction.

The woman added a wave to the smile, and I smiled back.

"Tell them we'll be happy to have coffee with them," MacPhearson said. He laid a credit card on the table and stood up.

"Thank you for asking us to join you," I said when we reached the Whitings' table.

They looked to be in their mid-fifties, judging from the wrinkles on the man's face and their salt-and-pepper hair. Hers was cut short and framed a plump smiling face. His started high on his forehead, and wire-rimmed glasses with tinted lenses rode atop a decidedly off-center nose.

The man stood, hand extended. "Caroline and Roger Whiting."

MacPhearson grasped the man's hand. "Doug MacPhearson, and this is Ginny Arthur."

"We missed each other at the sheriff's office the other day," Caroline Whiting said, "and before you ask, yes, Sheriff Duncan does call me Carol, but Roger prefers Caroline." She smiled at her husband, who frowned in return.

"I want to thank you for putting your statement on the computer," Caroline continued. She ignored her husband's frown, brushing it aside as she would a worrisome gnat. "It saved me a lot of work. What with the storm and the tourists, it was a bit hectic around there."

Mentally adding murder and a second death to the woman's list of things that would have made for a hectic day in a sheriff's office, I said, "No need to thank me. It was no bother, really."

"You going to be around long?" Roger Whiting asked.

"That depends on how long Ginny's willing to put up with me," MacPhearson said.

We all laughed, not the "we're having a good time" sort of laugh but a "searching for common ground" laugh.

"I hear you two have been doing some snowmobiling," Roger Whiting said.

"Some." MacPhearson pulled back as one of the wait staff set cups and saucers on the table. Close behind was another waiter holding a carafe of coffee.

Whiting made a circular motion, indicating that the waiter should fill the four cups. Moving forward, the solemn-faced young man did as directed.

Roger Whiting watched as the waiter carefully filled each cup and, when he had finished, waved him away.

"If you're going to be here through the weekend," Caroline said, "we'd love for you to come by the farm. Have dinner maybe?"

As the invitation was tenuous and our plans nebulous, the question went unanswered.

"I was looking at the map," I said. "It appears you have one of the larger farms in the area."

"Not larger, largest," Roger Whiting corrected. "My family was farming here before Michigan thought of becoming a state."

"We took a snowmobile run through Camp Whiting today," MacPhearson said. "Any relation?"

Roger nodded. "My great grandfather donated the land back in the early 1900s. It's one of the largest installations of its kind east of the Mississippi," he said proudly.

"According to the map, several areas are set aside for public use," MacPhearson frowned. "Has this changed since 9/11?"

"Some, of course." Whiting looked from me to MacPhearson. "We're seeing tighter security across the board."

Mac stirred sugar and cream into his coffee, a thing I had never seen him do. Headache coming back? I worried.

"Have to get my sugar high where I can get it," MacPhearson said. He nodded in my direction. "Ginny here vetoed dessert."

"If you want dessert, Mac, you can order it," I said testily, and damn if he didn't do just that.

MacPhearson signaled one of the temporary wait staff. Hesitantly, the man approached. "I'd like dessert," MacPhearson said. "May I see a dessert menu?"

The man shuffled from foot to foot. "Menu?" he asked in heavily accented English.

"Menu, man, menu." Roger Whiting pantomimed opening and reading a book.

Understanding spread over the waiter's face. "Menu," he said.

"They do have trouble speaking the language. One has to watch them all the time," Caroline motioned in the direction of the retreating waiter, "or the mistakes do pile up."

The waiter made a hurried retreat, grabbed a menu and, almost trotting in his haste, wended his way back through the tables. "For you, sir," he said softly, offering the menu to MacPhearson.

Roger Whiting took it instead, looked through it, then passed it to MacPhearson. "Just checking to see if he brought the right one." Whiting waved the waiter away. "Give the man a chance to look it over."

"No, no. I'll have this one, apple pie and ice cream." MacPhearson smiled at the waiter, who studied MacPhearson's pointed finger.

"Anything for the rest of you?"

The three of us shook our heads, and MacPhearson returned the menu to the waiter.

Roger Whiting talked about his farm, and Caroline pushed for a dinner date. We decided on Saturday, promising to come early enough to tour the farm.

We said our good-byes and headed for the kitchen and the back entry where we had left our outdoor gear. Music, laughter, and the hum of many voices poured from the bar area.

Mac and I stopped and looked inside. A harassed looking Linda was behind the bar, and to my surprise, the tall angular form and not-quite-smiling face of Lake County's Deputy Myra Johnson waited tables. Neither woman noticed us, nor did we try to catch their attention. The party-in-the-making we had observed on our ride over had taken over the motel bar. I said a silent prayer for Maggie Schmidt, a woman who would be missed by only a few of those present.

"And did you enjoy your pie and ice cream?" I asked. We had left the party to the partygoers and were in the back room, dressing for the return trip to the cabin.

"More than the atmosphere," MacPhearson said.

I gave him a quizzical look, but as we had left the motel and were in the parking lot, helmet and goggles in place, the look had been lost on MacPhearson.

Chapter Thirteen

As we had agreed to attend Maggie Schmidt's funeral, both Mac and I were in the kitchen before eight the next morning. I had started the coffee and was pouring the orange juice while, much to my surprise, MacPhearson began frying sausage and scrambling eggs.

"No bagels?" I quipped.

"Thought it was time for a change, Red."

MacPhearson's movements were quick and sure as he lifted the sausage links onto a paper towel. "So how about making the toast and bringing it to the table?" he asked.

Breakfast was as good as it smelled. Along with enjoying the meal, it provided the opportunity to continue my covert observation of the man who sat across from me. There was no evidence that Tuesday's headache might be returning.

After a minor skirmish around who would or would not drive my Honda, MacPhearson relented with a grudging, "You do know where the church is, don't you?"

I did and said as much. First though, we had another stop to make.

The yellow crime scene tape, a splash of color in the snow, flapped in the morning breeze. Even without it, the accident scene would have been hard to miss, and I pulled onto the shoulder well clear of the site. The two of us left the Honda and followed the broken shrubbery and a scraped tree trunk that marked the car's route.

The rutted tracks made by Maggie's Volvo and an overlapping set of footprints, both going and coming, were framed by the wind-blown tape. We followed where it led and stopped at the craggy edge that overlooked the frozen lake. My mind's eye saw the Volvo careen off the edge, saw it nose over, and the sound of the crash reverberated inside my head.

It had snowed little since Maggie's accident, and the weather had been cold enough to preserve the tracks. It was these tracks, the tracks that MacPhearson and I were now looking at, that told of how Maggie's Volvo had failed to negotiate the bend in the road. How the car had traveled across the shoulder, through the snow-covered vegetation, and over the precipice onto the frozen lake. What we didn't see were skid marks.

The slight dusting of snow urged caution, and I held tight to one of the sturdier shrubs that marked the edge of the bluff. Below, jagged edges of ice rimmed the impact site. Nature, in the form of zero temperatures, was busy repairing the damage, and a small white cross, nailed to a nearby tree, labeled this a place of death.

Outside the perimeter of the yellow tape, several pairs of foot-steps, some angled and some parallel to the tire tracks, told their own story. The larger, deeper rutted tracks of the tow truck, slightly downhill from those of the Volvo, could also be seen. Though Maggie Schmidt had been alone when she died, it had taken a small army to clear away the wreckage her death had left behind.

Neither of us spoke as we left the accident site and drove, very carefully I might add, into Pine City. The series of winding curves looked benign in the morning sun, but how had they looked to Maggie in the dark of night?

St. Paul's parking lot overflowed with cars, SUVS, and trucks of all types and models. In an adjacent field a tractor equipped with a snow plow was clearing away mounds of snow, creating a temporary parking lot to handle the overflow. Being one of this group, I praised the effort.

We crunched our way through what snow remained to where a long line of mourners waited to pay their last respects to Maggie Schmidt. Once inside, we found standing room only.

The organ swelled, and the voices of the congregation rose in joyful celebration for a life that had ended its mortal journey and for the soul that was beginning an eternity with God. True, there were many tearful faces, friends and neighbors who mourned Maggie's traumatic ending, but grieving had begun and, mercifully, would be short and healing.

The burial, which I learned from listening to the conversation around me, would be at the cemetery adjacent to the church. Due to the frozen ground, interment would be delayed and the body held at the mortuary until a thaw.

I moved closer to MacPhearson and linked my arm through his, watched as the coffin was loaded into the hearse. Why did I always feel so alone, so vulnerable at a funeral?

As if of one mind the crowd shifted, and we joined the congregation as it made its way to the tables loaded with food.

"Should have stuck to bagels this morning," MacPhearson said, lifting his heaping plate above the head of a runaway toddler.

"You don't have to eat it all," I said.

"We saw you standing in the back of church," Kim, or maybe it was Deb, said.

The two gave me a smile then turned their attention to MacPhearson. "I'm Kim and that's Deb and the boy standing next to Deb is Jimmy Wakefield," Kim explained.

"Jimmy Wakefield, sir."

Shuffling their overflowing plates, the two shook hands.

"They said she had been drinking and that she didn't have her seatbelt on," Deb said. The words rushed from her mouth as if having been held back by some invisible hand.

"What about the drinking and the seatbelt?" Mac asked.

"Maggie never drove anywhere without her seatbelt!" So emphatic were Kim's words, an explanation point danced in the air between us.

"And she wasn't drinking anymore," Deb added. "We talked about her drinking and her going to AA meetings."

"I asked her if working around all the booze in the bar was hard," Kim continued. "She said it sometimes was, but she promised

God, herself, and Ted that she wouldn't drink anymore, and when Maggie said she was going to do something, she meant it."

"When did Maggie and Ted get together?" I asked. I finished the last of my brownie, and Deb reached for my plate.

"I'm not sure, six or seven years ago. They both started working at the motel about the same time and just seemed to hit it off," Deb said, balancing my plate on top of hers.

"I remember Mom telling her if she didn't stop drinking, she'd have to fire her," Kim said. "Then Maggie moved in with Ted, and right after that, she quit drinking."

"And that's why we know Maggie wasn't drinking and that she was wearing her seatbelt, and whoever says different is wrong," Deb declared.

"Who's wrong?" Linda Braun asked. Her eyes moved from the twins to Mac and me.

"Everyone's wrong," the girls chorused in unison.

"And who's everyone?" Sheriff Duncan eased through the crowd to stand beside MacPhearson.

Deb gestured, the sweep of her arm taking in the whole room. "Anyone who says Maggie was drunk and not wearing a seatbelt. It just isn't true!"

Again a parade of exclamation points marched through the air. Not only did Deb believe the truth of what she said, she wanted the whole room to know. What had Maggie done to win such loyalty?

Duncan looked from mother to daughters. "Could we continue this conversation later?"

"Why?" Kim asked, coming to her sister's defense. "You don't have to take Deb's word for it. Everyone will tell you Maggie always wore her seatbelt and that she stopped drinking years ago."

"Girls! Later!" Linda interjected.

Deb turned from the group, bumping into Jimmy and sending the pair of paper cups he was holding tumbling through the air. Ignoring the hapless boy, Deb pushed past him and disappeared into the crowd.

"Jimmy," Linda said, "get something to mop up the spill before someone falls." Offering an apology, she went after her daughter.

With a sigh and a "Come on, Jimmy, I'll help you," Kim dragged Jimmy off in search of a mop.

Sheriff Duncan shrugged. "Guess the twins don't think Maggie's accident was an accident."

Standing guard over the puddle, which looked to be red punch, MacPhearson and I said nothing. That Maggie's accident had not been an accident was a conclusion Mac and I had already considered.

The thought was hardly digested before Kim and Jimmy came through the crowd, pushing a rolling bucket with a mop handle bobbing above it. The three of us, Sheriff Duncan, MacPhearson, and I, moved back a few steps to allow the cleanup crew room to work.

"You still wedded to the theory?" I asked the sheriff.

"You're referring to Maggie's death being an accident, I presume?"

I nodded I was.

"Can't say I am and can't say I'm not," Duncan said.

"But you must have an idea."

"And why should any idea of mine be of interest to you, Miss Arthur?"

I held up a hand in protest. "Since you all but accused Mac and me of getting the woman drunk, which I presume you consider to be the cause of the accident, I'd say we have every right to know." I looked around, hoping I had not been overheard. Though some were looking in our direction, most were intent on other conversations, the still-loaded tables, and the little ones running noisily underfoot.

"She got the liquor someplace," Duncan said.

"But not from us, and since you can't be sure of the time of death, Maggie could have gone any number of places before running off the road," MacPhearson added.

"She was coming from Judge Marfield's cabin," Duncan said.

"And how can you be sure?" Duncan said nothing and MacPhearson finished with, "You can't."

"Rhodes warned me to expect trouble from Miss Arthur, but he didn't say anything about you, Detective MacPhearson."

Mac shrugged. "Just asking a few questions."

"Just be sure you limit your involvement to a few questions, Detective, or do I have to remind you that you're out of your jurisdiction?"

"No need to remind me," MacPhearson said. He smiled, letting the corners of his mouth slide under his mustache, which meant . . . what? Hell if I knew, but I suspected MacPhearson had every intention of ignoring the sheriff's warning.

The conversation, with its accusations and veiled threats, came to an end as Linda and Deb joined the cleanup crew. Separated as we were by only a few feet, it was clear to see Deb had been crying.

"Time to go, Red." MacPhearson took my elbow and steered me toward the door. "I think we've all had enough melodrama for one day."

The wind had risen and was driving snow across the newly cleared field. Overhead, the sun looked ready to call it a day despite it being mid-afternoon, and heavy clouds scudded across the sky. The morning's bright promise was gone. Sensing the change in the weather, we hurried our steps.

I relinquished the driver's seat to MacPhearson and slid into the passenger's seat.

"Duncan sure is a testy son-of-a-gun," MacPhearson muttered.

"I can't figure if he thinks we really are involved in Maggie's death or is just grabbing at straws." Adjusting the seatbelt across my chest, I leaned against the headrest and shut my eyes.

"Could be a bit of both." MacPhearson drummed his fingers against the steering wheel as we waited for the line of traffic to start moving.

Before I could question MacPhearson further, a knock sounded on the driver's side window. Seeing Jim Wacker's smiling face, MacPhearson slid the window down.

"How about the two of you joining me for dinner tonight? Funerals always leave me wanting company."

Similarly disposed, we accepted the invitation.

As I had been earlier in the week, MacPhearson was duly impressed with Doc Wacker's home cum office. "This is some fine cabinetwork you have here," Mac said, running fingers over the cabinets and along the counter-tops as he made a second tour of the kitchen. "You do all this yourself?"

"Not me," Wacker said. "I'm much handier with people than with hammers and saws."

"It took more than hammers and saws to do this," MacPhearson said. His words, an obvious compliment, sounded as if MacPhearson knew whereof he spoke. Hearing them, I realized again how little I knew about the man.

Suggesting we have a drink in the family room before eating, Jim Wacker dragged Mac away from the kitchen. A fieldstone fireplace dominated one wall of the family room, while a pair of sofas and a scattering of overstuffed chairs promised comfortable seating. Autumn's bright reds and golds intermixed with green and brown pleased the eye. It was, instinct told me, a room created with love.

Jim struck a match to the kindling before bringing our drinks, a Bud for MacPhearson and a glass of wine for me, and settled into a much-worn lounge chair.

"Marty Shouldice did most of the carpentry work, he and his dad that is," Wacker said, "but Mary Ellen saw to most of the remodeling."

"Mary Ellen?" MacPhearson asked.

"My wife," Jim Wacker said. "Mary Ellen died last year. Guess that's why I like to be around people after I go to a funeral. Being I'm the only doc in town, I go to most of them."

"You said Marty Shouldice was one of the carpenters?" I asked.

"Marty and his dad."

"Any relation to Cindy Shouldice?" I took a sip of wine.

"Her dad," Wacker answered.

"She's one of the missing girls." I looked at MacPhearson. "You remember, I told you about them, Mac."

"Josie Leggit's the other one," Wacker added.

"How long have they been missing?" Mac asked, taking a pull from the bottle he held in his hand.

"Almost a year. The two went missing during spring break, which is always the first week in April."

"Anyone hear from them? Was there a ransom note?" Mac-Phearson asked.

"Nothing. Here one day and gone the next."

"They both disappeared at the same time?" I asked.

Jim Wacker looked from MacPhearson to me. "That's the primary reason Duncan thinks they're runaways." Wacker finished the Coke he was drinking and offered another round of drinks. I shook my head while MacPhearson nodded yes.

"And you say no one's heard from them?" MacPhearson asked again as he exchanged the empty Bud for a full bottle.

"No, Detective. Nobody has heard from them." Jim Wacker resettled himself in the lounger. "Why all the interest, Detective MacPhearson?"

Chapter Fourteen

"Cold cases are something of a hobby with me," Mac said.

The doctor gave MacPhearson a speculative look, watching as Mac's thumbnail bothered the Bud's label.

"Were they patients of yours, Jim?" I finished the last of my wine and set the glass aside.

"They were. In fact, I delivered both of them." A smile added additional wrinkles to Jim Wacker's age-worn face.

"What can you tell us about the missing girls? Finding a body in one's freezer does tend to make one curious."

"Sarah Frazier is not one of our missing girls, Ginny," Wacker chided.

"Nothing personal, Doc. Just fill us in on what everyone who lives around here already knows," Mac said.

"You can get most of what you want to know from newspaper accounts or the police reports." The doctor stopped, looked from me to Mac, and burst out laughing. "But I don't suppose Sheriff Duncan is into letting you see the department's records."

Mac joined in Wacker's laughter. "Didn't ask. But you're probably right."

"Their being patients of mine does present a problem." Wacker rubbed his brow. "What everyone already knows. Well, let's see. . . . The Shouldice and Leggit girls went missing last year during spring break. That's when the eighth graders go to Washington, DC." Wacker grew more somber as he talked. "I hear tell the two were damn near inseparable. Wherever one was, you'd be sure to find the other."

"Did the whole class go?"

"Can't say they all went, but certainly the majority."

"And both girls were supposed to go on the trip?" MacPhearson asked.

Wacker nodded. "But from all reports, they never got on the bus. Their parents thought the girls were on their way to Washington, and the teachers and chaperones thought they had decided not to go."

"How long before someone realized they were missing?" I asked.

"Two or three days, I think," Wacker said.

"The parents weren't worried when they didn't hear from their daughters? Two or three days is a long time," I said.

"Surely they had cell phones," MacPhearson said.

"They did, but as I understand, the girls didn't call home, and when the parents tried calling them, all they got was their voice mail."

"How did they get to the bus? They weren't old enough to drive," I said, adding another question to the mix.

Wacker held up a protesting hand. "Now you're asking about the hows and whys of things of which I have little or no knowledge."

Wacker pushed his way out of the chair. "Don't know about you two, but I'm hungry, and there's a big pot of chili on the stove just begging to be eaten."

The chili was good, as good as what I had eaten at Braun's, and was made even better with the cherry pie and ice cream we had for dessert. I groaned. Maybe tomorrow . . .

MacPhearson finished his last bite of pie and asked if there were other examples of Marty Shouldice's work in the house.

"You're eating off it and sitting on it," Wacker said. "Marty made the table and these chairs."

"His services must be in great demand," MacPhearson said. "One doesn't see such craftsmanship very often."

"You're right, work like this is fast becoming a lost art. Are you a carpenter, Mac?"

"I'm a putterer," MacPhearson admitted. "When I see this," he ran his fingers along the table's beveled edge, "I realize just how much of a putterer I am."

"Marty owns the local hardware store. You can see more of his work there."

"I'll have to stop by the hardware store. If I'm lucky, maybe he'll give me some pointers."

I offered to help with the cleanup, but Wacker insisted he could handle it. "I can put a few plates, bowls, and silverware in the dishwasher. Besides, it gives me something to do when I'm here by myself." He grinned at MacPhearson. "You putter around with hammers and saws, and I clean up peoples' messes."

We said our good-byes. The doctor added a hug for me. The show of affection pleased me for, despite our short acquaintance, I had come to think of Jim Wacker as a friend. Bundled against the cold, Mac and I hurried to the car.

Mac claimed the driver's seat, for which I was grateful. Though the falling snow was slight, the gusting wind swirled the flakes into a frenzied dance that twisted and swirled like fog in the headlights.

Pine City's lone traffic light glowed red in the distance. Along Main Street, the shop windows reflected the changing reds, greens, and yellows. Extensions of the traffic signal that blinked at us through the swirling snow.

"I'm glad you're driving," I said, hoping the apprehension that niggled inside me did not sound in my voice.

"Driving in snow doesn't bother me," Mac said.

I turned to look at him. The expression on his face, illuminated by the faint glow from the dashboard, supported his words.

"It's not just the snow." I waved at the windshield. "It's what the wind does to it. You can hardly make out the road, and it's impossible to see the middle line or tell where the edge is."

"Driving in snow doesn't bother me," Mac repeated with a grin.

Damn his arrogance.

I cancelled the thought, knowing it was more Mac's uncanny resemblance to David Arthur than his cocky grin that had triggered the untoward response.

We left the town and were traveling along the winding roads that led to Judge Marfield's cabin before either of us spoke again.

"Was it snowing like this the night Maggie had her accident?" Mac asked.

"It snowed some, but not much. There wasn't any snow to shovel in the driveway the next morning."

"And how about the wind, was it blowing like this?"

I thought hard, but had to admit I couldn't remember.

"How about drifts? Did you notice if the snow had drifted any during the night?" Mac persisted.

"I just can't remember, but if you want a guess, I'd say no. Otherwise, I think I would remember."

"I'm thinking the same thing. So let's say visibility was good the night Maggie went off the road."

"And where does that get us?"

"You tell me. Visibility was good. She wasn't drunk, at least she wasn't drunk when she left the cabin, and there were no skid marks."

"And because of the cold, they can't determine the time of death," I added.

"Wacker said there was alcohol in her stomach, but not enough in the blood stream to say she was legally drunk."

"And the twins say Maggie didn't drink anymore," I said, lengthening the list. "Mac, would it take more or less alcohol to impair a reformed alcoholic?"

Mac shrugged. "Beats me."

"Next time I see Jim Wacker I'll . . . What are you doing?"

Mac had pulled into the driveway of the Marfield cabin, but instead of pulling into the garage, he had pulled the Honda into the turnaround area and was headed back down the driveway to the highway.

"Just thought we'd take a look and see what the crash site looks like at night." Mac chuckled. "Interested?"

I admitted I was.

The snow continued to fall and the wind continued to blow, making it difficult to see beyond the front end of the Honda. Fearing we were on a fool's errand, my heart sank.

"Think positive," Mac chided.

"How . . ."

"Save it, we're about there."

And we were, heading into the curve that, if one failed to negotiate, led directly to the bluff that overlooked Big Pine Lake.

Mac stopped at the high point of the curve. "Maggie's car must have left the road about here."

"She was going too fast to make the turn," I said.

Mac grunted in reply and stepped on the gas. The Honda left the road, paralleling the ruts Maggie's car had made. Without warning, he brought our vehicle to an abrupt stop, thrusting me hard against my seatbelt.

"Don't want to disturb the crime scene," Mac explained.

A sudden glare of headlights illuminated the Honda's interior. With a shriek, I grabbed for MacPhearson.

Chapter Fifteen

Memories of another snowy night and another pair of headlights engulfed me. Though the vehicle on that other night had been a Ford Ranger, not a Honda, the man sitting beside me then as now was the redheaded Marion City detective, Douglas MacPhearson.

Timelines blurred, and the present faded. The sight and sound of that long ago night were real.

An engine roared and a monster truck with a snow plow spread across its front end loomed large in the windshield. I started to shake but could do nothing about it. I willed air into my lungs, but the tightness in my chest was unrelenting. Letting go of Mac's arm, I dug my fists into my eyes in a vain attempt to rid myself of the nightmare that engulfed me.

"Ginny."

Mac called my name, but I could not answer. Panic threatened. I pulled at my seatbelt, needing to escape the hovering snow plow. My fingers searched for the belt's release button as the lifted blade pushed against the windshield.

"No! No!" I abandoned my search for the release button and clawed at the harness that held me captive.

"Ginny . . . Ginny!"

Mac's voice sounded over my screams. Rough hands shook me. The screams stopped. The hands stopped shaking me, and a pair of arms circled tight around me.

"It's all right, Ginny. It's all right."

I tried to pull free, but he held me tight.

A knock sounded against the driver's window, and another voice, this one loud and demanding, asked, "Are you okay?"

I stiffened, pushed hard against MacPhearson's chest, tried to separate what was happening now from what had happened weeks ago. "Let me go . . . let me go," I sobbed.

"You're okay, Ginny," Mac said.

Okay? Hell, when had I been less okay? I pounded Mac's chest with clinched fists. Couldn't breathe . . . couldn't breathe. I needed to shout, to scream—to share my terror. Robbed of air, words would not come.

Another loud knock rattled the Honda's window. "You okay in there?" the voice outside shouted.

Mac lowered the window.

"Car trouble?" the talking head asked.

"No," Mac said, staring at the face framed by the open window.

"Deputy Schmidt," the man said, identifying himself. "Something wrong here? You having car trouble?"

"Car's fine," Mac said. "Just wanted to see where the accident happened."

"At night? In this weather?" Schmidt said, a note of skepticism in his voice.

"You're right," Mac admitted. "Can't see a damn thing."

"Then you'll be moving on," Schmidt stated.

MacPhearson looked through the Honda's back window to where a Suburban with winking red-and-blue lights sat. "We seem to be stuck here until you move, Deputy Schmidt."

As if not quite sure what his next move should be, the deputy stared from me to Mac. The silence, rapidly approaching a stalemate, continued. Mac's arm, the one wrapped around my shoulders, tensed. The endless moment ended when Schmidt turned away from the window. Feeling Mac's arm relax, I drew in a shuddering breath.

"You okay, Red?" Mac asked.

I nodded. Bouncing mentally between then and now, snow plows and police vehicles, I didn't trust myself to speak.

The deputy backed his Suburban onto the highway, executed a three point turn, and headed away from town. Together Mac and I watched the receding taillights, losing them when the car disappeared around a curve.

"Ready to go home, Red," Mac asked, "or do you want to have a look around?"

I stared through the windshield, wincing as fistfuls of snow hit against the glass. We were parked on a bluff overlooking Big Pine Lake, I knew, yet a part of me still heard the roar of the monster truck as it chased us across the parking lot.

Once more my pulse raced and my chest tightened. "I'm ready to go home," I said, in a voice I did not recognize as my own.

Mac backed onto the highway, and though the headlights tried to light our way, the darkness won. Mercifully, the drive to Judge Marfield's cabin was short.

MacPhearson pulled the Honda into the garage. Behind us the overhead doors slid shut, leaving the blowing snow outside.

The house was warm, but I was cold. Teeth chattering, I refused to give up my coat. Mac hurried me up the stairs, sat me on the couch, and lit the fire.

Anticipating the warmth to come, I tried to relax but couldn't do so. Mac coaxed the kindling into flame then sat beside me on the couch.

"Want to talk about it?" he asked.

I shook my head.

"How long has this been going on?"

"How long has what been going on?" I managed through chattering teeth.

"Wrong answer, Red," Mac said. "Gunshot wounds heal." Mac gently massaged my shoulder. "Other wounds, the ones inside our heads, are a different story, and sooner or later you will have to let them out."

But not now, not tonight, I thought.

Mac left the couch and went into the kitchen. I heard running water and the rattle of the coffee pot.

In the fireplace, the flames jumped from the kindling to the bark along the larger logs. Giving way to the fire's hypnotic pull, I struggled to let loose of the all-consuming terror of blowing snow, big trucks, and menacing snow plows. The flames in the fireplace became the winking red-and-blue lights atop Deputy Schmidt's Suburban and then the neon lights of the Sandcastle, the Marion City nightclub in whose parking lot the man behind the blade of the plow had almost succeeded in killing MacPhearson and me.

Mac pulled off my jacket and wrapped a down-filled comforter around me. I heard the rattle of cups, smelled the coffee, and felt the warmth of the ceramic mug as he pressed the cup into my hands.

His hands on mine, Mac lifted the mug to my lips. "Drink," he ordered.

I did. Choked as the brandy-laced brew found its way to my stomach.

I made a vain attempt to push the drink away, but MacPhearson tipped more of the potent liquid into my mouth. "Drink," he repeated.

I did, and when I finished Mac took the mug from my hands and set it on the table. I sighed, contented. Letting the coffee and brandy work their magic, I settled deeper into the couch and pulled the comforter closer around me. Mac was there beside me, and then his arms were around me, and then his lips were on mine.

I moved my head away but his followed mine, the weight of him pressing me deeper into the cushion.

"No," I said without conviction.

Mac moved away, and this time it was me who followed.

"Yes?" he asked.

My answer was to put my arms around him and pull him close. His kiss was warm, soft, then hard and demanding. I parted my lips inviting a closer union.

I groaned, appreciating the moment, anticipating what was to come.

"Say yes, Ginny."

I pulled him closer, relishing the feel of him against me, yes, I thought, oh, yes.

Mac moved against me, his hands roaming, seeking, touching.

I loosened my hold. Pressed my hands against his chest and shook my head. I couldn't speak, couldn't say the word that would make him stop. Coward that I was, I could only push against him and shake my head from side to side.

I lay alone in bed, but the emotional war I'd waged on the couch with Mac continued. Finally, exhausted from a battle that had neither winner nor loser, I slept.

My ringing cell phone jerked me awake. Set to both vibrate and ring, it danced across the polished surface of the bedside table. Wanting to catch it before it met an uncertain fate on the floor, I scooted to the edge of the bed and grabbed the instrument.

"Hello," I mumbled.

"Did I wake you?" Steve asked. "You sound half asleep."

Memories of last night's aborted lovemaking washed over me and guilt, like a wave of nausea, gripped my innards.

"I'm awake now," I said. I swung my legs over the edge of the bed, hoping the change in position would assuage the guilt.

It didn't. I attempted a laugh. It also fell flat. I looked at the clock. Its digital face told me it was well past seven.

"Are you going on or coming off?" I asked. Shift change was at eight.

"Going on," Steve said. He paused. "About this weekend, Ginny."

I sensed the hesitation in his voice and, knowing it brooked no good, decided not to wait for the shoe to drop. "You've got to work," I finished for him.

"No, I don't have to work."

My spirits rose. "Then you'll be up?"

That had been our plan, for the three of us to spend time together, to give MacPhearson the peace and quiet, the continued supervision he needed while he recuperated from his head injury. Only, due to Steve's erratic schedule, the "we" became "me," here alone with Mac.

"No. Afraid not, not this weekend. I . . ."

"But if you're off?" My smile faded, and I started to plead.

"Ginny." This time it was Steve who interrupted, and the shoe I'd been waiting on to drop hit the floor. "Mass General called. They've offered me the fellowship."

I took in a deep breath. It was what Steve wanted, to be accepted into a trauma surgery, critical care fellowship program. He had been interviewed by the Mayo Clinic in Minnesota and Florida and UC Davis in California. The months of waiting, the trips to check out each facility and be checked out by the powers that be had finally come to an end.

"They want me to fly out this weekend and work out the details. The program starts the first of April, so that doesn't leave much time."

Steve's voice rose and fell in my ear. I tried to respond to the excitement I heard in his voice. Wasn't this what I wanted for him?

"I'm sorry about the weekend, Ginny. Maybe next week, Saturday is Valentine's Day. How about I try and get up then?"

"I'm not sure Mac should stay here if you're not going to be here," I said, evading the Valentine's Day question.

"Is there a problem? Are his headaches worse? I talked with the doctor up there. He didn't seem to think there was a problem."

"Jim Wacker," I supplied, "and no, Mac's not worse. In fact, if anything, I'd say he was better." Despite what I was saying, I wanted to shout, "Read my mind! It's me I'm talking about, not Mac," but of course, I didn't, and he couldn't.

"Good, then that's settled. I'll try and get up for Valentine's Day. Say hi to Mac for me, and, Ginny, be happy for me."

I said I was, and closed the lid on the cell phone. Of course I was happy for him. But I sure as hell wasn't happy for me.

My eyes swept over the crumpled bed, the clothes I had tossed on the floor after escaping Mac's arms and the temptation of his lips. Even now, hours later, my skin tingled at the remembered touch of his hands . . .

"Damn you, MacPhearson!" I slammed the cell phone on the bedside table and pounded the pillow that lay beside me. Needing more than a pillow to vent the frustration building within me, I moved off the bed and circled the room. A pile of last night's discarded clothes shouted "Kick me." I obliged, stopping when my toe hit the bed frame. The coolness of the patio doors invited me close, and I leaned my forehead against the pane. Irrational as I knew it to be, I began the poor-me game.

Mass General was in Boston, and I lived in Marion City. We had talked about Steve having to move, had discussed what the separation would do to our relationship. Like most plans, though, it was a plan for the future.

Like a mantra, the voice inside my head chanted, "Poor me . . . Poor me . . . Poor me." A sigh moved through me, from the tip of my throbbing toe to the ends of my red hair. The future, no matter what I did or whether I accepted it, was six weeks away.

The glass warmed beneath my forehead, and I lifted my face and looked into the expanse of snow-covered pines, and farther on to the icy expanse of Big Pine Lake. Despite the dazzling effect of the morning sun, goose bumps rippled along my arms. Finding no solace in self-pity, I returned to the here and now. The here was where Mac and I were and where Steve was not.

Here was also an unmade bed, a scattering of dirty clothes, and a throbbing toe. I sat on the edge of the bed, pulled my knee into my chest, and inspected the latter.

Chapter Sixteen

Breakfast was a bowl of corn flakes, a banana, orange juice, a slice of peanut butter toast, and coffee, accompanied by a pair of extremely vocal Siamese cats.

"Sounds like you two have been alone too much lately," I said over the din.

Both responded with an even louder "Yowl!"

Feeling guilty, I invited both into my lap. I had carried a second cup of coffee into the great room and now sat cross-legged on the couch. Hera accepted my invitation, and I stroked her sleek coat as I stared absently into the fireplace. Fresh logs and kindling waited the touch of a match to bring it to life. MacPhearson had been busy this morning.

I had not emerged from my bedroom until after nine, having lingered over my shower, washing my hair, shaving my legs, and cutting my toenails, girly things that required extra time to do. No savory breakfast smells (except for coffee) had enticed me to hasten my efforts. A note on the kitchen counter explained the absence of the morning routine I had come to expect.

"Decided to do some looking around," Mac had written. "Back this afternoon. If you need me, my cell is . . ."

I sipped my coffee, enjoying the caffeine rush, and fished my cell phone along with Mac's note from the pocket of my jeans. Hera grunted her disapproval at being disturbed but resettled herself with little protest. I reread Mac's note, repeating his cell number as I entered it into my phone's memory.

I finished my coffee and set the cup aside. With a baleful look and a twitch of her upraised tail, Hera leaped off my lap.

"I know, I'm not very good company this morning," I admitted.

Hera said nothing, but Zeus, who had been watching from the coffee table, uttered a low growl.

"You trying to tell me something?" I asked.

Zeus jumped from the table and headed for the stairs. It didn't take an Einstein to interpret the cat's message.

Calling "Give me a minute, Zeus," I cleaned up the remains of my breakfast. No slouch in the kitchen detail, MacPhearson had left everything in ship-shape order, and I intended to do no less.

As I had expected, the problem was a personal hygiene matter.

I found a large heavy-duty trash bag, emptied the used litter, and after a thorough scrubbing, refilled the box with fresh litter.

My audience, watching my every move, inspected the results of my labors. Zeus, apparently satisfied, turned his back on the two of us and proceeded to do what cats do in litter boxes.

I lifted out the bottom grate of the carrying cage and placed it in the sink. Several feathers lay scattered over the surface. I scooped them into my hand. Small, mostly white in color and exceedingly soft, they had most likely come from either a pillow or a down jacket. Both being abundant in the cabin, I made a mental note to look for the source.

"I hope the two of you haven't been chewing on something you shouldn't have been chewing on," I scolded, tossing the feathers into an empty trash can.

I spent the next couple of hours doing my washing. I thought of checking Mac's room, but squelched the idea. Our relationship was already too personal.

Being I was on a roll, I pulled the vacuum cleaner from the closet and began shoving it across the floor. Busy hands and feet did not mean a busy mind, and as I ran the vacuum down the hall past Mac's bedroom door, I wondered what he would say when he found out Steve would not be up this weekend. Like a more infamous character, I decided to think about it tomorrow.

I found the makings of a turkey sandwich, which I ate standing before the patio doors. The morning sun had more than lived up to its promise. Riding high in the cloudless sky, its bright rays lent radiance to the landscape.

I ate the last of my sandwich and finished off a bottle of water. Tired of the domesticity that had filled the morning, I headed for the garage and my Honda. Now was the perfect time to have another look at Maggie Schmidt's accident site.

As MacPhearson had the night before, I pulled the Honda onto the shoulder several yards distant from where Maggie's Volvo had gone off the road. Though the sun was bright, the temperature hovered near zero, and before leaving the car I tugged the zipper of my jacket snug against my neck.

A set of tracks led from the shoulder of the road, past a stand of pines and through a scattering of low-growing vegetation before disappearing over the embankment. Another wider-based set, made by the emergency vehicle that had retrieved the car from the depths of Big Pine Lake, paralleled the first. Both sets cut deep into the layers of snow that, until Maggie's accident, had lain mostly undisturbed since the season's first snowfall.

The cold temperatures had preserved the crime scene, and I walked the tracks, staying well outside the perimeter of the yellow tape. I stopped where I had started, where Maggie's Volvo had broken through the hard-packed snow thrown by the blades of passing snowplows.

How fast had Maggie been going to have pushed through this first hurdle? I wondered. It had snowed little, if at all, the night Maggie visited the cabin. Had the wind been blowing, swirling the snow so as to make visibility difficult? If so, why hadn't she reduced her speed? Even in good weather prudence dictated the curve be taken at a slower speed.

I turned and surveyed the accident scene once more—the Volvo's tracks, the tracks of the tow truck, the coming and going of many pairs of feet. The Pine County Sheriff's Department, though not as large and perhaps not as sophisticated as Marion City's Police Department, knew how to preserve a crime scene.

Again I walked the tracks of the Volvo's final journey. They were straight and uniform in depth from the point of leaving the road to the spot where the car had plunged over the edge.

Had Maggie drank enough so as to ignore the most rudimentary safety precautions? If so, where had she done her drinking?

I stood at the edge of the embankment, adding to the list of questions raised by Maggie Schmidt's accident and damning the cold weather and icy water that made the time of death all but impossible to pinpoint.

"You back again?"

I started at the sound of the voice and turned from the embankment to see who had caught me so unaware.

"Careful, Miss Arthur. We don't want to add another victim to the county's casualty list."

Despite the cap pulled low on the man's forehead and his aviator-style sunglasses, I recognized the Pine County deputy. "I didn't hear you drive up." I looked past the deputy to the road behind him. It was empty.

"The Suburban's up the road near where you left your Honda," he said, watching as I looked past him. "It is your Honda? Isn't it?" Deputy Schmidt's thin lips moved upwards, lending a semblance of a smile to his face.

I nodded that it was.

Schmidt nodded in return. "Thought it must be," he said.

Having exhausted the small talk, silence settled between us. Though the afternoon sun had long since dispelled the swirling snow and blinking lights, last night's terror threatened to reassert itself. I felt unsafe trapped between the edge of the embankment and the Pine County deputy. Fighting a rising sense of panic, I urged my suddenly reluctant legs to move along the tire tracks toward the road.

"See everything you wanted to see?" Schmidt asked.

I chose not to answer, it being one of those "When did you stop beating your wife" type questions.

"You and your boyfriend seem mighty curious about this place. Both of you were here last night, and here you are again today." Schmidt's hand rested on his holstered gun.

I suspected the gesture as being a ploy to intimidate. It did, but I ignored it. Well, I tried. Holding the thought, I moved closer to the road.

"I hear that boyfriend of yours is a police detective from Marion City," Schmidt said. His hand left the butt of his gun to play with the zipper on his jacket.

"You heard right," I said. I watched the zipper of the red county-issue down jacket inch downward and moved another step closer to the road.

Deputy Schmidt rocked forward, the motion bringing him nearer to me. "Did you and that police officer friend of yours find what you were looking for?" he repeated.

My head shot up as I cued in to "that police officer friend of yours." Did Schmidt have a particular reason for calling attention to this fact or was I reading more into the deputy's words than was there? Focused on the deputy, I stepped into the wider, deeper rut made by the tow truck. My foot slipped. My arms flew wide. With the grace of a slapstick comedian, I fought to maintain my balance. Surprisingly, I did.

Schmidt's hand shot out. "Careful, Miss Arthur."

Be still, I told my heart, which was hammering away inside my chest. Fear? I didn't think so. Embarrassment? Maybe. Regardless of the cause, I wanted out of here, wanted to be anywhere where Deputy Schmidt was not. Mindful of the treachery that lay underfoot, I waved aside Schmidt's proffered hand and proceeded to make the thought a fact.

Shrugging, Schmidt withdrew his hand, dropping it over his holstered gun. Torn between wanting to watch the deputy's hand and needing to look at my feet, I opted for self-preservation. Another step and I was within spitting distance of the Pine County deputy.

"If you don't mind," I said. I stared at the lens of his aviator glasses. Both the afternoon sun and my own face stared back.

Schmidt didn't move. I took the coward's way out and walked around him. The sound of a truck braking caused the two of us to look at the road. It was MacPhearson's battered pickup and the detective himself who threw open the driver's door and jumped out.

"Is this a private party, or can anyone come?" Mac called.

I watched the still too-thin Marion City detective walk toward us, his presence breaking the tension that filled the air.

"You out sightseeing too?" Schmidt asked.

Mac looked hard into my face. Trying to read my thoughts? I wondered, and if he could, did he know how glad I was to see him? How much better I felt now that he was here?

"This seems to be a popular spot for the two of you," Schmidt said.

"For you, too," Mac said. He laughed and reached to shake the deputy's hand. "When I said I'd buy you a drink, I didn't expect you would be around so soon to collect."

Chapter Seventeen

It didn't take a mirror to tell me my jaw had dropped, or that my eyes were wide in disbelief. When had Mac and Norman Schmidt become drinking buddies?

"The two of us met at Braun's Motel. I stopped by there for lunch and ran into Deputy Schmidt," Mac explained. His face broke into a wide grin.

"And you offered to buy him a drink?" I looked from Schmidt to Mac.

Mac's smile faded. "Yeah, I did. I was alone, and as Schmidt was the only one I knew in the bar, I invited him to have a beer with me."

I doubted the surface value of Mac's smile, well aware that what you saw was all too often not what you got. As for Schmidt's, those damn aviator shades prevented me from seeing the whole of his face, but he definitely was not smiling. Whatever nonverbal communication there was between the two of them, I wasn't part of it.

"I was on duty and had to get back on the road," Schmidt explained.

"Well, the bar's open," Mac offered. "So why not follow us up to the cabin?"

"Hate to pass up another free drink," Schmidt said, "but I'm leaving this weekend to take Sarah's body to Rocky Ridge, and I still have a lot that needs doing."

"Long trip is it?" Mac asked.

"About two hundred fifty miles, but this time of year the weather can make the trip a bit iffy," Schmidt said.

"We can get together after you get back," Mac said. "How long will you be gone?"

"Don't know. Sheriff Duncan said to take as much time as I need." Schmidt's arms swung loosely at his sides. No more hand on gun, I noted. Had MacPhearson's presence caused the change in the deputy's demeanor?

"Just stopped to see if Miss Arthur needed help," Schmidt explained.

I said nothing. Whatever the reason Deputy Schmidt had in mind when he stopped, I was quite sure helping me was not on the agenda. Pumping me for information, like what Mac and I were looking for or more specifically what Mac and I had found, was nearer the mark.

"So, if there's nothing I can do," Schmidt looked from me to Mac.

I shook my head, but Mac, always ready with a quick comeback, quipped, "If Miss Arthur needs anything, Deputy Schmidt, I will take care of it." Unlike the cheery banter of before, Mac's last words had a decided edge to them.

Schmidt stared at MacPhearson for a long moment. He then turned away and headed along the rutted tracks to the road without, I might add, a single misstep.

Mac took hold of my elbow, ready to guide me over the uneven surface. I pulled free.

"There's something I want to show you." I led him to the edge of the embankment. "Take a look at the tracks left by Maggie's Volvo and tell me what you see."

"And when did you become interested in tire tracks?"

"Humor me," I said. I motioned him closer and pointed to the tire tracks, tracks that ended at the edge of the embankment, but seemed not to end at all.

"And what am I supposed to be looking at?"

"What you're looking at are tire tracks. What I want to know is what you see."

"I see . . ." Mac began.

"If you say tire tracks, Detective MacPhearson, I swear I'll push you over the edge."

Mac raised his hands. "No need to get physical, Red." Despite his protest, Mac hunkered down and studied the tracks. He looked for several moments, but said nothing.

"Don't you see it?"

Mac shook his head. He looked up at me, then back again at the tracks.

"It's as plain as the nose on your face," I shouted. "The tracks at the edge are deeper than the rest of the tracks."

"And that's supposed to mean something?"

"Of course it does. It means the Volvo sat here longer than at any other point along the route."

"You mean from the road to the edge here."

"And what else would I be referring to?"

MacPhearson stood up. "You might have something."

"You're damn right I have something, Mister Smart Detective. What I have is evidence that someone drove the car to the edge of the embankment, then got out and shoved the Volvo, with Maggie inside sans seatbelt, over the edge into the lake."

Mac looked at the tracks, his furrowed brow telling me he was thinking. Thinking I was right?

"Well?" I held my breath.

"There's only two sets of footprints, one coming and one going." Mac pointed to the overlapping footprints that paralleled the Volvo's tracks.

I grinned and, unable to help myself, laughed. "That's the beauty of it. What you think you see is two sets of footprints, one coming from the road to the edge of the cliff and one going from the edge of the cliff to the road, but what you're really seeing is three sets, two going from the edge of the cliff to the road and one coming from the road to the edge of the cliff."

MacPhearson looked skeptical.

"Now, before you say anything more," I held up a restraining hand, "we need to get someone up here who knows what they're looking at to take a look at those footprints."

"Three sets, you say?" MacPhearson said, looking and sounding even more skeptical.

I nodded and watched as Mac pulled his cell phone from his pocket and pushed in a number.

"I'll give Duncan a call and see what he says," Mac said.

Who cared if the Marion City detective was only humoring me? A victory was a victory, and I'd take one whenever I could.

"Duncan's sending someone out." Mac closed the lid on his cell. "Wants us to stay here until they get here."

I sighed, not a happy sigh, just one of relief. Even if my discovery did complicate matters, it gave us another avenue to explore. I must have voiced my thoughts out loud, thoughts Mac answered with a question.

"Us?"

"You and me and the sheriff. Unless I've misjudged Duncan completely, he's more than content to let Maggie's death remain a drunk driving accident."

We saw the county Suburban, heard a car door slam, and watched as a Pine County deputy, Myra Johnson, walked toward us.

"The sheriff said you had some tire tracks and footprints you wanted me to look at," Johnson said in greeting.

The deputy's clipped tone and unsmiling visage discouraged conversation, and I led the way to the edge of the embankment in silence. "Here," I said. I pointed to the tracks in question and hunkered down beside them.

Johnson followed suit. To her credit, she did not ask what it was she was looking for.

And after what seemed to be endless minutes of watching her look, I asked, "Well?"

Johnson said nothing. Alternating between the footprints and the tire tracks, she levered upright and walked their length, back and forth several times.

"What makes you think these tracks are different from the others?" she asked, pointing to the tire tracks nearest the edge of the embankment.

"The snow," I began. "We had some blowing snow last night, not enough that it accumulated to any depth. Fact is, the wind pretty much blew what snow there was here free of the tracks." I stopped, hoping for a response from the deputy, anything that might indicate she was following my train of thought.

Taciturn as ever, Myra Johnson said nothing.

"When you look at these tracks," I pointed to the tire tracks nearest the edge of the embankment, "there's still snow in them."

I shifted position, easing my cramping quads as I continued to point. "See for yourself. The snow's still there. The wind didn't blow it away."

Johnson grunted. "So, you think these tracks are deeper than the rest."

It was a statement, not a question. I started to laugh and settled for a grin.

Johnson rose to her feet and offered a helping hand, which I was quick to accept.

"You're thinking either something much heavier sat here or whatever made the other tracks sat here for a longer period of time," Johnson said.

I almost kissed her. Finally . . .

"The equipment's in the Suburban," she said, and walked back toward the road.

I laughed out loud. "Finally . . ." I repeated.

I joined MacPhearson. Together we followed Myra Johnson, catching up with her at the back of the SUV where she was busy selecting the equipment she needed for the castings.

"Need any help?" Mac asked.

Johnson shook her head. "I've got a call in for Deputy Bryant. He'll be along in a few minutes. The two of us can handle it."

The deputy's words were clearly a dismissal.

The sun had begun its downward spiral, and the wind was picking up when Mac and I reached the cabin. The air had taken on an icy edge, and the hot coffee, roaring fire, and the pair of companionable cats ensured our creature comfort.

I sipped the coffee and stroked the cats. Hera lay curled in my lap, and Zeus nestled snug against my thigh. As Zeus preferred Mac to me, this last did not last, and when Mac settled at the other end of the couch, Zeus skittered over the cushion to claim his favorite lap.

"Nice piece of work you did out there today, Red," Mac said as he propped his stocking feet on the table that fronted the couch. "Good cat," he murmured, stroking the purring Siamese. Trust the redheaded detective to give the two of us equal billing.

"It was the snow that did it," I explained. "The longer I looked at it the more convinced I was that something was different about those last few feet of tire tracks."

Mac continued to stroke Zeus. "If it pans out, the twins at least will be happy."

"Why shouldn't others be happy? People don't like hearing someone they know committed suicide," I argued.

"And you think they'll be happy knowing there's a killer loose up here?"

"They already know that," I grumbled. "Sarah Frazier sure didn't kill herself and climb into that freezer."

"That makes it worse." In spite of the topic, Mac grinned. "With two dead bodies, everyone will be talking serial killer before the next snowfall."

I threw a pillow at Mac, missing the grinning detective and hitting Zeus square in the face. With a loud yowl, the indignant Siamese leaped for the safety of another chair.

"Temper, temper, Red," Mac laughed.

I grabbed the other throw pillow, aptly named considering the use I had made of the first, and hugged it against my chest. "Any idea who the killer might be?"

"Not who, Ginny, why. Once we know that, who will be easy."

"I guess that means we'll be having more conversations with Sheriff Duncan. He doesn't like us, you know."

"Speak for yourself, Red. I spent a good portion of the morning mending fences with the local constabulary."

"I noticed, drinking buddies with Deputy Schmidt and who knows what with Sheriff Duncan." I sighed. Hera, tired of competing with the pillow, joined her boyfriend. "Besides promising them your first-born son, what did you offer to cause this change of heart?"

Mac laced his fingers behind his head. "Information."

"What information, Mister Detective?" Playing hard to get was one of Mac's tricks, and I had long ago learned playing the game was the quickest way to get Mac to open up.

Mac laughed. "I told Duncan about Rhodes's task force on human trafficking and suggested he give him a call."

MacPhearson sobered as he spoke. I knew about the task force. Marion City's mounting case load of missing kids had caused the city to suspect an organized trafficking ring as opposed to random runaways. Larry Rhodes, a lieutenant in the Marion City Police Department, had been named to head the group.

"But . . ." I started, then stopped. "We're not talking murder now, are we? We're talking missing girls, like Cindy Shouldice and Josie Leggit."

Mac nodded. "I convinced Duncan he should at least consider the possibility, and he agreed to give Rhodes a call."

I tossed my security pillow aside and turned to face MacPhearson. "Mac, that's a great idea. However did you think of it?"

"I'm a detective, remember? One whose hobby is cold cases, but you already know that. Truth is, I spent some time in the local hardware store. Introduced myself to the owner . . ."

"Marty Shouldice," I interrupted.

Mac nodded his head. "We had a long talk about woodworking and . . ."

"His missing daughter," I interrupted again.

"This story would be considerably shorter if you'd let me tell it," Mac said.

"Then tell it."

"Shouldice did talk about his daughter, and from what he said, Duncan didn't leave a stone unturned. Literally coerced the powers-that-be to call out the National Guard to search for the girls. They never found a trace of them, not one clue. Seems they disappeared from the face of the earth." Mac stared into the fire. "That is if you believe in such things, and I don't."

"Duncan seems to think they ran away."

"The two don't fit the profile, Red. Honor students, no problems at home or school . . ."

"So you're thinking it might be a case of abduction, kidnaping, human trafficking?"

"It's worth looking into." Mac got to his feet, stretched, and headed for the kitchen. "I picked up a pizza while I was in town. How about you making a salad while I get the oven going?"

I followed Mac into the kitchen. "That explains Duncan's change of heart, but what did you do to win Deputy Schmidt's heart?"

"Offered him a beer." Mac shoved the pizza in the oven. "Said he was on duty and couldn't, but when I suggested a rain check he was all smiles."

"That's all?"

"My charm," Mac said.

"Can't imagine that got you anywhere."

"Stick around, Red, and I'll show you."

Mac gave me a sober look, telling me that what had started as a joke had turned into something more serious. It being where I didn't want to go, I busied myself slicing tomatoes.

"Fact is, I saw Schmidt in the parking lot. Seems he wasn't in as big a hurry to get back on the road after all. He was talking to a couple of those guys we saw when we were snowmobiling the other day."

I paused the knife I was using. "It had to be the two I saw in the bar," I said and filled Mac in on my previous encounter with the snowmobilers.

The pizza—pepperoni, sausage, mushrooms, onion, green peppers, black olives, and anchovies on Mac's half, ugh—was as good as the salad I made to go with it. We took the last of our beers into the great room. Mac added a pair of logs to the fire, which soon rewarded us with a merry snap, crackle, and pop.

Mac leaned back against the couch and closed his eyes.

"You feeling okay?" I asked. His cheeks were hollowed and the lines that ran beside his nose seemed to have grown deeper.

"I'm okay," he said, "and you?"

"Steve can't make it up this weekend."

"Working?"

"Not exactly," I said and, without pausing, told him of Steve's upcoming trip to Boston and the surgical fellowship at Mass General.

"It's what he wants, isn't it?" Mac asked.

I nodded, but as Mac still had not opened his eyes, he couldn't see me.

A silence, broken by the snapping of the logs in the fireplace and the cats' contented purring, filled the room.

"Is it what you want?" Mac asked, so low I had to strain to hear.

He opened his eyes and looked at me.

"I don't know. Damn it all, I don't know."

Chapter Eighteen

MAC AND I PULLED INTO THE CIRCLE DRIVE that fronted the Whiting homestead at the agreed time—ten A.M.

The center section of the frame building was two-storied. Single-story wings abutted each side of the main building. Low and rambling, they gave the house the appearance of having grown more from need than design.

Caroline Whiting held open the oversized front door and called a welcome.

I slid from the passenger seat, holding onto the car door as I did. The house, building, structure, mansion maybe, being too much to take in at first glance, I could only stare.

"It is rather large, isn't it?" Caroline Whiting said. "But don't worry, Ginny, it has a way of growing on you. Roger wants everything big, and well, you can see the results."

As if cued by the sound of his name, Roger Whiting pushed past his wife and strode across the porch. "Glad you made it on time," he boomed. "I've arranged for the chopper to pick us up at ten-thirty. Only way to see this place is from the air."

"Roger," Caroline protested, "give them time to catch their breath, have a cup of coffee."

"No time, the chopper's already on its way." Roger Whiting took the pair of steps that led from the porch to the driveway in a single stride.

Caroline's hands beat the air in an attitude of frustration. "Lunch is at one," she called.

Ignoring his wife, Whiting continued toward us. He motioned to the Honda. "Leave your car where it is. Sam Leggit's picking us up in the Escalade. The landing pad's a couple of miles from here."

The words had hardly left Whiting's mouth when I heard the sound of an approaching vehicle. What else, a white Cadillac Escalade of course. Roger Whiting was, at the very least, an accomplished director.

A thick-shouldered, square-jawed man whose face spoke of years of outdoor living, brought the Caddy to an idling stop behind the Honda.

"This way, folks," Whiting said. He opened the rear door and motioned Mac and me inside. Whiting climbed in beside the driver, whom he introduced as his foreman, Sam Leggit.

Leggit looked over his shoulder. "Glad to meet you," he said.

Leggit, Josie Leggit's father? I wondered as the foreman slid the SUV into gear and pulled around my Honda.

"Like I always say, the only way to see this place is from the air." Whiting's face beamed with pride of ownership. "And believe me, it's something worth seeing."

Whiting tugged on the bill of his cap. Twin to the foreman's, it bore the logo of Whiting Farm.

As Whiting had promised, a helicopter, its slowly rotating blades causing only a minimal downdraft, waited for us. Never having been up in a chopper, I felt my stomach lurch in anticipation. Memories of amusement park rides, ones that had promised a thrill a minute but delivered only upset tummies, flooded over me. Adrenaline quickened my breath and sent my pulse to racing.

I glanced at MacPhearson, who looked for all the world like a kid being handed an ice cream cone. Knowing I would get no sympathy from that quarter, I took a longer look at the chopper. It was small, or at least it didn't look anything like the ones I watched on the nightly news stories about Iraq and Afghanistan. Large block letters along the side spelled Whiting Farm. Now why wasn't I surprised?

Whiting jumped from the SUV and opened the rear door. Motioning Mac and me to follow, he ducked his head and ran toward the chopper. Following directions, I reached the chopper a step or two behind Whiting and was boosted bodily into one of a pair of seats behind the pilot. MacPhearson followed after me, and Whiting climbed in behind us.

A pair of ear protectors was thrust into my hands. Setting them in place, I was rewarded by a decided reduction in the noise level. It did not last long, for almost immediately Whiting's voice sounded in my ears.

"Fasten your seatbelts," he said, "and we'll get off the ground."

I did as instructed, and the helicopter lifted into the air.

The sky, a cloudless vivid blue, rushed to meet us. I ordered myself to stay calm, and with a conscious effort relaxed my death grip on a conveniently placed grab bar.

"If you open your eyes, you'll see more."

It was Mac's voice, and after doing as he suggested, I was given a lesson on the mechanics of the communication system.

I felt my face warm. As the intercom was apparently an open system, I was sure Whiting had heard Mac's suggestion that I open my eyes.

Deciding to take the high road, I quipped into the small mike Mac had positioned close to my mouth, "They're open." I pointed to my eyes, added a grin and said, "All ready for the tour."

Whiting chuckled. "I promise you won't be disappointed, Miss Arthur."

Truth was, I wasn't.

"The farm covers most of Pine County and the two counties directly north and west of here. Camp Whiting borders us on the east, and Big Pine Lake marks our southern end." Whiting spoke into a mike, similar to the one Mac had pulled into place near my mouth.

I settled in, expecting to hear a grandiose description of what constituted the Whiting farm, but Whiting proved to be a better-than-expected tour guide. Despite his obvious pride, Whiting managed to hold his ego in check as he explained how the land we viewed from our moving sky box was used.

"A good deal of the acreage is devoted to apple and cherry orchards and some berries. Navy beans, soybeans, potatoes, and sugar beets along with Christmas trees are staples. Several acres on the east, those bordering Camp Whiting, I've leased to the state for research, and as I run a few hundred head of stock, I grow a variety of grasses, what you call hay, to hold us over the winter."

"Pretty impressive," Mac said. Silent until now, I wondered if he was as awestruck as I by the magnitude of the operation Whiting described.

"I guess it depends on what you grow up with," Whiting said. "As for me, it's what I know. All I know really. This land has been in the family since long before Michigan became a state, since the French, the Indians, and British were fighting over it, really. Can't imagine any other life or what that life would be like without the farm."

Roger Whiting spoke with a sincerity bordering on fanaticism, and I vowed to avoid future arguments. Though strong in many of my beliefs, I had the feeling Mr. Whiting was more bull-headed.

"What's over there?" Mac asked. He pointed to a stretch of land that lay to our left.

I followed his pointing finger, but restricted by the shoulder restraint I could see only the tops of trees and an expanse of snow-covered ground.

Whiting looked to where Mac pointed. "Beyond those trees there, you can see the fields where we plant what we need for feed. I let the snowmobilers use a few acres closest to the trees during the winter months."

"No, that's not what I'm referring to." MacPhearson twisted to look at Whiting. "Farther out, that part that's fenced. Where those buildings are." Mac moved to provide me a better view. "Is that some sort of storage area? Feed for your livestock? Apples maybe or potatoes?" Mac asked.

Whiting's face took on a stern look. "Nothing like that," he said. "That's where we house the migrants."

Mac's brow furrowed. "Kind of a long way from anything, isn't it?"

Whiting shrugged. "Transportation's provided when it's needed." His voice carried a note of finality.

"But I've saved the best for last." Whiting's face brightened. "Head up to the north pasture," he instructed the pilot.

The chopper turned abruptly right and picked up speed. My stomach lurched. "Does this hi-tech amusement ride come with barf bags?" I muttered, scanning the helicopter's interior. Fortunately for all aboard, the chopper leveled off, and my stomach returned to its anatomically correct position.

As Roger Whiting had predicted, he had indeed saved the best for last. There below us, their dark shaggy bulk clearly visible against the white snow, was a herd of buffalo.

"Where did you get them?" Amazement sounded in my voice, and for good reason; I was amazed. "Buffalo are supposed to be out west where there's cowboys and Indians."

"Not anymore," Whiting chuckled, clearly enjoying my amazed delight. "Today they're raised for food, bred with cattle for beefalo, or for the purest among us to preserve the species."

"Are they considered endangered?" Mac asked. The look on his face told me MacPhearson was as impressed as I by the immense shaggy beasts.

"If you mean are they on the endangered species list, then no, but there are a few groups who lobby they should be."

"How many buffalo are there?" I asked, unable to take my eyes off the herd. "Oh look, there's a calf trying to nurse from its mother." I looked at Whiting. "Do they call a baby buffalo a calf?"

Whiting laughed. "To answer both of your questions, the herd numbers around five hundred. That doesn't include the calves, which we'll round up and brand next spring."

"They look pretty big," Mac commented. "When were they born?"

"Late spring, early summer. Mating season's late summer and the gestation period is nine to ten months. The cows drop their young just a bit too late to be included in the spring tally. Seen enough?" Whiting asked.

"Never," I said. A big-city girl born and bred, I couldn't get enough of this glimpse into the past.

Whiting looked at his watch. "You can always come back, Miss Arthur, but for today I'm afraid we have to call it quits. Caroline's a bit short on patience, and my watch tells me it's nearly two."

The Escalade, with Sam Leggit inside, was waiting at the helipad when we touched down. With a thank you to the pilot to whom we were never introduced, I slid into Mac's waiting arms.

"Stomach okay?" Mac asked, hurrying us away from the chopper's downdraft.

"What makes you think my stomach's not okay?" I asked in return.

Mac laughed. "Asking for a barf bag is a dead giveaway."

"Just being prepared."

We were both laughing when we reached the SUV. Word play on the Boy Scout motto was a standing joke between us. I climbed into the rear seat. Further comments were lost in the closing of the SUV's doors and the revving of the engine as Sam Leggit made a U-turn and headed for the farmhouse.

Caroline greeted us at the front door. If she harbored any ill feelings toward her husband for our late arrival, she hid them behind a smile.

"I'm sure you want to freshen up before we eat," she said, taking my arm as I reached the porch. "There's a bathroom right down the hall."

I tried to thank her, but the woman had a death grip on my arm and continued to talk as she pulled me forward.

"Just give me your jacket, Ginny, and do you have a purse? I'm sure you will want to keep that with you."

I didn't, have a purse that is, and indicated the fanny pack fastened at my waist as I handed Caroline the jacket, cap, scarf, and gloves I was wearing.

"And here we are," Caroline said, pushing wide the door to what was obviously the bathroom. "Just call out when you're finished. I'll stay close so I can hear you."

Finally, the bathroom door was closed behind me. I sighed in relief. For one awful moment, I was sure Caroline Whiting intended to oversee my potty break.

I took a few minutes to run a brush through my hair and add a layer of gloss to my lips. Contrary to what Mac might think, I felt fine and, if I had to say, looked damn good.

True to her word, Caroline was waiting for me when I exited the bathroom. "Don't want you getting lost. People often do, this place being so big and all." Caroline laughed, and despite what I was beginning to think was rather odd behavior on the woman's part, I laughed along with her.

We entered what I learned later was not the dining room but an extension of the kitchen. Roger Whiting and MacPhearson were both there; each had a beer in his hand and each smiled a greeting as we approached the table.

"This room's a bit cozier than the dining room," Caroline said as she ushered me toward the table. "Sit anywhere you like."

As the table, which could easily accommodate twelve, was set for four, the decision was not difficult. I chose the chair nearest to where I stood. Mac pulled out the chair beside me, and Whiting moved to sit across from me. Caroline, after conferring with a woman who hovered near the stove, took the remaining place.

The woman came forward, platters of food in each hand. Expecting lunch, I could only stare at the meat and vegetables being set before us.

"Eat up," Roger Whiting said. "I can guarantee you won't find a better meal anywhere. Just about everything on the table was raised right here, and I guarantee you will have to look hard to find a better cook than Rita. Like I say, Whiting Farm is the best there is."

I watched the cook during Whiting's testimony. Her expression never changed. Thin to the point of being gaunt, her eyes were deep-set, her cheeks hollow. If she was as good a cook as Whiting claimed, she was obviously not eating enough of her own cooking.

"Rita's been with us for over ten years. Started doing the cooking when Josie began nursery school."

Rita's face paled. A feat I would have judged impossible given her sallow complexion.

"Rita came to us when she married Sam," Whiting said, ignoring the woman's discomfort. "Took us some time before she agreed to take over the cooking."

"She stayed home so she could look after Josie," Caroline explained.

"Well, that was a long time ago," Whiting grumped. "Rita's cooking for us now, and I for one intend to see she keeps right on doing so."

Talking didn't keep Whiting from eating. No sooner did he finish one plate than he was helping himself to seconds. A growing boy or a hard-working man? I studied the man at whose table I sat. True, he was tall, big-boned, solidly built, but there was also a fleshiness along his jaw and his shirt buttons strained over his chest. Roger was unfortunately still a growing boy and, if I had to guess, not quite as hard-working a man as he had once been.

Rita brought a second platter of meat and vegetables, traveling from table to stove to table. Was there no end to the amount of food? It was Caroline who called a halt to the parade with "You can serve the coffee in the den, Rita." This last when we, everyone except Roger Whiting that is, had refused dessert. It was apple pie, the apples having been grown on Whiting Farm, of course.

I was glad when we finally quit the table. Watching the man eat and listening to him brag was becoming hard to swallow.

As I walked from the kitchen into the hallway that Caroline assured me led to the den, I felt a prickle run down my spine. It was the feeling one gets when being watched. Turning to look over my shoulder, I saw that Rita was indeed looking at me. Though she said nothing, I somehow knew she wanted to.

Chapter Nineteen

BEHIND RITA, A DOOR OPENED. OUR EYES LOCKED, Rita's and mine, then with an indifferent shrug, Rita turned to greet the two women who entered the room. The moment was lost. Whatever had passed between Rita and me, if indeed anything had, was gone.

"That's a couple of the migrants come to help Rita clean up." Caroline eyed the trio as she spoke. "But come along, Ginny, I want to show you a little of the house before the men join us."

We passed a room Caroline called the den. Through the partially open door, I heard the drone of Roger Whiting's voice extolling more of the farm's virtues.

"I'd like to show you the dining room first." Caroline slid apart a set of pocket doors as she spoke.

It was indeed a dining room. A massive table, which could easily seat twenty or more, with matching chairs dominated the room's center. An equally impressive pair of sideboards stood against two of the walls, and an imposing China cabinet hid most of the third wall.

"All of the furniture was handmade from trees milled right here on the farm." Caroline ran her hand along the top of a chair. "More than a dozen governors, going back to the mid-1800s, have dined here."

Caroline's face glowed with pride as she surveyed the room. "Those pictures over the sideboards are Roger's great great grandparents."

It was indeed an impressive room, and I hopefully made all the right sounds as I expressed my appreciation of the heritage that surrounded us. Perhaps Roger Whiting did have the right to brag.

Caroline ushered me back through the pocket doors and across the hall to where a similar set of doors waited. Pushing them apart, Caroline announced, "And here we have the front or main parlor." She giggled. "I do sound like a tour guide, don't I?" Her eyes twinkled. "I never take Roger along when I give one of my tours," she confessed. "He thinks I'm a bit irreverent."

I walked to the center of the room and turned in a circle. Chairs, tables, sofas, too numerous to count, stood alone or huddled together in conversational groups. Pictures lined the walls and curios, knickknacks, or what my Grandmother Wickie called bric-a-brac, cluttered the tables and the mantel of an ornately carved fireplace.

"Seen enough?" Caroline asked.

"There's so much, I can't take it all in."

"That's the point. I told you Roger likes things big, which too often translates into too much."

Caroline made a sweeping gesture with her hand. "Have you ever seen so much junk in your life?"

I laughed. Perhaps there was more to this woman than met the eye.

She motioned me to one of the sofas. "Let's sit a minute. Most of the furniture in this room is not too comfortable, but I like this sofa. It's off to one side and lets you take in the room a bit at a time."

No sooner had we settled in than one of the migrant workers, who on closer inspection was more girl than woman, came through the pocket doors. She set a tray with a silver coffee service on a low table that fronted the sofa. Caroline nodded a dismissal, and the girl left. A shadow, she moved from the light into the dimmer recesses of the room.

I was back in the parking lot of the Braun Motel watching the snow shovelers move from light to dark, other shadows and another time.

"Thought you might enjoy this more than the whiskey and cigar smoke being served in the den." Caroline gave me a questioning look.

I pulled myself from that other time back to the here and now. "I do," I said, and I did. The coffee, like the meal, was some of the best I had tasted.

"Don't tell Roger," Caroline said in a hushed tone. "We don't grow this coffee on the farm." She laughed, and I joined in her merriment.

"Now tell me," she said, "what's this I hear about you suggesting to Sheriff Duncan the disappearances of the Leggit and Shouldice girls might be the work of an organized group? Human traffickers or trafficking, I think they're called?"

"Not me," I corrected. "Mac's done some work with a task force in Marion City that's investigating the problem. He suggested it might be something Sheriff Duncan might want to pursue."

Caroline frowned. The lines on her forehead deepening. "But surely not up here. You can't really think that sort of thing goes on in Pine County?"

"Crime exists everywhere, Caroline." Could this woman really be that naive? She did work for the Sheriff's Department.

Caroline sighed. "I know, but I just hate to see Sam and Rita get their hopes up. It's been a hard year for them, and you saw how Rita looked. I just don't know how much more of this she can take."

"There's no promises, no guarantees. It's just something new Sheriff Duncan needs to consider, something they need to investigate."

"But they've been hurt so much. When Betty Shouldice called here this morning and told Rita what Detective MacPhearson told Marty, Rita got so excited." Caroline offered to refill my cup. I shook my head no. "I just don't know how much more of this she can take."

"How much more of what can who take?" Roger Whiting's bulk filled the doorway.

Like a quick-change artist, Caroline's face went from morose to almost ecstatic. "Why, how much more our guests can take of this museum you call a home."

Whiting roared with laughter. "Woman, you just don't appreciate the finer things in life."

I wasn't at all sure I did either and was happy to learn that this last exchange marked the beginning of our leave-taking. Big, or at the very least long, like everything else at Whiting Farm, it was many minutes before our exodus was accomplished.

The setting sun and the lengthening shadows cast by the trees darkened the road, and night was upon us when we turned onto the highway.

"How are you doing, Red?"

I studied Mac's face and saw his familiar grin. "Just fine, Mac, just fine." Some things never changed, and I was beginning to realize that Douglas MacPhearson was one of them.

We continued down the highway, Mac holding the Honda at a steady sixty-five. Traffic was sparse, with only an occasional pair of headlights lighting the road. I fumbled with the radio dial but found nothing I liked and turned it off. The rhythmic hum of the tires against the pavement had a hypnotic effect, and my eyelids grew heavy.

"Take a nap if you want, Ginny. I can find the way home."

"No . . ." I yawned. "I'm not tired." Despite the denial and my best efforts, I fell asleep.

I sensed the Honda slow, the changed rhythm nudging me awake.

"Are we home?" I yawned. The unbroken expanse of highway and the forest of trees that bordered it answered my question.

"Is something wrong?" I looked at Mac. He was not smiling.

"I think we're being followed," he said casually.

Too damn casually. I looked out the back window.

"Thought I'd slow up and give that truck behind us a chance to pass," Mac said.

There were indeed headlights behind us. The idea of being followed made me nervous, and the way Mac kept looking in the rearview mirror instead of at the road made me more so.

Fifty, forty, thirty-five, the Honda's speedometer dropped. Still the truck, or whatever it was that followed us, did not pass.

"Refusing the bait, are you?" Mac said, and with a grin, slammed his foot hard against the accelerator.

Though there was no falling snow, nor did the truck appear as large as the monstrous truck we had encountered in the parking lot of the Sandcastle, my breathing quickened and my pulse responded to what was becoming an all-too-familiar adrenaline rush.

Beside me Mac continued the cat-and-mouse game, slowing to let whoever it was behind us catch up and pulling ahead when the distance closed between us. After several minutes of road tag, Mac settled back to an even sixty-five.

"Guess we'll just have to let whoever it is behind us pick the spot." Despite his calm tone, Mac's face had a hard set to it. The grin that had been present during the catch-me-if-you-can cat-and-mouse game was gone, and he seldom glanced in the rearview mirror.

Mac slowed for the curves and hilly terrain that marked the approach to Judge Marfield's cabin. "We're here." Remote in hand, Mac thumbed the button that opened the garage door and pulled inside. Behind us, the twin beams of a truck's headlights disappeared behind the lowering door.

Mac slid from the Honda, hurried past the pair of snowmobiles, and was inserting his key into the cabin door when I caught up to him.

"What are you going to do?" I whispered, fearful whoever waited behind the closed garage door could hear me. I was nervous, afraid. Who was out there? Why, and what were they planning on doing?

Mac pushed open the cabin door. To my surprise he went straight to the front door and threw it wide.

I followed after him. Like a limpet I stuck to him, stumbling when he came to a stop in the open doorway.

Throwing out his arm to prevent my falling, he called to the figure hunched over the steering wheel. "How about getting out of the truck and coming inside?"

The motion sensors, which had begun to dim, brightened as the figure inside the cab opened the door and climbed out. The light, full bright now, illuminated both the truck and the driver.

"Rita Leggit!" I said, as the Whitings' cook walked toward us.

Casting himself in the role of host, MacPhearson invited the gaunt, pale-faced woman inside.

"I'm . . . I'm sorry to bother you like this, but . . ." Glancing nervously from Mac to me, Rita Leggit stepped into the cabin. "But," she said again, "I just had to talk to you, to learn if what Betty Shouldice told me is true."

I led Rita into the great room. Wordlessly, she stared at the couches and chairs scattered around the room.

"Let's sit by the fire." I shot Mac a meaningful look. "That is, we can sit by the fire if Mac will light it for us."

Rita chose the same chair as had Maggie Schmidt. Not superstitious by nature, I had a strange sense of foreboding and fought the urge to ask that she move.

The fire was quick to catch and licked its way along the logs, breaking the silence with a loud pop.

I began the hostess routine, offering coffee or something stronger to our guest. Rita settled for the coffee, and Mac, as was usual with him, preferred a beer.

"And I'll get it," he said, heading me off at the stairs.

"The meal was delicious," I said by way of openers. "Caroline Whiting said you have been cooking for them for several years . . ." I let the sentence dangle.

"Over ten years," Rita answered.

"You went to work for the Whitings when your daughter started school?"

Rita nodded. She fumbled in the purse she clutched in her lap. "Nursery school it was. Living there on the farm like we did, Jocelyn, Josie we called her, didn't have much of anyone to play with." Finding the tissue she was looking for, Rita rubbed at the tears that ran down her cheeks.

"Coffee anyone?" Mac set the tray he was carrying on the table and handed a mug of the steaming brew to Rita and me.

"You lived on the farm back then?" Mac settled on the couch and lifted the bottle of beer to his mouth.

"Sam was living there when we were married. He's been Mr. Whiting's foreman for over twenty years. The house went with the job."

Rita's tears had stopped, and though she had not settled into the back of the chair, she was sipping her coffee. "All of the regular employees live at the farm. Mr. Whiting likes to keep us handy in case of an emergency."

"I noticed a large fenced area when we were up in the helicopter. Is that where the employees live?"

"Goodness no!" Rita exclaimed. "That's just for the migrants. Mr. Whiting doesn't like them wandering around the countryside. He says he has too much money invested in them to let anything happen to them."

"They stay there all the time?" I asked.

"When they're not working they do."

"But they don't all work at the farm." I thought of the extra help I'd seen at the Braun Motel.

"In the summer they do." Rita continued to sip her coffee. "Those who stay year round fill in at the resorts during the winter."

Impatience showed on Rita's face. "I followed you here to ask about Josie. Betty Shouldice told me you think the girls may have been kidnaped."

Mac held up a protesting hand. "Just another avenue I think Sheriff Duncan might want to consider."

"Betty said they kidnap young girls like Josie and Cindy so they can use them for prostitutes, and take awful, awful pictures of them to sell over the Internet."

Once more Rita's eyes brimmed over. I pushed a box of tissues forward.

"We don't know anything for sure, Mrs. Leggit," Mac said. "It's just something that should be considered. It's not a very nice thing, I know, but we don't live in nice times."

"Things like that don't happen here," Rita said.

Mac didn't answer. Truth was, things like this happened everywhere.

"I should have taken the girls to school that morning." Rita shook her head. "Mrs. Whiting asked me to run a couple of the migrants up to Cadillac. Said she could drop the girls off on her way to work."

"Caroline Whiting took the girls to school that morning? Not you?" I asked.

Rita was back to mopping her eyes. "Not the school, the convenience store. They said they wanted to get a few things before they got on the bus. Though I can't imagine what it could have been. The two of them spent weeks packing and repacking their bags." Rita sighed. "Mrs. Whiting said she offered to wait but the girls insisted they could manage. They each had a duffle and of course their backpacks, but the school was only a block away, so they probably could."

Rita mopped her face with a fresh handful of tissues. Clutching tight to her purse, she levered herself to her feet. I don't know what her actual age was, but tonight I'm sure she looked a dozen or more years older.

"Guess what Betty told me was true. Can't say that it's good news, nor is it something I wanted to hear," she said.

Mac helped Rita with her jacket, and the three of us walked to the front of the cabin. He pulled the door open. A flutter of snow and cold air swept inside. Sheltering behind Mac, I called a final good-bye as Rita walked onto the front stoop.

The sensor lights sprang to life. Rita paused, made a half turn and started to say something. It never got said. With a roar, the air exploded with the sound of one, two, three gunshots.

Chapter Twenty

Mac's arm hit my chest. Then pain, pain I later learned was caused when my forehead hit the hall table. Mac shouted, "Call the sheriff!"

The door slammed as I got to my feet. I called the sheriff's office and grabbed the door handle.

"Don't open the door, Ginny. Get on the floor and stay down," Mac shouted in his "don't mess with me" voice.

I ignored the warning. After what Mac had been through and was still going through, I had no intention of letting him face whatever was going on out there alone.

"Ginny!"

I continued to ignore the warning in Mac's voice, but I could not ignore the sensor lights that illuminated the front stoop. Already on my stomach, prudence and Mac's warning having dictated I do so before opening the door, I slid over the threshold, then over the edge into the darkness of the bushes that fronted the cabin.

"Where is Rita?" I whispered.

"She's here." Mac paused. "She's been hit, and she's losing a lot of blood."

The darkness worked to our advantage as it hid us from the shooter or shooters. It was also a disadvantage in that it prevented us from seeing the extent of Rita Leggit's injuries.

"I think she was hit twice," Mac said. "Once in the chest. I'm keeping pressure there, but haven't found the second wound."

I didn't need Mac to tell me the next few minutes were crucial. We had to get Rita in the house. Had to get her where we could do something about the bleeding.

The front door was invitingly open, invitingly close. It was also lit up like Times Square on New Year's Eve.

"Put your hand here, and I'll see what I can do about those damn lights."

We switched hands. Then Mac was gone, through the door in a blur of motion.

Blood oozed between my fingers. I pressed harder. The bullet wound was on the right side of Rita's chest under her breast. That the bullet had pierced her lung and that there was also an exit wound, I had little doubt. As Rita was lying on her back, I could only hope the pressure I was applying to her chest was sufficient to slow the bleeding on the underside.

I looked at the open door. Off to the side as I was, I could not see into the cabin. I listened, but heard nothing. Where was MacPhearson? What was he going to do about the lights? Shoot them out?

I winced at the thought. All we needed was more gunshots. Gunshots? I stared into the darkness beyond the lights. Besides the initial three gunshots, there had been no others. Were the shooter or shooters still out there? If so, why hadn't they come forward and finished us off? Surely they must know, or at least suspect, we were not armed.

I was still jumping from question to question when the yard went dark. Being out of the spotlight never felt so good.

"Support her head, Ginny. I'm going to drag her inside."

I did as directed, but careful as we were, Rita's body bumped over the edge of the stoop and again as we dragged her across the threshold. Once inside, I shouldered the door shut behind me.

Mac snapped on a flashlight. "Had to pull the circuit breaker," he explained.

I had Rita's jacket off and was examining her body for the second gunshot wound. "It's here, on her shoulder. Can't tell if the bullet hit the bone, but the bleeding's about stopped."

Leaving Mac to play doctor, I made a quick trip to the linen closet and returned with an armload of towels. Together the two of us packed the towels tight against the wounds in her chest and shoulder. The shoulder wound had stopped bleeding, but the wound in her chest, despite our best efforts, had not. I pushed my fingers into her neck. Her pulse was there, beating feebly against my fingers.

In the distance a siren sounded, stopping when it reached the driveway. Glaring headlights and rotating emergency lights poured through the windows and bathed the room in a macabre pattern of light and shadow. Not that the production was in line for an Oscar, but it sure impressed the sheriff when, gun drawn, he came through the door.

"What in hell is going on here?" he shouted, looking at me, then at MacPhearson.

Mac ignored the sheriff's question. "Are the EMTs here?" he asked and, without waiting for an answer, added, "How about you getting the lights, Ginny."

I handed the flashlight to Sheriff Duncan and took off for the utility room. Behind me, the EMTs barreled through the door.

A cacophony of yowls greeted me as I reached the utility room. I murmured a soothing response to the Siamese pair who, smart cats that they were, had taken refuge in their traveling cage. I groped along the wall for the breaker box, found it, and flipped the switch to the on position. I was rewarded with the sound of the furnace and water heater coming to life. Flipping light switches as I went, I headed back across the great room.

A pair of EMTs worked over Rita Leggit, who now lay on a stretcher. One tech adjusted the flow of fluids that dripped into her arm, while the other positioned an oxygen mask over her face and talked into a hand-held radio. Anxious moments that seemed like hours passed as the two positioned themselves at either end of the litter, and at the "ready to transfer" command from one, the pair lifted the stretcher and hurried from the cabin.

"Deputies Bryant and Bentley are on their way. So while we're waiting, suppose the two of you tell me what happened here."

"How about some coffee before we get started?" MacPhearson headed into the great room, stopping by the fireplace to add a pair of logs to the dwindling flames. "Don't know about you two, but I sure could use a mug."

"Talk first, coffee later," Duncan said.

I claimed the chair I had been sitting in earlier, leaving the couch and the Maggie chair for Mac and the sheriff.

With an audible sigh, Mac chose the end of the couch nearest to where I sat. "Rita Leggit followed us home," he began. "Wanted to know about the human trafficking task force."

"And what did you tell her?" Duncan asked.

"The same thing I told you and the Shouldices."

Duncan massaged his brow. "That's a tough pill for a parent to swallow, but it's hardly something someone would shoot someone for. More likely, it's something a parent would shoot someone for."

Duncan dropped into the Maggie chair, propped his elbows on his spread knees, and stared into the fire.

"We did talk about the day the girls went missing," I offered.

Duncan's gaze shifted from the fire to my face.

Guessing the sheriff was operating with a short fuse, I rushed the telling, finishing with, "Rita Leggit said Caroline Whiting didn't drop the girls off at school but at some convenience store." I waited for the sheriff to complete the story.

"Only they never made it from the convenience store to the school," Duncan obliged.

The thud of a burning log settling against another sounded loud in a room grown suddenly quiet.

"I talked to Lieutenant Rhodes," Duncan said. "Asked if he knew of any trafficking in this area."

The front door opened. Cold air and two Pine County deputies came into the room, their arrival delaying the questions I had wanted to ask.

"Kevin Bryant and Lamar Bentley," Duncan said, introducing the pair to MacPhearson. "We've got us a shooting. Rita Leggit's in bad shape. She's on the way to the hospital." He turned to MacPhearson.

"How about you showing us where the three of you were when the shots were fired so these two can get to work."

I moved toward the door with the four of them.

"How about making that coffee you talked about, Miss Arthur," Duncan said.

I thought of pointing out that MacPhearson had made the offer, but swallowed my frustration.

Their retreating footsteps and the bang of the front door closing followed me up the stairs. I started the coffee brewing, set out mugs, sugar, cream, and the cookie jar filled with Ardella Duncan's homemade cookies. The coffee maker was sounding its last gurgle when I heard the front door open. Hiding my curiosity behind a smile, I poured the steaming brew into the mugs.

"We were able to account for two of the three shots." MacPhearson shrugged off his jacket and slid into a chair. "One bullet messed up the doorframe. Another went through the open door and hit a picture hanging on the wall just about where you were standing, Red."

"I'd say you were damn lucky, Miss Arthur," Duncan said.

I sank into another of the chairs. My fingers went to the bump on my head, which had suddenly begun to throb. It could have just as easily been a bullet.

"Definitely a bump, Ginny," Mac said. He fingered my goose egg. "No need to grow your hair long to cover this one."

Mac's words were meant to comfort, still I mentally traced the scar over my ear, a souvenir from the intruder I'd surprised in Uncle David's apartment last fall.

"Haven't found where the third shot went, but it's probably somewhere near the door. We'll have another look tomorrow when it's light. Figuring the trajectory from the bullet holes, we were able to get a fix on where the shooter was standing."

Duncan helped himself to a cookie. "Damn good cookies," he said.

"Shooter or shooters?" I asked.

"Shooter," Duncan said. "We only found one set of footprints."

"And where was the shooter hiding?" I asked.

"In that stand of trees by the road." Duncan took a large swallow of coffee. "That puts him at about two hundred fifty feet from the house. Just about the right distance for an AR-15 semi-automatic rifle, which is what most of the locals carry."

"But you won't know for sure until you find the bullets," I said.

"Or the shell casings. Bryant and Bentley are out there looking, but chances are they won't find anything tonight, too dark and too damn much snow. They'll have another go at it tomorrow."

Duncan poured another mug of coffee and helped himself to another handful of cookies. "You two always create this much excitement, or is this something special you cooked up just for me?"

Duncan took the chair opposite me at the table. He still didn't look like he wanted to be friends, but he did look less unfriendly.

"If you're referring to my finding Sarah Frazier's body in the freezer," I said, "you can't possibly think I had anything to do with that."

"True." Duncan lifted his coffee mug, rested his elbows on the table, and brought the mug to his lips.

"Nor did we," I looked at MacPhearson, "have anything to do with Maggie Schmidt's accident."

"Jury's still out on that one," Duncan said.

I started to protest, but didn't. I'd wasted enough words on the subject.

Duncan set his coffee mug on the table. "I've heard what your boyfriend has to say about what happened here tonight, Miss Arthur. Now how about me hearing it from you?"

I looked at Mac. He was leaning against the back of his chair, arms crossed over his chest.

"Nothing fancy, just the facts," Duncan prodded.

"The three of us went to the door," I began. "Rita walked out on the stoop, stopped, then turned back toward the cabin as if she wanted to say something. That's when the shots were fired."

"Did you see Rita get shot?" Duncan asked.

I shook my head. "It happened too fast. I heard the shots. Mac hit me. I fell, and he pulled the door shut."

Duncan circled his mug on the table. "How light was it out there?"

"It was light, bright. The stoop light was on, and Rita was moving around; the motion activated the sensors."

"And it's your impression the shooter was shooting at Rita Leggit?"

My stomach did a slow flip-flop. "Who else would the shooter be shooting at?"

Chapter Twenty-One

I LOOKED FOR A SMILE, BUT DUNCAN WASN'T SMILING.
"I just asked you a question," I said.

"So you did, Miss Arthur. Now let me give you some answers. Number one," Duncan held up a thumb, "you come up here, and the first thing you do is find a body in your freezer."

I started to protest.

"Just hold it, Miss Arthur, I'm not finished." Duncan held up an index finger. "Number two, you entertain one of our local citizens, who leaves here and immediately takes a nosedive into a frozen lake."

I looked at Mac for help, but he was watching Duncan.

"And number three," Duncan held up his middle finger, "you hold a shootout in your front yard in which another of our local citizens is badly wounded, and from what the EMTs had to say, Rita Leggit will be damn lucky if she makes it."

"Common sense should tell you neither Mac nor I had anything to do with your Pine City crime spree." I hit my open palm against the table top; to hell with restraint.

Duncan pushed away from the table, picked up his jacket, and headed for the stairs. "If I was you, Miss Arthur, I'd watch my back."

"Let it go, Red," Mac cautioned.

The sound of tires crunching their way down the drive echoed through the cabin. "Why didn't you say something?"

"Nothing to say, Ginny. Duncan knows you're not involved in, what did you call it, the Pine City crime spree? From the way things are going, you had better hope that whoever is responsible is of the same opinion."

And that's how the day ended, except for the prayer I said before falling asleep, asking God for a better day tomorrow.

We left the cabin in plenty of time to make morning Mass at St. Paul's. Stopping at the end of the driveway, we waited for the lone car that constituted Pine County's early morning rush hour to pass by.

In the stand of pines that separated Judge Marfield's property from the road, three of Pine City's finest, Deputies Schmidt, Bentley, and Bryant, their eyes fixed on the ground, searched for the shell casings from last night's shootout.

"Wasn't Schmidt supposed to be on his way to the Upper Peninsula?" I asked.

"That was my understanding," Mac said, which I took to mean he either did or did not think the observation worth noting.

The mumble of voices and the swell of organ music greeted us as we entered the church, as did the frantic waving of one of the twins' hands, beckoning us to the seats the pair had saved for us.

Again we stayed after, enjoying sweet rolls and coffee with the congregation. Most of the talk was about Maggie Schmidt and Sarah Frazier, with last night's shooting at the Marfield cabin running a close third. Added to this conversational goulash was Kim and Deb's news that Rita Leggit had been airlifted to Mercy Hospital in Marion City.

Jimmy Wakefield was there, dogging Deb's every step. Was he the source of the twins' news? As he had the grace to blush when I looked his way, I suspected my guess was on target. Would the boy never learn?

Father Mike waved us over. "The news about Rita is not good," he said by way of greeting. His eyes did not twinkle, and his mouth was set in what could best be described as a grimace. He looked from me to Mac. "Marty Shouldice told me about that human trafficking task force they have in Marion City." Before Father Mike could say more or Mac could reply, a young mother with a yowling toddler claimed the pastor's attention.

"We'll catch you later," Mac said.

Father Mike nodded.

We worked our way to the front of the hall. A knot of young people, Deb and Kim among them, blocked the doorway.

"You are going to go, aren't you?" Deb, or maybe it was Kim, asked. The twin pointed to a colorful poster that dominated the vestibule wall.

"It's the annual Valentine's Day Dance and everyone's invited, even if you don't live here," the other twin said.

"Please say you'll come," the first pleaded.

"Girls," Linda admonished, "don't bother them so. Maybe they have other plans." The mother's smile took the sting from her words, as did her own invitation to attend. "It's a community-wide event, and everyone from around here, especially the tourists, are invited."

Promising to attend if we were still here, Mac and I edged around the growing crowd of teenagers who, from overheard conversational tidbits, were planning more than a dance.

We tried again to exit the hall and again were unsuccessful.

"Wait," twin voices called.

Escape being impossible, we waited.

"There's no school tomorrow, and we want you to go cross-country skiing with us," Deb continued, the girl's identity confirmed by Jimmy Wakefield's proprietary grip of her hand.

"There's plenty of snow, and Camp Whiting has opened more trails. Please say yes," Kim said, dragging the yes into two syllables.

"Not me," Mac said, shaking his head. "Snowmobiling is okay, but I draw the line at cross-country skiing."

"Then will you come, Ginny?" Kim pleaded. "We can get started early. Have lunch at a special spot we know and be back in time for dinner."

"We'll bring lunch," Deb added.

Mac laughed. "I think you should go, Ginny. Lunch, skiing, and you can't beat the company."

It was an offer I couldn't and didn't refuse.

As if by magic, the group of teenagers parted. Only now it was Father Mike who blocked the way.

"I'm saying Mass for the migrant workers at the Whiting farm this afternoon," he said. "The Shouldices and Leggits usually help, but since the Leggits, well, can't make it, how about the two of you joining us? It'll give you a chance to tell me more about that task force, Mac."

We agreed we would and made arrangements to drive out with the three of them.

"That is if we ever get back to the cabin in time to be picked up," I said, seeing Sheriff Duncan heading our way. We had escaped the hall and were crossing the parking lot to the Honda.

"Just the two I wanted to see," Duncan greeted. "The three I sent out to your place this morning found the shell casings and managed to dig out two of the three bullets."

"The other one was in the doorframe?" Mac asked.

"It was, but they couldn't get to the third one without doing considerable damage to the wall." Duncan shrugged. "If we need it, we know where it is."

"Can you identify what kind of gun the bullets came from?" I asked.

Duncan snorted. "The shell casings came from a thirty-nine-inch semi-automatic AR-15 rifle, which is what just about everyone in the State of Michigan owns."

"Are you saying you won't be able to find the gun?" I asked.

"If I get me a suspect, I'll examine his gun. Otherwise it will be like looking for a needle in a haystack."

We reached the Honda, and Mac clicked open the locks.

"I thought Schmidt was taking his niece's body up to Rocky Ridge today?" I left behind the subject of guns, which had apparently reached a dead end.

"He was, but Maggie's sister and her husband have decided to drive down after all. Seems they have some questions they want to ask me and Doc Wacker."

Duncan rested his hand on the open passenger door. "Now if I only had some answers, I might be able to clean up some of the mess around here."

I spent what time there was before Father Mike and the Shouldices arrived reading a mystery I'd found in one of the bookcases.

I propped myself against the pillows on my bed, doing my best to avoid the mirror that hung over the dresser. My goose egg had decreased in size, ushering in another phase of the healing process. I now had the beginnings of a shiner, which Mac prophesized would be "a beauty."

Mac found some tools and a few scraps of lumber and proceeded to demonstrate his prowess as a carpenter. I must say he did more than a creditable job, the repairs needing only some sanding, a touch of stain, and weatherproofing to blend in with the rest of the doorframe.

What made the afternoon memorable was what we later referred to as The Strange Incident of the Down Feathers.

It started innocently enough when Mac asked me about a handful of feathers that kept reappearing on his dresser. It didn't take long to identify Zeus and Hera as the culprits. Especially when we observed them retrieving the feathers from the wastebasket where Mac had thrown them.

Remembering the cache of feathers I had discarded in the utility room's trash can, our next step was to look there. We found nothing that remotely resembled feathers, down or otherwise. Could we assume Mac's feathers were my feathers? If so, where had the cats found them?

Fearing the worst, Mac and I spent what time was left before our ride was due looking for a possible source.

Fortunately or unfortunately, depending on one's point of view, we found nothing that bore evidence of having been chewed by feline teeth.

The sound of tires in the driveway told us our ride was here. Zipping jackets and grabbing gloves, we hurried outside. A round of greetings followed, and the five of us set off for the Whiting farm. The Incident of the Down Feathers we saved for another day.

Father Mike, turning to face the back seat, said, "Now, Mac, tell me what prompted you to suggest Marty and Betty contact that human trafficking task force."

"It wasn't just the Shouldices," Mac answered. "I made the same suggestion to Sheriff Duncan."

Father Mike gave an impatient wave. His chubby face wore a determined look. "Not who, Detective MacPhearson, why? Why did you make the suggestion? Is there some question in your mind that the sheriff mishandled the case?"

This time it was Mac who waved his hand, moving it back and forth as if erasing a blackboard. "Nothing of the kind. I'm sure Duncan did everything he could to find the girls."

Betty nodded. "Sheriff Duncan even had the governor call out the National Guard to help with the search."

"So why do you think this task force can do any better, especially after so long a time?" Marty Shouldice asked.

"I don't know if it can," Mac admitted. "But the task force has more resources. They can look for patterns. These two are not the only ones who went missing during the past year," Mac finished.

Beside me, Betty Shouldice tensed. I reached for her hand, which felt like ice. Though it may have sounded as if Cindy Shouldice was a statistic, she was Betty Shouldice's daughter.

"You're right about the Shouldice and Leggit girls not being the only ones to go missing." Father Mike sighed. "Truth is, there are at least four and maybe six others who have disappeared during the past year."

I started at the news. "How do you know?"

The chubby little priest chuckled. "You forget, Miss Arthur, we priests are laborers in the vineyard of the Lord. As such, our tasks are many and varied."

"Regular Father Browns are you?" I asked, referencing G.K. Chesterton's short dumpy fictional sleuth.

"Are you implying a physical or mental resemblance, Miss Arthur?"

My face reddened.

Father Mike waved away my embarrassment. "It's all a matter of communication. We priests do communicate with each other, you know."

"About missing girls?"

"About anything that concerns the well-being of our parishioners, and, yes, that includes missing girls."

Marty Shouldice braked the SUV, slowed, and turned into the drive that led to the Whiting farm.

Chapter Twenty-Two

In the gathering dusk the Whiting farmhouse, lights blazing through its many windows, looked even more impressive than it had in yesterday's sunlight.

"Quite the place, isn't it?" Betty Shouldice said. She freed her still-cold hand from mine. Would there ever be enough warmth to warm this mother's hand? Her heart? I wondered.

The farmhouse disappeared behind a forest of trees.

"Does your list of missing girls include Sarah Frazier?" As I said the girl's name, I felt my own self grow cold, the thought of the murdered girl lying in the depths of Judge Marfield's freezer a ready catalyst.

"No," Father Mike said. "Not being from this diocese, Sarah Frazier wasn't on our radar."

"This makes the Upper Peninsula off limits?"

"Not off limits," Father Mike explained. "It's just that we, the group of priests I'm speaking of, work within a specific geographic area, a diocese. Pine City is in the Marion City Diocese." Father Mike spread his arms. "Not that we don't exchange information statewide, but those meetings are few compared to those of our local group. Besides which, those of us looking into the disappearance of our young people is an unofficial group."

"Unofficially unofficial?" Mac asked.

Father Mike smiled. "Trust a detective to detect our little secret."

"From what Maggie Schmidt told us about her niece," Mac said, "Sarah Frazier doesn't fall into the same category as your girls."

"I agree," Father Mike's head bobbed up and down. "From what I understand, the Fraziers kept a tight rein on the girl. Given the nature of most teenagers, it's not surprising she didn't get along at home. My guess is she ran away after a particularly bad run-in with her folks."

"Or after discovering she was pregnant?" I offered.

"Both are possibilities," the priest agreed.

The SUV rolled to a stop, our progress blocked by a padlocked gate. A lone man stepped into the headlights.

"Welcome to Whiting Farm," called Roger Whiting. He pulled the gate wide and motioned us to a parking place.

At Father Mike's request, Mac grabbed a large backpack from behind the seat, and like soldiers on parade, the five of us marched into the building near where we were parked. Whiting, close on our heels, closed the door behind us.

An equal mix of men and women, about fifty I guessed, sat on rows of benches that lined the center of the room. Another guess put their ages as ranging from early teens to middle thirties. Swarthy-skinned with dark hair and eyes, they appeared to be of Spanish or Mexican descent.

Stepping to one side of the rows of benches occupied by the somber-faced congregation, Father Mike opened the backpack Mac had carried into the building and pulled out a stole. Draping it across his shoulders, the priest passed through a door into another smaller room. Seeing Whiting motion one of the bench-sitters in after him, I realized the room was a make-do confessional.

Movement near the wooden table at the end of the room drew my attention. The Shouldices were there, pulling vestments, an assortment of altar linens, a pair of candlesticks and their holders, a chalice, and ciborium filled with as yet unconsecrated hosts from the canvas bag.

Betty draped the linens over the wooden table while her husband placed the candles in their holders at either end of the makeshift altar. Next, at the end where he stood, Marty placed a pair of cruets. One he filled with wine and the other with water.

As I watched the tableau unfold, Roger Whiting laid a restraining hand on the arm of a waiting penitent and shook his head. The man slumped back on the bench. When the door to the confessional opened, Whiting pushed the door wider and called, "That's the end, Father."

Seeing how many still waited on the benches, there was no doubt as to who had made the determination.

With Marty Shouldice's help, Father Mike adjusted his vestments over his rotund figure and took his place at the table. With a broad smile, he began, "In the name of the Father and of the Son and of the Holy Spirit . . ."

Except for the responses integral to the service, the group of worshipers remained eerily silent. There was no music and no singing. Despite the priest's effort to make it otherwise, it was a joyless occasion, and I was almost glad when I heard Father Mike say, "Go in peace to love and serve the Lord."

Beside me Mac mumbled a fervent, "Thanks be to God." The words more epithet than praise.

Another voice, Caroline Whiting's, called a cheery, "Coffee and goodies, everyone." The cheerless service just ended, the invitation sounded out of place.

Mac and I waited while the Shouldices helped Father Mike out of his vestments and re-packed the backpack before joining the line at the refreshment table. Seeing their closed faces and listening to the silence, I had the distinct impression the congregation was here because they had to be and not because they wanted to be.

"Glad to see you so soon again," Caroline chirped, handing me a cup of coffee. "Father Mike comes out every week to hear confessions and say Mass for our guest workers. Sugar or cream?"

I shook my head. Not only did I not want either the sugar or the cream Caroline Whiting offered, I was happy not to be numbered as one of her guest workers.

"Makes it so much easier. That way we don't have to haul everyone into town." Caroline pushed a plate of cookies closer to me. "Terrible what happened to Rita." The woman leaned over the table, bringing her face nearer to mine. "Can't imagine why anyone would want to shoot the poor woman. Can you?"

I ignored the question, asking one of my own instead. "Have you heard how Rita's doing?"

Caroline shook her head. "Only that she's listed as critical. I understand the bullet did considerable damage to her lungs." The woman breathed a long sigh. "Sam called after the surgery. He said Rita was in the intensive care unit, but we haven't heard anything since."

Caroline offered another cookie. I refused and smiled a greeting at the girl helping Caroline behind the table. It was the same girl who had served the coffee yesterday afternoon.

"Hello," I said. "I'm Ginny Arthur. We met yesterday at the Whitings'."

The girl hesitated, seemingly unsure if she should or shouldn't acknowledge my greeting.

"Get along with you, girl." Caroline's words answered the question. "Time to pack up and go home."

Feeling I too had been rebuked, I moved away from the table. Sipping the coffee I held in my hand, I looked around the room for Mac. He was talking to a pair of guest workers, the same two who had served him his apple pie at the Braun Motel.

I worked my way through the crowd. Most were fastening their coats and pulling caps over their heads. Mac's pair was no exception. Urged on by Roger Whiting, they were intent on gaining the open door.

Except for the muted shuffling of feet and the clatter of a plate or two, the room was weighted by an oppressive quiet, as one by one the workers, for they were no longer either penitents or worshipers, filed from the hall. I watched them pass from light into dark. Close together, one behind the other, they became shadows in the gloom.

A chill passed through me. It was not the cold that crept through the open door but more the shadows' failure to bring a smile.

Mac helped himself to my coffee. "Recognize anyone?" he asked. He looked around the room at the remaining stragglers.

"The girl at the dessert table. She's one of the two who helped Rita in the kitchen yesterday."

Mac handed back my coffee.

"Anyone else?"

I shook my head. "Some may have helped with the cleaning and snow shoveling at the motel last weekend, but if you're looking for a star witness or a positive identification, I'm not your girl."

Mac grinned. "And if I'm not looking for a star witness, does that mean you are my girl?"

"Time to go," I said, refusing to recognize Mac's question.

Our good-byes were quick, and once outside, the cold night air dissuaded additional pleasantries.

We drove through the gate, which was open but not unattended. A lone figure waited, swinging it shut behind us. Was it my imagination or was there a collective sigh of relief when we reached the highway?

"You do this every week?" Mac asked, angling his long legs into a comfortable position.

"Every Sunday," Father Mike said. "Had to do quite a bit of talking before Whiting would even consider it, but he finally came around."

"Afraid you might persuade them to quit on him? Find someplace else to work?" Mac asked.

"There is no other place," Betty Shouldice said. "Roger Whiting holds the contract with the agents who supply the guest workers for this area."

"You're saying Whiting has a monopoly?" I asked.

"Guess you could call it that. Fact is, it was Whiting's dad, old man Whiting, who was the first to use contract labor."

"Do they stay all year?" I asked.

Betty shook her head. "Only the ones Roger keeps on for the winter season."

"Who chooses who stays and who goes?" Mac asked.

"I would imagine Roger does," Father Mike said. "He's quite demanding, and I'm sure he would want the best of the lot for the winter work."

"I wonder how the workers feel?" I mused.

"You'd think they'd be happy with the guarantee of year-round work," Betty offered.

"If what we saw tonight is an example of happy, I'd hate to see unhappy," Mac said.

"That gate," I said, "is it always locked?"

"I think it is," Marty said.

"Is he afraid they might get hurt, or . . ." Mac didn't finish.

"More like something might hurt them," Marty said. "He has that herd of buffalo that roam free, and there's plenty of predators out there."

"Like bears?" I asked.

Marty nodded. "Like bears," he said.

Or men with guns? I thought but didn't say.

What remained of the drive passed in relative silence with only the occasional comment about the brilliance of the stars, which, undimmed by city lights, showed us the way home. At the cabin the sensor lights, which last night had caused such panic, welcomed us home. Inside the Siamese offered a more arbitrary welcome. Out of patience with their human family, they yowled noisily around and between our feet and legs.

Due to the lateness of the hour, we skipped our nightly fire and settled for a quick drink before an unlit fireplace.

"Do you suppose they all have green cards?" I asked, savoring the fruity taste of the wine I was sipping.

"You suggesting Mr. Whiting harbors undocumented workers, Miss Arthur?" Mac tipped the bottle to his lips as he spoke.

"Undocumented, illegal, whatever. The question's still on the table."

"Then the answer is, I don't know."

"Can you find out? Like maybe through the task force?"
My answer was a ringing cell phone.

Chapter Twenty-Three

Recognizing the ring tone, I retrieved my cell phone from my shoulder bag and checked the caller ID.

"Say hello to your doctor for me," Mac called as I put the instrument to my ear.

He had guessed correctly, and wanting the privacy my bedroom offered, I headed down the hall.

I did not sleep well that night. Not that the conversation had gone badly, but then that depended on one's definition of "badly," Steve's or mine.

Steve had been excited, as well he might be, for the meeting in Boston had gone well, very well. Steve would begin the long-desired residency on April first. I had not asked what his last date at Mercy Hospital would be, or when he would be moving to Boston.

My thoughts were in turmoil when we ended the conversation. So much so that I couldn't remember if I had told him how happy I was for him. Surely I had? I was, wasn't I?

It was this last that caused my sleepless night. Being happy for Steve sure as hell didn't translate into being happy for me!

The sound of female voices startled me into a reluctant wakefulness from what little sleep I did manage. The digital display on the bedside clock read 8:15. Having watched the electronic display during most of the night, I knew I had slept no more than two or, at best, three hours.

The voices continued. Kim? Deb? What were they doing here?

Oh, yes . . . I had a cross-country ski date with the dynamic duo. Pushing aside the covers, I headed for the shower.

I emerged from my bedroom in record time, wearing a happy face and jeans over insulated underwear.

"You say Jimmy's coming, too?" I asked, breaching the first break in the conversational dam.

"Lots of us are coming," Kim said, "but I'm not sure how many."

"Jimmy's coming here," Deb affirmed. "The others will be meeting us along the way."

A knock at the door interrupted the narrative.

"That's Jimmy," Deb squealed, heading for the stairs.

"Better eat up while you can." Mac placed a plate of bacon, eggs, and a side of buttered toast at my place.

I wasted no time in following Mac's suggestion. On reflection, breakfast was one of the few sane moments I did remember about the day.

I joined the twins and Jimmy in the garage. The three had selected the equipment I would need for the day's outing.

Mac was there, adding his two cents worth of advice, such as "stay together," "take frequent rest stops," "drink plenty of fluids." He handed me a thermos of hot chocolate and held my poles while I added the thermos to my backpack.

With a wave of good-byes to the homicide detective, the four of us headed into the woods. Should I have stayed home? I dismissed the thought. The die was cast.

Although not new to cross-country skiing, it had been several years, and the muscle memory I planned on to see me through the day was slow to return. On the positive side, the day was full of sunshine and teenage laughter.

We paralleled the snowmobile trail Mac and I had traveled, picking up fifteen or twenty boisterous teenagers along the way.

The morning passed swiftly, and we broke for lunch at the same picnic area as had Mac and I. A group of five or six snowmobilers occupied one of the tables. Eyeing the invading horde, they made a hasty escape.

The voices of the teenagers who now claimed the tables almost, but not quite, drowned out the sound of the departing snowmobiles. Was it my imagination, or did two from the group linger longer? The faces of the two beer drinkers from Braun's Motel came to mind, but faded when these last two disappeared down the trail.

The twins had packed enough food for the four of us, but I found that Mac, besides the thermos of hot chocolate, had included four shiny red apples. Since the twins' offering was either sweet or salty, the apples were a welcome treat.

"We'll be leaving the main trail and heading up toward Little Pine Lake," Jimmy explained. "It's an uphill climb, but it follows the edge of the lake up toward the bluffs that rim the northwest edge."

"It's worth the climb," Deb interjected. "Once we break free of the trees, the view is awesome."

Kim smiled broadly. Did she sense a reluctance on my part? "As clear as the weather is today, Ginny, you'll really be glad you came."

My muscles were telling me otherwise, and I suggested—well, insisted—we plan another break midway through the climb.

We left the picnic area, leaving the remembered snowmobile track after about fifteen minutes of what had finally become familiar alternating arm and leg movements. I was able to use the skis and poles instead of brute strength to propel my way through what was mostly soft powder. That is, I was able to do so until we reached the steeper grade that led to the summit and the spectacular view the twins had promised.

Time for that break. I sidestepped into a denser stand of pines and allowed a group of teenagers to pass. Jimmy, my appointed watchdog, followed me into the trees.

"Tired?" he asked.

Reluctant to waste breath on mere words, I nodded. I gestured up the trail and mouthed, "How much farther?"

"We're about halfway to the top," he said. His goggles hid most of his face, but his lips moved upward into a grin. "We're past the worst. All that's left is a couple of smaller slopes with some level spots between."

I sighed my relief and was rewarded by the sound of his laughter.

We rested about ten minutes, which my arms and legs told me was not near long enough, when Jimmy insisted we rejoin the group. Wrapped in silence in a forest of towering pines, we brought up the rear, the far rear.

The trail broke from the trees to skirt the edge of Little Pine Lake, and as Jimmy had promised, the incline was less severe. To my right lay the spectacular view I'd also been promised. I stepped nearer the edge.

"Don't get too close, Miss Arthur," Jimmy cautioned. "The snow's not solid there."

The wind had picked up. Was blowing toward us. So loud was it, I almost missed his warning, but Jimmy's restraining hand stopped my sideways drift.

"The wind blows the snow over the edge," he explained. "This late in the season it builds up. Looks solid enough, but believe me, it's not. Best not to take any chances of the ground falling out from under you."

Jimmy pushed his ski pole into the cornice and gave a downward thrust. A large section of snow and ice fell free of the trail. I watched it spiral downward, watched it dislodge small rocks as it plummeted to the larger rocks that bordered the shore of the lake. I needed no further convincing and moved away from the edge.

We continued to climb, the wind stronger as we reached the summit. Blowing out of the northwest, it blew away the voices of our trail mates.

Standing nearly seventy-five feet above the lake, I could see the entire perimeter. The snow-laden pines and the white-edged oaks, maples, and birches provided a study in mostly black and white. The brilliant cloudless blue of morning had faded into a winter white, and darker storm clouds were gathering in the northwest corner.

The wind stung my face, tugged at my clothes, and pulled the words from my mouth. Standing as I was in the midst of the laughing faces of the young people, I could only guess as to what they were saying.

"Time to start back," Jimmy shouted in my ear, but it was less the words and more his moving into position for the downhill run that told me what he said.

I stole a few more minutes staring at the stark scene before me. The wind-whipped snow on the surface of the lake was a frenzied dance of white-skirted ballerinas, the creaking tree branches a wildly clapping audience.

Regretfully, I gave in to Jimmy's increasingly urgent beckoning.

As before, we were at the tail end of the procession winding its way down the slope. I watched them go. Singly and in pairs, they slid down the tract. Most used their poles to avoid a headlong encounter with disaster. Others ignored caution. Poling vigorously, they moved at breakneck speed past their more cautious companions.

The plan, as the twins had explained earlier, was to keep to the edge of the lake until joining with another trail that led through the trees to the county road. Here several of the parents had been cajoled into picking up the group. Knowing it was important that we not keep our ride waiting, I set my mind to remembering how one controlled the rate of descent on cross-country skis.

Suddenly, as if a giant hand had brushed them aside, the skiers ahead of us fell and scattered. Some made untidy heaps of flailing arms and legs, fluttering scarfs, long narrow-bladed skis, and upturned poles. Others more fortunate or perhaps more agile escaped into the trees. From the midst of the melee came the snowmobiles. There was one, two. Roaring up the trail, louder now than the blowing wind, they crested the last rise.

Jimmy, skiing near the outer edge of the trail, moved sideways in an attempt to avoid a collision. I watched in horror as the outcropping of snow that extended from the rocky edge gave way. Jimmy was gone.

I screamed, or I think I did. The boy's vanishing form imprinted on my mind, I swung sideways, following those who had made it into the trees. A snowmobile passed by me.

Another swerved to intersect my path. Poling as if possessed, I dug into the hard-packed surface. I didn't look back. Ahead lay the promise of safety. Behind was the certainty of disaster.

The first of the low-hanging pine branches dusted me with a layer of snow. My heart sang. I had made it. Only I had not. A loud roar told me the snowmobile was upon me. Still, I did not look back, not even when the machine cut across the backs of my skis, bringing me to an abrupt halt. My boots sprung free of their fastenings, and I was catapulted into the stand of trees I had thought a refuge.

I loosened my grip on the poles and tried for a tuck position. Miraculously, my head missed the largest of the trees. My shoulder did not, the impact throwing me sideways. I lost my tuck position and hit the ground on my stomach and slid forward. A toboggan on a downhill run, I came to a stop in a dense thicket of saplings and low-growing vegetation.

Behind the goggles that covered my tightly closed eyes, my lids twitched. Each breath was painful. Spinning round and round like a child's top, my stomach lurched. Was I going to be sick?

Despite the pain in my chest, I took in several slow even breaths. I tried for deep but the knife-like pain persuaded me otherwise. Slowly, my stomach ceased its aerobatics. I opened my eyes and was rewarded by a glimpse of broken branches. I succeeded in moving both arms and legs. Entangled as I was, the movements were slight. The vines and shrubs that had in all likelihood saved my life were now a prison.

Knowing I would need help, I attempted to call out. Mistake!

I took to listening, a thing I should have been doing, but who's perfect?

The first thing I heard, rather didn't hear, were the snowmobiles. I listened more intently, aware as I did of the wind whipping the pine boughs and rattling the barren branches of the oaks and maples.

Snow-laden clouds hung heavy above me, and daylight was ebbing away. I fought an imminent panic attack and made another feeble attempt to free myself. The exertion was too much.

Think, think, I commanded. Then I heard them, the cries and calls for help of those others who had been with me.

Visions of fallen bodies, tangled arms and legs, waving scarfs and broken ski poles crowded together inside my head. How badly were they hurt? Had some escaped the marauding snowmobiles? Possibly made it to safety? Had they been able to summon help?

This last brought hope and a rush of adrenalin. I made a greater effort to free myself. Heard branches crack and felt an arm break free. Using my newfound freedom, I tore at the vines encircling my other arm and soon had it free.

The exertion was not without consequence. My chest hurt like hell.

I lay still. Gusts of wind swirled the snow around me. Around me too was the sound of voices.

"Kim, Tom, Mark, Debbie, Susan, Olivia, Shelly, Jimmy, Deb," teenage voices calling one to another. "Are you hurt?" "My leg . . . my arm . . . damn, I've broken my pole." The voices—did I hear Jimmy's?—floated by on the wind.

Hands tugged at me, and other voices called my name. "Ginny, Ginny, wake up. Are you hurt?"

Behind the goggles, my eyes fluttered open. "I'm not sleeping," I said. Why would they ask such a question?

I brushed at the snow that blew across my face. Bracing on an elbow, I struggled to lever upright. A sharp pain, as if someone was kicking me in the ribs, brought a gasp.

"Lie still," a voice commanded.

"Please tell them to stop kicking me." I gasped. The effort to talk was too great.

More hands fussed over me and more voices talked to me. "I'm putting on a neck brace, Miss Arthur." My neck was clamped round, making turning my head an impossible task.

"We're putting a backboard under you, Miss Arthur," another voice said as a board slid into place.

A needle pricked my flesh. "What?" I asked.

"Something to help you relax," the now familiar voice said.

The explanation was followed by a shouted, "Ready to transport."

I was being lifted, heard a flap-flap sound. One I knew, but could not identify.

Chapter Twenty-Four

Bright lights stared down at me. I tried to move my head but couldn't.

"Don't move."

"Mac," I said.

"Ginny," Mac answered.

John? Marsha? John? Marsha? I giggled as lines from some long ago movie echoed in my head.

"And what's so funny?" Mac's face came into view. He wasn't smiling.

I abandoned the giggle. "Where am I? What happened?"

"You tell me, Red," Mac answered. He still wasn't smiling, but the frown was gone.

"What happened to Jimmy? Deb, Kim?" I amended.

"The girls are fine. They're in the waiting room, waiting for the okay to see you."

Ah! That explained a great deal. If the girls were in the waiting room, they must be fine, and I—we—were in the hospital. I frowned. There was a flaw in my reasoning.

"Jimmy?"

Mac's frown reappeared. "Not so good. Jimmy's in surgery. Leg's broken for sure, and maybe an arm, but the worst is his ruptured spleen."

The fog lifted from my memory. "I saw him fall, go over the edge." I tried to lift my hands as I offered the explanation, but Mac held one and the other wouldn't move. Clear plastic tubes snaked from clear plastic bags suspended above me. Was this why I felt so spacey?

I tried again to move my head, but as before, it wouldn't move.

"Just hold on, Red. They're reading your X-rays now."

Another voice, Jim Wacker's, called a greeting. "That collar can come off, and we can take away the backboard."

"So I'm okay?" I asked.

"Depends on what you mean by okay," Doc Wacker said.

I grumped an unladylike response, causing both Mac and Doc Wacker to laugh.

"What it means, Ginny, is that you don't have any neck or back injuries. Your shoulder's banged up, but nothing's broken." The doctor shook his head. "You're lucky you didn't hit the one they just put back together."

"Now that I know what's not wrong, mind telling me what is wrong?"

"Oh, I'd say a couple of broken ribs and a concussion."

"I didn't hit my head," I said.

"That lump on your head tells a different story," Wacker said.

Foolish girl that I was, I tried for a deep breath and gasped at the pain that followed.

"Broken ribs, remember?" Wacker reminded.

"When can I go home?" I asked. What this conversation needed was a change of subject.

"Not until tomorrow at the earliest." Wacker waved away my protest. "I'd say you were damn lucky, young lady. So don't let's hear any more complaints."

I bit back further protest.

Wacker took my silence for acceptance. "That's a good girl. Just do what you're told, and I'll see you in the morning."

With a promise to send someone to remove the neck brace and backboard, the Pine County Coroner was gone. Consider yourself lucky not to be needing that part of Wacker's professional services, the rational part of me argued.

"How many were hurt?" I asked, having decided to leave the other thought alone.

"Surprisingly few, five, six maybe, I don't know the exact number," Mac answered.

"It was awful, Mac. All those kids . . . they tried to get away, but those damn snowmobiles just kept coming. Mowed them down like dominoes, pins in a bowling alley." An awful thought entered my mind. "Was anyone killed?"

Mac shook his head. "Jimmy got the worst of it. Mostly what we have are a couple of broken legs, a broken arm, and a lot of bumps and bruises."

"So most of them got away?" I asked, wanting the assurance of a second affirmative response.

Again Mac nodded. "And as soon as they could use their cell phones, they called for help."

"Anyone know who the snowmobilers were?"

"Duncan's been asking, but so far I don't think he's got much in the way of answers." Mac massaged the back of my hand with his thumb. "You got any answers?"

"There were two snowmobiles. But with their helmets and goggles, the drivers looked alike. Even the snowmobiles looked alike. Unless the kids recognized them, Duncan will have a hard time identifying them."

"About as much trouble as I'm having identifying the rifle that shot at you last night, I suspect," a grim-faced Duncan said, entering the cubicle where I lay. "With the exception of Jimmy Wakefield, who's still in surgery, I've talked with most of the kids. Now it's your turn. What can you tell me about what happened up there?"

"Has anyone said how Jimmy's doing?" I asked.

"Only that he's holding his own," Duncan said. "What about you?"

"A couple of broken ribs and a bump on the head," I answered.

Duncan gave me a speculative look. "So, are you up to telling me what happened up there?"

Careful not to take a deep breath, I told Duncan about the snowmobiles.

"Did they seem to be aiming at anything or anyone in particular?" Duncan asked.

"Hard to tell. They were lined up, one behind the other."

"But they did come up the hill?"

"The lead one did. Came right at Jimmy and me. That's the one that ran Jimmy over the edge."

"And you?" Duncan asked. "What did you do when you saw Jimmy fall?"

"I made a run for the trees, and I would have made it, if that damn snowmobile hadn't clipped the end of my skis."

I tightened my fingers around Mac's hand.

"Just a couple more questions," Duncan said. "Did you see where the third snowmobile went?"

"Third snowmobile?" I reran the scene, but to no avail. "I can't remember there being a third snowmobile."

"Okay." Duncan swiped his hand across his face. "What happened after you fell off your skis?"

"I got tangled in some ground cover."

"But you managed to free yourself?" Duncan asked.

"Only my arms."

"Not your legs?" Duncan asked.

"I don't think I even tried."

Duncan pursed his lips. "Any chance those snowmobiles might have been after you?"

I stared at Duncan. "What are you suggesting?"

"I'm not suggesting anything, Miss Arthur. Just trying to fit the pieces together."

Duncan had hardly left when a nurse pushed aside the curtain and came into the cubicle with, "Doc Wacker says we can do without the collar and backboard." She smiled. It was an infectious smile, and despite all that had happened, I smiled back. "He also said you'd be spending the night with us."

Her nimble fingers freed me from the cervical collar. "The orderly will be right in to move you into the other wing. Bed's waiting for you."

"Have you heard how Jimmy Wakefield's doing?" I asked.

Her smile broadened. "He's out of surgery and in the intensive care unit. Word is, he's stable and should be right as rain in a few days."

I gave Mac's hand another squeeze. "Thank you, God," I whispered.

Mac followed with, "Amen."

The move was accomplished without incident, and Mac was contemplating his choice of chairs when the door to the room banged open.

"Ginny," the twins chorused. They ran to the bed, one on either side.

"We know about Jimmy and the others," Deb said. "Now we want to know about you."

"I'm sure my story is no different than theirs. I made for the woods and had just about made it when one of the snowmobiles ran over my skis."

"It hit you?" Kim cried.

"No, no, just my skis. I was thrown forward and landed in some underbrush."

"Ouch," Deb said.

"Do you remember us being there?" Kim asked.

A glimmer of something niggled inside my head, then was gone. "Afraid not," I said.

"We're the ones who found you," Deb said.

"Not really," Kim corrected. "It was the helicopter. It was hovering in the air. That's what led us to you. You were laying on the ground beside a tree."

"Ginny said she was tangled in some bushes." Mac looked to me for confirmation.

The girls shook their heads.

"Not when we found her," Deb insisted. "She even had a blanket wrapped around her."

The door to the room swung open. "Thought I'd find you here," Linda Braun said.

"We wanted to find out how Ginny was," Kim said.

"And did you?" Linda asked.

"Sort of," Kim said.

"They still won't let me see Jimmy," Deb complained.

"And that won't happen tonight. Move. It's time to go."

"So, the two of them found me."

"Someone found you," Mac corrected, "and that someone covered you with a blanket." Mac lowered the back of the recliner. "Time to go to sleep, Red. If you don't shut up, they won't let me stay, and I don't relish having to sneak back in."

Chapter Twenty-Five

THE QUESTIONS THAT NEEDED ANSWERS were still in need of answers when sunlight flooded my hospital room.

"Good morning," Mac said brightly.

"And what's so good about it?" I grumped.

Mac laughed. "Are you one of those people who need a jolt of caffeine before they can be civil?"

"Not usually."

"Good. Then it's safe to talk to you."

"Only if you tell me what's going on around here."

Mac levered the recliner to full upright. "And what makes you think there's anything going on around here?"

"You and I both know that what happened at Little Pine Lake yesterday was no accident, and what were medics doing there? If the kids called 911, which I'm sure they did, it should have been the county EMTs who responded."

"Hold it," Mac said.

But I was on a roll. "And the shooting, that most certainly was no accident, and while we're at it, we might as well toss in the body in the freezer and Maggie Schmidt's nosedive into Big Pine Lake."

"Are you through?" Mac asked.

I wasn't, and after a couple of shallow breaths added, "Are you afraid something more might happen? Is that why you spent the night here? Don't keep me in the dark, Mac. I have a right to know."

"I know you do, Ginny. Only I'm as much in the dark as you are."

"I hope it's not my patient who's in the dark." Jim Wacker, an impish smile on his face, strode into the room.

Doctor-like, he proceeded to shine pinpoint lights into my eyes, hold up fingers that needed counting, and ask such mundane questions as who's the president, what's your name, and what day is it?

Though right on the day, I was wrong on the date. But Wacker was satisfied and wrote the discharge order.

"You need to give me a call if you notice anything out of the ordinary." Wacker grew serious. "We took skull films yesterday, but something might crop up later."

"I promise," I said. Buoyed by my imminent discharge, I tried a deep breath.

"Can't do much for those ribs. You'll just have to tough it out until they heal."

Tired of being the topic of conversation, I asked, "How is Jimmy today?"

"I spoke to his surgeon on the way in. He said Jimmy had a good night, and plans are to move him out of the unit this morning." Wacker shook his head. "Seems like God blesses both cats and kids with nine lives."

"Are you including those others who were out there yesterday in your assessment, Doctor Wacker?" I asked.

"And you too, Ginny Arthur." Wacker dropped his bantering tone. "Just see that you don't use them up too fast."

With a wave of his hand and "I'll send the nurse down to check you out," Wacker left the room.

Anticipating an early escape, I swung my legs over the side of the bed and stood up. A wave of dizziness swept over me. Steadying myself against the bedside table, I waited for the room to stop spinning.

"It's going to take a while before you get your sea legs back," Mac said. He handed me the plastic bag that held my clothes.

His face came into focus. "Guess you've been here," I said.

"Been there, done that." Mac grinned his familiar grin. "Need an arm, Red?"

The close quarters of the bathroom were both a curse and a blessing. A curse because I kept bumping into things, the jarring causing my ribs to scream a protest. A blessing in that the confined space provided multiple surfaces for leaning if another attack of vertigo threatened. Fortunately, this last did not happen, and I was soon dressed and ready to leave.

I gave the jacket I had been wearing a cursory look. From the numerous tears and puncture wounds, all bleeding down feathers, it would need a major overhaul before it could be worn.

Both the discharge nurse and the sheriff arrived at the same time.

Allowing that we were on the nurse's turf, Sheriff Duncan waited while she completed the discharge procedure. The nurse, who looked to be not much older than the twins, reviewed each item in turn and, after getting my signature on the document, said I was free to go.

The three of us settled in to wait for the wheelchair, which the nurse insisted was the only way I was going to get out of the hospital. Mac reclaimed the lounger, the sheriff a molded plastic chair, while I, still on patient status, got the bed. From this vantage point, I looked first at Mac, then at Sheriff Duncan. I settled on the sheriff.

"How about answering some questions?" I said.

"Shoot," Duncan said.

I would have preferred a different metaphor but chose not to argue the point. "What do you think happened at Little Pine Lake?"

"Strange you should ask. That's what I was going to ask you."

"I asked first, so you tell me."

"I'm thinking someone around here doesn't like you, Miss Arthur," Duncan said.

"Seems Mac's of the same opinion. He's appointed himself my bodyguard."

"Judging from what's happened since you arrived on the scene, I'd say you need one," Duncan said. "The big question is, why?"

"It has to be something that happened since Ginny came here," Mac said.

Duncan nodded. "Unless Miss Arthur has a secret past she's not telling us about."

"I have no secrets, past or present."

"Then how about we start from when you arrived at Judge Marfield's place?" Duncan said.

"I had nothing to do with that. I walked in, opened the freezer, and there she was," I said a bit testily.

Duncan's hand came up. "Hold it, Miss Arthur. This is a fact-finding mission, not a witch hunt. Sarah was Maggie's niece," he said, continuing his "fact-finding" mission. "You found the girl's body, and Maggie comes calling. She wants to hear the details from you." Duncan paused. "Nothing unusual there. Families always want to know all there is to know about the death of a loved one."

I shifted a pillow, trying for a more comfortable position. "Actually Maggie came to apologize," I said.

"Apologize for what?" Duncan said.

"For the way you acted that day at the motel."

"Now look here, Miss Arthur."

"Oh, I know, it was your way of telling me to keep my nose out of police business," I interrupted.

"And did she apologize?" Duncan asked.

I nodded. "She did. We talked about Sarah, how she didn't get along at home and about her leaving Rocky Ridge. I think Maggie just wanted someone to talk to."

"She had her brother, and Ted Williams," Duncan said.

"She did talk to Ted, but not to her brother. Seems Norm Schmidt was thick as thieves with Sarah's family and was sure to tell them where she was."

"Schmidt sounds like a real gem," Mac said. "Not only was he willing to rat out his niece, he wasn't too happy about us poking around the accident site."

"That's news to me," Duncan said.

"Fact is, he was Johnny-on-the-spot whenever we went near the place."

"And it was your suggestion that we take a closer look at the tire tracks," Duncan said, looking at me.

"And until I did, you had Maggie's death pegged as a suicide."

Duncan shrugged his shoulders. "Oh, I had some doubts, but nothing concrete until you nagged us into taking another look at those tracks."

"Could be that's why Ginny has a bull's eye pinned on her back," Mac said.

"Could be," Duncan agreed.

"Was that reason enough to shoot up the house?" I asked. "And if so, why shoot Rita Leggit? She didn't have anything to do with finding Sarah Frazier's body in the freezer or Maggie Schmidt taking that dive off the cliff."

Duncan pursed his lips. "Seems to me those three shots were all aimed at that open door."

"And yesterday?"

"How about letting me finish, Miss Arthur? Everyone I've talked to agrees that one of the snowmobiles was aimed directly at you."

I felt my shoulders sag.

"That target getting heavy, Red?" Mac asked.

The door opened, and an orderly pushing a wheelchair came into the room. "You ready to leave, Miss Arthur?"

He was a Jimmy Wakefield look-alike, with a smile that filled his whole face. Unfortunately, the smile did little to assuage my fear. Mac was right, the target was heavy and was growing heavier by the minute.

As we planned to detour by Jimmy Wakefield's room, Mac insisted on doing the pushing, and the boy bid us a reluctant farewell.

Jimmy was propped up in bed, or at least propped as much as a leg and arm wearing plaster casts would allow.

"I really feel better than I look," he said by way of greeting.

"And how do you feel?" I asked.

"The incision hurts, but only when I laugh," Jimmy said.

"That makes us a pair," I said. "You can't laugh, and I can't breathe."

We shared war stories, each of us giving an exaggerated account of our battle scars. "I saw you fall," I finished, keeping the "I was afraid you would be killed" thought to myself.

Jimmy looked disgusted. "I do a lot of ski jumping and really did think I could make it. The elevation at the point I went over the edge wasn't all that great, and I should have been able to fly far enough to miss the rocks."

"Doc Wacker said the two of us have nine lives but that we're using them up too fast."

Jimmy grinned. "The doc's always telling us that." He frowned. "But I would have made it if that snowmobile hadn't clipped the back of my skis."

"Same here, the snowmobile hit the back of my skis and sent me flying," I said.

"Then you know how it feels. You just stop all of a sudden, then boom." Jimmy made a diving motion with his free hand.

"The twins said there were medics on hand, not the county EMTs," Mac said. "You know anything about that?"

"The medics were there, and a helicopter too," Jimmy said. "Did you see the helicopter, Miss Arthur?"

A flap, flap, flap sound echoed somewhere in my memory. "I'm not sure," I said. "Things are a bit fuzzy yet."

Duncan, who until then had only been listening, said, "The medics were on the scene when we got there. The Guard was running a training exercise, saw what was happening on the ridge, dropped the training part, and went to work."

"Nobody called them? They were just there?" Mac asked. "Pretty convenient if you ask me."

The two men, police officers both, exchanged knowing looks.

A nurse came and shooed us from the room. "This is a hospital, Sheriff," she said. "Let's let the patient get better before you start grilling him."

Mac wheeled me across the parking lot to where the Honda was parked.

"There's more going on inside my head than I can process," I complained when I was settled in.

"That's your mind saying it's time to shut down. Give yourself a rest," Mac said.

I took his advice, closed my eyes and . . .

We pulled into the garage. Mac helped me from the car and, when I asked, handed me the plastic bag with my jacket.

"I want to see if it can be repaired."

Pulling the jacket from the bag, I laid it over the hood of the Honda. Dangling from the zipper pull was a silver unicorn.

Chapter Twenty-Six

I STARED AT THE SMALL CHARM. IT COULDN'T BE. Yet it was.

"Mac." My voice broke.

"Ginny?" He called my name and then was there.

I pointed to the silver unicorn.

"Anybody could have put it there, Ginny."

"Not anybody, Mac, only Uncle David."

"You can't know that," Mac said. He put his arms around me, and I leaned against him.

"What am I going to do, Mac? How can I find him?"

"There's nothing you can do, Ginny. If David Arthur is here, the next move is his."

Mac was right.

I pulled free of Mac's embrace and worked the charm off the zipper pull. Holding it tight, I headed for the cabin door. Mac, following close behind, insisted I go no further than the couch. In short order several pillows supported my broken ribs, and the curtains were drawn over the windows to cut the sun's glare. It was this last for which I was most grateful, as a bass drummer with nothing better to do than practice the boom-boom-booms for which the instrument was best known had taken up residence inside my head.

"Hungry?" Mac asked when I was settled to his liking.

I started to shake my head but thought better of it.

"Head hurt?" Mac asked, a worried look on his face.

I closed my eyes. Between my ribs, my head, and the waves of nausea that had come out of nowhere, I wasn't sure what felt worse. I tried willing the trio away. It didn't work.

"Take this," Mac said, handing me a couple of pills.

Eager for the relief they promised, I popped the pair into my mouth and washed them down with the glass of water he held to my lips.

"Little sips," he cautioned. "I'm making you a cup of tea. That should settle your stomach."

Mac was right. The pills dulled the headache, and the tea settled my stomach. With the unicorn still tight in my fist, I closed my eyes, but neither the pills nor the cup of tea dulled my restless thoughts. Inside my head the drum boomed an incessant David Arthur . . . David Arthur . . . David Arthur.

I poked into the corners of my mind, searching through the stored memories of the tall red-haired man. Somewhere there had to be a key, a clue that would unlock the mystery of his disappearance, something that would tell me where he was today.

I must have slept, for I woke with a start.

"Are you okay?" Mac was beside me.

"Larry Rhodes knows," I said.

Mac shook his head. "We've been through this before, Ginny. Your Uncle David skipped town after the police uncovered his art smuggling ring. If Rhodes knew anything about his disappearance, do you think he'd risk his career by not telling what he knew?"

"You're not listening, Mac. Uncle David's here. I know he is."

Mac moved to the center of the room and circled round, pausing to stare into each of the four corners. "Come out, come out wherever you are," he called sotto voce.

"Then why does he show up whenever I'm in trouble? Answer me that, Mister Smart Detective, the shooting in the parking lot last fall, after my surgery, and yesterday on the ski trail?"

I shoved at the pillows that had once offered comfort but now held me prisoner. "And where's my cell phone?" I demanded.

"And who are you going to call?" Mac asked.

"Larry Rhodes," I shouted. "Someone knows where David Arthur is, and that someone is Larry Rhodes."

Mac's shoulders sagged. "Stay still, Red, I'll get your cell."

"Does that mean you agree with me?"

"Hell no! But even I know it's pointless to argue with a redhead."

I watched Mac's retreating back. Had I won the argument or only the first round? Freeing myself from the eiderdown cocoon, I wiggled to a sitting position.

"Comfortable?" Mac asked, handing me the phone.

"Yes," I mumbled. I suppressed a grimace. What's a little lie between friends.

"Yeah, I just bet you are," Mac retorted. He chose a nearby armchair and settled into it.

"You're staying?" I asked.

"And miss this show?" His face wore no expression, but his arms crossed tight over his chest spoke volumes.

"Suit yourself," I said, and punched in Rhodes's number.

I waited through a series of rings, so many I thought I was about to be transferred to voice mail, when Rhodes's familiar voice answered. "Rhodes here."

"This is Ginny. Got a minute?"

"For you, Ginny, I'll take the time."

Mac continued to stare. Refusing to be intimidated, I stared back.

"You still there, Ginny?" Rhodes asked.

"I found a unicorn . . ." I launched into the story about the down jacket and the silver unicorn.

Rhodes laughed. "So?"

"So, Uncle David's the only one who would have put it there."

"Just a minute, Ginny."

"No, you wait a minute." I rushed on. "Whenever I need help, Uncle David's there. He was in the parking lot when I got shot last fall, at the hospital following my surgery, and yesterday he was on the ski slope when the snowmobile tried to run me down," I said, repeating what I had told MacPhearson.

"How about telling me more about the ski slope and the snowmobile?" Rhodes said.

"No! Not until you tell me about Uncle David, Larry. Where is he?"

"Mind if I ask if you're okay?" Rhodes's voice held an anxious note.

"I'm okay. A bump on the head, that's all."

"Where are you?" Rhodes demanded. "The hospital?"

"Judge Marfield's place. I'm sitting on a couch, and a redheaded detective is sitting across the room glowering at me."

Rhodes's sigh was audible. "Did you discover this unicorn before or after you hit your head?"

"Oh no you don't. Doc Wacker checked me out, and there's nothing wrong with my head."

"Let me talk to MacPhearson."

"No! You and I are talking, and I want some answers."

"So far, I haven't any answers to give you."

"Try harder," I snapped.

"Just because someone keeps showing up at opportune times and keeps dropping silver unicorns along the way, what else makes you think this unknown someone might be your Uncle David?"

"Well, there's the little matter of the National Guard air rescue unit," I said.

"National Guard air rescue unit?" Rhodes repeated.

"Seems I didn't rate the more prosaic EMT unit, which, I might add, is the usual first responder in these situations."

"Situations?" Rhodes asked, paraphrasing me yet again.

"This is a winter sports area, and the EMTs are specially trained to handle emergencies. Calling in the National Guard just doesn't happen."

"And it happened?"

I repeated my earlier statement. Was I, like Rhodes, turning into a parrot?

"Besides which, there's also the manner in which the twins found me," I said.

"The twins found you?" Again Rhodes parroted my words. My suspicions were confirmed. We were indeed a couple of birds, chattering one to the other.

I sighed. "The Braun twins found me tucked up nice and neat in a survival blanket, which, need I say, is not standard equipment for teenagers on an afternoon cross-country ski jaunt."

"I take it the question is, who wrapped you in the blanket?" Rhodes said.

Finally, Lieutenant Larry Rhodes, head of the Marion City Crimes Against Persons Unit and recently appointed head of the newly formed Task Force on Missing and Trafficked Persons, was thinking like a police officer.

"Right. I was tangled in some underbrush, then the twins were there telling me help was on the way."

"The twins moved you?" Rhodes asked.

"The twins didn't move me."

"And . . ." Rhodes prompted.

And then, like sunlight bursting through clouds, I knew. There had been a third snowmobile, and the driver of the third snowmobile had been Uncle David, and it was Uncle David who had rounded up the stragglers and herded, not chased, the teenagers into the safety of the woods.

I paused for another breath, wincing at the pull on my ribs. "There were two snowmobiles," I said. That there was a third snowmobile and that the driver was David Arthur I'd save for another time. "One came at me, and the other ran Jimmy off the cliff."

"Snowmobiles? Blankets? Twins? I think you'd better rethink your story, Ginny. It's got way too many holes."

"No," I said. "It's time for you to tell me where David Arthur is and where he's been hiding for the past three years."

"I can't tell you what I don't know, Ginny," Rhodes said.

"Then I guess we have nothing more to say," I said, and broke the connection.

I looked to where Mac sat. "He's lying," I said.

Chapter Twenty-Seven

Fearing more pain or, worse, more dizziness, I undressed slowly. Why had Larry Rhodes lied to me about Uncle David?

I slid into bed. "One can protest too much," I told the darkness as I fell into a deep, dreamless sleep. With so many villains chasing me in real life, there was little need for them to haunt me in Morpheus's realm.

I woke early the next morning, feeling better but not good. A quick shower and a comfortable set of sweats, the top being loose enough to camouflage my bouncing breasts. After struggling to get my bra fastened, it had proved too constrictive.

Mac was on duty in the kitchen. My nose told me the coffee was ready, and the rattle of the cereal box announced the rest of the menu.

"Not up to cooking this morning?" I asked.

Mac responded to my cheery greeting with a questioning look.

"Your head?" I asked.

"Nothing's wrong with my head. It's yours I'm worried about," Mac retorted.

"There's nothing wrong with my head."

"Does that mean you've given up the idea of your Uncle David being loose around here?"

I spooned a helping of cereal and blueberries into my mouth. "You've obviously had a bad night."

"You're not answering my question."

"And Larry Rhodes didn't answer mine either," I snapped. Patience, patience, Ginny, I told myself. Getting mad at Mac would accomplish nothing.

"What does Larry Rhodes have to do with your Uncle David? In case you've missed the point, David Arthur is the topic under discussion."

"Oh, were we having a discussion? It sounded more like an inquisition," I said, louder than necessary. I shoveled another spoonful of fruit and cereal into my mouth. Milk dribbled down my chin, and I reached for a napkin.

"Okay, Red. So you think Rhodes knows where your Uncle David is."

I crumpled the napkin and laid it beside my bowl. "I think he's known all along."

Mac shook his head. "So, what are you going to do about it?"

"Nothing. Knowing Uncle David is here is enough." I stared down at the lone blueberry swimming in a pool of milk. "I don't remember buying blueberries."

"Women," Mac growled. "There was a package in the freezer."

"Didn't Duncan say he wanted my statement today?" I asked with a smile.

Mac pushed his bowl aside. "And what else do you have in mind for us to do while we're in town? Somehow I don't think Sheriff Duncan is the only item on your agenda."

Having no agenda, I let the question go.

We entered an almost empty reception area. Missing was the bustle I had come to associate with police departments. Reminding myself I was not in Kansas, or more precisely Marion City, I waved a greeting to the woman who guarded the inner door.

"Glad to see you're up and about," Caroline Whiting said. "I heard you, along with half of our freshman class, were in the hospital." Caroline's face expressed what could best be described as shocked sympathy.

"I tried to tell her she needed to lay low for a few days, but . . ." Mac shrugged his shoulders, "what can you do?"

"Detective MacPhearson's right. You belong home in bed, Ginny, what with your fractured ribs and a concussion."

So much for confidential information, I thought.

The ringing telephone ended the conversation. "Go on in," Caroline said, buzzing open the door that led to the inner office.

"Pine County Sheriff's Department, Caroline Whiting here. How may I help you?" The sound of Roger Whiting's wife's voice, mistress of Whiting Farm and today's gatekeeper for the Pine City Sheriff's Department, followed us through the door.

"That lady wears a lot of hats," Mac said when the door had closed behind us.

Sheriff Duncan's "Come on in" cut off my response, but not my thoughts. Caroline Whiting did indeed wear many hats.

Mac and I skirted the empty desks to Duncan's office.

"You give everyone the day off?" I asked.

"Afraid not," Duncan grunted. "Fact is, I could use a few more deputies."

"You're looking for volunteers?" I asked.

"If you're thinking of volunteering, Miss Arthur, forget it," Duncan said. "I sure as hell don't need anyone with broken ribs and head injuries." Duncan looked from me to Mac. "And I'm including you on that list, MacPhearson."

Mac held up a hand. "Whoa, I'm not the buttinski type, and I sure don't remember volunteering to help, so what's the beef?"

Duncan picked up a pen that lay on his desk, then tossed it back. "It's been a long couple of days, and I don't think the ones coming up will be any shorter."

Dark circles rimmed his eyes, and his uniform shirt looked like yesterday's model.

"Our staff isn't all that big—Myra Johnson, Kev Bryant, Norm Schmidt, Bentley, Ramos, and Carol Whiting. That's the lot. I've got everyone except Lamar Bentley and Juanita Ramos looking for anyone who was within hailing distance of Little Pine Lake Monday." Duncan wiped his face with a heavy hand, as if trying to rid it of the fatigue that showed there. "But you're not here to listen to my complaints."

Duncan pushed back from his desk. "So, let's get you started on that statement. Remember how to work the computer?"

I said I did and followed Duncan into the outer office.

"Might as well use the same computer you used the other day." Duncan looked at me. "Remember which one it was?"

I pointed to a computer and settled into the chair behind the desk. At the touch of my finger on the space bar, the screen lit up. "All set," I said.

"Then I'll leave you to it," Duncan said, and with a dismissive nod reentered his office.

I shoved my gloves into my jacket pockets, pulled my arms free of the sleeves, and tossed the parka across a corner of the desk.

I had no trouble recalling the sequence of events that led to my being dumped into the tangle of vegetation. From there on it was a different story, a short story as I had no intention of sharing my conviction that David Arthur had been the driver of the third snowmobile. My fingers hovered over the keyboard. Amorphous half images of what may or may not have happened flooded my mind. The twins were there, I knew, only because they had told me they were. The helicopter ride? Not really.

My fingers slowed. I read over what I had typed, ran the spell check, and gave the print command.

While the printer did its thing, I picked up my jacket from where I had tossed it. A scattering of down feathers fell to the floor. Not wanting to give the overworked department more to do, I scooped up the feathers and shoved them into the pocket of my sweat suit. Had this jacket been the source of the loose feathers in the cabin? Was my jacket the Siamese pair's chew toy? I lifted my statement from the printer tray and headed for Duncan's office.

"Not much here," he said, dropping the lone sheet on his desk.

"I can't tell you what I don't know," I said.

My response warranted a grunt. "Seems you don't remember much of anything."

"I remember there were two snowmobiles." I crossed my fingers and sucked in a shallow breath. Was I finally getting the hang of lying, of broken rib breathing?

"There's nothing here about what happened after you got free of that underbrush." Duncan stabbed the report with his index finger.

"The twins said they found me lying beside a tree, covered with a blanket, but I don't remember freeing myself from all that shrubbery."

"And I don't suppose you happened to be carrying a blanket with you?" Duncan asked.

"No blanket," I said.

"Or being moved down to where the helicopter could airlift you out?"

I shook my head.

Duncan massaged his pursed lips between thumb and forefinger. It was a thing I'd seen him do before. Habit? I wondered. "But you're sure about the two snowmobiles?"

"There may have been a third," I admitted. Was it better to tell half a lie than a whole? I wondered.

"Most of the kids say there were three snowmobiles," Duncan said. "The two that went after you and Jimmy Wakefield and a third one that chased the kids into the woods."

"They may be right," I said. "They were closer to the woods than I was."

"Well, if you can't remember seeing a third snowmobile, can you remember anything that might help identify either the snowmobiles or the drivers?"

I shook my head. "I was too busy trying to get away."

Duncan laid his hand on the report. "Then I guess this will have to do." He pushed the sheet toward me. "Sign it, and you're free to go."

I picked up the pen Duncan had earlier discarded. "I know you told me, but will you tell me again how it was that the medics from Camp Whiting instead of the EMTs picked Jimmy and me up?"

"Simple," Duncan said, "they were there, saw what was happening, and picked you and Jimmy up."

"And why were they there?"

"Some sort of training exercise. They hold one every few weeks."

"And the kids? I saw the snowmobiles run through a bunch of them."

"The medics called for extra choppers. Air-lifted out the kids along with you and Jimmy." Duncan drummed his fingers on the desk. "Why is it so important who picked you up? The important thing is you were picked up and taken to the hospital in a more-than-timely fashion. Seems you should be grateful about that and not so damn curious about who did it or how it came about." Duncan pointed to the report. "Are you going to sign that statement or not? If so, let's get it done. There's other things I need to be doing."

Chapter Twenty-Eight

"Looks like you're busy," I said. I indicated the blinking lights on Caroline Whiting's telephone console.

"About normal. Tourists usually hit the downtown area around noon, but being tourism is the lifeblood of the area . . ." Caroline laughed, leaving the sentence unfinished.

"Were you here Monday afternoon?" I asked.

"When the kids started calling about the attack of the snowmobiles?"

"Sounds like someone's been watching too much science fiction."

"Attack might be a bit strong," Caroline admitted, "but what else would you call it?"

Her grin faded. "I took the 911 calls Monday afternoon. First from the kids, then from the parents. Really tied up the phones, I can tell you."

"Did you send the EMTs to Little Pine Lake?"

"I sent every available unit there was to send. From the way the kids and then their parents were carrying on, you'd think every kid in Pine City was either dead or dying." Caroline shook her head as another pair of calls came through. "And if I don't want a repeat of Monday, I'd best get back to work."

"Find out what you wanted to know?" Mac asked when we were in the Honda.

"I know the EMTs were called and that they responded to the call. I also know they weren't the first on the scene. The National

Guard, who just happened to be handy, were the first responders. From what Duncan said, they were also the last. Seems the National Guard air-lifted out all the casualties, not just Jimmy and me."

"And like he said, you should be damn glad they were there. Things may have turned out differently, especially for Jimmy Wakefield."

"I know, I know. Must be I've been hanging out with too many cops lately. Coincidences are beginning to bother me."

Mac grinned. "You got a particular cop in mind?"

"This is serious business, MacPhearson."

"I know, I know." Mac's words echoed mine as his grin broadened to a smile.

"And don't make me laugh. It hurts my ribs."

Traffic was heavy with the noon hour rush of which Caroline had spoken.

"How about having lunch in town and stopping by the hardware store afterwards? I need some finer sandpaper to finish the repair job on the doorframes."

Thinking we could grab a quick lunch proved a pipe dream. Being flexible people, we chucked plan A, eat lunch, and adopted plan B, buy sandpaper.

The hardware store, except for the area showcasing Marty Shouldice's woodworking skills, had few customers. There, the aisles were crowded, and mingled voices called, "Did you see this?"

"This is just what I've been looking for."

"Wouldn't Mom just love this?"

I mingled with the tourists. Finding a set of bowls I knew would be just right for Grandma Wickie, I waved Mac away. He could pick out his sandpaper by himself. I picked up the set of matching bowls. Prize in hand, I headed for the counter.

MacPhearson was already there, deep in conversation with Deputy Myra Johnson, the two sharing an intimacy greater than their brief acquaintance should have allowed. "Is this a private conversation?" I asked, looking first at MacPhearson then at Deputy Johnson.

"I was just leaving," Myra Johnson said. Turning, she headed for the back of the store.

"Just checking on the tire casts she made the other day," Mac said. "You getting these bowls?" He took one and rubbed his fingers over the polished surface. "Marty Shouldice sure does fine work."

"Jealous?" I studied Mac's face. Was this a convenient twist in the conversation, or was Mac really interested in the wooden bowl?

"Jealous? Yes, I am. No matter how hard I tried, I'd never be any more than a carpenter. Marty Shouldice is a master craftsman."

"And Myra Johnson, is she a carpenter or a master craftsman?"

"If she's got what she says she has, I'd have to put her in the master class."

"The way you two were cozied up, one wouldn't think tire tracks."

Mac's blue eyes twinkled. "Jealous, Red?"

I felt my face redden. "Curious." I reclaimed the bowl Mac was holding and set the four on the counter. "And what did Deputy Johnson have to say about the tire tracks?"

Mac laughed. "That the Volvo sat at the edge of the drop-off before going over the edge."

I heard Mac's words but saw the Pine City deputy standing close, too close, beside him.

"Can I help you?" Betty Shouldice asked.

I pushed the thought aside and shoved the set of bowls across the counter. "I'd like these."

"And I'll take this sandpaper," Mac added.

"We were going to have lunch in town, but," I motioned to the front of the store, "couldn't find a place that didn't have standing room only."

"That's how it is at lunchtime around here, and that's not a complaint. My only suggestion is that you get something at Ardella's and take it home. Better still, how about having lunch with us?"

She paused to ring up the two sales. "We're getting things together to send to the human trafficking task force you told us about." Betty looked at Mac. "We could use your input."

"Oh, I don't think . . ." I started.

"Thank you for the invite, Mrs. Shouldice," Mac interrupted, "and yes, we'd like to join you for lunch."

Hoping I'd put the bottle of extra strength Tylenol in my shoulder bag, I pushed my aches and pains to the back of my mind. Though I wondered why Mac had overridden my refusal and accepted the invitation, I said nothing. Curiosity may have killed the cat but satisfaction brought it back. Close on Mac's heels, I began to purr.

We followed Betty Shouldice to the back of the store, to a room filled with sunlight that streamed through a set of French doors. A large oval table dominated the center, and cabinets along with a stove and refrigerator lined the remaining walls. More than a kitchen, it was a showcase for Marty Shouldice's carpentry skills.

"Take any chair you like," Betty Shouldice said. "Father Mike's bringing the sandwiches, and there's potato soup warming on the stove."

"And where would you like these sandwiches, Betty?" the priest asked, coming through the door. "Ardella says there's ham, turkey, and salami along with extra condiments if anyone wants more. She also said to tell you that the morning catch was extra good today. Those fishermen must have been at it early. Brought in perch, bluegill, Northern pike and some walleye."

"You take up advertising in your spare time, Father?" Betty laughed. "Just put the sandwiches on the counter by the soup bowls. I'm serving buffet style."

"We're all here except the doc," Marty Shouldice said, "so how about we get started. Father Mike, will you say the blessing?"

We paused as the priest led us in prayer, and after helping ourselves to the soup and sandwiches, Father Mike and Myra Johnson, the Shouldices, Mac and I settled around the table.

"Glad you two happened by," Father Mike said, wiping a dribble of soup from his chin. "We're reviewing the report on our missing girls. I talked to Lieutenant Rhodes as you suggested, Mac, and he said it sounded like something the task force would be interested in hearing more about. Since I have to be in Marion City for a meeting with the bishop tomorrow, I thought I'd hand-deliver the report. I want to be there in case they have any questions."

Mac nodded. "Sounds like a good idea, Father."

"Sorry I'm late." Jim Wacker strode into the room. "Either I'm seeing more patients than usual or I'm getting slower," he said, helping himself from the buffet. "Ardella make these?" The doctor took a bite from the sandwich he held in his hand. "That lady sure makes a damn fine sandwich."

The doctor pulled a chair away from the table and sat down. "Quite a group you have here, Father."

Father Mike nodded his thanks. "I asked us all here so we could go over the report the Marion City task force asked for. Seeing it's your idea, Mac," the priest looked in MacPhearson's direction, "how about telling us if we missed anything?"

Mac nodded he would.

"Then how about I start." Betty Shouldice set a tray of coffee mugs on the table. "I drove Cindy out to the Whiting farm about four the afternoon before the girls were supposed to leave. We went directly to the Leggit place. Josie was there. I didn't see Rita, or anyone else for that matter."

"How about phone calls? Did Cindy call you that night or in the morning?" Father Mike asked.

Betty mopped a tear from the corner of her eye. "Cindy called me the next morning. Said Mrs. Whiting was taking them into town because Rita had to drive a couple of the workers to Cadillac."

"Anything unusual about that?" Mac asked.

"Not unusual," Betty said, "but she didn't do it very often. Usually just tended to things around the Whiting house."

"With a place as big as that, you'd think Mrs. Whiting would have enough to do without working outside the home," I said, voicing an earlier observation.

Jim Wacker laughed. "Staying home is not Caroline's thing. Soon as their kids were in school, she found herself a job."

"The Whitings like to keep track of what's going on," Myra Johnson offered. "Working in the sheriff's office gave Mrs. Whiting ample opportunity to do that."

"Can't think of a better information source," Marty Shouldice agreed.

Father Mike rapped his knuckle on the table. "Time's getting away from us, folks. Myra, let's hear what you have to say."

The deputy propped an elbow on the table and leaned forward. "That trip to Cadillac must have been a last minute thing. Caroline Whiting knew Rita had to have the girls at school by seven-thirty as the buses were scheduled to leave at eight."

"And did they leave at eight?" Mac asked.

Myra nodded. "There were three buses, each full of overexcited kids, chaperones, and enough luggage to sink a battleship."

"There must have been a lot of confusion," I said, picturing buses, kids, and assorted adults.

"There was. I was there checking on a couple of last minute runny noses. That's probably why no one missed the girls," Jim Wacker said.

A heavy silence descended on the group, broken by Father Mike's "You questioned Caroline Whiting, Myra. How about filling us in on what went on after Rita Leggit left for Cadillac."

Myra stared into her coffee mug. "Caroline took the girls into town. Said it wasn't a problem as she was going into town anyway."

"But she didn't drop them off at school," I said.

"No." Myra Johnson shook her head. "The girls wanted to be dropped off at the convenience store. Said they had a couple of things they needed to pick up."

"I find that hard to believe," Betty Shouldice said. "Those two had been shopping and packing and shopping and packing for the better part of a month."

"And that's the last Caroline Whiting saw of the girls?" I asked.

"That's what she said," Myra answered.

"And you questioned the people at the convenience store?" Mac asked, looking at the deputy.

"More times than I care to count," Myra said. "Nobody, and I mean nobody, remembers seeing the girls at the store."

"How did they get from the convenience store to the school?" Mac asked.

"Caroline said they planned on walking. The store is only a block from school," Myra answered.

"If both girls had backpacks and duffle bags," I said, looking around the table, "wasn't that a lot to carry even if it was only a block?"

"I did question Mrs. Whiting about that. She said she offered to wait, but the girls insisted on walking. She thought they may have wanted to change clothes or maybe put on more make-up."

"Much as I would like to think Cindy wouldn't do such a thing," Betty let out a long sigh, "I'm not naive enough to think she wouldn't."

Jim Wacker thumped his empty coffee mug on the table. "So, whatever happened, happened at the convenience store."

Chapter Twenty-Nine

Myra Johnson set out a plate of what smelled suspiciously like fresh-baked chocolate chip cookies. "Here's my contribution to today's lunch," she said, breaking the silence that followed the doctor's words.

"And a fine contribution it is," Father Mike said. He took a bite, savoring the taste. "Now, tell us what Rita Leggit had to say when you interviewed her."

"Not much, other than she drove to Cadillac that morning," the Pine County deputy answered.

"Did she say who sent her?" I asked.

Myra brushed cookie crumbs from her fingers. "She said it was Caroline Whiting."

"I thought Sam Leggit or Roger Whiting usually made the arrangements for the migrants," Marty Shouldice said.

Myra shook her head. "I didn't get into that. Just checked to see who fed the girls breakfast and who drove them into town."

"What time did Mrs. Leggit leave the farm?" Mac asked.

Father Mike ran his finger down the paper that lay on the table in front of him. "According to your report, Myra, Rita left the Whiting farm with the migrants about five-thirty."

"Isn't that early?" I said.

"The workers were scheduled for the morning shift. Takes over an hour to get to Cadillac from the Whitings'," Myra said.

"Did Caroline make breakfast at the Leggits'?" I asked.

Myra shook her head. "Rita dropped the girls off at the Whitings'. The last time she saw either her daughter or Cindy Shouldice, the two were drinking hot chocolate in Caroline Whiting's kitchen, and Caroline was making pancakes."

I pictured the scene, two girls talking excitedly about the upcoming field trip, a mother wishing she could share these moments with her daughter, and Mrs. Whiting flipping pancakes on a hot griddle. My stomach knotted. What was wrong with the picture? Was it that I already knew what the future held?

"I have the medical records you suggested we include with the report, Mac." Jim Wacker handed a large envelope across the table to Father Mike. "If the task force needs anything more, tell them to give me a call."

True to form, Wacker began cleaning up the table.

"Have you heard anything more about Rita Leggit?" I asked.

Jim Wacker stopped shuffling dirty bowls, paper plates, and napkins and looked at me. His expression told me more than his words. "Rita's not doing well, Ginny, not well at all."

I rested a hand on his arm. "I'm so sorry," I said.

"Aren't we all," Jim Wacker said. "Aren't we all."

"What do you think, Mac? Have I got everything the task force will need?" Father Mike asked.

Mac moved to stand beside Father Mike. He scanned the reports, then fingered through the papers on the table. "Everything looks good, and I'm glad to see Wacker got you the medical report."

"Thanks for suggesting it, Mac. Much as we don't want to think about it, there's always the possibility of having to identify a body." Father Mike ran chubby fingers over his face. "Sometimes the answer to our prayers isn't the answer we want."

"Amen," I heard Jim Wacker say.

"Is it just you or will the other priests in your group be meeting with Lieutenant Rhodes?" I asked.

"There'll be three of us. Between us we've identified five missing teenagers, all girls, who fit the profile Mac suggested." Father Mike looked from me to Mac. "Unfortunately from what Lieutenant Rhodes told me, I gather our five are not even a drop in the bucket."

"I see you have a copy of the police report." Surprise sounded in Mac's voice as he looked through the file. "Duncan pulled out all the stops on this one, county deputies, the state troopers, and the National Guard."

"But they never found them," I murmured.

"They never found them, not a trace, nothing. It was as if they had vanished from the face of the earth," Father Mike said.

He tidied the papers and slid them into a briefcase. "Let's hope the task force has better luck." He waved good-bye and headed for the door.

I looked across the table at Myra Johnson. "Your cookies sure didn't last long," I said.

"Glad they didn't. My waistline can't take too many." She brushed crumbs from the table, catching them on a paper plate. "Did MacPhearson tell you about the tire casts?"

"He did," I said. "Any idea how long the car sat there?"

"Can't say, but the impressions near the edge were definitely deeper than those leading up to the edge. Temperatures got into the forties the day before the accident. Thawed the ground some, not much, but enough."

"And the tracks leading up to the edge?"

"Hardly broke the surface," Myra said.

"What about the footprints?" Mac, who had moved to our end of the table, asked.

"Lots and lots and lots. Norm Schmidt was first on the scene, and along with the tire tracks, he did preserve the footprints he made going to and coming from the edge of the cliff."

"Did you notice anything special?"

Myra Johnson shook her head. "Too much overlapping."

Doing my best to hide my disappointment, I asked, "Where do you go from here?"

Johnson looked from Mac to me. "I guess we need to find out where Maggie did her drinking and who she did it with."

We followed the Pine County deputy from the hardware store, pausing to ask Jim Wacker about Jimmy Wakefield.

"Rumor is he's going home tomorrow, so I'd say he's coming along just fine."

"Then it's okay if we stop by to see him this afternoon?" I asked.

"He'll be glad for the company. Being confined to a hospital bed is not Jimmy's thing."

"Surely his friends have been visiting him," I said.

The doctor laughed. "So many and so often, his doctors have written a no visitors order."

"That must cramp his style," Mac said, "especially if it includes that pretty little girlfriend of his."

"It does, but those twins have figured a way to smuggle Deb in."

Doc Wacker and Mac both laughed. I tried, but didn't quite succeed.

"Ribs giving you trouble, Ginny?" Jim Wacker asked.

"Not too bad."

"Don't believe a thing she says, Doc. She's popping Tylenol on the side, and who knows what else."

"How much are you taking, Ginny?" Jim asked in his doctor voice.

"I took a couple at lunch, but I hadn't had any since breakfast."

"And the headache, how is that? Any blurred or double vision? Are you dizzy?"

"Slow down, Doc. The Tylenol's taking care of the headache. And those other things you mentioned? I don't have any." Mentally, I crossed my fingers. I had admitted to the headache, but admitting to being dizzy might put me back in the hospital.

Wacker frowned, enhancing his doctor look. "Mac says you lie a lot."

"Not about my head," I said.

Mac snorted.

"Are you insinuating?" I shot back.

"You two keep that up, and I'll put you back in the hospital, Miss Arthur, and send your friend here back to Marion City." Wacker's laugh lessened the threat his words posed. "Go see Jimmy Wakefield. He can do with some cheering up."

I watched the doctor's retreating back. It was a slow retreat, as many Pine City residents used the chance meeting to consult with the town's only physician.

"Want some fish?" I asked.

Mac gave me a puzzled look.

"You know, those scaly things that swim under the ice?"

"Get in the car, Red. Those things that swim under the ice will keep until after we visit Jimmy."

Bypassing the receptionist, we headed into the surgical wing and down the hall that led to Jimmy Wakefield's room.

I tapped on Jimmy's door, which was open a crack, then pushed it wide. "Hope you're decent, Mr. Wakefield, because you've got company."

The look of surprise on the young man's face changed to one of pleasure. "How did you get in? The nurses said I couldn't have any visitors."

"We snuck in when their backs were turned," Mac said.

"You're looking better today," I said, grabbing the lounger Mac was eyeing.

Settling back, I listened to Jimmy and Mac chit-chat about hospital food (bad), the weather (cold but sunny), and the possibility of Jimmy going home tomorrow (a maybe).

"Only I have to go home in a wheelchair. Fat lot of fun that's going to be."

Mac laughed as the boy described his hapless plight. "I would think anything's better than being in the hospital," he said.

"Oh, home's better than the hospital, but I'm not too sure about the wheelchair."

Jimmy gave the two of us another baleful look. "I had all the songs picked out for the dance this weekend. Deb even has a new dress."

"There's always the wheelchair tango," Mac suggested.

Jimmy looked puzzled. "A wheelchair tango?"

"You know. You just sit there and do a little wiggle." Mac did a shimmy and shake.

The teenager seemed to consider the idea. "Think Deb will go for it?"

"You can always try it out and see," Mac said.

"What do you remember about the snowmobiles that ran us off the hill?" I asked, changing the subject to a topic higher on my priority list.

"Not much really. Everything happened so fast," Jimmy said.

"Start from when you first saw the snowmobiles," Mac suggested.

Jimmy screwed up his face. Did he really think making like a prune made it easier to remember? Must be it did, for his eyes widened, and he started to talk.

"There were three . . ."

I picked up on the "three." Memory had not failed me; there had been a third snowmobile.

Jimmy continued his narrative, telling a story that was, by now, all too familiar.

"Did you recognize the drivers?" Mac asked.

Jimmy shook his head. "They all wore helmets and ski masks. I wouldn't have recognized my dad if he had been one of them."

"Okay, let's think about the snowmobiles. Can you remember anything about the one that ran you over the edge? Color? Make? Dents or scratches?" Mac said.

"I never thought about the snowmobiles. Sheriff Duncan kept asking about the drivers, but now that you ask me about the snowmobiles, there was something different about the one that came at me."

Mac and I waited as Jimmy did another of his prune imitations. Only this time it didn't work.

"Don't push it, Jimmy, but if you think of anything, let us know." Mac pulled a card from his wallet. "Here's my cell number. Call me if anything comes to mind."

Behind us the door opened.

"Hi, Mom," Jimmy said.

Tears welled in the woman's eyes. "I just heard," she said. "Rita Leggit died this afternoon."

Chapter Thirty

Sarah Frazier? Maggie Schmidt? Rita Leggit? My vision blurred, and the room tilted. I sank deeper into the chair.

"Are you okay?" Mac asked. He looked from me to Eve Wakefield, seemingly uncertain as to which of us he should direct his question. Being as I was already seated, Mac took hold of Mrs. Wakefield's arm and eased her into the other chair.

"I talked to Doctor Wacker in the hall." The woman's voice broke. "Rita was such a good woman. First Josie and now this. Poor Sam, how will he ever bear it?"

Doc Wacker came through the door, his voice sounding over Eve Wakefield's sobs. "He will, Eve. Sam Leggit's a strong man."

The doctor looked at Jimmy. Like his mother's, the boy's face was wet with tears. "How are you doing, son?"

Jimmy reached for a handful of tissues. "Fine, sir," he answered. "The doctors say I can go home tomorrow."

"Well, that's good news, and we can sure use some of that around here."

Wacker gave me a critical look. "And I suggest you go home and get in bed, Miss Arthur, and if you don't, I'll find you a bed in the hospital."

Knowing it was futile to argue, I started to rise from the chair and found my self-appointed bodyguard close at hand.

"No need to find a bed, Doc." Holding tight to my arm, Mac-Phearson led me from the room.

"You don't have to . . ." I protested.

"Cool it, Red," Mac said, pulling the door shut behind us.

Conversation was nonexistent as we left the parking lot, and sparse until we reached the highway.

"Still dizzy?" Mac asked.

I shook my head, but said nothing. My mind was an empty vessel. Another death was more than a body, at least this body, could bear.

I leaned against the headrest. "We forgot the fish," I said.

"Tonight you get chicken soup," Mac said, pulling into the drive that led to the cabin.

As fate would have it, we had neither.

Mac activated the remote. The door groaned upward, and we rolled between Mac's pickup and the snowmobiles.

I swung open the passenger door and levered myself from the car. My aching muscles, like the closing garage door, groaned a protest. The thought of a hot shower or perhaps a long soak in the hot tub lured me forward.

Ahead of me, Mac unlocked the cabin door and pushed it open. Focused on the curative powers of hot water, I failed to stop when he stopped and ran full tilt into his ramrod-stiff back.

"What the hell!" he said.

I massaged my bruised nose. "Wh . . . what?" I stammered.

"Call Sheriff Duncan, Ginny, and stay out here. Someone paid us a visit while we were gone."

Responding more to his tone of voice than his words, I reached for my cell phone and punched in the emergency number. Mac pushed the door to behind him. Reflexively, I held out my arm to prevent the door from closing as I waited through an unfamiliar dispatcher's, "Pine County Sheriff's Department, how may I help you?" message.

Having caught a glimpse of what lay behind the partially closed door, I said, "This is Ginny Arthur. I'm calling from the Marfield cabin on Big Pine Lake. There's been a break-in. Detective MacPhearson is checking out the crime scene and is requesting back-up."

At the dispatcher's request, I repeated what I had said. Receiving the assurance that help was on the way, I followed Mac into the cabin.

The echoing sound of MacPhearson's expletives did not prepare me for the scene that met my eyes. Chairs were overturned, drawers open, and their contents strewn about the floor. The door to the laundry room stood open.

Unsure of what I might find, I moved cautiously across the littered floor, announcing my presence as I went. The meows grew louder as I entered the laundry room and grew to a crescendo when I knelt before the travel cage. Behind the half open wire door, Zeus's and Hera's blue eyes indicated their readiness to either protect their territory or flee from danger.

Responding to my solicitous overtures, the pair left the relative safety of their cage to twine themselves around my legs. Satisfied I was friend and not foe, they retreated into the carrying cage and nestled into a pile of feathers.

"I told you to stay in the garage."

I rose to meet what I knew would be an accusatory look. I wasn't disappointed. I offered no excuses, as I knew Mac would accept none.

"They okay?" He nodded to the pair in the cage.

"Fine." I waited for him to say something—anything. Mac said nothing.

"Well?"

Mac shrugged. "If you're about to ask about the rest of the house, it looks just like what you see here."

"Anybody?"

"Whoever was here is gone."

"But why . . ."

Bang! Bang! Someone was at the door.

The someone was Deputy Norman Schmidt, who, like a bad penny, kept turning up.

"Got a call from the dispatcher. Said you reported a break-in." Schmidt moved to the center of the room. Hand resting on his holstered gun, he surveyed the surrounding area. "This is how you found it?"

I was tempted to say no but knew now was not the time for levity.

Mac's sentiments did not mirror mine. "We found it like this," he said with exaggerated nonchalance.

Schmidt's jaw tightened. "You check the rest of the house?"

Mac nodded.

"Any sign of an intruder?" Schmidt asked

And did he think we'd be standing here if there was? I thought.

Patience personified, Mac answered with another shake of his head.

"Mind if I have a look around?" Schmidt asked.

Mac waved him forward, and as if anxious to rid himself of our company, the deputy pounded up the stairs. Finding the sudden noise disturbing, the cats uttered a raucous cry.

"Will he find anything?" I asked.

"Maybe how the intruder or intruders, which seems more likely, gained entry. I didn't check, just made sure they weren't still here," Mac said.

"They?" I asked

"One person could have done all of this, but from the looks of things, I'm guessing there was more than one."

I thought of the two from the motel bar, the men in the snowmobiles. Could it have been them? I dismissed the thought. Jumping to conclusions was not a good idea.

"Anything missing?" I asked.

Mac shrugged. "Hard to tell." He looked around. "Anything missing down here?"

"Hard to tell."

Another bang bang, and an authoritative "I'll get it" from Norm Schmidt, killed what little there was of our conversation.

A rush of cold air and dimming sensor lights ushered Sheriff Duncan into the cabin. Side by side, the pair of red-jacketed officers moved toward us.

"What have we got here?" Duncan surveyed the room as he spoke.

"An apparent break-in from the looks of it," Schmidt said.

"Anything missing?" Duncan looked from me to MacPhearson.

"Haven't had time to look around," I said.

"Nor should you have," Duncan said. He fixed on MacPhearson. "I'm assuming the same doesn't apply to you?"

"I did look around," Mac said, "but only to see if whoever did this was still here."

"And?" Duncan prompted.

"Nobody here, Sheriff," Schmidt answered. "I checked as soon as I arrived on the scene."

"Any idea how the intruder gained entry?" Duncan looked from MacPhearson to Schmidt.

"Couldn't tell from my initial walk-through," Schmidt answered.

"Same here," Mac admitted.

Duncan nodded. "Get hold of Bryant and Johnson, Norm. Tell them to get out here." Duncan looked at us. "When they get through, the two of you will need to take a look and see what's missing."

The cats yowled.

"Should have guessed those two would still be here." Duncan glanced toward the laundry room. "You might as well collect them. It's another night at Braun's Motel for all of you."

This time I left without so much as a toothbrush. The inconvenience did not extend to the cats.

As Mac readied the traveling cage for transport, Duncan handed me a can of cat food. "Don't want these two disturbing the guests. Linda would have my hide."

"Any idea who may have done this?" I fitted the halves of my jacket zipper together and pulled up the tab.

"Probably kids looking for something with resale value," Duncan said.

I pointed to the television and stereo system; though no longer in their usual place, the component parts seemed to be all there.

"That's portable and easy to get rid of," I said, debunking his theory.

Duncan shrugged. "You asked for a reason. I gave you a reason."

"Schmidt sure got here fast," Mac said, as we headed for the door.

"That's what he's paid to do, get to the crime scene in a timely manner."

MacPhearson stared at the Pine County Sheriff. "I understand he was also the first on the scene of his sister's accident."

"Not surprising, this is Schmidt's beat. That is what you big city cops call it, isn't it?"

"It was you who came the night I found the body in the freezer," I said.

"And so I did, Miss Arthur, but I wasn't responding to a 911 call."

It was full dark when we left the cabin. The Honda's headlights raced ahead, punching holes in the night.

I fiddled with the radio. Music blared from the speakers, and I adjusted the volume.

"Is the break-in related to the disappearance of the two girls, one or all of the three deaths, or the attack of the snowmobiles on Little Pine Lake?"

My words were a statement meant for speculation, which Mac proceeded to do.

"So how about we put them in order," he said.

"First the girls disappeared," I began. "Then I found Sarah Frazier's body in the freezer . . ."

"Enter Sheriff Duncan," Mac interrupted.

"Enter Sheriff Duncan," I repeated. "Then Maggie Schmidt takes a nosedive off the cliff . . ."

"After leaving the cabin," Mac interjected.

"Then Rita Leggit gets shot as she's leaving the cabin and later dies from her wounds," I said.

"Then the snowmobiles run you over, and now the break-in," Mac finished.

He negotiated a sweeping curve. Ahead the lights of the Braun Motel glowed in the dark. Inside the Honda Mac's cell phone trilled.

Chapter Thirty-One

Mac checked the caller ID, flipped up the cover plate, and sounded a cheery, "Hello, Jimmy, what's up?"

Making sense of a one-sided conversation is difficult. Making sense of Mac's grunts, okays, and a couple of are you sures was impossible.

"Jimmy said there was a dent along the side of the snowmobile that ran him off the cliff," Mac said when he broke the connection.

We made a second circle of the parking lot.

"Does he know who owns it?"

"So far he only remembers the dent."

A car pulled out, and Mac slid the Honda into the empty space. "Is there something special going on around here we don't know about?"

Though I was unable to answer Mac's question, the twins eagerly filled our knowledge void.

"Valentine week is always busy," Kim said.

"Mom likes it when we're busy," Deb added.

"She must really miss not having Maggie here. I hear she could almost run the bar and restaurant single-handed," Mac said.

A shadow passed over the girls' faces. "She could, and even with the extra help from Mr. Whiting's migrants, it just isn't the same," Deb said.

"Did you bring Zeus and Hera?" Kim asked.

Mac swung the cats' traveling cage into view.

"Sounds like you're more anxious to see those two than either Mac or me," I chided.

"Oh, no," the pair chorused.

"Why haven't you two got Ginny and Mac settled?" Linda Braun called from the doorway.

"I've got your key cards," Deb said, hurrying from behind the registration desk.

"Sheriff Duncan called, said you would need a couple of rooms," Linda explained. "They're connecting. Is that okay?"

"Fine," Mac and I said in unison. Were we spending too much time with the twins?

We turned to follow the girls, but turned back as Linda continued with "Rick told me about Rita. I feel so sorry for Sam. First his daughter and now his wife. Will this madness never end?"

Linda massaged her forehead with a thumb and forefinger. "I haven't told the girls. After what happened at Little Pine Lake, I thought I'd wait." Linda made a shooing motion. "You'd better follow the girls; they'll be back here looking for you if you don't."

It took the pair to get us to our rooms, one holding the electronic key cards and the other the cats' carrying cage.

"You're in here, Detective MacPhearson." Deb unlocked the motel room door and turned on the lights.

"And you're in here, Ginny," Kim said, opening the connecting doors. "Should I put the cats in with you?"

I agreed she should and followed Kim into the next room. Deb, talking all the while, followed after us.

"You and Detective MacPhearson are coming to the dance, aren't you?" Deb flopped belly down on the queen size bed. "We're getting off school early on Friday to decorate. If you want, I can add your names to the list of volunteers."

The twin flipped over and propped herself against the headboard.

"They used to have a live band," Deb continued, without waiting for an answer, "but that was way before our time. All I remember is the DJ. He's real good and plays all sorts of music, so there's sure to be something you and Detective MacPhearson can dance to."

"Want me to let the cats out of their cage, Ginny?" Kim asked.

"Of course, I won't be doing much dancing, what with Jimmy in a wheelchair, and me with a new dress." The corners of Deb's mouth drooped. "But the doctor said he can go to the dance, so we'll at least get to listen to the music," the girl ended on a brighter note, a note which faded with her next words.

"Jimmy told me about Rita Leggit," she said. "I don't think Mom knows, unless Sheriff Duncan told her. Kim and I thought we'd wait until the bar settled down."

I looked at Deb's young/old face. Would I have a daughter like her one day? I wondered.

"Should I put the cat's cage in the bathroom?" Kim asked.

I covered my ears. "One thing at a time," I pleaded.

"You are going to the dance?" Deb pushed away from the pillows, a worried look on her face.

"What about the cats?" Kim demanded.

Behind me, I heard Mac laugh. It was too much. "Yes, you can let the cats out, and yes, you can put their cage in the bathroom, and yes, we'll probably go to the dance, but I need to check with Detective MacPhearson first."

Deb scrambled off the bed. "Let's ask him now, Ginny." The girl turned her attention to MacPhearson. "You are going to the dance, aren't you?"

"Do I have a choice?"

"If you don't, you'll be the only one in town who isn't going," Kim said, adding fuel to her sister's argument.

"Go, go," I cried, "and if you don't, the answer is a definite no."

Except for Deb's parting shot, "Don't forget you're decorating the hall on Friday," this last did the trick, and the pair hurried from the room.

"Reminds me of home," Mac said.

For a moment I envied the large family in which Mac had been raised. My parents had been killed in an automobile accident when

I was a toddler, and it was Grandma Wickie and Uncle David who had raised me. Now there was only Grandma Wickie.

I wrapped my fingers around the silver unicorn that hid among the feathers in my pocket. "Uncle David," I sighed. "Where are you?"

I had a bowl of soup and Mac a sandwich in the bar. As late as it was, the lounge was filled to near capacity. Along with Roger Whiting's migrant workers, Linda Braun and Ted Williams, Juan and Rosa Torres shared the late-evening workload.

Rosa, who admittedly was not a waitress, had taken on the chores of short order cook, while Ted Williams was helping Linda behind the bar. Juan Torres, wrapped around with a too-big apron, bussed tables. A cosmopolitan crew, they had evolved into a well-oiled machine.

"Those two men sitting over there," Mac pushed aside his empty plate and nodded toward a table at the far end of the room. "They look like the same two we saw when we were snowmobiling."

I started to turn but was caught midway by Mac's, "Don't turn around."

Sensing the cop mode, I pushed my napkin off my lap, twisting around as I bent to retrieve it.

"They are," I said, returning to upright. "I've seen them several times, here in the bar, out in the parking lot, and the other day when I was skiing."

Mac frowned. "And if I'm not mistaken, they're the same two Norm Schmidt was talking to the other day."

"And?"

"Nothing, just an observation."

I slept well that night. Mac had been adamant about the connecting doors being left open, but if I was a target, which both Mac and Sheriff Duncan insisted I was, this was not the time to argue.

We had a late breakfast in the kitchen, where Linda joined us for a midmorning coffee break. Despite his having worked late into the night, Ted Williams was also there, the rhythmic chop-chop of his knife against the cutting board blending pleasantly with other kitchen sounds.

"Quite a crowd you had last night," Mac said.

Linda agreed. "Being we're the only place in town open past midnight, we draw the tourist trade from the whole area."

Ted, who had interrupted his chopping to scramble eggs and fry sausages for our late breakfast, slid the plates in front of us.

"Are you usually this full during the middle of the week?" Mac looked at Linda over a forkful of eggs.

"Not usually, over the weekend, yes, but not during the middle of the week," Linda answered.

"The twins said it was because of the Valentine dance," I said.

Linda laughed. "The dance is a drawing card, but no matter how many dances we had, if we didn't have snow, we wouldn't have tourists."

"Must be hard to staff with the weather determining the number of tourists you may or may not have," Mac said.

"Fortunately, Roger Whiting has resolved that problem. Until he started keeping a few of the migrants here over the winter months, we were dependent on local help." Linda sipped from her coffee mug. "When local help is available, things work fine, but being it's both weather-dependent and seasonal, it just doesn't work for families who need a regular income."

"How long has Whiting been keeping workers over the winter?" I asked.

"About five or six years. It was just after Bob, my husband, left for his last tour of duty." Linda paused. "He and Roger used to sit up nights discussing the help situation. It was one of the things the two of them planned to tackle when Bob came home from Iraq."

Again Linda paused, and though she didn't say it, I sensed she was thinking, only he didn't come home.

My cell phone rang. I checked the caller ID. It was Sheriff Duncan.

"The Fraziers are in town," I said, after breaking the connection. "They want to see the cabin. I said we would meet them there after lunch, two or three o'clock. That should give us time to put the place back together."

We settled the bill, picked up Hera and Zeus, and were on the road within minutes.

We started in the great room and the kitchen area, where, surprisingly, nothing seemed to be missing, and had the cabin looking almost presentable when a knock sounded at the front door.

Mac played host, leaving me to finish wiping the last of the fingerprint powder from the kitchen cabinets. The door opened, and I heard their voices, first Mac's, then another, deeper pitched than Mac's. It was the third voice, a woman's voice, that caught my attention. Had I not known, I would have sworn Maggie Schmidt was in the cabin. The closing door almost, but not quite, muffled a fourth voice, Norm Schmidt's.

Leaving behind several smudged fingerprints, I walked to the stairs and looked over the railing. Mac and our three guests stood clustered before the fireplace. Mac, still playing host, motioned for them to be seated, while Deputy Schmidt made the introductions.

"This is my sister, Angie, and her husband, Len Frazier," he said. "They'd like to talk to Miss Arthur about their daughter, Sarah."

"And my sister Maggie," Angie Frazier said in what I had to stop thinking of as the dead woman's voice.

I hurried down the stairs. "I'm Ginny Arthur," I said, extending my hand.

Besides sounding like Maggie Schmidt, the woman who took my hand had the same gray hair, lined face, and slender build as her sister, and when she released it, I noticed too that her bony fingers had the same nervous flutter.

"I'm Len Frazier, Miss Arthur." Not as gray-haired as his wife, the man had the weather-worn face I suspected endemic to Michigan's northern population. Though not tall, the man's presence dominated the room.

Chapter Thirty-Two

There were no takers to Mac's offer of coffee or beer. Just a general shuffling as our guests settled into chairs and couches. It came as no surprise when Angie chose the ill-fated Maggie chair.

As before, I allowed superstition to reign and settled into another of the armchairs.

Mac pulled a straight-backed chair from across the room and slid in beside me. He neither lit the fire nor made another offer of drinks.

Angie Frazier opened the conversation in Maggie Schmidt's soft, halting voice. "I hear you found our daughter's body, Miss Arthur."

"I did." I did not point to the laundry room where the ill-used freezer had once stood. Surely her brother or Sheriff Duncan would have told the parents the grizzly details. Len Frazier's next words told me someone had.

"I understand you found Sarah's body in a freezer." He looked around the room.

"Sheriff Duncan had it hauled away, Len, but if you want to see it, I'm sure Duncan won't object," Schmidt said.

"I don't think we need to, Norm," Angie Frazier said hesitantly.

"Norm tells us you were the last one to see Maggie alive, Miss Arthur, that she visited you here the night she died," Len said, changing the subject from daughter to sister-in-law.

"Ginny and I were both here," Mac corrected. "Have either of you talked with the sheriff or with Doctor Wacker?" he asked.

"We talked to Doctor Wacker. He showed us Sarah's body. Said she died from a blow to the head. That she was pregnant when she died." Len Frazier looked from Mac to me, his voice flat, as if reading a list of nutrients on a box of cereal. "And we know Maggie was killed when her car went off the cliff and hit the ice on the lake."

"They think the Volvo stopped at the edge of the cliff. That it sat there," Norm Schmidt added.

"I don't understand," Angie Frazier said. "Are you saying Maggie drove to the edge, then just sat there? In the car? Waiting?"

"Not me, Angie. It's what the evidence tells us." Schmidt's fingers picked the edges of his jacket. "There's some around here who think Maggie's death might even be a homicide," the deputy finished.

Angie gasped. "Murdered? Both of them?" Tears fell from the woman's eyes, and her fluttering hands stifled a keening wail.

"Angie," Len Frazier admonished. "Murder, suicide, accident. Whatever, it's up to the sheriff to figure it out."

Angie's shoulders sagged. Her mouth opened, then closed.

"What we really want to know, Miss Arthur," Len Frazier continued, "is whether or not Maggie talked to Sarah before she died. Did Sarah tell her who the father of the baby was? Did she say why she left home?"

The mother looked at me through tear-filled eyes. "Please, Miss Arthur, if Maggie said anything at all to you about Sarah . . . anything at all."

"Only that she talked to Sarah on the phone. Sarah was supposed to call when she got to Pine City, but Maggie said she never called."

"Maggie told you this?" Angie asked.

"She did."

"Sarah didn't say anything to Maggie about being pregnant? Why she left Rocky Ridge?" Len Frazier persisted.

"If she did, Maggie didn't tell us," Mac said.

Norm Schmidt cleared his throat. "I didn't know Sarah was coming to Pine City, or that the two of them had made arrangements to meet."

"How about Maggie's boyfriend? Williams, isn't it?" Len Frazier asked, turning to the deputy.

"Ted Williams said he knew Sarah was coming and that Maggie had planned to meet with her," Schmidt said, fiddling with the zipper on his jacket. Were the man's hands never still?

"You talked to this Ted Williams?" Len Frazier asked. "Did he say where Sarah and Maggie planned to meet? Was it here, in this cabin?"

The deputy shook his head. "I didn't talk to Ted Williams. What I told you I got from Sheriff Duncan's report."

Len Frazier stared at his brother-in-law for what seemed an over-long moment.

"If you want," Schmidt said, "we can go by and talk to him." He brushed at a couple of feathers that fell from his jacket.

Len Frazier seemed to consider the offer, then shook his head. "Not now," he said. "Maybe later."

Frazier rose to his feet. "We've taken enough of your time." He extended his hand to Mac. "Thank you for letting us visit."

Angie Frazier pulled her coat around her, picked up her purse, and slid to the edge of the Maggie chair.

Her face was still wet with tears, and she had difficulty speaking. I wrapped my arms around her and hugged her tight. It was the only positive thing that came from the meeting.

Hera jumped into my lap and shoved her face hard against my neck. "What's the matter, cat?" I asked.

Hera yowled her answer, leaving her meaning open to interpretation. Mac, on the other hand, spoke a language I did understand.

"Strange how they kept asking about the baby's father," he said. "Being they come from such a small community, learning who his daughter was seeing shouldn't be all that difficult."

"Rocky Ridge," I said, "the place where everyone can do what he wants to do when and how he wants to do it."

Mac nodded as if in agreement, but said nothing.

Hera continued to butt my neck.

"What do you want, cat?" I held the protesting feline at arm's length.

Hera wiggled free, hit the floor on four paws, and swished her upright tail.

I trailed the cat to the laundry room. Both food and water dishes were empty. Surprisingly, this did not seem to bother Zeus, who lay curled inside the traveling cage.

"You too lazy to ask for your dinner?" Like any self-respecting Siamese, Zeus ignored me.

I fed and watered the cats, then returned to the great room. Mac was still sitting on the straight-backed chair. "That Frazier's one cold fish," he said, picking up our conversation where it had been interrupted.

"Either Norm Schmidt or Sheriff Duncan could have answered their questions," I said.

"Oh, I'm sure Frazier talked to both his brother-in-law and the sheriff."

"Then why come here?" I resettled myself in the armchair. "If it wasn't for his being a couple of hundred miles north of here, I'd suggest he might be revisiting the scene of the crime."

"Did you get the feeling Norm Schmidt was somewhat intimidated by his brother-in-law?" Mac said, ignoring my comment.

I remembered the deputy's constantly moving fingers, his apologetic answers to Len Frazier's questions. "You might be right."

I propped a pillow behind my back and listened as the conversation replayed itself inside my head. "Do you think Maggie may have committed suicide?" I asked, freeing the thought from a jumble of words.

"It's a possibility." Mac clasped his hands behind his head, stretched long, and crossed his ankles. "She could have driven to the edge of the embankment, unfastened her seatbelt to get comfortable, and drank her bottle of whiskey."

"And when she was drunk enough, drove off the edge," I finished.

Mac leaned forward, uncrossed his ankles, and rested his elbows on his knees. "Could have happened that way. Only according to Doc Wacker, her blood alcohol level doesn't support that scenario."

Mac gave up his chair and bent to light the fire. "What say we finish cleaning up this mess and see if we can discover what it was our intruders were looking for?"

Which is what we did, the "clean up the mess" part. What it was the intruders were looking for proved to be more elusive. So much so, we gave up looking and spent what remained of the day soaking in the hot tub.

Splashing shafts of yellow over the ice-covered lake, the sun seemed more to "settle" than to "set." Giving in to the lethargy spreading through me, I sank deeper into the hot tub.

"Time to get out." Mac stood and grabbed his towel. "Beat you inside," he said.

I ignored the challenge, reluctant to face the cold cruel world that waited outside the tub.

Mac's call, "We're about to get company," got me moving.

"Who's coming?" I asked, shivering inside the blanket in which I had wrapped myself.

"Father Mike," Mac said. "He called to say he would stop by to tell us about his trip to Marion City."

Mac's words lent wings to my feet. No way was I about to let the pastor of St. Paul's Church see me in a string bikini.

I rummaged through the closet and pulled out my last pair of clean jeans and a University of Michigan sweatshirt. A relic from my law school days, it was warm, baggy, and oh so very comfortable.

Coming up for air after foraging the depths of the closet, I was still missing a shoe. I surveyed the mess. Some of it was mine, but most was the result of the recent home invasion. Still searching for the missing shoe, I tossed my dirty clothes into a corner and, painful as it was, continued my hands-and-knees search of the closet. Finally I triumphed. The shoe was in the far reaches of the closet, where my laptop should have been but wasn't.

I shoved my stockinged foot into the missing sneaker and stood up. A quick look around the bedroom did not produce my computer.

Another fruitless trip into the closet and I was forced to admit, my computer was not in the bedroom.

Had I left it on the kitchen table? In either of the great rooms? I shook my head. I had not used the computer since coming to the cabin.

I ran a comb through my hair, dabbed some concealer on the worst of my bruises, touched my lips with gloss, and headed for the great room.

"Have you seen my laptop?" I said.

Mac, who was busy adding logs to the fire, looked up. "I was about to ask you the same question."

"Your computer is missing, too?" I sank to the couch. "It doesn't make sense. Why our computers and nothing else?"

"Sense or nonsense, they're both gone." Mac dusted tree bark from his hands. "I took a look in my truck. The files I brought with me are also missing."

I shook my head. "Any ideas, Detective?"

Mac urged the fire along with a blast of air from the bellows. "I'd say it wasn't things our uninvited guests were after, it was information."

"There's nothing on my laptop that could possibly be of interest to anyone but me."

"Same here, but whoever took the computers and my files doesn't know that."

Chapter Thirty-Three

THE SAVORY AROMA OF THE CASSEROLE CONVINCED the priest to stay for dinner.

"Didn't plan on being so late," he said, "but after Rita died . . . just couldn't bring myself to leave Sam alone."

"Does Sam have other family?" I asked over the clatter of dishes and silverware.

"None that I know of and no other children. Josie was their only child."

Conversation slowed to a trickle as we ate. Not until Mac had poured each of us a mug of coffee did Father Mike open the subject that was the reason for his visit.

"That Larry Rhodes is one sharp cop," the priest said with a grin. "Not only did he keep that task force meeting on track, he got more information out of my fellow priests than I have in all the years I've known them."

"The trip was worth it then?" Mac asked.

"In that it brought what we priests have long thought to be true to the attention of those who can do something about it, yes. Did it bring us any closer to finding our missing girls? Well, I'm not sure." Father Mike raised his hands in a hopeless gesture.

"How many of you met with Rhodes?" I asked.

"Three of us," Father Mike answered.

"All of you with reports of missing girls?" I asked.

Father Mike nodded. "Six of them. One from each of four other parishes and two from here."

Father Mike paused as if marshaling his thoughts. "Taken separately, the cases aren't all that special and, as Lieutenant Rhodes pointed out, kids go missing every day."

"And what makes your six special?" Mac asked.

"You hit the nail on the head the first time we talked about Josie Leggit and Cindy Shouldice, Mac. They don't fit what is euphemistically referred to as the 'profile.' " Father Mike made hooking motions with the index and middle fingers of both hands. "Except for what seems to be a universal complaint about computers and cell phones, these kids had no problems at school or at home."

For the first time since Father Mike had introduced the subject of the missing girls, he favored us with a smile. "The Holy Spirit does indeed work in strange ways," he said. "This time there's someone willing to be His hands and feet."

I returned Father Mike's smile, not because of its infectious quality but from the idea of Larry Rhodes being an agent of the Holy Spirit.

"I know our missing girls are not the only cases the task force is investigating," Father Mike said, "but hopefully this new information will give them something they can use to help catch whoever is responsible for their disappearance."

"Then Rhodes is definitely classifying these six as human trafficking victims?" I asked.

"That's the impression he gave."

Father Mike left soon after. Mac and I finished the kitchen cleanup and poured ourselves another cup of coffee, each with a dash of brandy, and settled before what was left of the fire.

"Do you think the task force will have any better luck in finding the girls than Sheriff Duncan?" I asked.

"Classifying them as human trafficking victims will help."

Mac sipped at his coffee. "The place to start is the beginning, and that means reviewing the material Father Mike put together for the task force."

"Too bad we don't have a copy."

"Oh, but we do." Mac grinned. "The file's laying on the back seat of your Honda. Father Mike gave me a set after the meeting at the hardware store."

Mac dropped the file in my lap. I had settled on one end of the couch and had cleared the coffee table of everything except our coffee mugs.

"How about you start." Mac moved to add another log to the fire. "You're a faster reader, and we only have one copy."

I did as bidden, sliding each sheet on the coffee table as I finished. I felt the couch sag under Mac's weight but didn't look up as I read through the sheriff's report that Myra Johnson had supplied. Next were Doctor Wacker's notes, along with each girl's medical history. Father Mike had added additional information on the family history, and the Leggits and Shouldices had supplied the girls' school records. Not just words on paper, the report breathed life into the two thirteen-year-olds.

Cindy, blonde and blue-eyed, favored her father rather than her mother, while Josie, though her hair was brown like her mother's, was a pleasing mix of both parents. I put aside the pictures and picked up Myra Johnson's report and turned to the statements made by Rita Leggit and Caroline Whiting. If there was a clue to the girls' disappearance, it had to be here.

I finished reading the women's statements and waited for Mac to finish.

"If they were snatched, it would most likely have been at the convenience store," Mac said, dropping the last of the sheets on the table.

"Not necessarily." I riffled through the pages, found the one I wanted, and handed it to Mac. "Anything strike you as odd about this?"

"Nothing leaps out at me," Mac said. He looked up from the page I'd handed him.

"It's that bit about Rita Leggit having to drive those migrant workers to Cadillac."

"Could be everyone else was busy," Mac suggested.

"But sending Rita Leggit to Cadillac the same day her daughter was leaving on a field trip, a planned field trip? On a day she had not one but two girls to get to school on time?"

"One, two, what difference does that make? Caroline Whiting was there to drive them to school." Mac gave me a quizzical look.

"It's a mother thing. Rita Leggit should have been the one to take Josie and Cindy to school, and Caroline Whiting should have been the one to drive the migrants to Cadillac."

Mac said nothing.

"And from all reports, Roger Whiting was mighty selective about who he trusted with his migrant laborers," I added.

"You're jumping to conclusions again, Red," Mac said.

"How about you jump to some conclusions of your own, Mr. Detective?" I snapped. "Isn't that what detectives are supposed to do, detect?"

"We need to look into the convenience store angle first," Mac said.

I jumped to my feet.

"Where are you going?" Mac demanded.

"To bed. It's late." I threw the pillow I had been clutching onto the couch.

"I take it you don't like the convenience store angle."

I sat on the edge of the coffee table, bumping knee to knee with MacPhearson. "The convenience store angle has been worked to death, Mac. Nobody saw the girls there. How do we know that Caroline Whiting even dropped the girls off at the convenience store? All anyone has is her word."

Mac stared at me so long I looked away.

"How are you feeling, Red? Ribs sore? Head hurt?" he asked softly.

"I'm fine," I said. Only I wasn't. I turned away, blinking back the tears that flooded my eyes.

"Look at me, Ginny," Mac said.

"No."

"Yes," Mac said, and pulled me toward him.

"No," I said, pushing against him.

"Relax, Red. I'm not going to bite."

"That's not what I'm afraid of."

"What are you afraid of?"

I was in his arms, held tight but not too tight against his chest. His chin rested on my head, and his hands moved up and down my back.

"Relax, Ginny. You've had a rough few days, and worrying about what may or may not have happened to the Shouldice and Leggit girls isn't helping."

I began to cry. Not just a few tears rolling down my face but the sobbing, chest-heaving scene that sent a torrent of tears over my cheeks and into Mac's sweatshirt. I tried to pull away, but Mac pulled me closer.

"Let it out, Ginny."

Truth is, I couldn't have stopped crying if I had tried. What was wrong with me? Again I tried to pull away, but Mac's arms continued to hold me tight against him. He didn't say anything, just sat there, holding me while I cried my crocodile tears. I stopped finally, and he loosened his hold.

"Better?" he asked.

"I need a tissue," I sniffed.

Mac handed me the box.

I mopped my face and blew my nose. "Your shirt's wet," I said, fingering the front of his sweatshirt.

"That's the hazard you run when you hold a crying girl in your lap," Mac said with a half grin.

"I'm not sitting in your lap," I protested.

Mac's eyebrow shot up. "Want to be?"

I declined the offer. "Mac . . ."

Mac's hand raised in protest. "Let it be, Ginny. You needed to cry, and I wanted to hold you."

I searched his face. Saw the scar, and the lines deeper now and permanently etched. Looked into his eyes, which, usually a clear blue, were the deeper hue of sapphires.

The voice inside my head said, "Back off, run."

I wrapped my arms around MacPhearson's neck. "What am I going to do, Mac? What am I going to do?"

Chapter Thirty-Four

IF THE DARK CIRCLES THAT HUNG BELOW MY EYES hadn't told the tale of my tortured night, the tangled bed clothes were ample evidence. Groaning, I swung my legs over the bed, my only hope being the restorative powers of a hot shower.

The shower worked (somewhat), and I left the bedroom feeling I just might survive the day.

I followed my nose to the kitchen. It did not deceive me, and when Mac placed a plate of golden fried French toast liberally sprinkled with powdered sugar, a side of bacon, a glass of orange juice, and a mug of coffee before me, I was almost glad it was morning.

Though silence did not reign over the table, the conversation was somewhat stilted.

"The French toast is good," I said.

"Thank you," Mac said.

"Looks cold out," I said.

"No new snow," Mac added.

"No snow," I repeated.

This last brought a grin to Mac's face. Seeing it, I smiled.

"Now that the small talk's out of the way," Mac's grin widened, "how about we get around to the topic we seem to be avoiding?"

My smile faded.

"And before you get bent out of shape, Miss Arthur, the subject that needs discussing is whether or not we're going to help decorate the hall for the dance tomorrow."

"Douglas MacPhearson, you're impossible," I said, allowing myself a laugh.

"My dear Regina Arthur," Douglas MacPhearson said. "On the contrary, anything's possible if one puts his mind to it."

We arrived at the municipal building only to find there was no place to park. Circling around the block, Mac finally located an empty spot, and we walked the three blocks back to the auditorium.

Decorating was in full swing, with people from barely-able-to-walk toddlers to octogenarians who looked in better shape than I felt. My muscles, as well as my cracked ribs, were constant irritants, and if I had any illusions as to how I looked, the twins soon set me straight.

"Ginny," they said in unison.

"We're glad you came, even if you don't look so good." Deb frowned. "Maybe Mom's got something you can use to cover your bruises. Purple and yellow really don't suit you."

"You two are a big help."

For the remainder of the afternoon I tied red ribbons to loops of tinsel and glued red paper hearts to every inch of available wall space. I caught sight of Mac once or twice standing high on a ladder, stringing yards of tinsel and bows across the ceiling.

When we finally got together, Mac said, "Let's get out of here before those look-a-like slave drivers find more for us to do."

I seconded the idea. We rescued our coats from the jumble piled on a corner table and headed for the stairs. Blocking our way was Deputy Norm Schmidt, along with his brother-in-law Len Frazier and the two men from the motel. Deep in conversation, they seemed not to notice us. We attempted to skirt around them, but it was a futile attempt. Norm Schmidt saw us. "You part of the work crew?" he called.

"We've done our part, but if you're here to volunteer, I'm sure the Braun twins can find something for you to do."

The deputy shook his head. "Just showing Len the local sights." He indicated the other two men. "Bumped into these two outside and invited them to come along." Schmidt looked at Mac. "You remember them? Mark Pricheck and Ron Vorhies? They're the two I was talking to at Braun's the other afternoon."

Mac nodded and offered his hand, which the two men accepted.

"How is Angie today?" I asked Frazier.

"Just fine, Miss Arthur," he said. "I'll tell her you asked after her."

"Angie's at Williams'," Schmidt said. "Ted offered to let her go through Maggie's things."

"You talked to Williams?" Mac asked Frazier.

"I did."

"Not that it did any good," Schmidt said.

"They're a chummy bunch," I said, watching the four walk farther into the room.

"Just the local constabulary offering a bit of northern hospitality," Mac said.

"Looks like more than hospitality to me."

"You're jumping to conclusions again, Red."

We were on the street, heading for the Honda, when a called "What have you two been up to?" caught our attention.

"Stringing tinsel and hanging paper hearts," I said when Jim Wacker reached us.

"Those Braun twins volunteer you for the job?" Wacker laughed. "That pair's a two-woman chamber of commerce."

"Shouldn't you be home seeing patients?" Mac asked.

"Been there, done that. Truth is, I'm out buying some of that fish Ardella Duncan's been pushing." Wacker hefted the sack he was carrying. "Got some great looking walleye here. How about helping me eat them?"

The doctor's kitchen was warm and welcoming, and as on his previous visit, Mac made the same appreciative sounds as he ran his fingers over the table, chairs, and cabinets.

"Marty Shouldice does have a way with a piece of wood," Wacker said. His jovial smile faded. "Seems your Lieutenant Rhodes is good at what he does, too. Hear it took him less than a couple of hours to convince Father Mike and his fellow priests he walks on water."

"He's a good cop," I said, "but walk on water?" I was sitting at the table while Jim pan-fried the lightly battered fish.

"How does rice and green beans strike you?" he asked.

The menu was agreed upon, and it was not long before we were seated at the table. In pushing the ice fishermen's bounty, Ardella Duncan had done us all a favor.

"What else have you heard about the meeting?" Mac said. We had moved to the family room and were enjoying our after-dinner coffee. "I'm especially interested in that part about Rhodes walking on water."

Jim chuckled. "That's probably an exaggeration on my part, but Father Mike felt confident the task force would get to the bottom of the girls' disappearance. He never did buy the theory that Josie and Cindy ran away."

"He stopped by the cabin yesterday on his way back from Marion City. Told us much the same thing," Mac said.

"Mac had a copy of your report," I said. "After Father Mike left, we went over it."

"And?" Jim prodded.

"Mac thinks they need to take another look at the convenience store."

"Is that skepticism I hear in your voice, Miss Arthur?"

"Ginny thinks the convenience store is a dead end," Mac said.

"And you don't?"

"I don't think anything should be considered a dead end until it proves to be one."

"What Mac's failing to point out," I interrupted, "is that the only one who claims the girls were ever at the convenience store is Caroline Whiting. There's absolutely nothing in the report that corroborates her story. Who's to say Caroline Whiting didn't spirit them away?"

Jim Wacker set his coffee mug aside. "What makes you think that might be the case, Ginny?"

Unlike Mac, Jim Wacker sounded like he might believe me. Feeling more confident, I repeated what I had told Mac the evening before.

"And what's your objection to Ginny's premise, Mac?"

"None, and I agree it's time to look at other angles."

"Like maybe Caroline Whiting is not telling the truth," I said.

"Why would Caroline lie?" Jim asked. "She has nothing to gain by the girls' disappearance."

"Maybe it's not Caroline," I said. "How about Roger Whiting?"

"And what would he gain by their disappearance?" the doctor asked.

Mac held up his hand. "Hold it, you two. Let's not go running off on tangents." He cradled his coffee mug in his hands. "Considering Larry Rhodes thinks the case worth pursuing, how about we look at it from the task force's perspective?"

"Human trafficking, sweat shops, prostitution, forced labor." My mind raced as I listed the possibilities. "And Roger Whiting works with contract laborers," I finished.

"Slow down, Ginny." Wacker held up both hands. "Same question, what would the man have to gain by involving himself in such a thing?"

"Lose, not gain. Maybe it's something Roger Whiting might lose."

"Go on, Ginny," Mac said. "What has Roger Whiting got to lose."

"His farm, for starters," I said. "The recession must be hard on him. With unemployment being what it is, even the farmers must be feeling the crunch."

"They are," Jim admitted. "Several of the smaller farms have been especially hard hit."

"And Roger Whiting, with all the acreage he runs, must have tremendous overhead," I said, warming to the subject. "Imagine the number of laborers he needs to keep that place going."

"And labor is expensive," Mac added.

I nodded agreement. "The cost of which Roger Whiting would go to any lengths to reduce."

Jim Wacker shook his head. "I'm not liking where this conversation is going."

Chapter Thirty-Five

Wacker looked from Mac to me. "Are you suggesting the Whitings are also responsible for Rita's shooting?"

"Can't say, but whoever was responsible, my guess is Ginny was the target," Mac answered.

I placed our empty coffee mugs on the tray that held the cream and sugar. "What if the Whitings thought Rita was passing along information they didn't want passed along?" I argued. "Wouldn't that make her or all three of us a target?"

"Then how do you explain the snowmobile that tried to run you over?"

"I can't." Despite Mac's question, I was convinced I was headed in the right direction.

I woke the next morning to a banging on my bedroom door and the sound of Larry Rhodes—Larry Rhodes?—calling, no shouting my name.

"Coffee's on, sleepyhead. If you don't come out, I'll be in to get you," he called.

I groped my way from sleep to awake, pushed upright, and shook the fog from my head. Surely I must be dreaming. Larry Rhodes here?

"Ginny, are you decent? I'm coming in." Saying this, the Marion City Police Lieutenant made good his threat.

"So, you are awake," he said, a grin spreading over his face.

"What are you doing here? And yes, thanks to you I am awake."

"Then get dressed, we have a lot to do today." And with, "Bacon's ready, and Mac's breaking eggs," Rhodes left the room.

I pulled on yesterday's jeans and sweatshirt, decided to forego such amenities as a shower and brushing my teeth or hair, and hurried down the hall to the kitchen. Along with Mac, who was busy at the stove, and Larry Rhodes, who was seated at the table drinking coffee, it seemed I was having breakfast with the Pine County Sheriff and the county coroner.

I slowed my steps, ran fingers through my unkempt hair, and debated returning to the bedroom for a more complete toilet. Mac's call of "Eggs are on" tipped the scales.

"About time you joined us," he said. "The rest of us have been up for hours."

Deciding the time of day warranted no comment, I said to Rhodes, "Did you drive up this morning or last night?"

"Neither," he said, around a mouthful of eggs and bacon. "Helicopter."

Ladylike, I swallowed my bacon and eggs before asking, "Why the rush?"

"Decided we needed a strategy meeting." Rhodes pushed aside his empty plate. "After hearing what Father Mike had to say about your missing girls, the task force decided to take a closer look."

Duncan frowned. "It's not like we've been sitting on our hands up here."

"I know, and that's one of the reasons I'm here."

A bang at the door, the door whose frame Mac had so recently repaired, brought the table conversation to a halt.

"That must be Father Mike," Duncan said. "He said he'd be here after morning Mass."

Mac answered the door, returning with the usually jovial priest. Only this morning, his smile was missing.

"Time we got down to business," Rhodes said.

Feet shuffled, backs stiffened, faces sobered as he looked around the table.

"First thing we need to clarify is why we're meeting here and not at your place." Rhodes looked at Duncan. "And the reason is, we'll be taking a closer look at the Whitings."

"Won't Deputy Schmidt get suspicious with all the coming and going at the cabin?" I asked.

"No need to worry about Schmidt," Duncan said. "He's busy with his sister and her husband. They're leaving tomorrow to take Sarah's body back to Rocky Ridge. Johnson's covering this part of the county."

"We're especially interested in why Rita Leggit drove the workers to Cadillac the morning the girls disappeared," Rhodes said.

I started to say it was Caroline Whiting's story that needed looking into, but was stopped by Rhodes's let-me-finish look.

He pulled a file from a briefcase sitting beside his chair. "Another thing you need to know, Sam Leggit came to see us yesterday."

"And?" Duncan prodded.

"Apparently, Roger Whiting keeps a tight rein on his laborers." Rhodes riffled through the file that lay before him. "From what Leggit says, Whiting holds the paperwork on the migrants, and nobody leaves unless he authorizes it."

"I'm not surprised," Father Mike said. "Those migrants of his are the most depressed bunch I've ever met."

"And that compound of his is always locked," Wacker said. "Whenever I'm called out to treat one of the workers, either Whiting or Sam Leggit are there to let me in."

"They never smile," I said, "and neither he nor Caroline have anything good to say about them." I looked at Mac, who nodded agreement.

Rhodes looked around the table. "Sounds more and more like a forced-labor situation."

"And what does that have to do with Cindy Shouldice's and Josie Leggit's disappearance?" I said.

"We know there's an organized group that deals in human trafficking in western Michigan. We suspect the victims are brought to Marion City from smaller communities like Pine City, funneled into the pipeline, and transported out of state. Usually they go to Chicago, then St. Louis, and from there to either Atlanta or Houston."

"Missing girls? Migrant workers? How do the two tie together?" Wacker asked.

"Different sides of the same coin, Doctor Wacker," Rhodes said. "There's the farmer who contracts for itinerant workers with an agent who deals in laborers who may or may not be legal. In the case of trafficked persons, however, the workers are almost always illegal. On the other side of the coin are the lowlifes who snatch kids and pass them along to those who specialize in a more perverse form of trafficking. They're most likely girls, but the market for boys is increasing."

"And you suspect Roger Whiting of being involved in both?" Father Mike said.

Around the table, already somber faces grew more somber as the weight of Rhodes's words sunk in.

Rhodes nodded. "The evidence indicates this might be the case."

"But why?" I asked.

"Money," Rhodes said. "These kids bring a hefty price."

"But surely Roger Whiting isn't that hard up," Father Mike said.

"On the contrary," Rhodes said. "After talking to Sam Leggit, the task force did some digging into Mr. Whiting's finances."

"And you found what?" Wacker asked.

"Things are tight for the Whitings at present, second mortgages and the like." Rhodes tapped his finger on the papers that lay before him. "So tight that, unless Whiting comes up with some creative financing, he'll probably lose the farm."

"That farm has been in the Whiting family since before Michigan was a state. Surely Roger must own the land free and clear," Father Mike said.

"I think Roger, as did many others, thought the bubble would keep on getting bigger and bigger. Then . . ." Rhodes's voice trailed off.

"I do know Whiting bought a lot of new equipment, experimented with some hybrid crops that didn't pan out," Duncan said. "Carol likes to talk, and I'm usually of a mind to listen."

Rhodes closed his file folder. "The task force is looking into all of this. As for the rest of you, I'll be seeing each of you individually throughout the day. In the meantime, it's business as usual. Just keep your eyes and ears open and your mouths shut."

"What about Sarah Frazier? How does her death fit in with all of this?" The group was breaking up, but I wanted more answers.

"As a trafficking victim?" Rhodes asked.

I nodded.

Rhodes's expression softened. "We can't eliminate the possibility, Ginny, but the evidence suggests she's more likely a runaway."

"So, you're going to ignore the fact that someone murdered her and probably her aunt?"

"That's my problem, Miss Arthur," Duncan said, "and I can assure you, we won't be ignoring the deaths of either Sarah Frazier or Maggie Schmidt."

Good-byes were quick and perfunctory. Alone with Rhodes and MacPhearson, I said, "It was Sam Leggit who led you to suspect the Whitings might be involved in trafficking?"

"It was. The information he provided was the key the task force needed. Up to then, we knew the where, suspected the why, but didn't have a clue as to who."

"And how were Josie and Cindy made to disappear, and without a trace?" I said.

"My guess is, the same way I got from Marion City to here," Rhodes said.

"Helicopter?" Mac and I said together.

"And I understand Roger Whiting has one," Rhodes said.

Rhodes, who had booked a room at the Braun Motel, pulled on his jacket. "I hear everyone in town is going to a dance tonight. That include you two?"

"The twins would have our heads if we didn't show up," I said.

We agreed to meet at the motel for dinner and said our goodbyes. I walked Rhodes to the door.

"Any more Uncle David sightings?" he asked.

I shook my head. "No." I wanted to say more, but this was neither the time nor the place.

I joined Mac in the kitchen where dirty dishes waited.

"Do you think the task force suspected Roger Whiting before any of this happened?" I asked, loading the last of the plates into the dishwasher.

"Hard to say, but from the way Rhodes tells it, I'd say, not until after Sam Leggit talked to them." Mac brought the frying pan from the stove and set it in the sink.

"Was it because of Rita?" I filled the sink with hot water and added a squirt of detergent.

"Or maybe his daughter," Mac said.

My hands stilled. I looked at Mac. "Surely, Sam Leggit didn't suspect the Whitings had anything to do with his daughter's disappearance?"

"In this world, Red, anything's possible."

In another room, my phone began to ring.

I hurried down the hall to my bedroom, followed the ring tones to my shoulder bag, and reached inside.

"What time does that dance of yours start?" Steve said in my ear.

"About eight," I said, "but we're having dinner with Rhodes at the motel at six."

Shoulder bag in one hand and the phone pressed tight to my ear with the other, I waited, refusing to consider if Steve Brock's question meant he would or wouldn't be there.

"Not sure I can make dinner," he said, "but I'll be there for the dance."

My knees wobbled, and I sat on my unmade bed.

"I know I should have called sooner, but I wasn't sure until the last minute. You know how that goes."

I did know, the never knowing, the waiting until the last minute.

"How formal is this dance?" Steve asked.

"This is a tourist area. Just about anything that covers you will do."

"And what will be covering you?" Steve asked.

I warmed to his not-too-subtle question. "Guess," I teased.

Chapter Thirty-Six

Despite all that had happened during the past two weeks, it was a merry group that gathered around Linda Braun's kitchen table. The twins had done their part, folded the red napkins into hearts, and added a foil-wrapped chocolate heart to each place setting.

"Looks like a party," Rhodes said.

"It is," the twins chorused, as they placed an arrangement of silk roses in the center of the table. Their dresses, each different from the other, were a mix of black and white and red and pink.

"That the new dress you've been telling us about?" I asked Deb.

"Like it?" she asked. She moved away from the table and executed a quick turn, showing off the black and white ankle-length dress. "I knew everyone would be wearing red, and I wanted something different."

"I like it, and not everyone's wearing red." I duplicated Deb's turn, showing off my black slacks and cream-colored sweater. Soft and clingy with a not-too-daring décolletage, I had chosen it not for Deb's approval, but for Steve's.

MacPhearson, who had been observing the scene from his seat at the table, moaned softly. "With two such beautiful women at the dance, how am I ever going to choose a dancing partner."

"How about choosing me?" Kim asked, smoothing down the skirt of her pink-and-red dress.

Mac rose to his feet and bowed in Kim's direction. "Miss Braun, will you do me the honor of letting me escort you to the Pine City Valentine Dance tonight?"

Kim fluttered her mascara-darkened lashes. "Why, Detective MacPhearson, I'd be delighted to have you as my escort," she drawled, the southern accent bordering on burlesque.

The exchange brought howls of laughter from not just the group around the table, but from the kitchen staff and several waiters waiting to pick up their orders.

Kim, her face flushed, hurried from the kitchen. Mac, still standing, held my chair as I settled into the seat.

"If I haven't already told you," he said quietly, "that sweater does become you."

The empty chairs at the table began to fill. Rhodes was there, as was Sheriff Duncan and Jim Wacker. Linda came and went as the demands of ownership allowed. One chair remained empty, Steve's.

"How about I take all of you to the dance?" Sheriff Duncan suggested. "Parking's going to be a problem."

A murmur of assent went around the table.

"Linda, you able to shake loose?" Duncan asked.

"Afraid not, Rick, at least not until the dinner crowd thins out. Ted's offered to stay late and tend the bar." Linda looked around the room. "I'd like you to take the girls, though, wherever they are."

"Will do." Duncan smiled. "Just remember, I'm saving the last dance for you."

Linda laid an affectionate hand on the sheriff's shoulder. "Not to worry. I should be there long before then."

Duncan gestured to the rest of us. "You all meet in the lobby. I'll pick you up in front."

In the general hubbub that followed, I missed him. Not until I felt his hand on my arm and his whispered greeting did I know he was there. Steve brushed his lips over mine. The lock of dark hair that seemed always to hang over his forehead, the familiar smile that played at the corners of his mouth, the twinkle in his eyes, all the things I loved about the man, including the man himself, were there.

"I do like what you're wearing," he said, running his hands over my arms. He leaned closer. "But I'm going to like it more when you're not wearing anything at all."

"Have you had anything to eat?" I asked, breaking the intimate mood.

Steve laughed. Gave me a hug and another, longer kiss. "No, I have not eaten, but a pair of look-a-likes said they would fix me a plate to go."

Steve called a greeting to Rhodes then turned to MacPhearson. Doctor fashion, he said, "You're looking good, Mac. Feeling okay? No more headaches?"

"I'm feeling fine, Steve." Mac raised his hands, warding off more questions. "No headaches or blurred or double vision." Mac grinned. "So you see, Doctor Brock, sending me up here was a good idea."

The two men in my life, which seeing them together was a fact I could no longer deny, stared overlong at each other. Not until the Suburban's horn sounded outside did they break eye contact.

Nirvana's *Smells Like Teen Spirit* sounded from the auditorium. I braced myself for the increased volume that would surely come when the doors were opened. I was not disappointed. The persistent beat of the music, coupled with the sound of too many people crowded into too small a space, threatened early onset of deafness.

With one hand holding tight to Steve's hand and the other grasped firmly in Mac's, the three of us snaked our way through the crowd. After dodging a series of bent elbows attached to constantly shifting bodies, MacPhearson came to a stop. There, defying probability, was an empty table. The four of us—Rhodes was close on Steve's heels—took advantage of our good luck.

The DJ switched to *My Funny Valentine*. Showing their appreciation, several gray-haired women partnered by balding men took the floor. As the twins had promised, there was indeed something for everyone.

Rhodes took advantage of the reduced volume. "Are the Whitings here?" he asked. "The Shouldices?"

I looked around the overcrowded room. "Can't tell, but if anyone would know, it's sure to be the twins."

As if hearing their names, the two emerged from the crowd. Close behind was a wheelchair-bound Jimmy Wakefield.

"Are you really going to dance with me, Detective MacPhearson?" Kim called as she neared the table.

"Would I let you down?"

Kim frowned. "Sometimes people say things they don't mean."

"Not me," Mac said. He rose from his chair. "Ready?"

Kim's smile was shy, almost embarrassed. As the bouncy beat of *Popular,* one of the hits from the Broadway show *Wicked,* poured from the sound system, the two wove their way through the tables to the dance floor.

Jimmy maneuvered closer to the table, pulling Deb on his lap as he did.

"That's one way of assuring the two of you have a seat," Steve said. He offered his hand to the young man. "Steve Brock."

"Jimmy Wakefield," Jimmy said, reaching to shake Steve's hand.

"Tried tackling the dance floor yet?" I asked.

"We have," Deb said proudly.

"Deb does the dancing," Jimmy explained. "I just sit and jiggle the chair. You know, do that wheelchair tango Detective MacPhearson told me about."

"Wheelchair tango? I'll have to ask Mac about that one," Rhodes said. He took another look around the room. "Have either of you seen the Whitings or the Shouldices?"

"The Whitings are sitting with the mayor and his wife," Deb said.

Jimmy pointed in the direction of the dance floor. "It's the table in the middle of the room nearest the dance floor. If you walk around the edge of the floor, you can't miss them."

"How about the Shouldices? Know where they're sitting?"

"They're not sitting anywhere," Deb said. "Mr. Shouldice is tending the bar, and Mrs. Shouldice is helping with the buffet table." Deb turned to Steve. "Is that the dinner Kim and I fixed you?"

"It is," Steve said, bringing a forkful of vegetables to his mouth. "Thank you. It's very good."

Rhodes's eyes fixed on the bar. "Which one is Marty Shouldice?"

"The man standing at this end of the bar, the blond one," I said.

Rhodes studied the man for several seconds before shifting his gaze to the buffet table. "And his wife? Which one is Betty Shouldice?"

"I don't see her. She must be in the kitchen," Deb said. "Want us to get her for you?"

"No thanks, I'll catch her later," Rhodes said. He turned to me. "If that doctor of yours isn't going to ask you to dance, how about taking a turn around the floor with this old man?"

Aerosmith's *Crying* replaced Johnny Cash's *Ring of Fire* as we took the floor. We merged with a press of humans whose every body part except their feet seemed to be moving.

"Where are the Whitings sitting?" Rhodes asked, his lips nudging my ear.

I jerked my head in the direction of a table some distance from where we were doing our best to dislocate both shoulder and hip joints.

"Hold on." Rhodes grabbed my arm and added a series of leg movements to our already moving bodies. "When we get there, introduce me," he breathed in my ear.

I nodded I would, and with a shift of hips and several quick two-steps, we were standing beside the Whiting table.

Another oldie from the Big Band era cleared the floor by half and dropped the sound nearer conversational level.

"Caroline, Roger," I said, "this is Larry Rhodes, a friend of mine from Marion City."

The two men shook hands, and Caroline invited us to join them. "Can I get you something from the bar?" Roger asked, his hand raised to summon a waiter.

"You're a friend of Ginny's?" Caroline asked.

"I grew up with Ginny's dad and her uncle," Rhodes said. "I like to think I'm more family than friend."

"A surrogate uncle?" Caroline asked, looking from me to Rhodes. "How nice."

The waiter appeared beside the table and with a softly worded, "Sir?" waited.

"Two of the same," Roger Whiting said, indicating his and Caroline's half empty glasses. Roger looked from me to Larry Rhodes. "And what will the two of you have?"

Rhodes ordered a Bud, and I asked for a glass of white wine.

"You do know what we are drinking?" Caroline asked the waiter, who was jotting notes in a small notebook.

The waiter nodded his head.

"Well, then," I heard Roger demand, "what are we drinking?"

"Scotch and water, sir," the waiter answered, his face darkening as he spoke.

"Put this round on our tab and be quick, our guests are thirsty." Roger waved the young man away.

"He's from my farm. Extra help I keep on hand for emergencies. Unless you keep a constant check on them, you never know what they might bring you," Whiting said. His expression changed from scowl to smile. "Now tell me, Mr. Rhodes, are you here to ski, snowmobile, or fish?"

"Just visiting, Roger, and it's lieutenant not mister."

Chapter Thirty-Seven

THE GLENN MILLER NUMBER ENDED ON A downbeat. The dancers moved off the floor, and a moment of welcome silence followed.

"Are you with the National Guard, Lieutenant Rhodes?" Roger Whiting asked, slipping in the question before the next selection began.

"The Marion City Police Department, and it's Larry, Roger."

"And here's one for the younger crowd." The DJ paused, letting the momentum grow. "Let's all dance to Lady Antebellum's *Need You Now.*"

A roar of approval and the sound of rushing feet drowned the first notes as the teenagers crowded the floor.

"My, such a noise," Caroline shouted. She offered each of us a smile. I was the only one to reciprocate.

Along with the waiter bearing the drinks Whiting had ordered, the mayor and his wife chose that moment to return to the table.

Another pair of chairs were found and the drinks served, the service quick and attentive. Even in a town as small as Pine City, it paid to be at the top of the pecking order.

Our proximity to the dance floor made conversation near impossible. Still, introductions were attempted. Rising to the occasion, Rhodes shook hands with Gerald and Sally Van Haven. I settled for a wave, having already met the mayor and his wife on one of my trips to Ardella Duncan's meat market.

The mayor's lips moved, and Rhodes shook his head, the performance ending when Rhodes raised his hands as in denial.

"What was that all about?" I asked when Rhodes was seated, tipping my head close to his as I did.

"The mayor wanted to know if I was here to help Duncan with Pine City's current crime wave," Rhodes answered.

A hand touched my shoulder and a different head bent close to mine. "They're playing *Just a Girl*," Steve said, "and since you're my girl, how about dancing with me?"

The evening passed in a blur of good food, a sparseness of conversation due to the throbbing beat of the music, and the shuffling feet of the dancers. Hoping for an intermission which never came, as not one but two DJs had been hired for the evening, I sought refuge in the women's lounge. If it was peace and quiet I wanted, I didn't find it.

Waiting in line for one of the stalls, I felt a pull on my arm. It was Kim.

"Detective MacPhearson's a great dancer," she said. She giggled, a lilting, little-girl sound. "He knows all the right moves."

I laughed. "You're right about that, Kim. MacPhearson definitely knows all the right moves."

Kim looked puzzled. "Detective MacPhearson's been moving in on you?"

Too late, I realized I'd backed myself into the proverbial corner. I hastened a verbal retreat. "Of course not. Mac's just a friend. I only meant . . ." What did I mean? ". . . he really does know how to dance."

Kim frowned.

A stall opened up, and I grabbed the swinging door. The look on the girl's face told me she wasn't buying what I was selling.

Another teen favorite, *Single Ladies,* by Beyoncé, had just begun when I left the restroom. I watched Deb roll Jimmy's wheelchair onto the floor. The kids scattered. Taking advantage of the space, Jimmy executed a series of quick turns. Catching Deb's hand on the last go around, he swung the laughing girl into his lap. Almost as quickly as she had landed, Deb was up. Her black-and-white skirt flying, she danced circles around the wheelchair.

Amid the smiles and clapping hands of their peers, the two continued their performance, Deb moving to the rhythm of the music and Jimmy making the chair shimmy and shake. If prizes were being given for the most popular couple, it would go to this pair.

The music ended, and the floor cleared. Smiling at the sea of faces turned in his direction, the DJ mopped his brow with an overlarge red handkerchief. The quiet did not last long. From the depths of the speakers that surrounded the room came the muted strains of U2's *One*.

A familiar arm circled my waist. "How about it, Ginny. I ordered this one just for us." The music wrapped round us as I followed Mac onto the dance floor. His arm tightened around me, and with his red head close to mine, he crooned the lyrics in my ear. Closing my eyes, I joined my voice softly, oh so softly, with Mac's and the singer's.

The music ended as music does. Yet I was reluctant to move from Mac's embrace.

"Up for another dance?" he asked.

I lost myself in the depths of Mac's blue, blue eyes. What was happening to me? To us?

Ike and Tina Turner's *Proud Mary* filled the auditorium. The spell was broken.

Steve came forward from the edge of the dance floor and took my hand. "My turn, Miss Arthur."

We found the beat and moved to the rhythm of the music. Steve did not smile, nor did he speak. Like Proud Mary, we just kept on rolling.

The music ended, and we found our way to the table. Rhodes was there, as was Sheriff Duncan and Linda Braun. Steve pulled out a chair. I sat down, and he went to the bar. Whether it was thirst or the need of an alcoholic stimulus, I sure wanted that drink.

"Everything under control at the motel?" I asked, looking from Linda to Duncan.

"Ted's tending bar," Linda said. "The restaurant's closed but will serve appetizers and sandwiches from the bar until closing time." She smiled at Duncan. "Ted convinced me I wasn't needed."

The sound of a clock striking midnight followed by the familiar strains of *Sentimental Journey* came from the speakers.

"This one's for us." Duncan pulled Linda to her feet.

As many with young children had already left the dance and the gray-haired balding contingent stayed and visited, there was not the usual crush of people hurrying to leave the auditorium. The teenagers, the mainstay of the cleanup crew, were noisily clearing tables and dumping trash.

"Great dance," Mac said, claiming a chair at the table.

"Kim tells me you were a good dancing partner. How did she put it? Oh, yes, said you knew all the right moves."

"I've been accused of worse," Mac said.

"Accused of what?" Linda asked. Duncan pulled out a chair, and the motel owner sank gratefully into it. "It's been a long day," she said. "Now, Detective MacPhearson, tell me what it is you've been accused of, and I'm hoping it's that you know where those twins of mine are. I haven't seen them since I got here."

MacPhearson shook his head. "Afraid not, Mrs. Braun. Haven't seen them since Deb and Jimmy's performance several dances back."

Linda's eyes swept over the table. "Any of you seen them?"

I told of having seen Kim in the restroom, but had to admit to not having seen her since.

"This is not like them. They knew I was coming." Linda stood, seeking a better view of the auditorium. "And how do you hide a boy with two casts in a wheelchair?"

The answer was, you don't. This sent Rhodes, Mac, Steve, and me in search of the misplaced trio.

The search was quick. Even in a room as large as the municipal auditorium, there were only four corners. I volunteered for the girls' bathroom and Steve the men's. Mac and Rhodes searched the bar area and the kitchen, while Duncan and Linda disappeared into the cloakroom. They reappeared almost immediately, each with a coat in hand.

Eve Wakefield and Betty Shouldice came from the kitchen.

Duncan's long strides outdistanced Linda's as he hurried to meet the two women. "I understand you're taking Jimmy and the Braun twins home tonight, Eve. Any idea where they are now?"

The lines on Eve's face deepened. "I can't remember when I last saw them, but we agreed to meet by the stairs when we finished cleaning up."

A cry came from beyond the bar.

"Get Doctor Wacker," Marty Shouldice called. "We've found Jimmy, but he's unconscious. Looks like he's been hit on the head."

Eve Wakefield gasped.

"I don't think he's badly hurt, Eve. You know how a cut on the head bleeds." Marty Shouldice grabbed the mother's arm as she hurried by.

"I'll have a look at him," Steve said, pushing past the pair.

"Get me a glass of water," Betty Shouldice said to one of the group of wide-eyed teenagers. They had given up cleaning and were watching the drama unfolding around them.

"I'm sure Jimmy's going to be okay, Eve," Betty Shouldice said. She had joined her husband, and the two of them helped Eve to a chair. "The doctor's with him."

Duncan, who had followed Steve into the storeroom behind the bar, reappeared in the doorway, cell phone in hand. "Help's on the way," he said to an anxious Eve and an equally anxious Linda.

Duncan wrapped his arm around Linda. "Don't worry. The girls can't have gone far. We'll have everything straightened out in no time."

The look on Linda's face said she didn't believe him, and if I were a betting woman, my bet would be on Linda. The memory of another pair of missing girls was much, much too fresh in my mind.

Steve came through the storeroom door, pushing a pale-faced Jimmy in his wheelchair, a towel wrapped turban-style around his head.

"Jimmy!" Eve Wakefield rushed to meet her son. "What happened to you?"

"He's fine." Steve interrupted the dialog between the anxious mother and her son. "He's lost some blood and needs a few stitches, but it's nothing you need worry about."

"Someone called for me?" It was Jim Wacker. "Just got the message. One of our partygoers finished the dance with a tumble down the stairs." Wacker looked at the mix of emotions that showed on the faces of the assembled group. "Since I've told you what's going on downstairs, how about telling me what's going on upstairs?"

"Someone knocked Jimmy Wakefield on the head, but Steve Brock took care of him," Duncan said.

"Deb was with me," Jimmy said. "We went into the storeroom to get more trash bags. Did someone hit Deb on the head, too?"

"She's not in the storeroom, son," Duncan said. "Let's find someplace quiet, and you can tell me what happened."

Duncan took the wheelchair from Steve and headed for the kitchen. "There's a pantry out back." Duncan looked at Rhodes. "Mind coming along, Lieutenant?"

Eve Wakefield moved next to her son's wheelchair. "I'm coming, too," she said.

Duncan nodded an affirmative.

"And me," Linda said, following the group.

Duncan sighed. "Okay, but no more." He swung the wheelchair around and headed for the kitchen.

Rhodes nodded at Mac, who nodded in return and followed after the group.

"Nobody's questioning my patient without me being there," Steve said.

I watched the group disappear into the kitchen. What the hell, I thought, and joined the parade.

Behind me I heard Jim Wacker call, "Wait up, Ginny. If you think I'm going to miss this show, you're badly mistaken."

It wasn't much of a show. Duncan tried to make it interesting, but Jimmy didn't cooperate. His answer to whatever question Duncan asked was the one liner, "I don't know." After several repetitions, far too many to count, Duncan gave up.

"Do you know where Deb is?" The boy's eyes met Duncan's.

"No, son, we don't, but we sure as hell are going to find out." The sheriff turned to the boy's mother. "Eve, I'll have Deputy Ramos drive you and Jimmy to the hospital. She can wait while they do what they need to do and then take the two of you home."

"But . . ." Eve Wakefield started.

"No arguments, Eve." Duncan looked at the group that surrounded him. "I'm in charge, and what I say goes." His voice dropped to a mumble. "At least I think I am."

The three police officers exchanged glances. "How about you two coming with me to headquarters. I told Johnson and Bryant we'd meet them there. Bentley will be along to take over here."

"I'll stay with Doctor Wacker. Can't see as you'll be needing me at headquarters," Steve said. He looked at me. A question was there, but he didn't ask it.

"Ginny stays with me." Finality sounded in Mac's voice. "Whatever's going on around here, I don't want her any part of it."

The target, which I'd discarded for the evening's festivities, was back. Heavier now than before, it caused my shoulders to sag.

Linda remained at the auditorium. "If the kids saw anything or heard anything, they're more likely to talk to me than to Bentley," she argued.

Though it was obvious Duncan wasn't happy about leaving Linda behind, he agreed.

In the privacy of the SUV, it was obvious, too, that Rhodes had a definite plan in mind.

"If what I suspect has happened, the girls are already en route to Marion City."

"But why . . ."

Mac's hand closed over mine, stopping my protest.

Speaking into his cell phone, Rhodes asked, "You've got the airport covered?" Nodding as if satisfied with what he was hearing, he added, "Judging from when the girls were last seen, I'd say less than an hour."

Rhodes snapped the phone shut. "Vengeance is the Lord's," he said, "but never underestimate a father's wrath."

Chapter Thirty-Eight

MYRA JOHNSON, KEVIN BRYANT, AND RINGING telephones met us at the municipal building.

"I've been checking the 911 calls," a grave-faced Johnson greeted. "There's been several explosions at the Whiting farm."

"Explosions? Whiting Farm?" Duncan looked from Johnson to Bryant, a confused look on his face.

"And why in hell aren't the State Police picking up these calls?" Duncan asked, looking as if the answer to this last question would answer the first two. Clearly exasperated, the sheriff lifted a ringing phone with a terse "Please hold," pressed a button on the console, and slammed the handset into its holder.

"Want I should forward the incoming calls to the State Police, Sheriff?" Bryant asked.

"Hell, yes! Carol should have done that before she left on Friday." Duncan paced the aisle between the desks as the ringing phones were reduced to blinking lights. "Now, tell me what's going on."

The deputies looked at each other. Bryant nodded, and Johnson began.

"When we got here, Kev started answering the phones, and I checked the 911 calls. A man, he didn't identify himself, said there had been several explosions at the Whiting farm, and the buffalo herd was stampeding."

Duncan interrupted, "That shouldn't be a problem, there's plenty of pasture out there. The herd will run itself out." He looked at his two deputies. "Is there more?"

Johnson moistened her lips. "The caller said the explosions had driven the buffalo toward the workers compound. Said the compound was locked, and that the herd had overrun the place before he could get the workers out. He asked us to send all the help we had."

"And?" Duncan prompted.

"I relayed the information to the State Police," Johnson finished.

Duncan stopped pacing and stared at his deputies. "And why wasn't I called?"

"You were already on your way in, Sheriff. You had just called in to tell us about Jimmy Wakefield and the Braun twins," Bryant answered.

Duncan paused, as if weighing his thoughts. "Did you try to get hold of Roger Whiting?"

"We tried, but he's not answering his cell or home phone."

Rhodes, who had retreated to an inner office, returned to the room, cell phone tight against his ear. "Whiting's helicopter is on the ground. Landed in a private field north of Marion City just like Sam Leggit said it would. The SWAT team is there. Seems the pilot isn't offering any resistance."

Rhodes fell silent, as did the rest of us, the blinking lights of the phones mute testimony to our barely restrained impatience. A minute passed, two. Feet shuffled, and nervous glances were exchanged. After another almost unendurable moment, Rhodes smiled.

"They've got the girls. They're unconscious, but their vital signs are stable. They're en route to Mercy Hospital as we speak." With a final "Keep me informed," Rhodes broke the connection. "Anyone here know how to get hold of Linda Braun?"

Grinning broadly, Myra Johnson asked, "Want I should give her a call, Sheriff?"

The sheriff shook his head at the grinning deputy. "No need to act so smug, Johnson, and yes, go ahead and give Linda a call. She's probably still at the auditorium."

Duncan watched his deputy punch in the number. "And when you get her, Myra, I want to talk to her."

The tension in the room, which had lessened considerably, rose again when Duncan's cell began to ring. Duncan flipped the lid, but before he could get the phone to his ear, Jim Wacker's voice boomed from the small phone.

"What the hell's going on over there? I've been trying to get hold of someone. First, all I got was a busy signal, and now all I'm getting is the damn State Police." The doctor's usual calm demeanor had deserted him.

"You got a problem, Doc?" Duncan asked. He switched the phone to speaker.

"Damn right I have. We're being overrun with casualties, mostly migrant workers from the Whiting place. Seems that herd of buffalo Roger keeps out there went berserk and overran the workers compound."

"How many casualties, Jim?" Duncan asked.

"I'd say about twenty. Mostly broken bones and lacerations but some—seven, eight—need emergency surgery. Good thing that doctor friend of Ginny's is here. Not too often we have us a trauma surgeon on hand when we need one."

"Anyone able to tell you what's going on out there, Jim? All I know is that the State Police are there." Duncan paced as he talked.

"Most aren't in any shape to do much talking. We can handle what casualties we have. Any more, they'll need to send to other hospitals." Jim Wacker drew in an audible breath. "Didn't mean to come across like gangbusters, Rick."

Duncan laughed. "It's not like you haven't done it before, you old curmudgeon, but I do have some good news." Duncan relayed the information about the Braun twins and, after another exchange of friendly insults, cut the connection.

"I've got Mrs. Braun on the phone, Sheriff." Deputy Johnson handed her boss the receiver.

"Myra tell you the good news, Linda?" Duncan asked. His broad grin faded. "I'm sure you do, but . . ." Duncan frowned. "I don't think it's a good idea for you to drive down there alone."

Rhodes called, "Tell her our department's helicopter's on its way, and she's welcome to ride back with me."

Duncan relayed the news. Rhodes, returning to his cell, made the necessary arrangements.

"Can't tell you how much I appreciate this," Duncan said.

Rhodes waved away the sheriff's words. "I'm just glad everything turned out as well as it did. Only hope the outcome is as good for the other two." Rhodes's expression hardened. "Tell the Shouldices I'll be in touch. After what Sam Leggit's told us, I'll need to have another talk with them. Can't promise anything, but knowing where to start is a big help."

"And it's time I saw for myself what's going on at the Whiting place," Duncan said. "Bryant, you get on out there, and Johnson, you stay here and get a lid on things." The sheriff headed for the door. "Too bad you won't be with us on this one, Lieutenant. Might be us small town hicks could teach you big city cops a thing or two after all."

Before Rhodes could answer, Duncan's phone rang again.

"It's Father Mike. He wants to talk to you, Ginny."

I took the sheriff's phone and, after a few minutes of listening, said, "Mac and I will be right out, Father.

"Father Mike is getting the overflow of casualties from the Whiting farm." I handed Duncan the phone and looked at MacPhearson. "You up to more volunteering, Mac?"

Duncan brought the Suburban to a stop before the auditorium, where a smiling, teary-eyed Linda Braun waited. Rushing forward as Rhodes exited the SUV, she threw her arms around him and hugged him tight.

"I didn't believe . . . couldn't accept the fact they were gone." She stepped back, looked Rhodes full in the face. "Then you found them."

"It's not me you should thank, Mrs. Braun. It's Sam Leggit," Rhodes said, shaking his head.

Linda smiled through her tears. "Sam may have helped, but I know it was you who put the pieces together."

She pushed past Rhodes. "And you, Rick Duncan, why didn't you tell me what was going on?" Her voice lost its strident pitch. "Oh, Rick, I was so scared."

Duncan drew her close, muttered words none of us could hear, then pushed her from him. "Time to go, Linda. Rhodes is waiting to take you to the girls. We'll talk when the three of you get back."

Duncan hit the accelerator and, ignoring the speed limit, covered the distance between the auditorium and the Braun Motel in record time. Pulling into the parking lot, he braked to a stop behind the Honda. "That Rhodes, he's okay. Had all his ducks in a row before the dance even started. Told us to sit back and let everything play out. Just wish he had let us know about a damn buffalo stampede."

"Is that why Rhodes told you not to tell Linda what was going on?" I was out of the Suburban, looking at Duncan through the driver's open window.

"He said it would be better that way. Wanted to keep things looking as normal as possible." Duncan's fist pounded the steering wheel. "Hardest damn thing I ever had to do in my life."

Duncan mopped his face with his palm. "If the two of you are through standing there," he said, "how about getting your car out of my parking place. I need to let Ted and the others know what's going on."

"And you," I started in before Mac had the Honda in gear, "did you know what was going on?"

"I knew there was going to be a dance," Mac said.

"Mac!" It was not his name I called, but a cry of anger and frustration.

"Okay, Red, I get the message. The answer is, no, I didn't know what was going on."

"You really expect me to believe that?"

"Believe what you will, but Larry held the cards close to his chest. Only those who had a need to know knew what was going on, and I wasn't one of the need-to-know group."

My mind filled with what ifs. Rhodes had been lucky things went as planned. What would have happened if they hadn't? But prudence dictated I keep my mouth shut.

We entered the church through the double doors that led to the vestibule. Instead of the chaos I had expected, the atmosphere was calm, almost serene.

"Glad to see you two made it," Father Mike greeted. "I hear the Braun twins are doing well, and at last report, it appears all of the migrant workers have been evacuated from the compound. If you ask me, not that anyone has, I'd say the evening's turned out much better than we had any right to expect."

What we didn't know was that the night was not yet over.

We moved into the church proper, where several migrant laborers had taken refuge. Some held rosaries in their fingers, the beads clinking softly as they prayed. Some were in pairs, others alone, all with heads bowed over clasped hands. Though the lights in the vestibule shone brightly, here the light was dim, and shadows danced in the flickering glow of the votive candles.

We moved back into the vestibule, Father Mike closing the church door behind us.

"Any idea how many migrants are here?" I asked as we headed for the social hall.

"My guess is about fifty," the priest answered.

"How did they know to come here?" asked the more practical MacPhearson.

Father Mike chuckled. "Truth is, I got a call just as I was about to head out for the dance. Some man, I didn't recognize his voice, and he didn't say who he was."

My mouth tightened to a thin line. How many more times would I hear this same refrain?

"He said there'd been some explosions out at the Whiting farm. That the buffalo had stampeded and overrun the workers compound." Father Mike shook his head. "I tried to question him, but he wasn't having any of it. Just kept saying I should open the church and get enough supplies to take care of fifty to sixty people."

The social hall was a picture of ordered disorder and Ardella Duncan the drill sergeant. With her rapidly moving arms and pointing fingers, the Pine City butcher moved her troops with the ease of a traffic cop directing traffic.

"How's it going, Ardella?" Father Mike called.

"Fine, just fine, Father," Ardella said. "Thanks to the Guard we got fifty cots almost before I asked and plenty of sheets, blankets, pillows, and towels to go with them. The ditty bags are the ones we keep for tornado victims. We've set twenty-five beds up here for the women and another twenty-five downstairs for the men."

Ardella looked me up then down. "Sure you don't need one of them, Miss Arthur? You're not looking all that good yourself."

My hand went to my face, the woman's expression telling me the make-up I had so carefully applied earlier in the evening was long gone.

"It's not as bad as it looks," I said. Shaking my head, I declined the offer.

Ardella made a dismissive, well-I-offered, gesture, wrinkled her nose, and sniffed loudly. "From the smells coming from the kitchen, I'd say the ladies are ready to feed this bunch." She laid a hand on the priest's shoulder. "So, if you'll excuse me, Father, I need to get this crowd rounded up and fed while the food's hot."

Ardella Duncan moved across the hall, barking orders as she went.

"Every church needs an Ardella Duncan," Father Mike said, "and frankly I don't know what we'd do without her."

That and a super efficient local grapevine, I thought. I looked around the room, noting several casted limbs and several others with bandages on arms, heads, and legs.

Father Mike followed my gaze. "Could have been worse, Ginny. Seems the fence around the workers compound diverted most of the buffalo herd, and Wacker tells me if it hadn't been for that doctor friend of yours, we would have lost a good number of those who were hurt."

"Steve Brock is a fine surgeon, and trauma is his specialty," I said. Not only was trauma Steve's specialty, it was his life, his love. Without it . . . I silenced the thought, not wanting to go where I knew it would lead.

Mac and I helped serve the food and, at Ardella's direction, led each of the migrants to the cots the resident drill sergeant had assigned. As Father Mike had predicted, by the end of the evening, an evening which had stretched into the middle hours of the morning, Ardella had a list of names, a description of the injuries, and the treatment each had received.

I was tired beyond belief. The migrant workers, the group to which I had been assigned, were all tucked into their respective cots. The ladies, promising to return in the morning, had closed the kitchen for the night. Ardella, exercising the privilege of rank, had announced "lights out."

Dimly glowing night lights led my way to the church. I needed a place to wait while Mac finished with whatever it was Ardella had assigned him to do, a place where I might find peace and quiet. A place to rest my weary bones, hurting ribs, headache, and a heart heavy with doubt.

I sank into a rear pew, leaned back, and breathed in the scent of candle wax, of incense, of the mingled scents of people gathered together.

Behind me, the door opened. I turned to look. A shadow, like the shadows I had seen earlier, moved down the aisle.

"Mac?"

Chapter Thirty-Nine

There was no answer.

"You're not funny, Mac." Before the echo of my voice died, I knew the shadow was not Mac's.

I turned, verified another fact. Except for the shadow and me, the church was empty.

I pressed hard against the pew in front of me and groped for a weapon, wanting something, anything that might protect me. Protect me? What was I thinking? Did I really expect to find a gun, or maybe a knife, secreted in a book rack in St. Paul's Church?

I shifted focus to the shadow, opened my mouth, and closed it. My last call had gone unanswered as, I felt certain, would another. I tried anyway.

"What do you want?" I asked. My voice quivered. Well, hell, I was afraid. Alone, at night, in a church where the only light was a row of votive candles.

My groping fingers found the edge of a hymnal. I pulled it from the rack. It wasn't much in the way of a weapon, but beggars can't be choosers.

"You need to come with me, Miss Arthur."

The voice was low, vaguely familiar, one I should have recognized, but in my heightened state of anxiety, I didn't.

"Now!" The man separated himself from his shadow. "I said now, Miss Arthur. Move out of the pew, into the aisle."

What did one do in this situation? My mind sorted through the bits and pieces of information Uncle David and Larry Rhodes had given me over the years. I took another look around. The church was still empty. I crossed screaming off my mental list. Don't get in a car with a stranger was another. Yet somehow I knew this man was not a stranger, and the aisle of the church was not a car.

The man gestured impatiently with his hand. I took a better look. It wasn't his hand. It was a gun. Unlike my Smith & Wesson, the only gun with which I was familiar, this man's gun was bigger, much bigger.

Seeing it, the last piece of remembered advice from both David Arthur and Larry Rhodes fell into place: Never give up your gun.

Unlike the man's shadow, his gun did not waver. If I had my Smith & Wesson, would it waver in the candlelight? Dumb question. I didn't have my gun. I had a hymnal.

I cocked my arm back and threw the book at the man's extended arm. Fortunately, it was a hard-cover book. Unfortunately, I had forgotten another piece of advice. Always aim for the largest mass.

The book missed, and Roger Whiting was on me.

"Unless you want me to use this, turn around and put your hands behind your back."

I stared at the business end of the gun Whiting held close to my nose, and did as he said. I thought of many things—running, screaming, kicking, kneeing him in the balls—but rejected them all. Though not a great deal taller, Whiting easily outweighed me by half. I turned around and put my hands behind me.

Whiting secured a plastic tie around my wrists, grabbed my upper arm, and pulled back.

"Now, Miss Arthur, you have a choice. Either keep quiet, or I put a gag in your mouth."

I opted for keeping quiet.

Whiting pushed me ahead of him into the vestibule, then through the church doors into the parking lot.

I shivered. I had no coat, scarf, hat, or gloves. Worse yet, I had no shoes. Wanting to rest my tired feet on the padded kneeler, I had kicked off the sandals I had worn all evening. Though right for dancing, they were never intended for running the length and breadth, the upstairs and downstairs, to which Ardella Duncan had subjected her troop of volunteers.

I stumbled, cried out as my feet skidded over the snow and ice.

"What did I tell you about keeping quiet?" Whiting's grip tightened around my arm.

The reminder was sufficient, and I swallowed the next cry.

A large SUV skidded around the corner of the church and came to a stop before us. Whiting pulled open the back door and shoved me forward. "Get in and lay on the floor," he ordered.

Stiff with cold, I was slow to respond. With a grunt of displeasure, Whiting grabbed me around the waist and, as if I were a sack of grain, heaved me onto the floor. Another pair of plastic ties secured my ankles, and a blanket was thrown over me. It smelled of the aforementioned feed and of other things I didn't want to think about, but it was blessedly warm.

A pair of doors slammed shut, and the SUV rolled forward. At first, except for the drone of tires against the pavement, I heard nothing. Then, as I became acclimated to my surroundings, I heard a pair of voices coming from the front seat. One was definitely Roger Whiting's, and the other definitely female. It was, I concluded after more minutes of listening, a voice I had not heard before.

It wasn't the twists or turns that suggested where we might be heading, but more the length of time it took to get there. The final circling turn before the motor fell silent told me I had guessed right. We were at the Whiting farm.

Was the woman in the seat ahead of me Caroline Whiting? I didn't think so. Caroline's voice was higher pitched with a whiney hint, a child-about-to-pout-when-it-didn't-get-its-way voice.

Speculation ceased when the back door flew open.

"Sorry, Miss Arthur," Roger Whiting said. "I'm afraid I'm going to have to gag you after all."

A large wad of something was stuffed into my mouth and several strips of tape wound tight around my head. The vigor with which Whiting went about the task convinced me he was neither sorry nor afraid.

The door of the SUV slammed shut, leaving me both blind and deaf. Panic threatened, but reason won. If I could neither see nor hear, could I be seen or heard? Dismissing the question, I went to work. It was that, or lay and wait for whatever it was Roger Whiting and the unknown woman had planned for me.

Others might have considered how much time they had in which to complete the task, but not me. I wiggled closer to the front seats and pushed my hands as far under the seats as my bound arms would allow. I went about the task as if I had no time at all. That at any minute either the woman or Roger Whiting would be back.

It took several more tries and several more wiggles before I found what I was looking for, that sharp something one always cuts their fingers on when searching for things that get lost under the seats of cars. Buoyed by this initial success, I went to work sawing through the plastic ties that bound my wrists.

It was slow going. The stretching and turning exacerbated the damage to my ribs and made each breath a challenge. At last, success rewarded my efforts. My hands were free. I went to work on the tape that held the gag in place. I thought to yank the tape away in one quick motion, then thought again. Slow and careful was a better choice.

After the gag was gone, I worked on my feet. Free at last, I reached for the door.

Even though my senses were far from being on full alert, I knew to exit the SUV on the side away from the house. What I almost forgot was the dome light. Yanking free the bulb, I released the door catch and opened the door. Exhilarated by my new-found freedom, I grabbed the blanket and slid from what I now knew was a Cadillac Escalade.

My exhilaration was short lived. The blanket did little to keep out the cold, and I was still shoeless. I had to get somewhere warm, and I had to do it fast.

I made my way to the end of the Escalade and looked at the house. It offered both the warmth I needed and the threat of being recaptured. The former being the immediate need, the latter a possibility, I chose the former and took a longer look at the house.

Except for a porch light, which lit the front entryway and the steps leading to it, the area was wreathed in darkness.

Suspecting and fervently hoping the door would be unlocked, I looked at what lay between me and the house. There were no trees, no shrubs, nothing. Where were the shadows when I needed them?

My feet were fast freezing to the ground. If I were going to act, it had to be now. Throwing caution aside, I dashed across the open expanse, up the stairs and across the porch. I paused for breath and turned the handle. The door opened.

Light from the porch poured in ahead of me, making the hallway a yellow brick road. I followed it, hoping the outcome would prove as favorable for me as it had for Dorothy.

I closed the door, and the yellow brick road disappeared. Alone in the darkness, I tried to remember the layout of the house. There was, I knew, a pair of pocket doors on either side of the hallway. One set led to the dining room, the other to the parlor. Both rooms, according to Caroline Whiting, were seldom used except for large gatherings. Would one of them provide the safe haven I sought?

They would, the voice inside my head said, but as usual, I ignored it and continued to inch my way down the hall. Roger Whiting had brought me here, and I meant to find out why.

The hall led to the kitchen. The room was dark, but light seeped from beneath a door at the far end. I hung back, sensitive not just to the light but to the voices from behind the closed door, voices that belonged to Roger Whiting and his wife Caroline.

"After all I've done for you," she said. "How could you?"

There was the sound of shuffling feet. Then nothing, as both Caroline and I waited for Roger's answer, an answer that did not come.

"I've put up with your schemes, yes, even been a partner in most of them, but damn you, Roger, I will no longer put up with your philandering. This last was the last. The last. Do you hear me?"

Surely Whiting must have heard her, for Caroline was yelling loud enough to be heard in the next county. Still, he did not answer.

"And with her. Her!" Caroline's voice cracked like ice in a glass, logs in a fire. "Why not use one of the migrants? One whore is as good as another. You should know. You've had plenty."

"Now, Caroline, let's be reasonable. I'm sure we can work things out. Just give me the gun."

Gun? I looked for a place to hide. The blanket clutched tight about me offered no protection against bullets.

Bang, bang, bang!

Not caring who or what was the target, I ran back up the hall. My only thought being, should I seek refuge in the dining room or the parlor?

Remembering the number of tables, chairs, and sofas that cluttered the parlor, I slid open one of the pocket doors and rushed inside. It was a good idea. I had found a hiding place that offered several places to hide. Running pell-mell into an unfamiliar room was not. The crash of the lamp hitting the floor was louder than a brass band.

My hand found the arm of a horsehair sofa. Its back was against the wall, and I crawled behind it, edging the sofa forward with my shoulders as I did.

Running steps thundered into the room. An overhead light came on. Beneath my blanket, I stopped breathing. Did they see me?

Footsteps drew near, then retreated. Maybe they couldn't see me.

Again I heard the sound of approaching footsteps. Lighter sounding than the first, I guessed it was a woman. Caroline Whiting? The woman in the Escalade?

"She's got to be in here, Roger," a woman said. It was not Caroline Whiting.

"Keep looking, Juanita. We've got to find her."

"You told me she was tied up. That she couldn't get loose," the woman called Juanita said.

The sofa moved away from me. I shrank deeper into the blanket.

"You can get up, Miss Arthur. Time's running out, and you're causing us considerable delay."

The blanket was pulled from my face. Roger Whiting stared down at me. Beside him stood Deputy Juanita Ramos. I rolled to my knees and, using the back of the sofa for leverage, stood up.

"Seeing as how the flex ties didn't hold you, I'm afraid we'll have to try something different. We have a ways to go, and I can't run the risk of your getting away again."

Roger's gun hand was steady, his voice calm. A look passed between Whiting and the deputy, a look that sent the deputy scurrying from the room. Whatever that something different was, I knew it wouldn't be pleasant.

I moved from behind the sofa. "Why are you doing this, and why me?"

Getting no response from my captor, I sat down.

"Why am I doing this, and why you? Two questions, but just one answer, Miss Arthur."

Whiting backed up to a chair across from me and sat down. Using his free hand, he pulled a cigar from his pocket.

I watched his every move, from the unwrapping of the cigar to the striking of the match against his thumbnail, not as one amazed at the trick but as a cat stalks its prey, waiting the opportunity to strike. Ever cautious, Whiting presented no such opportunity.

"Caroline would never let me smoke in here, but since she can no longer object, I might as well enjoy myself."

The arrogance of the man. I don't know if I hated him more for what he was doing to me or for what I suspected he had done to his wife. Whichever it was, I had the feeling my fate would be similar to Caroline's. Though I had not liked the woman, I felt a kinship with her.

Whiting smiled as he puffed on the cigar. "Let's see," he said. "Why you? The answer's simple." Whiting leaned forward. "You got in my way. You found the Frazier girl's body and proceeded to stir up a real hornet's nest. Then you got hold of Rita Leggit. Heaven only knows what that woman told you. Never can trust a woman to keep her mouth shut." Whiting settled against the back of his chair and took another long pull on the cigar.

"Does that last include Caroline?" I looked at the door. How much longer before Deputy Ramos came back? How much longer could I keep him talking? How much longer did I have before . . .

"Caroline." Whiting gazed at the ceiling as if seeing his wife. "Oh, I think she would have kept quiet. She had as much to lose as I did."

"And what would that be?"

Whiting sprang from the chair. "This." He gesticulated wildly, spreading ash and bits of burning tobacco. "All of this, Miss Arthur. Things were going fine until you came along and bullied the sheriff into taking another look at the Shouldice and Leggit girls' disappearance. Just couldn't leave it alone, could you? Had to stick your nose in where it didn't belong. Why in hell didn't you just stay in Marion City?"

Whiting drew deeply on his cigar. "And that buffalo stampede! Why did you stampede the buffalo?" The words mingled with the smoke that escaped his mouth and nose. He leveled the gun in my direction. Despite the emotional outburst, his hand was surprisingly steady.

"I didn't stampede your buffalo."

"Then who did? That police officer friend of yours?" Whiting stubbed out his cigar in what was probably an expensive candy dish and looked through the open pocket doors. "Where in hell is that woman?" he thundered. Roger Whiting's patience was running thin.

"Why don't you just kill me here and get it over with?" I goaded and, taking advantage of the situation, added, "What's another dead body in a house as big as this?"

Whiting laughed. "Because, Miss Arthur, the fate I have planned for you is far more interesting than a simple shooting."

"I don't think so," another voice said.

Chapter Forty

"Stay where you are, Ginny," Uncle David ordered.

I rose from the chair. A doubting Thomas, I had to touch him, feel him before believing what my eyes were telling me. It was a bad decision.

Work-roughened hands grabbed me and pulled me against a well-padded chest. "If you don't put that gun down," Whiting threatened, "I'll put a bullet through Miss Arthur's head."

I struggled, tried to break free, but Whiting held me tight.

"Be still," he said, "or I might just shoot you anyway."

"Do as he says, Ginny," Uncle David said.

Out of options, I did.

"We seem to be at a stalemate." David Arthur's casual tone denied the gravity of the situation. "And since we are where we are, what would you suggest we do next?"

Roger Whiting laughed, the sound more threatening than the gun at my head. "For starters, I suggest you put down your gun and move away from the door."

As directed, Uncle David moved away from the open door and dropped his gun into a cushioned chair, closing the distance between us as he did.

"Now, that's better," Whiting said. Pushing me ahead of him, he circled around Uncle David.

I watched Uncle David's face, older now and more careworn than when I had last seen him, and caught the twinkle in his eye.

Hoping I was reading him correctly, I faked a stumble and, like a rag doll, folded myself over Whiting's arm.

Encumbered by the spineless creature I had become, Whiting struggled to readjust his hold, looking down as he did. It was but a moment's distraction, but it was the moment David Arthur needed. A chopping blow to Whiting's gun hand, a numbing kick to his knee, and the proud owner of the Whiting farm was down.

"Move, Ginny," Uncle David shouted.

I did. Running through the open door, across the hall, and out the front door. Being in the cold was definitely preferable to being inside where the climate was much too hot.

I looked over my shoulder, expecting to see Uncle David behind me.

He was not there.

Inside the house, a gun roared.

"No . . . no!"

Reversing direction, I ran back through the front door and straight into Uncle David's arms. "You're alive!" I was crying and laughing and holding him tight.

His arms were around me. "It's okay, Ginny. It's okay."

"When I first saw you, I thought . . ." I held him tighter. Oh, hell, what did it matter what I thought? What mattered was he was here.

I pulled back, ran hands and fingers over my wet cheeks and under my dripping nose. "I heard a shot."

"Ginny, Ginny. I'm okay. I'm okay."

I stared into his face. His lips were a hard line, his eyes unreadable. "Is he dead?"

Uncle David nodded.

"I think Caroline Whiting's dead, too," I said. We were standing in the hall, and Uncle David's arms were still around me. "There's another woman here, too, Juanita Ramos, one of Sheriff Duncan's deputies."

"We've met. Ran into each other about the time you and Mr. Whiting were discussing your future."

"She's one of them. We have to do something before she gets away."

"You haven't changed a bit. Still the stubborn, head-strong redhead you always were." He gave me a final hug and released me. "Everything's taken care of. What we have to do now is find you a coat and some shoes."

He found the hall closet and rummaged through the coats that hung there. "This should do," he said, handing me one.

A pair of shoes followed. Not shoes exactly, more boots, but they met my shoeless needs.

"Sheriff Duncan's on his way. He'll take over here and see you get back into town."

"Are the State Police still here? Duncan's deputies called them about the explosions."

"The State Police are here, and the National Guard as well. It's been a busy night, Ginny."

We entered the kitchen. Juanita Ramos's dark eyes flashed above a mouth taped closed with duct tape. More tape secured her arms and legs to one of the wooden kitchen chairs. Had it been only a week since Mac and I had eaten there?

"You're right about Caroline Whiting," Uncle David said, returning from the room that adjoined the kitchen.

Ramos's eyes shot daggers, if eyes can shoot daggers, as David Arthur checked the duct tape that held the deputy to the chair. Apparently satisfied, he headed for the hall. "Let's get out of here, Ginny. We've done about all we can do."

Reluctant to face the staring eyes of the Whiting ancestors that lined the dining room walls, I chose the hall and sat on the stairs that led to the second floor . It was also one of the few places without a body, dead or otherwise. With a long sigh, I lowered myself to one of the steps.

"Spit it out, Ginny," Uncle David said, massaging my hunched shoulders.

"Why? What good will it do?"

"Because you need to tell me." He rested his hands on my shoulders, letting his strong fingers work their magic. It was not the questions I feared. It was the answers.

I needed to move, needed to put distance between me and the man who had been more father than uncle for most of my life. I rose from the steps and, in my overlarge boots, stomped the length of the hall. "Okay. Tell me. Are you here to stay or will you be leaving again?"

He said nothing for what seemed like forever. Just sat there looking up at me from where he sat on the stairs.

"I need to know," I said softly, the anger draining from me.

"You're right, Ginny, you need to know, and the answer is no, I won't be staying."

"When?" The word stuck in my throat. "When are you leaving? Where will you go? How long will you be gone?"

"Whoa! One question at a time." He laughed, breaking my heart. "You asked when I would be leaving. The answer is soon. The boss doesn't like us staying around once the job is finished."

I started to speak, but Uncle David held up a restraining hand. "And where will I go? Truth is, I usually don't know until I get there. Now for the tough one. How long will I be gone? Depends on how long it takes to get the job done, a couple of weeks, a couple of months, or even a couple of years."

"Those times you were gone when I was growing up, they were part of what you're doing now?"

"They were."

"Are you here now because of the migrant workers, the missing girls, a possibility of the Whitings being involved in human trafficking?"

"No, that's not why I'm here," he said.

"Then why?"

He shook his head. "I can't answer that, Ginny, and before you ask, I can't tell you who I work for."

I settled on the step below his. "You do seem to show up when I need you. What more can a girl ask?" I laid my head against his knee.

His arm came around my shoulders, and he rested his cheek against my head. Neither of us spoke, content to spend what time was left in the companionable silence of love.

The play of headlights followed by pounding footsteps announced Duncan's arrival. Quick to respond, Uncle David was at the door before the sheriff reached it.

"Bryant's on his way," Duncan called as he came through the door. He looked first at Uncle David, then at me. "You going to need to see a doc?"

"Where's Mac?" I demanded, ignoring his question.

Another rush of footsteps answered my question. Mac was here, and before I could ask any more, he was across the hall, and I was in his arms.

"Ginny, Ginny. Are you all right?" He studied my face. "Doesn't seem to be any new bumps or bruises."

"I'm okay, Mac."

"We looked everywhere, but you weren't anywhere. We found your coat and your shoes in the church." Mac held me even tighter. "Why in hell did you take off your shoes?"

I pushed against his chest, not hard, but the message got through, and Mac loosened his hold.

"How did you know to come here?" I asked.

"Duncan called, said you were here at the Whiting place with David Arthur."

My gaze shifted from Mac to Uncle David. His head close to Duncan's, the two conversed in low tones. Though I couldn't hear the words, their expressions piqued my interest.

The twins were okay, as were most of the migrant workers, so why the long faces? What was going on that I didn't know about?

I approached the two men, scrutinizing each in turn. I didn't like what I saw.

I backed away. "Don't think you're going to ship me back to town, because it's not going to happen."

I clomped back to the stairs and sat down. "So, fill me in. It's me the bad guys are after, and that gives me the right to know."

The three (Mac had joined forces with the other two) looked from one to another as if deciding who would do the talking.

The stalemate was broken when Uncle David reached into his pocket and pulled out a vibrating cell phone. Moving out of earshot, he brought the phone to his ear. The precaution proved unnecessary. Drowning out any other sound were the whirling rotor blades of a helicopter.

The blast of sound had barely registered before Deputy Kevin Bryant barged through the open front door. His mouth moved in rhythm with his wildly gesticulating hands but to no avail. His words were lost in the roar of the hovering chopper.

I stood up, then sat down. The four who crowded the door combined with the noise level discouraged action. From the advantage of stair-step seating, I saw Uncle David dash from the house and grab at the rope that hung beneath the hovering bird. Once again the motor's roar assaulted our ears. In the blink of an eye, David Arthur was lifted up and away.

"Uncle David! Uncle David!" I rushed for the door.

Mac's arms caught me. "He's gone, Ginny."

"I hear all hell's breaking loose at Camp Whiting," Bryant shouted, the distraught deputy's voice rising over the noise of the retreating chopper. "Any idea what's going on out there, Sheriff?"

Duncan heaved a great sigh. "Yeah, afraid I do. From what David Arthur has told me, it seems we have a group of terrorists from Rocky Ridge intent on raiding Camp Whiting's arsenal."

Chapter Forty-One

Duncan was not into answering further questions. What he was into was giving orders.

"You'll have to look after Ginny, MacPhearson." Duncan looked at Mac. "If you need transportation, take Bryant's Suburban."

Duncan turned to his deputy. "I want you to get hold of Johnson. Tell her to bring the crime scene van and get over here. Have her give Bentley a call. When he finishes at the auditorium, he can go to the office."

Duncan frowned, as if checking a mental list. "And Johnson needs to give Doc Wacker a call. Tell him to bring plenty of body bags. Busy as he's been tonight, he's not going to like this last bit at all."

"Anything more I can do?" Mac asked. "Since Ginny's okay, there's no need for us to rush back to town."

"Matter of fact, there is," Duncan said. "How about dropping Ramos off at the jail?"

Before Mac could answer, Duncan's cell phone rang.

The sheriff's gruff "Hello" was followed with "They're there? On the base? I'm on my way." Without a backward look, Duncan ran from the house.

Though no Rhodes scholar, I had no trouble figuring this one out. Whatever agency Uncle David worked for, it was this, the raid on Camp Whiting's arsenal, not the Whitings' involvement in human trafficking, that had brought him to Pine City. "Be careful," I whispered.

Mac and Kevin Bryant came from the kitchen, a sullen-faced Juanita Ramos sandwiched between them. Her hands were cuffed behind her, and the tape was gone from her mouth.

I have worked with several guilty clients, some of whom showed remorse and others who showed none at all. Deputy Ramos was one of the latter. Knowing she most likely had a part in the twins' abduction, I too felt no remorse.

"Thought I'd get started," Bryant said. He had returned from having locked Ramos in the Suburban, carrying a box bearing the Pine County logo. "This one's going to take some time."

Mac joined me on the steps. "Care to tell me what happened at the church?"

And so I did, telling him about the shadow that wasn't him, the gun that wasn't mine, my escape from the Escalade, and how once again Uncle David saved my life.

"Tell me again," he said when I finished, "why did you leave your shoes in the church?"

"I didn't have time to put them on."

Mac slid his arm around me, and I laid my head against his shoulder. It had been a long day.

"Why did Whiting and Ramos go to the church?" I yawned. Not only had the day been long, the night seemed even longer.

"Other than wanting to kidnap you?"

"Be serious, Mac."

"Father Mike said they were checking on the workers, and were probably looking for you. You were a loose end, Ginny. You knew too much."

"I thought Ramos was with the Wakefields. How did she hook up with Whiting?"

"I'm guessing it was at the hospital. I'm also guessing the two of them were involved in trafficking. When they saw what had happened to the workers, probably figured everything was down the drain," Mac said.

"Who set off the explosions that stampeded the buffalo? Roger Whiting accused us, you and me, but . . ."

MacPhearson shook his head. "My guess is it was those would-be terrorists, Frazier, Schmidt, and those two from the motel, Pricheck and Vorhies. They needed a diversion while they broke into the National Guard armory."

I thought of the body in the next room, of Caroline Whiting laying dead in the back of the house, and of Juanita Ramos locked in the back of Bryant's SUV. "Best laid plans," I mumbled.

Tires crunched on the driveway. Myra Johnson, carrying a box similar to Bryant's, came through the door.

"You look worse every time I see you," she said by way of greeting.

Proving I could, I got to my feet. "Did Sheriff Duncan tell you about Roger Whiting?"

Johnson motioned to the set of pocket doors that led into the parlor. "Said the body was in there."

Another set of tires crunched in the driveway. Another car door slammed, and another pair of footsteps echoed across the porch.

"Send the doc back when he's finished with you," Johnson said, heading down the hall.

"I'm getting too old for this," Wacker complained, coming through the door. He stopped and looked me up and down.

"Don't say it," I said.

Wacker shook his head, then looked at the two sets of doors. "Is there someplace without a body where I can have a look at you?"

"If you don't mind several pairs of ancestral eyes staring at you, the dining room's our best bet," I answered.

Mac slid the doors apart. The three of us trooped inside, and Wacker motioned me to a chair. A few minutes and a few questions later, he pronounced me fit to travel.

He repacked his bag and turned to Mac. "As soon as you drop off your prisoner, I want you to take this girl home and put her to bed."

I opened my mouth, but Wacker cut me off. "Any arguments, young lady, and I'll get Sheriff Duncan to lock you up with Ramos.

It's a jail cell or your bed. Even that whiz of a doctor you brought along can't fix a head full of scrambled brains."

Knowing Wacker meant what he said, I followed Mac to Bryant's Suburban.

A soundproof partition separated us from a still sullen-faced Ramos, and I took advantage of the privacy.

"If you take the highway that circles Little Pine Lake, we can get close enough to Camp Whiting to see what's going on."

"Nothing doing, Ginny. It's jail then back to the cabin."

"Will you at least stop by the hospital?" I said, my thoughts on Uncle David. "If there are any casualties, they will have sent them there."

"Fine! First the jail, then the hospital. We can pick up that boyfriend of yours. Let him take you home and put you to bed."

I stopped talking. Silence may be golden, but tonight it hung between us like a lead weight.

Mac turned into the parking lot of the municipal building, drove around to the back, and pulled up to the rear door. A light burned over the door, illuminating an emergency call button. Slamming the SUV's door behind him, Mac walked the short distance to the building's rear entrance and punched the emergency button.

Norm Schmidt opened the door. Behind him were Len Frazier, Mark Pricheck, and Ron Vorhies. All four held guns, and all four guns were pointed at MacPhearson.

Ignoring my heart's erratic beating, I slid down the window.

"I think I'll stay out here," I heard Mac say.

"I don't think so, Mister Big City Police Officer. We want you inside and your girlfriend with you." Schmidt leveled the gun at Mac's chest.

Mac shook his head and shook his head and continued to shake it. My brain was slow to function, but self-preservation, both mine and Mac's, told me what to do. I raised the window, grabbed the wheel, and bumped from one bucket seat to the other.

Several bullets hit the vehicle. Due to the foresight of the Pine City Sheriff, none penetrated the SUV's extra plating or bulletproof glass.

Spurred by another round of bullets, I jammed my foot against the accelerator, swung the Suburban in a wide arc, and made a run at the open door.

Would Mac anticipate the moves? Get himself out of harm's way? More importantly, would Schmidt stay where he was?

I stopped short of impact. Both Mac and Schmidt had disappeared. Was I wrong to hope for the best?

I shifted into reverse and tapped the accelerator. There were few cars. Few places for Mac or whoever else was out there to hide.

Headlights shone through the windshield. Friend or foe? I decided foe and met this new challenge head on.

It was a game of chicken, one the Suburban easily won. The oncoming car slid sideways. More intent on finding Mac than adding victims to my hit list, I did not give chase. Growing small in the side mirror, the car, Pricheck's and Vorhies's familiar heads visible through the fleeing vehicle's rear window, exited the parking lot. With a sense of pride, I cheered the vanishing taillights.

Busy patting myself on the back, I almost missed the figure running toward me. Gun in hand, he took aim and fired. Schmidt? Frazier? Again my heart thumped in my chest.

The running figure disappeared behind a car. Trusting the technology of bulletproof glass, I stood my ground. The figure reappeared around the opposite side of the car, extended his arm, and fired. In the periphery of my vision, I saw another someone fall.

I stomped the accelerator, aimed for the shooter and the car behind which he was hiding. I was not wearing a seatbelt. Being as such safety measures were low on my list of priorities, I braced for the impact.

The SUV's airbags deployed as we hit, knocking my head against the headrest. Doctor Wacker wasn't going to like this, I thought.

The SUV's door was wrenched open. Hands grabbed me and dragged me from the seat.

"What in hell were you trying to do?" Mac shouted. "Kill me?"

"You were shooting at me," I argued.

"I wasn't shooting at you. I was shooting at Len Frazier," Mac said.

Another part of my brain kicked in. "You don't have a gun."

"Schmidt did."

I swivelled around, taking in the whole of the parking lot. "Did I hit him?"

"He jumped clear before you hit the door." Mac put his arm around me. "You're shaking, Ginny."

"If I didn't hit him, how did you get his gun?"

"He dropped it when he jumped clear of the Suburban. What difference does it make? I have it, he doesn't."

"He's a police officer, Mac. They always carry a back-up piece." I looked beyond the Suburban and the smaller vehicle wrapped around the grill.

"Is Frazier dead?" I said.

"He's not shooting at us, is he?"

Answering Mac's question, a bullet hit close beside us.

Chapter Forty-Two

We dropped to the ground and rolled under the Suburban. "Frazier?" I asked.

"I shot him. He's down." Mac's voice was firm, his tone positive.

"Those two friends of his are gone, too," I said. "They drove off just before you started shooting at me."

"That leaves Schmidt." Mac inched his way from under the car and came to his feet behind the open door.

After several minutes of listening and looking, Mac beckoned me to follow. "Get in the Chevy, Ginny," he said. "I want you out of harm's way until I know where the bastard's hiding."

I needed no urging. Mac followed, shoving me ahead of him into the passenger seat. If Schmidt was within shooting range, he wasn't shooting.

Mac backed the Suburban off the car that had molded itself to the front bumper. We circled the parking lot, stopping by the back entrance.

"I need to check out the jail," he said.

He didn't take long.

"If Schmidt's still around, he's not in there," he said.

I slid from the SUV. "Bentley called. He's on his way."

More than on his way, he was here. Entering behind us, Bentley pulled the door shut. "What's Juanita doing in the back seat of Bryant's Suburban?"

The question told us how far out of the loop the deputy was. His face mirroring disbelief, we brought him up to date.

"We need to get Ramos into a cell," Mac finished. "Can't let her freeze to death out there."

Bentley banged his fist against the desk. "Serve her right if she did."

Sitting where I had sat on other visits, I picked at some stray feathers that littered the desktop, stopping when the two police officers reentered the room. Ramos's face wore the same sullen expression, and her hands were still cuffed behind her.

"The cells are through here, Detective MacPhearson," Bentley said.

The trio disappeared, and I went back to picking at feathers, stilling my hand when I heard the clang of metal on metal. "Best laid plans," I said quietly.

"That's Schmidt's desk," Bentley said when he and Mac re-entered the room. "You can always tell where Schmidt's been by the trail of feathers he leaves behind."

My fingers froze.

"Schmidt's first jacket had something wrong with the zipper, and the one the company sent to replace it is always shedding feathers." Bentley looked from me to MacPhearson. "Either of you know where he is?"

"I'm hoping he and Frazier are laying out there in the parking lot." MacPhearson checked Schmidt's gun. "And now that Ramos is taken care of, it's time we had a look for them."

I went back to picking up feathers. Was Schmidt's jacket the source of the cat's carefully hoarded store? If so, where did the cats get them? Schmidt had not been inside the cabin until . . .

The door banged shut.

"We found Frazier, but not Schmidt," Mac said, "and Frazier's damned lucky it's as cold as it is out there. If not, he probably would have bled to death."

Leaving Bentley to mind the store, Mac and I followed the ambulance to the hospital.

"Doc Brock's with Frazier. They're on their way to the operating room as we speak," Wacker said in answer to our questions. "Frazier's in bad shape, but as fine a surgeon as Steve is, I'd say he's got a better than even chance of making it."

"You get any other shooting victims tonight, Jim?" Mac asked.

"Other than the two I brought back with me from the Whiting farm, we got a few from Camp Whiting, but they mostly take care of their own out there, and Norm Schmidt came by. Had a gunshot wound in his arm, but the bullet only grazed him. We patched him up, and he left. Forgot to take his jacket though."

Wacker pointed to a plastic bag in the corner of the staff lounge.

"He said there was some shooting over by the municipal building. You two know anything about that?"

"We were there," Mac admitted.

"Schmidt and Frazier tried to kill Mac and me," I said, "but Mac shot both of them."

The door to the lounge swung open, and Duncan came into the room. "Bentley tells me you two have been up to your usual shenanigans," he greeted.

Though some stories are embellished by frequent telling, the story of the shoot-out at the Pine City Municipal Building stayed the same.

"And the SUV?" Duncan asked when we finished.

I raised my hand. "Guilty," I said.

"You a drag race queen? A member of a demolition derby?" Duncan asked.

I waved away the sheriff's attempted levity. "You were at Camp Whiting?"

Duncan nodded. "Want to know about that uncle of yours, do you?"

"Is he okay?"

"Everything and everyone is okay, well almost," Duncan amended. "Seems a group of Rocky Ridge right wing militants decided to add to their store of weapons by raiding the Guard's armory."

"That's why Uncle David was here," I said.

"I expect that's part of it. What part I'm not sure, but he sure as hell threw a monkey wrench into the plans of those would-be terrorists."

"Was it Uncle David who called about the buffalo stampede and the migrant workers?"

"My guess is it was, and he was probably the one who rescued you out at Little Pine Lake."

Not probably, Sheriff Duncan, I thought, it was Uncle David. David Arthur had been riding the third snowmobile, and David Arthur had left behind a silver unicorn.

"Jimmy Wakefield thought he recognized one of the snowmobiles," Mac said. "Anything come of that?"

"So far no luck," Duncan said. "Chances are it's a rental, so it might take a while."

"What about the explosions at the Whiting farm and the buffalo stampede?" Mac asked.

"A diversionary tactic. That militant bunch thought they'd keep us busy while they helped themselves to the Guard's weapons," Duncan said.

"I take it they weren't successful," Mac said.

"About as successful as John Brown was at Harper's Ferry," Duncan said.

Having gotten so far, but not quite far enough in my assumptions cum speculations, I asked, "What about Sarah Frazier, and Maggie, and Rita Leggit, how do they tie in with all this?"

"I think their deaths were a way of tying up loose ends, or more specifically, loose tongues. Frazier was one of the ring-leaders of the Rocky Ridge bunch. He couldn't be sure how much his daughter knew and what she may have told Maggie or what Maggie may have told you. From what Sam said, neither he nor Rita knew about any plans to raid the National Guard armory."

"Did Roger Whiting shoot Rita?" I asked.

"Not sure yet whether it was you or Rita the shooter was aiming at, but most likely it was that helicopter pilot, Al Vort, who did the shooting," Duncan said. "His service record qualified him as an expert rifleman."

Duncan reached for his coffee. "According to Lieutenant Rhodes, Vort's done some talking since they arrested him. Sounds like he's what you might call Whiting's right hand man for dirty deeds. Brought in the migrants, especially the illegals, and ferried out the youngsters when there was a call for young flesh."

"And Ginny, as usual, stuck her nose in too many places where it didn't belong," Mac said.

"I didn't know anything about anything," I protested.

"Try telling that to the Whitings and Schmidt and company," said Duncan. "My guess is, it would be a hard sell."

Deciding I'd rather be hung for a sheep than a lamb, I shared my thoughts about Schmidt, his jacket, the down feathers, and Sarah Frazier's death.

"Might as well tell you. Can't do any harm now," Duncan said. "We found several feathers in the freezer with Sarah Frazier's body. They've been checked, and they did come from Schmidt's jacket. My guess is Frazier told Schmidt to look out for his daughter in case she tried to hook up with her aunt. Schmidt did. Probably got to her first and decided to hide her out at Judge Marfield's place. He knew the cabin was empty. What he didn't know was that you would be moving in."

"And you think Schmidt killed Sarah and put her body in the freezer?" Wacker asked.

Duncan nodded. "With what we have, Doc, we shouldn't have any difficulty tying him to Sarah Frazier's death."

"What about the footprints and tire tracks at Maggie Schmidt's accident site?" I asked. "Is there enough there to connect Schmidt to Maggie's death?"

"The more I think about it, the more I'm liking Norm Schmidt as the killer of both his niece and his sister," Mac added.

"As do I," Duncan admitted. "Only most of what we got there, except for a few down feathers, is circumstantial."

"The feathers, they're from Schmidt's jacket?" I asked.

"And the alcohol in Maggie's stomach?" Mac added.

"The feathers came from Schmidt's jacket. The alcohol in Maggie's stomach?" the sheriff paused, "Schmidt's big enough. He could have forced her to drink it."

Duncan finished what was left of his coffee and banged the mug on the table. "Schmidt and those two friends of his better enjoy their freedom while they can," he said, "because they sure as hell won't be enjoying it much longer."

Before the three of us could speculate further, Steve Brock came into the room. His face was drawn, his eyes bright. "The patient's going to live," he said, "but I'm not as sure about the surgeon."

Steve looked at me. "If it hadn't been for the dance, I wouldn't have seen you at all this weekend." Steve took my hand, and Mac, Doc Wacker, and Duncan made excuses and left the room. "Seems my work has a way of interfering with what time we have together."

"And it's always going to be that way," I said, hoping he would say it wouldn't but knowing he couldn't.

"When are you leaving for Boston?" I asked.

"They want me there by April first," Steve said.

"That doesn't give us much time," I said.

"Do you need more time, Ginny?"

I pushed aside the lock of hair that hung over his forehead. I had done it many times before but knew I was doing it now for the last time.

"Don't look so sad, Ginny. It's not the end. It's the beginning. For me it's Mass General, and for you it's Mac."

"No," I said.

"Yes, Ginny. I've watched the two of you together for weeks. Maybe you couldn't see what was happening, but I could."

I leaned into his shoulder. "I didn't mean for it to happen."

"Shhh," Steve said. "All I've ever wanted is your happiness. If that means being with Mac, well . . ."

"And for you? What makes you happy?"

"Doing what I'm doing, Ginny."

Steve hugged me, and then he was gone.

In the silence of the empty room, I asked myself how I could love one man and yet be willing to exchange this love for another's. It was a question not easily or quickly answered. One to ponder for weeks, months, or maybe even years.

Wacker came into the room. "That doctor of yours tells me he's spending the night with his patients."

"He's not my doctor," I said.

"Figured as much." Wacker wrapped an arm around my shoulders and gave me a hug.

"How can a heart hurt so much and still not hurt?" I asked.

"Now wouldn't I be a millionaire if I had the answer to that one?" Wacker said.

We both laughed, and were still laughing when Mac came into the room.

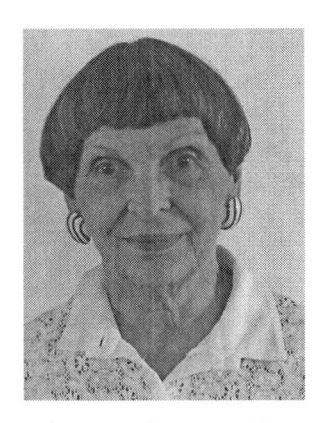

About the Author

Called Barb as often as Barbara, Mrs. Kiger was born in Michigan but moved south with her husband and most of their six children in 1979. A nurse by profession, she began writing seriously after losing her sight in 1985. Her work has appeared in magazines and anthologies, the most recent being William B. Toulouse's *Amazingly Simple Lessons Learned After Fifty*. "Beginnings," a short story, received Honorable Mention in the Tallahassee Writers' Association 2002 Seven Hills Contest, and appeared in that year's *Fiction Review*. *Cold Storage* is her second published novel and follows the continuing adventures of Ginny Arthur that began in *Payback*.